Br

"With *D*
and

—David Liss, Edgar® Award–winning author of
The Devil's Company

Praise for Hank Schwaeble and *Damnable*

"Flat-out fabulous . . . *Damnable* kept me breathlessly glued
to the pages from start to finish. Fast-paced, edgy, and gripping."   —Cherry Adair, *New York Times* bestselling author

"Hank Schwaeble is a new, talented voice on the scene. He
writes with a confidence that could be called swagger if it
wasn't so good. *Damnable* is a powerful tale . . . fresh and
irresistible."
—Thomas F. Monteleone, award-winning author of
The Blood of the Lamb

"Hank Schwaeble steps into territory usually dominated by
Dean Koontz . . . and solidly holds his ground. Suspenseful,
inventive, and consistently surprising."
—Gary A. Braunbeck, Bram Stoker and
International Horror Guild–award winner

"Fast-paced and tension-ratcheting . . . a page-turner sure to
satisfy the most fickle supernatural-thriller junkie."
—Deborah LeBlanc, author of *Water Witch* and *The Wolven*

"Hank Schwaeble's *Damnable* is a first-rate fusion of horror,
suspense, and noir. There are plenty of creeping chills and
chilling creeps here for every fan of the dark. Schwaeble takes
the horror-action novel to the max."
—Tom Piccirilli, award-winning author of *Shadow Season*

continued . . .

Jove titles by Hank Schwaeble

DAMNABLE
DIABOLICAL

DIABOLICAL

HANK SCHWAEBLE

JOVE BOOKS, NEW YORK

THE BERKLEY PUBLISHING GROUP
Published by the Penguin Group
Penguin Group (USA) Inc.
375 Hudson Street, New York, New York 10014, USA
Penguin Group (Canada), 90 Eglinton Avenue East, Suite 700, Toronto, Ontario M4P 2Y3, Canada
(a division of Pearson Penguin Canada Inc.)
Penguin Books Ltd., 80 Strand, London WC2R 0RL, England
Penguin Group Ireland, 25 St. Stephen's Green, Dublin 2, Ireland (a division of Penguin Books Ltd.)
Penguin Group (Australia), 250 Camberwell Road, Camberwell, Victoria 3124, Australia
(a division of Pearson Australia Group Pty. Ltd.)
Penguin Books India Pvt. Ltd., 11 Community Centre, Panchsheel Park, New Delhi—110 017, India
Penguin Group (NZ), 67 Apollo Drive, Rosedale, Auckland 0632, New Zealand
(a division of Pearson New Zealand Ltd.)
Penguin Books (South Africa) (Pty.) Ltd., 24 Sturdee Avenue, Rosebank, Johannesburg 2196,
South Africa

Penguin Books Ltd., Registered Offices: 80 Strand, London WC2R 0RL, England

This is a work of fiction. Names, characters, places, and incidents either are the product of the author's imagination or are used fictitiously, and any resemblance to actual persons, living or dead, business establishments, events, or locales is entirely coincidental. The publisher does not have control over and does not have any responsibility for author or third-party websites or their content.

DIABOLICAL

A Jove Book / published by arrangement with the author

PRINTING HISTORY
Jove mass-market edition / July 2011

Copyright © 2011 by Hank Schwaeble.
The Edgar® name is a registered service mark of Mystery Writers of America, Inc.
Cover art by S. Miroque.
Cover design by Rita Frangie.
Text design by Kristin del Rosario.

ISBN: 978-0-515-14961-6

JOVE®
Jove Books are published by The Berkley Publishing Group,
a division of Penguin Group (USA) Inc.,
375 Hudson Street, New York, New York 10014.
JOVE® is a registered trademark of Penguin Group (USA) Inc.
The "J" design is a trademark of Penguin Group (USA) Inc.

PRINTED IN THE UNITED STATES OF AMERICA

10 9 8 7 6 5 4 3 2 1

ACKNOWLEDGMENTS

This book couldn't exist without the wonderful efforts of my tireless agent, Bob Fleck, and my editor with a heart, Tom Colgan. And, of course, it wouldn't have been nearly as much joy to write without my first reader and essential critic Rhodi, who always keeps everything so positive.

CHAPTER 1

❖

THE GUY AT THE BAR WITH THE WINNING SMILE AND FLAW-less hair was on the small side, so Hatcher decided he'd have to kill him.

He dropped his eyes to the note one more time before crumbling it and stuffing it into the pocket of his jeans.

> *Roses are Yellow*
> *Falcons are Blue*
> *I know a fellow's*
> *Been looking for you*
>
> *Side alley, Chief. Four balls.*
>
> —*Mr. E*

A runny splash of moon reflected off the indigo Pacific, the churn of waves flashing silver as they broke on the beach. Hatcher inhaled a briny whiff of sea breeze. It carried a chill in through the patio, managed to cause goose bumps on his arm even as it dissipated under the ceiling fans that blew hot air down from the lights.

Three months. Hatcher liked Venice Beach. The weather was tame. The people managed to be friendly while still leaving you alone. Nobody ever asked what his last name was. Nobody seemed to care about anything except soaking up the sun and having a good time.

He took in a breath, exhaled half of it. Mr. E was still grinning, scraping nuts from a bowl and shaking them in a loose fist, for all appearances quite invested in conversation with one of the blonde barmaids as she rested a tray of empty glasses against her hip. Long-sleeve white shirt, untucked, cuffs turned once and hanging open; black vest, unbuttoned. He looked completely at ease. Not even so much as a glance in Hatcher's direction. Hadn't made noticeable eye contact when he walked in, hadn't looked over from the moment he'd taken a stool.

It was a Thursday night. Crowd was light. Two couples sharing a booth. Half a dozen regulars scattered around the bar, dropping comments out of the sides of their mouths while they watched a football game. Two young gals conspired over drinks at one of the tables, talking behind cupped hands about stuff that made them giggle. Patio was empty. Place wasn't very big. The guy seemed to be alone.

Yes, Hatcher concluded. No doubt about it. Way too slight a build. He'd have to kill him. And quick.

There were other options, of course. There always were. Just not good ones. It was still several minutes till. He could slip out, walk right off the patio, vanish into the cool California night. Zero Residual Presence. He sure as hell knew how to do that. But that was a tactic, not a strategy. It didn't solve the problem, only kicked the can down the road. Or maybe just along the curb a few feet. That was the trouble with running. You never knew how far away you were really getting, because behind every problem was a person, and people had a way of giving chase.

On the other hand, if the individual you pegged as doing the chasing was incapacitated, the distance you could put between you and your problem was likely to be much bigger.

Besides, it was rarely better to run from a fight. Engaging an adversary created some control over the dynamic. Running meant you were either scared to make a stand or content to let yourself be hunted. That pretty much established where you were on the food chain.

Not that engagement was a foolproof strategy. Killing the guy wouldn't necessarily solve anything. But it would sure address the food-chain issue. There was a term for it in the military. Decisive Intervention. In this case, the idea would be to turn the tables, be the predator rather than the prey. What sucked about it was he'd still have to move on. In the civilian jungle, the guys with badges were at the apex. They hunted in packs.

And considering he'd dropped one from a rather tall building not that long ago, he figured he'd already used up whatever breaks he could hope for when it came to taking on cops.

The guy took a swig of his beer, popped some more peanuts into his mouth. Didn't glance over once.

As much as Hatcher would have loved to hear what the guy had to say, he knew that was an option he had to dismiss outright. This was no simple messenger. The wording of the note clearly meant the sender was military. Ex-military, most likely, but definitely a soldier. And he wanted Hatcher to know it. *Chief* referred to Hatcher's highest attained rank, chief warrant officer second class. *Four balls* was army jargon for midnight, when the twenty-four-hour clock was all zeros.

But it was the way the note seemed designed to bait him that was most bothersome. Like the author was determined not to give him a chance to ignore it. Like he wanted to make sure his quarry showed up outside in an enclosed area looking for a fight at a specific time. *Roses are Yellow, Falcons are Blue*. Operation Rose Garden had comprised three phases—white, yellow, and red. It was during *Yellow* that Davis, moronic fucker that he was, screwed the pooch and nearly got the entire team killed. The guy was such an egomaniac, his nickname was "Mister I." Only a child would entertain the possibility of that being a coincidence.

Falcons are Blue was the clincher, though, the reference that really stuck out. Blue Falcon was phonetic slang for BF, which stood for *buddy fucker*. It was a moniker slapped on someone who ratted out a teammate.

And in Spec Ops, if you called someone a BF out in the field you were as good as marking them for death.

Hatcher sensed heavy footfalls approach. Heard the familiar labored breathing behind him before he felt the weight of a hand on his shoulder.

"Hey, Jake. What do you think of small and lethal?"

It was the owner, Dennis, standing next to him with his usual jowly half smile. He was a flabby guy with a red waft of hair and an equally red beard, like a cross between Santa and Satan. He always seemed to be winded. And he always seemed to have some new toy to share.

He held his hand up, dangling something in front of Hatcher's face.

Hatcher drew back a bit, saw it was a tiny holster with a little gun handle sticking out, swinging on the end of a chain. He shifted his gaze over the man's shoulder to the flat-screen TV suspended in the corner. A cable sports channel was running down scores, with a headline ticker across the bottom. The time on the ticker read 2:53 EST. Seven till midnight, Pacific.

"Wait till you see how cool this is," Denny said. "C'mon back to the office."

"I'm about to go on break. There's something I need to take care of."

"Well, come back there when you're done, okay?"

"Sure, Den. Give me a few minutes."

"Not gonna forget, are you? Make me sit back there waiting? I've got a new DVD to show you. Better than the last one."

Early on Hatcher had pegged Dennis as a guy who was more or less full of shit. Harmless, though. Geeky. Always wore the same jeans and an XXL shirt with the name of the bar plastered across the front of it. The Liar's Den. One of the bartenders had intimated Dennis didn't actually own the place, but had a small percentage of the company that did and ran it for his brother-in-law, who owned the other 95 percent. Denny did his best to create a different impression. Referred to himself as the owner in practically every conversation, same way he was always mentioning some new injury he'd sustained playing a sport. Pretty active for a guy who couldn't lift an eyebrow without sounding like he was on life support and who spent his days practicing magic tricks and playing on his computer. But he paid Hatcher under the table and didn't ask a lot of questions, so Hatcher liked him, even if the big goof seemed to have some sort of weird man-crush on him.

Liked the bar's name, too. It fit.

"I won't forget."

Dennis lifted his hand off Hatcher's shoulder and dropped it again with a convivial slap before heading off, each breath still crying out for some WD-40. "Darn good man."

Hatcher glanced over at the guy who'd passed him the note, thinking, *Not really.*

The vibe he was getting from the guy at the bar really bothered him. The fella was just so pissant scrawny. A guy who, for all appearances, Hatcher was inclined to think he could snap like a number two pencil. Yet considering the implications of the message he'd sent, the shrimp wasn't showing the slightest bit of nerves.

Big men, at least the pugnacious ones, were used to pushing people around. Even if they didn't have big mouths—and the dangerous ones usually didn't—they knew how to use their size to win the psychological battle, how to project it, to get inside the other guy's head. They were all about intimidation. If a fighter can persuade the other guy he's going to lose, chances are it will become a self-fulfilling prophecy. Small guys learn that early from the bullies, naturally attempt to imitate it when dealing with others, try to act bigger than they are. But in wanting to come across as tough they tend to overcompensate, act louder, more obnoxious. Little man's disease, they call it.

A small guy who acts as cool as the other side of the pillow, though, that's different. Truth was, it didn't matter what this one wanted. No way Hatcher could afford to take any chances. Guy like this has danger writ large over every inch of him. Obvious, but only if you knew what to look for. Like a coral snake: all venom, no hood.

There were three possibilities, not mutually exclusive. One was that his little friend was armed. That was less of an option than a certainty, the more Hatcher thought about it. Armed, and the type who knew how to use whatever he was carrying. An expert. He'd have to be. A gun or knife in the hand of a small guy might make him cocky, but it wouldn't make him calm unless he knew how to use it and *knew* he knew how to use it. This guy was the definition of calm.

Possibility number two was that he was an extremely skilled fighter, the world-class kind. Hatcher doubted it. Nose was straight, lips were thin and delicate, face was free of scars. Skilled fighters get their skills from fighting. Nobody escapes every fight unscathed. Add to that the fact this guy obviously knew something about Hatcher's background, and it became even less likely. A fighter good enough to be that confident would be smart enough not to take an opponent with Hatcher's training for granted. Wouldn't be letting his attention drift so freely to flirt with another barmaid, like he was now. Not after passing a note as provocative as the one in Hatcher's pocket.

That left a third possibility. Hatcher checked the time once more, then gestured to the waitress who had passed him the note. New gal with blonde hair, been there less than a month. Always smiling at him. Had a way of filling a T-shirt and cutoffs that made her look like sex was her business. She so resembled the woman he'd moved out to L.A. for—only to have her take off on him a couple of months ago—that he had to struggle not to call her the wrong name.

"Lori, if Denny comes looking for me, tell him something came up and I'll see him tomorrow."

Or not, he told himself, thinking about how the bar's name really did nail it.

The woman flashed him an okay sign, nodding as she wiped down a table.

Hatcher walked out through the patio and crossed the strand. He stopped a few feet past the pavement, angling himself to peer into the alley next to the bar.

Most of the buildings along the beachfront were adjacent to one another—side walls touching if not outright shared—due to square footage being such a premium on the strip. Even so, gaps popped up here and there, and one of them was along the north side of the bar. The neighboring building was a long, flat structure divided into a T-shirt mart and a smoothie shop. There was a narrow alleyway between it and the bar. The space was blocked off by a wrought-iron gate. Other than some garbage cans, it looked empty.

Hatcher moved in closer, checked the chain. It was wrapped around the gate, fastening the edge to an iron post attached to the wall. A large steel lock connected two of the links. A twisting loop of barbed wire sagged along the gate's top like a thorned slinky.

The alley was used for trash. The entry on the opposite side was blocked by a wooden fence. The fence, like the gate, was high and barbed so vagrants and drifters couldn't climb over and camp out after-hours; at least, not without expending serious effort. Unless someone was going to scale one of them and negotiate the wire, the only way in was through the bar itself. And the side door always remained locked.

An ambush was beginning to look unlikely. Unless he was missing something.

Hatcher stared at the neighboring building. Unlike the bar, it was only one story, with a flat roof surrounded by a parapet. A bit too high to see over from where Hatcher stood, and he doubted improving his angle would help. If he backed farther out onto the beach, the row of palm trees bordering the path would block his line of sight. And the section of wall extending above the roofline provided plenty of concealment even if it turned out the trees didn't. He would need a higher vantage point.

There were two second-story windows on the bar's alley wall that were useless, covered by a giant banner advertising medical marijuana for a place three or four blocks up, earning Denny a few hundred extra bucks a week. The bar did have a balcony facing the beach, but the alley side of it was jammed with busted patio tables and beach umbrellas. It would take a bit of noisy effort to make room for a view. And it was getting close to midnight. Four balls.

If someone was up there, using the parapet for concealment, they'd be expecting Hatcher to come into the alley, so their attention would be directed there. They were likely to be hunched down right behind the wall adjacent to it, waiting to hear the door open, checking their watch. That alley would command their attention.

Hatcher scanned the twin storefronts, sliding his gaze to his left. There was no alley on the opposite side of the adjacent building, but near that end somebody had parked a motorcycle. Even in the wan moonlight, he could see the words Harley-Davidson written across the large gas tank in stylish lettering. Jet-black paint, with red-and-white script and striping. California license plate.

The promenade was relatively clear. To the north, he could just make out the large geometric shapes representing a body-builder poised to dead lift, an abstract landmark forming the gate to Muscle Beach. A few pedestrians were loitering in the distance beyond that, but with the shops closed and the sun long down, the walkway was all but deserted. Hatcher wasn't sure who the motorcycle belonged to, but it almost had to be someone in the bar. Maybe even *GQ* Danger Mouse himself, a possibility that made the decision about what to do next easier.

The seat of the bike looked just high enough. A glance in each direction, and Hatcher starting moving swiftly toward it, adjusting his trajectory along the way, checking the bar and rooftop one more time. He broke into a trot for the last few feet, took two running steps and used the third to launch himself off the bike's seat. Stretching his hands out as far and high as they would go, he managed to hook his fingers over the edge of the cement parapet and hang on. He pulled himself up the rest of the way with his arms until he could lean his chest across the top, was forced to reach his arm down the other side of the wall to get a better grip and swing his leg up.

But something reached for him instead, grabbing him by the throat.

"Well, I'll be damned," said a cartoonlike voice, high and squeaky.

Hatcher felt himself get dragged over the edge of the parapet onto the roof, head jammed forward, unable to look up. His neck was being crushed and he couldn't breathe. The gravelly surface of the roof passed beneath him, the tips of his shoes scraping behind him as he tried to get footing. A gargantuan forearm blocked most of his view. He clawed and punched at it feebly, the unexpected constriction of his arteries and windpipe sapping his strength.

"They said you'd be here, few minutes before midnight, and whatd'ya know? Here you are! Un-fuckin'-believable."

The pressure was building in his eye sockets, and the stranglehold around his neck made his head seem on the verge of popping right off. Thinking about anything other than getting air to his lungs and oxygen to his brain was next to impossible. But despite the chaos in his skull, he remembered feeling arms this steely on him once before, remembered being in the grip of something similarly massive, similarly strong. And that voice, taunting him. Even with his thoughts scrambled, there was no mistaking it.

"Heard you got out . . . Took a while to track you to Cali. Knew I'd find you eventually. You didn't think I'd forget our little score, did ya?"

Hatcher couldn't speak, had no desire to. Getting air was all that mattered. His head was swimming, the tension in his skull unbearable. His chest felt ready to split open.

"Read all the papers, saw you'd managed to get away from

those crazy broads and mess Valentine's shit all up. Realized you took care of that cop Maloney, too, when I saw he turned up on a slab. But didn't see one mention about ol' Lucas Sherman anywhere. So I shook Valentine's mouthpiece down for a couple grand and got outta Dodge."

Sherman raised him by the throat, clasping his other hand around Hatcher's neck. He managed to lift Hatcher completely off the ground, so that his feet weren't even touching.

"I have to think of you every friggin' time I look in the mirror, you know that? I got three different rips on my scalp cause a' you. And I have to see them every goddamn morning. That's why I decided I was going to have to get some payback. And you know what they say. Paybacks are a bitch. *Bitch*."

Consciousness seemed to be drifting away, floating across a growing chasm, barely maintaining contact with his mind. A survival instinct was telling him he had to do something, and that he had to do it within seconds or he'd pass out. Passing out meant dying. It was as simple as that.

Problem was, at the moment, passing out seemed like the only thing he could do.

Hatcher forced himself to relax, to let his muscles go loose. He pushed his right leg back, felt himself swing a bit, pushed it back farther. Then he brought it forward in an arcing kick, jerking it with his whole body.

The instep of his foot found its target. A square shot right between the legs.

Sherman barely flinched. Hatcher felt the clamp of fingers tighten around his neck.

"Ever since that little number the state did on me, that whole chemical-castration thing, it's just not the same, ya know? Shot to the nuts now is kind of like getting frogged. All it does is piss me off."

As if to put an exclamation point on it, Sherman lifted Hatcher higher and slammed him down onto the roof. Tiny shards of gravel stabbed into the back of Hatcher's head and shoulders, though the sting of them seemed unimportant compared to the desperate need to breathe.

Fighting off a panic reflex, Hatcher mustered enough strength to punch at Sherman's elbow, brought down a hard chop to his forearm. He struck again and again, riding a last gasp of adrenaline, trying to find a pressure point, to weaken the man's grip. It was like hitting padded granite.

"Been on a kick-ass 'roid regimen, new stuff someone turned me on to. Comes in through Mexico. That, and daily doses of HGH. Been pumping twice a day, harder than ever. The whole time, looking forward to this."

He slapped a palm over Hatcher's mouth and nose, pressing hard, leaning his massive frame forward to put all of his weight into his arms, pinning Hatcher down. The other hand kept squeezing Hatcher's throat.

Deprived of all air and lacking blood flow, Hatcher's vision began to fade, collapsing into a shrinking tunnel. Ambient noise grew muffled, the sound of his own pulse filled his ears.

Sherman was simply too strong, stronger than he had been, and bigger, too. Way stronger, way bigger. Hatcher felt himself start to flail, arms and legs moving frantically, without focus. His hands clawed fiercely at Sherman's skin, raking strips of it, to no avail. Only the pain in his upper back and scalp, the scores of sharp points of gravel digging into the skin like talons, enabled him to cling to consciousness. But not for much longer.

The pain. A thought flickered, sparked by the stabbing pricks in his back.

He threw his arm out, slamming his hand against the rocky roof. Bits of gravel bit into his flesh as he clawed through them. His fingers finally settled on one the size of a stick of gum. It had a thin edge. It would have to do.

Barely cognizant of his actions, Hatcher whipped his hand back toward the hand clenched around his throat. He pressed the edge of the rock hard against the inside of Sherman's wrist, just beneath the meat of his palm. Then he slashed upward.

Everything finally went dark. For a moment, darkness was all there was, all it seemed there would ever be. But then Hatcher heard something echo through the liquid-stuffiness of his ears, something like a screaming string of cuss words.

Blood surged into his head, filling it, overwhelming him with vertigo. He realized he could breathe again about the same time he realized he was no longer being choked. His skull felt engorged. His limbs felt numb and useless. He gasped for air as he tried to roll over and vomit.

"Goddamn motherfucker!"

Hatcher finished retching and blinked several times. He looked over to see Sherman holding his forearm out in front his body, cradling it in his other hand, wide-eyed. His flesh was split from just below his wrist to roughly a few inches short of the crook of his elbow. Blood was streaming out and spilling onto the roof.

"You little . . . *son of a* . . . you cut me! Look at this! *You cut me!*"

Still struggling for air, Hatcher crawled on all fours toward the nearest edge of the roof, coughing. He collapsed when he reached it. It took some effort to prop his shoulders against the wall. The concrete was hard and unforgiving against the back of his head. Gravel shards dug into his lower back, dozens of slivers stuck to his palms. Their sharp tips scratched at his throat as he tried to rub it. He was still having trouble getting enough air. He felt ready to vomit again any moment.

Sherman was looking down at his wound. The lower half of his forearm was drenched in blood. Thick crimson sheets of it rolled off like paint. He flexed his fist several times, causing more red to flow.

"This is gonna scar bad," he said, tilting his head to glare at Hatcher before his expression gave way to a menacing smile. "That's another one. Ya know, before I was just gonna choke you out. Now I'm gonna rip that sorry pimple of a head of yours off while you're still breathing. Then I think I'll shove it up your ass."

One chance, Hatcher told himself. That was all he was going to get.

"What'd you say?" Sherman asked.

Hatcher tried to clear his throat, swallowing painfully, the muscles in his neck bruised and raw.

"I said, did you get that voice in prison? Must've been a popular guy, from the sound of it."

Sherman's smile widened. He wiped his hand on his jeans, then took off his shirt and wrapped it tight around his lower arm, tying it off.

"I'll give you this, ass-wipe. You got balls."

"Too bad you don't, Princess."

The smile remained on the big man's face, but the eyes were

narrower now, hate and rage streaming through the slits the way water blasts through a pressure hose. Hatcher let his body settle lower, wishing he had a better plan, but thinking, times like these, you gotta take what the other guy gives you.

He took a breath, still trying to work through the pain in his throat. He forced himself to focus. *He doesn't protect his groin.*

Sherman crossed the roof toward him, flexing that hand several more times. The shirt was already saturated with blood.

Even in his dazed state, Hatcher couldn't help but notice that Sherman's chest was just plain enormous, two giant peachy slabs of polished marble, squared off at the edges, the abs below them rippling like large stones implanted beneath the skin. Sherman was more than three hundred pounds, easy, and not an ounce of visible fat anywhere on him.

One chance, Hatcher reminded himself.

Sherman bent forward as he came to a stop, straddling Hatcher's body, thrusting his arms down to snag Hatcher's throat. Hatcher slid down along the gravel as he did, his hips almost directly below Sherman's, his body between the man's ankles. He waited for Sherman's knees to bend, feeling those viselike hands wrap themselves around his neck again. The pain was immediate and excruciating.

Just . . .

A . . .

Little . . .

Lower . . .

Now.

In one continuous motion, Hatcher pulled his knees in toward his chest, curling his back, and planted his heels firmly into Sherman's crotch. Then he exploded his quadriceps into a full extension.

And prayed he had enough strength left.

Jesus, this guy is heavy.

Hatcher's legs buckled, but he continued to press hard and Sherman unsteadily rose into the air. For a fraction of a second, Sherman hung there, balanced, and Hatcher thought he was going to come crashing down on top of him. But then he let go of Hatcher's throat, throwing his hands onto the wall to catch himself before he slammed into it, and Hatcher was able to complete the move by rolling back, pressing against the gravel with his elbows, using inertia, extending his body and legs as far as he could. Sherman's body started to flip and he pressed himself up, a gymnast on a pommel horse, almost managing to break the momentum, until one arm slipped forward and he toppled over the edge.

Hatcher heard a thump a second later, the sharp crack of bone hitting pavement mixed in.

Massaging his throat, Hatcher lay there for a count of twenty, waiting for his airways to loosen, allowing his lungs to fill with air and his heart rate to settle. When he was certain the stars he was seeing were all in the sky, he pulled himself up and leaned over the parapet.

Sherman's body was laid out like a crime scene reenactment. The side of his head was red and pulpy. One arm was resting on its elbow, hand in the air, sort of floating in a seesaw movement back and forth. His head lolled vaguely to one side.

Crouched next to him was the guy from the bar. The look on his face struck Hatcher as one of professional intrigue, a big-game hunter examining a felled beast not his own, his eyes fixed in detached interest as he took in the size and majesty of the exotic creature stretched out before him. He gave a slight shake to his head, and what looked like a bemused chuckle, before looking up at Hatcher and pulling his cheeks into a smile.

"Nice work," he said. He jutted his chin, gesturing with it. "Check your six. Third of a click."

Hatcher twisted to peer over his shoulder. Beyond the roof of the building to his rear, across Pacific Street, two people stood on a motel balcony, a man and a woman, watching from a third-floor railing that overlooked the street. The man was wearing a suit, tan, expensive-looking. He was trim, with short, silvery hair. The woman was younger, blonde, wearing a gray skirt and dark blouse. They were too far away for Hatcher to make out any other details about them, except that they had clearly been there for a while.

But he was pretty sure he recognized the woman.

The man in the suit seemed to nod in his direction, then turned to walk away. The woman lingered a moment before following. They disappeared into a nearby room.

Hatcher looked back down to the walkway. Sherman was still there. So was the other guy.

"You're wondering who I am," the guy said. "Friend or foe."

Hatcher coughed, his throat still sore. He didn't think he had another fight in him, and certainly not if it was against someone skilled. Or armed. Or both. "Now that you mention it."

"You can just call me Mr. E."

Hearing it aloud gave the moniker new meaning. Hatcher's gaze drifted over to the Harley. He could see the license plate. MRE HD.

"Cute."

"I thought so. So, do you want me to finish him off for you?"

Before Hatcher had a chance to process the question, Mr. E snapped his arm straight, pointing it out and down at an angle. The move triggered a mechanism up his sleeve that released a large dual-bladed knife into his hand, a smooth handle in the middle. The man twirled the blade baton-style, weaving it through his fingers back and forth. Then he spun it in the air like a pinwheel, loosely centered against his palm, and dropped suddenly to a knee, catching the blade so that the tip of one end was poised directly over Sherman's chest, maybe a centimeter above it. Maybe less. It didn't look to Hatcher like the guy he knew as Mr. E had even broken eye contact during the move.

"Well?"

Not on the same team as Sherman after all, Hatcher realized. Unless this Mr. E switched sides easily and often. He had to admit the proposition was an attractive one. Sherman was a homicidal psycho freak, a threat to pretty much everyone and anyone. There was no reason to think he wouldn't keep gunning to settle things with Hatcher until one of them was dead anyway. Knife boy was offering him a gift. Killing a murderous sociopath like that was a no-brainer.

Too much of one.

"No," Hatcher said.

Mr. E shrugged, spun the blade with a flourish again, and then somehow made it disappear up the sleeve of his out-stretched arm.

"Why don't you get down from there. There's someone I'm supposed to take you to see."

I know a fellow's been looking for you. "And who would that be?"

"William Bartlett."

Hatcher chewed on the name for a moment. "*General* William Bartlett?"

"The one and only. Know him?"

"I've heard of him."

"Well, it's mutual. He's waiting. And he's with someone else, someone you definitely do know."

The sea breeze picked up, gusting in, mussing up the guy's hair, the howl forcing him to pause until it died down.

"Gal by the name of Vivian. Used to be married to God."

The one who called himself Mr. E smiled, mocking lips on a face brimming with unspoken knowledge. "That is, until you had a hand in her divorce."

CHAPTER 2

"HOW MUCH FARTHER?"

"HOW MUCH FARTHER?"

The kid sitting next to him was in his early twenties, at the most. Maybe even his teens. He offered him a reassuring smile, noticed the kid was staring at the digital clock readout above the radio: 12:17. He'd picked the boy up just after midnight. The strip was good for that.

"Not much," Perry said.

The Mercedes followed the twin beams of light as they cut a swath atop the winding asphalt. The road snaked in ascending curves through the hills, a slack of ribbon unspooling ahead of them. A barrier of trees to each side gave the route a mazelike quality.

"When we get there, I was thinking I might open this nice bottle of cab I have. A '97 Diamond Creek." Perry shifted his frame behind the wheel, twisting to face the younger man. "Do you know much about wine, Daryl?"

His passenger thought for a moment, eyes roaming the dashboard. "Darin. I'm pretty sure I told you my name was Darin."

"Sorry," Perry said, rebuking himself. The traffic had been loud, so it was excusable. And the odds of that being his real name were practically zilch anyway. But still. "Are you a wine drinker, Darin? The '97 is excellent."

Darin started to say something, then angled away. He stared out the side window, his body quiet.

"What was that?"

"Nothing," Darin said.

Perry nodded, reiterating that the '97 was a good vintage, then segueing into the weather. He had little doubt his lean, lithe passenger had wanted to declare he wasn't a homosexual. Such protests weren't uncommon, in his experience. Usually when they popped up he would make a point of agreeing, explain how he understood completely, assure the young men—and they were always rather young—that it was obvious they were straight, how he could tell right off. Fashion a comment about how he never really thought otherwise. He was just looking forward to some good company, some stimulating conversation over drinks. Whatever reason they had for hanging around outside that bar, for approaching the car and getting in, it wasn't *that*. He was just happy to make a friend.

The little speech was ready to go. The kid would likely raise the objection again. But really, who was he kidding? Hadn't he made a point of mentioning how much he enjoyed some museum in San Francisco recently? As if *that* wasn't intended to send a message.

Perry hummed softly to himself, the lyrics to the tune bringing a smile to his lips as they cascaded over his thoughts.

See the pyramids a-long de-nial . . .

He felt good. This was the part of the Game that got his juices flowing, the almost giddy feeling of anticipation. He was so thankful for his life, so grateful he had money and the freedom that came with it. He never questioned that he deserved it, that he'd *earned* it, but he also never let himself forget how fortunate he was compared to those like Darin. He had brains, and he'd used them to get what he wanted. Poor schmucks like the one next to him had no intellectual gifts, or at least none they used. As a consequence, they had no power. Nothing to offer but their bodies.

And for that particular commodity, it was always a buyer's market.

Perry shook his head silently. Disgusting, really.

The road doglegged, becoming a long driveway that forked into a teardrop turnaround. At the tip of it sat a block-shaped sectional protruding from the hillside, the elevated portions supported by solid round stilts.

"Well," Perry said. "Here we are."

Darin studied the edifice without expression. Trying not to look impressed, perhaps, but unable to hide his interest.

"What do you think?"

"I think the architect laughed all the way to the bank."

Perry waited several seconds before responding. "I designed it myself."

Darin nodded, as if the information didn't surprise him at all.

Perry was still trying to determine whether the remark had been an insult or a clumsy joke as he swung the car around the circle and parked near a set of white steps. He got out and waited at the base of them until his guest, frayed shoulder pack slung over his back and adopting what seemed like a painfully slow gait, finally joined him. The code to the keyless entry was Perry's birthday, year first, then day, then month. Keying in the numbers, he considered making a comment about the view and how it looked in the moonlight, describe the vista as it appears on a clear day, the rocky shadows of the mountain slopes, the cobalt blue Pacific visible in the divides, but sensed his new acquaintance wasn't impressed by such things. The kid was dressed in what Perry supposed was street-cool. Untucked gray shirt, baggy jeans, zip-up hoodie with some sort of graffiti-look design on the back. Fingerless black gloves.

But he did look clean. No hint of tweaking. Even if his taste in clothes suggested he was no stranger to that kind of thing.

The locking mechanism disengaged with a metallic hum, then the sliding clunk of a bolt being thrown.

"Please," Perry said, closing the door behind them and gesturing toward a sofa. "Make yourself at home."

The young man plodded into the house, absorbed the surroundings with measured glances. The main living area was open; a large island kitchen in full view on the far side and a dining area with an oversized table to the left. A wide stairway off to the right ascended to a loft area with a pool table and television overlooking the living room, a short half wall separating them. Next to the staircase, a brief passageway led to a master suite, two posts of a large bed visible through an open set of French doors a considerable distance from where they stood.

Perry strode toward the back, gesturing insistently that his guest take a seat. "Now, how about some of that wine?"

He stopped just short of the kitchen. "You might find this interesting," he said. Bending down, he slid two fingers between the inset ring of a trap door and lifted it.

"This wine cellar is spiral. The staircase was handmade from a single piece of red cedar."

Darin stood, swinging the pack over his shoulder like a lumberjack about to decamp.

Shit, Perry thought. *I've spooked him.*

"Oh, just look at me," he said, lowering the cellar door shut. "Not much of a host. I haven't asked you if you're hungry or if you wanted something other than alcohol."

"I need to use your bathroom. Is there one in the bedroom?"

Smiling, Perry swept his arm toward the door at the end of the hallway and began to move in that direction, not bothering to mention the closer bathroom near the stairs.

"Of course, help yourself. You don't even need to ask. If you don't mind, while you're in there I'm going to get out of these slacks, maybe put on some jeans. Relax a little."

"It's your home," Darin said.

Perry ushered him into the master suite. It was, by any standard, the showcase of the house. Cavernous but somehow still cozy. Perry reveled in the regal dimensions, the statement it made about someone who could claim such a chamber. But he'd been careful with the décor. The key was not to appear ostentatious. To find that balance of richly furnished but tastefully restrained. Still, there were some things he couldn't resist. In addition to the super-ultra king-sized bed, the area comfortably accommodated a full sofa and an Indian rosewood coffee table, a mahogany writing desk big enough to play ping-pong on, and an eighteenth-century armoire. A custom-made water feature of imported stone took up most of one wall, babbling gently in the background.

On the other side of the room, a large archway offered access to the bath. A curve of stylish brass craned out over a gigantic bowl sink, surrounded by veined granite and deeply colored marble. The rest of the bathroom lay hidden around the corner, extending back toward the main part of the house.

Perry watched as Darin swept his eyes from right to left, taking it all in. He had to be in awe—had to be—but his face was all poker. A second of standing there, orienting himself, then Darin headed for the archway.

A six-foot mirror leaned against the wall near the entry to the bath, framed in wide thick planks of brown-black wood. He paused in front of it. He seemed to be studying its design, admiring it, but Perry knew better. Little doubt the kid was checking himself out, making sure he looked good. Wanting to be at his most attractive for what the rest of the evening held in store.

To be gay, he thought, was to be vain.

Perry watched him cross into the bathroom and glance around the corner. He imagined the young man's impressions of the place, of the luxuriousness of that shower, the pebbled stone floor behind the glass, the twin showerheads, the rock bench. This was another part of the Game he loved. He smiled and turned to enter the closet.

If the bedroom was his favorite room in the house, the closet was a big reason. It was the size of a small motel room. Modular organizers along the walls, sliding foot drawers, a three-sided mirror angled around a stepped platform. Nothing captured his sense of who he was like this room.

He nudged off his shoes, then slid off his trousers and hanged them on one of his valets. Shrugged off his shirt, boxers, and socks, dropped them each in a separate hamper compartment. He placed his shoes carefully on a rack and straightened his spine to inspect himself in the three-way. Not bad for fifty. Damn good, in fact. His cock especially. Hanging there, slightly engorged on its way to erect, mildly tingling with excitement, it looked manly. He allowed that perhaps his stomach could be flatter, his muscles a bit more toned, but to be leaner at his age meant time in a gym. That was for losers. Corded, sinewy bodies required too many hours, hours that he spent making money instead. He had a small workout room in the house, did twenty minutes of aerobics a day. That was enough. He had a Game to play.

One of the wardrobes held a drawer with new packs of individual boxer briefs. He opened one and pulled it over his legs, snapping the band around his hips. They felt fresh and tight, a feeling he loved. New underwear was part of the ritual.

Reaching up, lifting his heels to stretch, he felt along the top of the wardrobe until he found the latch. Hooking his finger around it, he pulled firmly, listening for the click. He held on to it and reached into the space above one of the shelves near his chest and pressed a button that looked like the head of a bolt in a line of several. The wooden frame crept a tiny bit, a loose, swaying feeling under Perry's weight. He lowered himself onto his heels and placed a hand along the side of it. The entire section glided open on graceful hinges.

God, he loved this closet.

He'd told the contractor this modification was to be a safe room, a tiny enclosure to provide a haven in case of a home invasion. Totally off contract. Four feet wide, five feet deep. He didn't want it on any of the plans, demanded all copies of the blueprint and spec revisions be handed over upon completion, and insisted those documents be kept to a minimum in the first place. A small bonus ensured no permits would be needed and no public record of the modification made. The contractor never blinked. Perry was convinced the guy actually swallowed the whole spiel.

And now it was his Sacred Space.

An overhead fluorescent bulb flickered on, bathing the compartment in a white glow. A sense of reverence, of holiness, washed over him as his eyes caressed the contents. It was the closest thing to a religious experience he knew, worshiping at this altar.

Each wall had its own theme, its own function. The wall on the left was a Memorial. A commemoration of his body of work, photos arrayed with great care. High-quality digital printouts in chronological order. The wall on the right held his souvenirs, his trophies. Some stood on small shelves, others hung from hooks. The back wall was dedicated to his tools of the trade. Mostly knives.

There were four rows of cutting instruments, as he liked to think of them. It was a term suited to what he saw as his particular avocation, his calling. The top two rows were held in place by magnetic strips. The lower two rows were for more specialized implements, some displayed in custom cases. These were secured to the wall on individual holders. Hanging along each side was a vertical row of handcuffs and manacles, an assortment of different size bracelets connected by chains of varying lengths.

Below the rows was a narrow table with a single drawer. He tugged open the drawer and examined the contents, which were neatly organized for quick access. First things first.

He removed a small glass jar of clear liquid and set it on the table, then retrieved a box containing an old-fashioned atomizer with a mesh bulb. Another narrow case held a syringe, which he removed and set out next to the atomizer.

Although he'd tried many methods in the past, some crude,

others highly sophisticated, he found the simple approach of spraying an aerosolized solution of procaine to be the best. It was easy to acquire, easy to use, and most important, as long as an opioid antagonist was administered in short order, unlikely to result in death. Having them die early on was no way to play the Game. Death signaled the end. Rendering his subjects unconscious was intended to mark the beginning.

One of his early discoveries was that it was not as easy to induce unconsciousness as he'd thought. In fact, he learned it was actually quite hard—far more difficult than the way he'd seen it done in movies and on television. The most reliable methods required an administration of something narcotic, orally or intravenously. There were problems either way. Slipping something into a person's food or drink turned out to be far trickier than he'd anticipated. Some people had a habit of barely touching their beverage, others would sip it so slowly for so long the effect was diminished. And the wait while someone nursed their drink was just too excruciating to endure. On the other hand, injecting someone with a needle usually triggered a violent reaction. He'd been punched and kicked and almost stabbed once with his own syringe trying it that way. Not to mention, of course, the potential for damage to some of his exquisite furniture, a risk that couldn't be overlooked. And then there were the dosage issues. A few had never woken up, robbing him of the best part. Like being handed a forfeit after training and prepping for a win. It just wasn't right.

But he was always learning, and he had finally discovered a much more practical manner of delivery. He could spray his little concoction without touching the person, usually under the pretext of wanting his playmate to smell a wonderful fragrance. Two strong puffs, and that was usually it. The eyes would saucer, a look that seemed to be equal parts confusion and horrifying realization. The hands would shoot to the throat. Some rough coughing would ensue. A few violent shakes of the head, often a gasping noise, and then the legs would buckle. At this point, another spurt to the face was sometimes thrown in, just to be safe.

Lift him to the bed, apply a cuff to each arm, secure the legs at the ankles, and the hard part was done. From there it was simply a matter of reviving the sap. Arranging the instruments took a few minutes, but that was enjoyable work. After that, it was all fun. The purest kind.

Perry realized he'd just sighed. He truly loved what he did, ridding the world of degenerates. Making money was satisfying, and he certainly enjoyed the things money could buy, but nothing matched the thrill of the just kill. The Game was all there was. It gave him purpose.

His pulse thumped with excitement at the thought of plying his special trade again, but at the same time a familiar calm settled over him as he prepared the procaine solution and assembled the atomizer. He decided he would take extra care in selecting which implements to use tonight. This one would be special.

The cuts were always planned to inflict maximum pain. He wasn't about senseless acts of violence. No, the Game demanded more. This was punishment. Punishment for being an insult to decency, to normalcy. It required they all suffer, all he captured, and suffer they did. They suffered pain, they suffered humiliation. Suffered so many times, in so many ways. The humiliation came first. He would degrade them through sexual acts, rub their noses in their depravity by forcing them to face what they were, violating their bodies the way they violated the laws of nature. Over and over, repeating it for hours. He prided himself for having the confidence to do what it took. Many, he knew, would be unable to engage in such acts, would anguish over the implications. Not him. He knew he was not one of *them*. He was doing this for a greater cause, a greater good. Defiling them for a reason. The exhilaration he experienced was out of asserting his will, of demonstrating his sexual superiority. His ability to climax several times was simply an example of his exceptionalism, of the tremendous control he had over his own body and the limitless power of his will, not evidence of any deviant prurience or unnatural proclivities. No, he was definitely not one of them. He was a true man.

And there was work to be done.

Normally, he would reach for the large crescent-shaped amputation knife. Its curved blade allowed for the deepest cuts, and its angled tip was ideal for exploring pain centers beneath flaps of partially flayed skin. But he decided tonight he would use the antique European circumcision knife, a rare piece he'd acquired a few years earlier via private auction. Dating to the late eighteenth century, it had a carved bone grip (perforated to decrease weight), a gap bolster exposing the tang, a case-hardened blade, and a beveled cutting edge. The triangular shaped cutting edge rounded out its unmistakably pre-Victorian look.

Perry stared at the antique instrument. There was something magical about a good knife from any period, ancient or modern. Something primal. The craftsmanship, the functionality, the ability of the blade to cleave, to separate a whole into constituent parts. A new, pristine blade was a joy to hold, but the historical ones, the specimens with a pedigree, those were practically narcotic. They were like holy relics. Inspirational artifacts. Instruments forged centuries earlier only to find their true purpose, finally, in his hands.

Highlights of what was to come danced through his thoughts. The begging, the screaming, the pleas to God. He took particular satisfaction in those. A sodomite hoping for divine intervention? Ha! There was no God, he would tell them. Order, civilization, even love—it was all a delusion. His great discovery, one he knew few before him had ever made, was that reality was his to shape. That existence was the Game. He was a player. The rest, perhaps every last one of them, were pawns.

The object of the Game was to impose your will on those pawns, and in doing so, create something wonderful: justice.

He removed the knife from its case, tilted the blade in various directions to feel its heft, its balance. He realized he was grinning. He couldn't help it. There was an unusual smugness to this Darin kid, mostly unspoken but still there, like with that crack about his house. A lack of respect that cried out for special treatment. And this instrument seemed wonderfully suited for the job. Poetically so.

The timekeeper in his head told him he'd left Darin alone long enough and that he needed to make an appearance. He stepped back from the compartment and gently closed the wardrobe, stopping it just short of catching. He pulled on a pair of loose pajama pants and slid the atomizer into the front pocket.

Emerging from the closet, he noticed a faint wobbling of light from the bathroom. It only took a second for him to realize Darin must have lit a candle.

How sweet, he thought. Annoying that a guest would be so presumptuous, act so at home, but still sweet. In a pathetic sort of way.

"Everything okay?" he said, padding into the room, voice raised a notch.

The sound of movement whispered from across the room, soles falling on the bathroom tile, then Darin came into view. He walked into the bedroom carrying a candle, holding it out in front of him.

Perry slid his hand into his pocket, fingers sliding over the nozzle of the atomizer, feeling the bulb.

"There's something I wanted to show—"

The words died in Perry's throat. His eyes locked onto the object in the young man's hands. It wasn't a candle, he realized. Well, it was, but it wasn't. It was a hand. A severed human hand, whitened and waxy. Darin held it palm out, digits extended toward the ceiling, a flame burning from the middle finger. It cast a glow that reversed the normal shadows of the young man's face.

The room seemed to tilt. Perry took a step to catch his balance. The floor stretched. He staggered to the bed, which now seemed a moving target. He pulled his hand from his pocket, dropping the atomizer, and stabbed his arms toward the mattress, stumbling. He slid to his knees against the edge, stared mutely at the person holding the flame.

His body felt heavy, all dead, rubbery weight, but his mind was like air, lighter than air, a balloon. His thoughts were just sounds, faint vibrations echoing away, voices disappearing over some distant cliff, too far off for him to hear what they were saying.

He stared at the flame until there was nothing to see, just the darkness behind his lids.

PERRY'S EYES SNAPPED OPEN BEFORE HIS MIND REGISTERED any conscious thought. He blinked. A vague feeling of panic sizzled beneath his scalp. Too many realizations hit him at once, not allowing him to focus on any of them.

He was in his bed, on his back. He was naked. The room was dimly lighted. He was unable to move his arms or legs; at least, not able to move them much. There were bands of pressure around his wrists and ankles. The restraints were tight. There was a stinging pain in the palm of his right hand.

He wasn't alone.

The pieces were forming a whole. He'd been drugged somehow, knocked out.

And now he saw it was Darin in the room with him, not far from the foot of the bed. Standing at the mirror.

Stay calm, he told himself. *You're smarter than everyone else, more aware. You're not a mere pawn. This was all part of the Game. Everything was part of the Game. It's just a new challenge. What's a Game without a challenge?*

He swallowed. The dryness in his throat made it hurt.

He tried to make himself speak. It was harder than he expected.

"Darin," he finally said. The weakness of his voice alarmed him. He swallowed again, said it louder.

The young man didn't respond, didn't acknowledge he'd even heard him.

"Darin, let's talk about this. I don't think you realize who . . ." He caught himself, thought carefully about what to say. "You don't want to do this."

Calm, calm, calm. Focus. The Game had evolved, that's all. It was an unexpected twist, but really nothing more than a test of his skills. How to play the next move depended on what his opponent's motivations were. If this Darin kid were a serial killer, he could suggest a partnership. Money and resources to enjoy his hobby in style, satisfy his cravings in comfort. Maybe the kid was on his own mission, ridding the world of degenerates himself, and the Game was offering Perry a chance to morph into team play mode. Unlikely, but he couldn't rule it out. There was also the chance this was just a heavy-handed robbery. If so, he would have to convince Darin that he needed to physically retrieve his stash of money, persuade him that the restraints had to be removed. The prospect that concerned him the most, though, the one he knew would be the trickiest, was if the kid was some kind of vigilante, maybe someone related to one of those many degenerates Perry had taught a lesson. In that case, the play would have to be that he had the wrong man, pretend to understand why he was out for justice and offer to help. All compassion and empathy.

Regardless, all scenarios would end up with the kid dead. Very dead.

Yes, he told himself. All part of the Game.

And now his surprising adversary was backing away from the mirror, not even glancing down as he drew near the bed. Darin picked up a knife from the nightstand. Perry recognized it—long, utilitarian blade, contoured handle, stored on the top row of the magnetic strip, second from the left—just as Darin clamped down on his wrist, pulled the wrist strap down to expose flesh, and screwed the point of the knife into the meat of his palm. Perry let out a yelp. The kid set down the knife and dug his index and middle fingers across the wound, curling the fingertips with a scooping motion, turning them up toward the ceiling to minimize the dripping.

"You're right," Darin said, heading back to the mirror. "I don't. But you know what they say, if you want something done right . . ."

For the first time, Perry realized Darin had been smearing his blood on the glass. Drawing something. It looked like a large, vertical oval. Not an oval, exactly. Longer. Thinner. More like a cunt.

"See? I knew it." Perry swallowed again, trying to get some moisture into his mouth and throat. "Why don't we talk about this, Darin? Just you and me, okay. Sit down next to me and talk. I care. Let me show you how much I care, how I want to help."

"Do you, really now? Want to help, I mean?"

"Yes," Perry said. "Yes, I do."

"Then tell me where you normally dispose of the bodies. You must have a good location, close by. It might save me some time. Unless you want to deal with it later."

Perry blinked. Almost two decades of play and he had never faced anything like this before. For the first time since he'd become aware of the Game, he was actually afraid of losing. Was that even possible?

"I have no idea what you mean. This is all some big mistake."

"If you could hear yourself through these ears, you might realize how ridiculous you sound and just shut the hell up."

"Listen, you have to believe me, I—"

"I know what you are. It's why I'm here. I was admiring your knife collection. Nice. That particularly large one will come in handy. The memento wall next to them was a bit cliched, but I guess there's something to be said for honoring traditions."

"Please, you *have* to listen—"

"Shhhh . . . just stop. I need you to be quiet now. I'll use the hand again, if I have to."

The hand. Perry's gaze jumped to the coffee table. He remembered the candle, remembered how it was the last thing he saw, remembered the way the flame seared an image into his head, crowding out everything else.

"Is that how you drugged me?"

"That's one way to look at it. Now, stop talking."

"Look . . . whatever it is, whatever reason you're doing this, we can come to an arrangement. I have money. Lots of money."

"I have a good idea of how much you're worth."

"Then you know I can wire money anywhere. Just let me get to my computer. Thousands. Hundreds of thousands."

Darin's lips pulled tight, spreading into an ironic grin that Perry didn't like. "That won't be necessary."

"You said yourself you don't want to do this. Don't be a killer."

"Tell me something, since you won't *shut up*: how many?"

"I don't—"

"Men. Boys. *Victims.* How many did you rape and torture and dump into a hole somewhere?"

"Listen to me! You've got the wrong guy—"

"Your first one was in 1998. He was seventeen. Turning tricks for money to feed his habit. His picture didn't make your wall. That part came later. Ritual evolution."

Perry said nothing. A vigilante. Worst of all possibilities.

"You don't even know, do you? You've lost count. Don't get me wrong, I'm not judging. Just illustrating why you've already been judged."

Darin retrieved the knife and circled to the foot of the bed. Perry's legs were tied down, leather cuffs around the ankles. His feet were pale, tinged with blue from veins webbed just beneath the surface, his toenails thick and yellowing. Darin stabbed a short, deep cut into the top of each foot midway down, near where the cuneiform bone met the metatarsal. He scraped his forefingers into one of the cuts and went back to the mirror, tracing an outer line around the curve on one side. He returned, repeating the act with blood from the other foot.

Perry grimaced and grunted each time, but didn't cry out. His mind raced to think of a new strategy. Nothing came to him.

He watched as Darin made another approach and leaned over him from the side. The steel of the knife flashed once in the dim light, then Perry felt it stab him between two ribs. Not deep, but enough to make his body seize up, force him to gasp.

This was something he had trouble grasping. In all his years of playing, he never expected to meet someone else who seemed aware, someone like him, another player. He never contemplated the words now pictured flashing on the screen. Game Over.

Fingertips dripping once again in blood, Darin stood at the mirror and made another mark, one Perry couldn't quite discern. Then he spoke in a hushed tone, barely audible.

Perry didn't understand the words. They were foreign, alien. Unrecognizable gibberish. When he was finished, Darin picked up the hand from the coffee table, struck a match.

The wick above the middle finger blazed with an unnatural brightness as Darin held it forward. But instead of reflecting it, the area of the mirror inside the blood outline seemed transparent, clear glass giving view to a dark tunnel of some sort. A passage.

A figure moved behind the glass. Large, imposing, covered in shadow. Perry caught glimpses of a hide, tight and smooth, skin the color of arterial blood in milk. But as it moved the blackness seemed to envelope it, to follow it. An occasional glimpse appeared through brief gaps in the darkness, but it seemed otherwise impervious to light.

The shadow raised an arm and reached toward the glass. Rather than stopping on contact, it moved right through.

A large hand emerged, long fingers, nails like small talons. It was like someone reaching up through water, and Perry realized that it wasn't actually coming through the glass, but rather stretching it. A smooth membrane coated the arm as it extended forward. A foot stepped out next, a knee moving with it.

Then the contours of a face appeared against the surface.

Perry felt his heart smashing against his breastbone, pounding to be let out. This was wrong, he thought. Wrong, wrong, wrong. Things like this weren't real. His entire existence had been a testament to that, to the fact the material world was all there was, that reality was a tangible substance he could shape with his will. It was all a Game, nothing more. There was no such thing as the supernatural. No spirits, no ghosts, no demons. Certainly no Devil, and definitely no God.

Was there?

The head of the thing pushed out into the room, stretching the glassy film as if it were a thin sheet of elastic. It was enormous, a gargantuan skull with a pair of massive horns spiraling out from the top at opposing angles. Triangular face, huge jaws. But the details of its features remained unclear, obscured by the glassy membrane now smoothed over it.

It stepped out onto the floor and leaned forward. Perry's eyes followed it as it straightened its spine, its head almost reaching the twelve-foot ceiling. In two giant strides it was at the bed, tilted over the mattress, studying Perry with a feral grin, its heading canting back and forth slightly.

It raised its hand, floating a large palm over Perry's body, before clapping it down on his chest. Perry felt his lungs seize. The spot it touched burned, burned freezing cold, colder than he could imagine ever being. The cold spread in a wave down his left arm, into his ring finger. The entire limb tingled painfully, the stinging sensation of pins and needles. But his finger hurt the worst.

Then the figure withdrew, retreating until the surface of the mirror snapped back into place. The glass shuddered, a pool of liquid smoothing itself out, before hardening to normal.

Seconds passed. Perry was having trouble catching his breath, his pulse far ahead of his respiration. He stared at the mirror until he remembered Darin. He snapped glances around the room.

Just as his hopes started to rise that the boy may have left, Darin stepped out of the closet. He was holding several knives from Perry's collection. He had a towel draped over his shoulder.

Darin laid the towel out on the coffee table near the bed, arranged the knives on it in a neat row. The huge amputation knife, a long ridged carving knife, a butcher knife.

"You're going to kill me," Perry said, the words coming as a surprise to his own ears.

"Not tonight."

Perry blinked. Not tonight? Was this another twist? Had he been too quick to assume it was all over? He could feel the relief rain down like a warm shower. Premature, perhaps, but he didn't care. There was still hope. Maybe he was still the player, still at the controls. Maybe.

He twisted his neck, raised his head. The knives were arrayed like a set of surgical instruments.

"What, then?" he asked.

"You want the simple answer or the complex one?"

Perry opened his mouth but wasn't sure what to say. The Game had taken him so far into uncharted waters he was uncertain what was expected of him.

"Let's keep it simple," Darin said. "I've got one more thing to do, then I'm going to undo your restraints."

"You're going to let me go?"

"More or less."

Yes, Perry thought. Yes, of course. How silly he'd been, ready to assume the worst. This was still the Game he knew. It had merely changed course. All he had to do now was learn the new rules.

"Then what?" he asked.

"Then . . ." Darin tugged the fingerless gloves off his hands one at a time. His hands were wrapped in gauze. Blood had seeped through the palm area of each.

"Then those hands of yours are going to use those knives there, and do what you might call 'a surgical number' on this body," Darin said, tapping himself.

Perry couldn't be certain he heard correctly, was even less certain he could believe any of it. He started to speak several times but worried he may say something wrong, something that would make the crazy boy change his mind. Things were being played out on a different level now, one he was unfamiliar with. There was still a feeling he could lose.

Darin took off his jacket, then his shirt.

Perry's attention immediately went to his left arm. The first

thing he noticed was its color, or lack of it. The skin was an unnatural shade of pale, almost ghostly. Purple veins spidered the
length of it. It was like the arm belonged to someone else, like
someone had cut the real one off and sewed this in its place. A
tattooed word ran the interior length of the forearm. *Coagula.*

"Now, I want you to listen closely. In the morning, you're
going to find a note over there." Darin gestured vaguely toward
the coffee table, toward the arrangement of knives. "It will tell
you exactly what you're supposed to do."

"In the morning?"

"You heard me."

Perry stared at the coffee table for several seconds. "But,
didn't you say you want me to use the knives on you?"

"That part will be done by the time you read the note."

"I don't understand."

"You don't need to."

A prolonged silence, then Perry said, "You also said there
was one more thing."

Darin's face was impassive, all business, the only expression
on it one of boredom. He said nothing.

"Before you let me go," Perry added. "You said you had one
more thing to do before you let me go."

"Yes, I did, but there's really no point discussing any more of
this."

"Darin—"

"In case you hadn't guessed, my name's not Darin. I'm sick
of hearing it already."

He picked up the candle and lit the blackened tip of the middle finger. He moved toward the bed and held it out, placing it
directly between them.

"And as for that 'one more thing,' all I can say is, talk to the
hand."

CHAPTER 3

A LIGHT-SKINNED BLACK GUY IN A DARK BLACK COMMANDO sweater answered the door. Black cloth pads sewn on the shoulders and elbows. Black pants tucked into black boots. Hair high and tight, shaved on the sides well above his ears. A little taller than Hatcher, with long limbs and bulky hands. He had an HK model 93 hanging from his shoulder, also black, with a collapsible stock. Finger not quite on the trigger but not far from it, either. He eyed Hatcher with a smug familiarity, as if he knew him but was getting a good look for the first time, then stepped back and cleared a path.

It was a small beach motel room with twin beds. Dorm style, intended to be cheap and efficient, designed for tourists on a budget. The wall next to the door had an AC unit with a top vent beneath a single window overlooking the breezeway. Simple watercolors of sand dunes and starfish set beneath robin's-egg blue skies and orange suns adorned the other walls that had once been a powder-puff blue but now just seemed a dingy shade of drywall white.

On the left, a man in a tan gabardine suit rose from a chair. He was short but sturdy, with hair a chalky gray color so intense it was hard to imagine another ever covering the same head. He wore a bone-colored shirt open at the collar, exposing a tuft of more gray at the bottom of the V. It reminded Hatcher of a scarecrow with stuffing about to escape.

The woman was seated across the small circular table, closer to the bed. What she was doing there, Hatcher couldn't fathom.

The man held out a hand. Hatcher hesitated before raising his. It was hard to refuse to shake hands with a major general.

"You're one hell of a warrior, son," the man said, slapping

his palm into Hatcher's and giving it a firm shake. "One *hell* of a warrior."

The words carried a solemn tone of enthusiasm, but were spoken more like an observation than a compliment. Delivered like someone trying to make a point.

When Hatcher didn't reply, the man added, "I'm Bill Bartlett. Given your background, I'm guessing you've heard of me. I believe I was in your chain of command at one point."

Hatcher's gaze drifted to the woman. A silver crucifix dangled from her neck, but nothing else about her suggested the nunnery. Blonde, legs crossed, hemline just at the knee. He realized he was staring, but figured no one would think it unusual. She didn't get up. It had been a while since they'd last seen each other.

Vivian Fall looked right at him, held the eye contact. Exactly what was going on behind those aqua blue eyes was hard to divine. The anxiety was easy to spot, but it was mixed with something else. Could have been suspicion, could have been concern. Maybe even a little resentment thrown in. She may have been happy to see him; he couldn't think of a reason for her not to be. But she didn't look happy to be there, that was for sure.

"I believe you know Ms. Fall. She, of course, owes you a debt of gratitude for saving her. She's left her order, in case you didn't know."

"I need to use your bathroom," Hatcher said.

If Bartlett was surprised by the lack of acknowledgment, he didn't show it.

"Certainly."

The general gestured across the room, giving a directional nod. Hatcher crossed toward a recessed area off the back wall. There was a sink adjacent to a separate bathroom. He turned on the water and bent over to rinse his hands and splash his face.

The cold was bracing. He raised his head to look in the mirror, rivulets running down his face and dropping off his chin. His cheeks were still a bit flush. He had several scrapes around his jaw. A cut on his forehead, a bump on the bony corner over his left eye. A smear of blood coated one of his ears, not quite dry yet. There were red marks on his throat. He could almost make out the imprint of Sherman's hands.

He rinsed his hands again, splashed water on his face a few

more times, and toweled himself dry. His skin left dark streaks on the cloth. He noticed tiny bits of gray gravel in the sink.

There was a knock at the door. Hatcher watched in the mirror as black sweater guy opened it and Mr. E walked in.

"Street's clear," E said. "Parking lot, too."

Bartlett nodded, his gaze shifting over to Hatcher. Hatcher tossed the towel onto the counter and stepped back into the main part of the room.

"Sorry for all that," Bartlett said. "I trust you're no worse for the wear."

Hatcher took another couple of steps, stopped next to the guy in the sweater. He narrowed his gaze for a passing moment, eyes on Bartlett, then shot his arm back in a tight arc.

The side of his hand knifed against sweater guy's throat, just a hair below the Adam's apple. He followed it up with a palm strike to the face, this time with the right arm, rotating his torso into it. Without pausing, he grabbed the rear end of the HK's leather strap with one hand and ripped the buckle open, yanking the weapon away as the guy in the sweater doubled over and made hacking noises. Hatcher snapped the rifle up and aimed it at Mr. E's head, freezing him in place.

Mr. E already had an arm cocked back behind his ear. Knife loaded between his fingertips, ready to be launched.

"Whoa! Whoa! *Whoa!*" Bartlett said. "Just calm down now!"

"You lured me into an ambush," Hatcher said, eyes still locked on E's. "Served me up to a homicidal maniac lying in wait. Color me unhappy at the moment."

"I understand," Bartlett said, patting the air in front of him. "You have a right to be upset. But you need to hear me out. Hear *us* out."

Hatcher raised the rifle slightly, lining the sight up directly between his eye and E's. "I'm listening."

Bartlett shook his head sympathetically. "We can't talk like this. Put the weapon down. No one here meant you any harm, soldier. You have my word. Surely, the word of a general officer still means something to you."

As if it ever did, Hatcher thought.

"Tell Mini Mack the Knife to lose the blade."

Bartlett looked over at Mr. E, who shrugged. He slowly lowered his arm. His hand disappeared behind the edge of his vest, and when it emerged the knife was gone. He wiggled his fingers for emphasis.

Hatcher was about to tell him that wasn't good enough, but realized the guy could have a dozen other weapons stashed on him for quick access. Probably did. He'd already seen one stashed up the man's sleeve. He wasn't in the mood to do that dance right now.

Or was he? Worn out as he felt, he could also tell part of him wanted the little shit to try something. Just so he'd have an excuse.

"There," Bartlett said. "Edgar won't start anything if you don't. On my honor, one soldier to another. Now . . . do you mind?"

"Tell him to stand down."

Bartlett gave Edgar another little nod, pursing his lips and knitting his brow as he did, and the smallish man moved across the room, giving Hatcher a long look on the way to the back. He leaned against the counter near the sink, half sitting on it. His expression seemed like a collection of reactions to small amusements, but there was definitely anger swirling behind those eyes.

The guy in the sweater was on all fours, sounding like he was trying to dislodge a hair stuck in his throat. Hatcher glanced down at him, then over to Bartlett. The general stood his ground with an avuncular easiness, an expectant cast to his face, a calm patience to his bearing. He might as well have been waiting on a free refill. There was cool, and then there was *cool*. Something wasn't right.

"The weapon," Bartlett said. He held out an arm. "Hand it over, son, so we can talk. Please."

Hatcher watched him, studied the man's posture. Open, trusting. Confident. His gaze drifted off Bartlett and over to Vivian. She wasn't happy—eyes a bit wide, staring intently—but she didn't look terrified. If he sensed anything coming off of her, it was something like shame.

He shifted his attention back to Bartlett. Hatcher lowered his arms and let the muzzle of the HK tilt toward the floor.

"How many years were you on active duty, General?"

"Thirty-three."

Hatcher nodded. "Most of your commands were of combat regiments and SF teams, right?"

"Most of them, yes."

"Oversee any psyops? Fourth Airborne, maybe? JTF? Delta Force?"

Bartlett grimaced. "I'd prefer we have this discussion after you lay down arms, soldier."

"Yeah, I bet you do."

Hatcher looked down at the HK, then spun around, jerking the barrel in the direction of Mr. E. He squeezed the trigger.

The firing mechanism made an audible click as the pin slammed into place. But other than that, nothing else happened.

The room was quiet except for the persistent hacking of sweater guy. Then Bartlett coughed a little laugh into his hand, shaking his head.

"How did you know?"

"The tactics were sloppy, and you don't have a rep for sloppiness." He dipped his head to the guy on the floor. "Your man here gave me too much of an opening. Bad positioning, let me get too close. He wouldn't be on your personal detail if he was that lax."

"Very astute, Hatcher. Anything else? Or is that your entire after-action report?"

"Knife boy over there seemed to be holding back a chuckle. Some inside joke."

Eyes on him, Mr. E hitched a shoulder. He seemed mildly entertained, but mostly apathetic.

"Let's see if I can follow the script," Hatcher said. He tossed the HK onto the closest of the two beds. "You have one of your guys deliver me to a psychopathic freak for some kind of test, to see if I can take him. You arrange a stadium view, want to see firsthand how I handle myself. Then, figuring I will be more than a little pissed about being the evening's main event, you give me a chance to blow off steam, prove a point in my head, feel like I made a statement. And in doing so, you establish a basis for trust, a chance for me to see you empathizing with my anger, then show good faith by complying with my demands. You demonstrate you care, ask me nicely for the weapon like you expect me to live up to a bargain, and I'm supposed to come away from this believing you're someone who prefers to play it straight, and who has confidence in my character and understands me. Confidence I'm then supposed to feel obliged to prove worthy of. Am I close?"

"You can't blame me for wanting to avoid getting things off on the wrong foot."

"Things got off on the wrong foot when you tried to feed me to Roidzilla out there."

"Calvin"—Bartlett dipped his his head toward the one on the floor still trying to get up—"the man you just took some of your anger out on—had a clean shot. He was instructed to end it if it got out of hand."

Hatcher started to ask what the hell his definition of getting out of hand was, but said nothing. Instead, he looked down at Calvin, who was trying to pull himself up off his knees, his body too distracted by the coughing and wheezing to make much progress. That was enough to prompt Bartlett to wave a hand toward Mr. E, who crossed in front of Hatcher and helped Calvin to his feet. Hatcher had given the man a nasty chop to the windpipe. Blow like that probably warranted medical attention. He wondered if maybe he should have tried something less harsh.

On the other hand, he thought, resisting the urge to rub his own throat, fuck him.

"You don't have enough information to understand," Bartlett continued. "Yet. But the long and short of it is, I had to know."

"Had to know what?"

"Vivian insisted I give you a chance."

"Okay, that's it . . . I'm walking out that door if you don't tell me exactly what this is all about. And I mean, right now."

Bartlett held Hatcher's gaze for a prolonged moment, clearly a man not used to being spoken to in such a manner. The muscles in his jaw made tiny fists at the edges. Then his face seemed to relax, and his mouth formed a happy shape that looked something like a precursor to a smile. His eyes dropped to his fingernails as he checked them.

"Are you by any chance a student of World War Two?" he asked. "Did you ever study it?"

"A little. In school."

The man's eyebrows squirmed slightly, like furry worms greeting each other. "Ever hear of Operation X-Ray?"

"No."

"Few people have. It was an example of thinking outside the box, a plan to attack Japan that was being tested roughly around the same time as the Manhattan Project." The general paused, looking directly into Hatcher's eyes. "I'm sure you're familiar with that one."

"I know as much about it as the next guy. If the next guy knew what they teach you in junior high."

Bartlett nodded. "Compared to Manhattan, X-Ray was rather low tech. It was thought up by a dentist, of all people. The plan was to unleash canisters containing thousands of bats—to drop bat bombs, if you will—over Tokyo. The bats were to have tiny incendiary devices attached to their legs."

Hatcher shot a glance over to Mr. E. He was leaning back near the door, poker-faced. Calvin was in a chair, still holding his throat.

"I can't say I understand where this is heading, General."

"I'm getting there. The idea was simple. Once the bats were loosed, they would immediately seek shelter in crevices and crannies, in attics and under eaves, anywhere dark they could insinuate themselves. Tokyo was made mostly of wood. The trickiest part was designing a workable mechanism to start the combustion. Once they had one, the army tested the plan on a deserted mining town in Utah. They set the delay on the devices for two hours. Within minutes after detonation, the entire town was up in flames. But before X-Ray got the green light, they pulled the plug on it. The A-bomb had been successfully tested. And that project was a lot more expensive. They weren't going to waste all that money and all that science in favor of dropping bats."

"Fascinating. But I still have no idea what you're trying to tell me."

"I know what you did, how you fought to keep Demetrius Valentine from fulfilling a prophecy of apocalyptic proportions. That you saved Vivian here from being . . . *violated* by the demon prince known as Belial."

"I killed some bizarre animal Valentine had engineered, or whatever. That's all I know for sure."

"Yes, well, you certainly don't need to affect an air of skepticism with me."

"I'm not 'affecting' anything. I killed a creature grown in a lab by a rich nut case. You can read the police report."

"That would be like directing someone to the Warren Commission findings for the truth about JFK's assassination. Are you really going to stand there and tell me you don't believe that what you encountered, the thing you killed, was a demon hybrid inhabited by Belial? Don't get me wrong. I can see why you wouldn't want to. She also explained the price you paid for protecting her. And that means you'd also have to believe that in touching it, in having contact with the crown prince of Hell, you've rendered yourself unclean. Damned."

"Look, General, I'm tired. My neck feels like somebody used a blood-pressure cuff on it. My head felt better the time my M9 exploded and the slide ricocheted off my face. Just tell me what the hell I'm doing here."

Bartlett let his gaze linger on Hatcher for several moments. Then he dipped his head toward Vivian. She reached down next to the bed and lifted a canvas satchel. The bag rose slowly, twisting as she floated it over the bed, sagging in the middle from its weight. Vivian turned it over and dropped its contents onto the mattress. Something hard tumbled out. It sunk a couple of inches into the comforter with barely any bounce. She pulled back and set the empty canvas on the table.

"I don't suppose this means anything to you," Bartlett said.

It was a piece of engraved stone, a corner section of something larger, maybe a foot across and eighteen inches long. At least a couple of inches thick. Rough and jagged where it had been broken off, but flat and squared at the bottom corner and along the unbroken edges. The surface was dark and smooth. There were symbols carved into it.

Hatcher stared at it. "Should it?"

"No, but it was worth asking. This is a plaster cast of something I came into possession of about six months ago. Don't ask how."

"What is it?"

"The real one is a sandstone tablet, dating back two, but more likely close to three, millennia."

"Millennia?"

"Yes. The composition of the stone is consistent with other relics that have been unearthed around excavation sites near the Temple Mount in Jerusalem. There are even gold flecks embedded in it, something that suggests it was in the temple itself for some time. The inscriptions are in what is known is *lingua ma-litia*. Do you know what it says?"

"I'm sure I would, if I had any idea what that meant."

"It's the language of demons. Similar to Enochian. Very few humans have ever even heard it. The only known person to have spoken it was Solomon."

"The Solomon from the Bible?"

"That Solomon."

"And you think I can read this?"

"No, but it couldn't hurt to ask. We've had a hard time trans-lating it."

Hatcher looked at the engraving. There were symbols and characters carved into rows of text. To his untrained eye, it looked like a combination of Greek and hieroglyphics.

"So?"

"Best anyone can tell, it talks about the creation of a gate. A portal." Bartlett pointed a finger, swept it over the some of the markings. "It references a being banished to Hell, then coming back. A Hellion."

Hatcher said nothing for a long moment. He didn't like the way that sounded. It reminded him of things he'd heard before. From the Carnates. Gorgeous women who had everything. Except souls. That hadn't turned out so well.

He dropped his eyes to examine the tablet once more. "I still don't see what this has to do with me."

"Two weeks ago, a Markhor goat was stolen from the Los Angeles zoo. A rare specimen. Enormous. Almost six feet tall at the shoulders."

"Okay."

"Fingerprints recovered from the cage matched a serial rap-ist from Seattle. They found his body a few days ago. His geni-talia were missing. Surgically removed, you might say. So was his right hand. No sign of the goat."

"I guess with one gone, he wouldn't need the other any-more."

"This isn't a joke. Do you know how he was killed? He was hanged."

A crude comment about being hanged but not hung came to mind, but Hatcher was able to keep it from popping out.

"And?" he said.

"The right hand of a hanged criminal is used as something called the Hand of Glory. An implement of magic that can be used to render a person immobile, put them almost instantly into a hypnoticlike state. It can also be used to open that person up to a spiritual possession."

"Still not getting how I fit in."

Bartlett nodded to Edgar, who retrieved a folder from the table and pulled out a sheet of paper. He handed it to Bartlett. Bartlett held it out for Hatcher to see. It was a drawing of a creature with a human torso and goat's head.

"Are you familiar with this?"

"It looks like the Devil sat for a sketch artist."

"It's called the Baphomet."

"If you say so."

"It is an icon of demon worship. A powerful symbol. A goat's head, a human torso, goats legs, wings. An authentic one, the kind suitable for conjuring a very specific demon, requires very specific body parts. One is the penis of a rapist."

"I'm not following."

"Did you happen to catch the Apocalypse exhibit at the museum here some weeks back? Pity. Several of its displays contained unmistakable references to what's happening. Imagine, Hatcher, if a passage to Hell were opened. A doorway. Imagine demons being set loose on this world, streaming into it like the bats I just described. Each of them containing the equivalent of a ticking incendiary device. Thousands of bats out of Hell, working their way into our society, then once in place unleashing hellfire everywhere. Imagine death and mayhem and damnation here on Earth, the world literally burning. What would you say if I told you that was a very real possibility?"

"I'd say insurance companies would be looking for another round of bailouts. Then I'd ask again what the heck you think it has to do with me."

Bartlett glanced over to Vivian, who stared back at him with eyes that conveyed more than just a look.

"Vivian's agreed to explain the rest."

Bartlett gestured to Edgar with a snap of his head. Edgar stood. He left Calvin on the chair and picked up the stone. After wrestling it into the satchel, he slung it over his shoulder and scooped up the HK. He gave Hatcher a toothy grin as he walked past.

Then all three of them walked out of the room. Calvin was hunched forward and a little shaky, but except for Bartlett's palm in the small of his back, he didn't get much help.

The door shut behind them, leaving Hatcher and Vivian alone.

Hatcher watched the door. Neither of them spoke. The silence stretched past a minute, extended through two, started bearing down on three.

"Do you think they're standing out there, listening?" he said.

Vivian shook her head, held up a finger as she cocked her jaw, directing an ear toward the door. After another moment, some of the tension seemed to dissipate from her body.

"I just wanted to be sure."

She pushed herself off the bed. Her eyes grew shiny and her lips started to quiver with the intensity of a prayer. Then she rushed forward and threw her arms around Hatcher's neck. She cupped the back of his head, pressed her mouth over his. Her tongue twirled and flicked.

A few seconds later, she pulled back and took a breath. Squeezing him close, she rubbed the side of her face into his chest. Hatcher lowered his lips to her crown, inhaled her scent. Coconuts. Same shampoo she always used. He still had some left.

"God, I missed you," she said.

CHAPTER 4

THE THING ABOUT WATCHING THE CHILDREN OF BEAUTIFUL
women play, Morris mused, was they way their squeals and
giggles helped him visualize the exquisite agony that lay in
store for them. A lifetime of it. Finding the corpses of their
young mothers always had that effect.

That part was almost as exciting as anticipating the fun he
was going to have with the mothers themselves. Almost.

The sun was just breaking over the horizon as he strolled the
sidewalk. New town, as always. The walk from the bus station
to what he assumed was the main commercial strip hadn't taken
very long. He enjoyed the practiced routine, the ritual of arrival,
of getting his bearings. And he liked this time of day, especially
for scouting locations. The streets were mostly empty, the risk
of someone trying to mug him was low, and police finishing
their graveyard shifts or just settling behind the wheel of their
cruisers with tall cups of coffee steaming in their hands always
seemed uninterested in a white male in an orange windbreaker
and orange cap. Most people in his situation would be inclined
to dress inconspicuously, Morris knew. But he didn't care. He
loved the color orange. So much so he couldn't stand to see
anyone else wearing it. It was his.

Besides, he was practically charmed. Police rarely gave him
a second glance. He often chalked it up to his attention to detail,
his savvy way of defying expectations. But part of him knew it
was more than that. He was special.

He spied a Laundromat on the other side of the street and
crossed at the next intersection. Twenty-four-hour, coin-
operated. Empty inside. He leaned close to the large windows
and shaded his eyes, quickly taking in the rear corners, the spots
near the ceiling. No cameras that he could see. Security cams

weren't a disqualifier, but they did limit the amount of time he could safely spend in a place, particularly one like this. They also made him wary of his demeanor, and self-consciousness cramped his style. He didn't want to be watched while watching.

The air inside was warmer and damper than on the street. It smelled of fragrant soap and mildew. Two rows of machines. Dryers along the walls, washers back-to-back forming a row down the middle. Tables at each end and along the wall on each side where there was a break in the row of dryers. He glanced up at a clock above a wall-mounted vending machine selling tiny boxes of detergent and fabric softener. He could come back around three, if he decided to use this location. But the sun was going to be shining, and the day had clear and warm written all over it. Perfect park weather. And there was plenty of time to find a dog.

Laundromats were okay. They were especially reliable in rain or snow or just plain cold weather, a place he could loiter without drawing too much suspicion. All he needed was a cheap laundry bag and a book or magazine. Newspapers, he found, didn't really do the trick. Over the years he observed that women got a little chary around a solitary man reading the local rag. Maybe it was a cliché, maybe it was some false reality learned from spy movies, maybe in the internet age it simply marked you as unusual. All he knew was that something about it seemed to clue them in, make them notice him. Paperbacks were the best. Sports magazines worked almost as well. He was a harmless-looking guy. Most of him. He knew his mere presence wouldn't cause alarm, not if he seemed to have a reason to be there.

That was, as long as he could keep them from noticing his right hand, keep them from wondering why it never strayed from his jacket pocket, the one bulging like it was about to split a seam.

But finding attractive mothers with children in tow at a Laundromat was hit-and-miss. The most desirable location for that, bar none, was a park. The catch was, parks were ideal if and only if he had a dog in tow. This was a lesson he'd learned early on. Take a dog to a park, and nobody looks at you as being by yourself. Nobody even looks at you at all, just your dog.

Walking a dog through a residential subdivision was a bit different. People in those tended to wonder why they hadn't seen you walking the dog before, always seemed to want to ask questions about whether you were new to the neighborhood. Most important, people in neighborhoods took notice. But in the park, a dog was like a backstage pass, letting you go where you wanted, get as close as you wanted. You were conspicuously invisible, cloaked in nonthreatening purpose. Like someone walking into an office building with a hard hat on his head and a phone handset hanging from a tool belt.

So all he had to do was find the nearest park and steal a dog before three. Easy peasy. And if that didn't work, he'd hang at the Laundromat.

The day was off to a good start. He could feel its potential with each breath, the morning air practically swollen with it.

He headed down the main strip, continuing away from the bus station. It was still quiet, but people were beginning to populate the sidewalk in places. Here and there, merchants were unlocking doors and setting items out in front of their shops. The angle of the sun was glistening off glass, creating long shadows and brightening an immaculate sky. Morris sucked in another contented breath as he saw a school bus turn onto the road and disappear over a crest far ahead. Something about this town felt tailor-made for him. Like he was destined to be there—like this was, as was so often the case with him, the right place at the right time.

About a mile and a half later, he reached a municipal park. Open, with expanses of grass dotted by a few clusters of trees. A brunette was sitting on a wood and concrete bench alongside a jogging path, flipping through a magazine. Large dark sunglasses. Scarf wrapped over her head, knotted below her chin. Very attractive. His eyes fixed on the creamy smooth flesh of her legs, crossed at the knee. He followed the lower line of the top one along its delightful slope, the shape hugged by her dress, curving into the tight round bulge of her ass.

Women were the greatest joys, he thought. So much fun in one package, so easy to dispose of. Every man should own one, and often.

A small dog paced a few feet away from the bench at the end of a leash, glancing about, looking a bit anxious. Morris immediately wondered if the woman had children. This town! He could hardly believe his luck. He veered onto the grass, set a course to pass directly behind her.

She stuck the end of the leash out in front of him as he was about to go by, causing him to stop abruptly. Her hand stayed there, the black canvas loop suspended near his navel. Morris stared down at the woman. She was still leafing through her magazine. Hadn't even glanced his way.

"This is what you're looking for, isn't it?" she said. After a pause she tilted her sunglasses down, swiveled her head toward him. Green eyes sparkled above the shades. "Well?"

Morris had a hard time following. Was she offering him her dog?

A roll of emerald irises. "Oh, good gobbling geezers . . . take the damn thing, will you?"

Slowly, Morris removed his left hand from his pocket. She dropped the end of the leash into it

"Thank you. Since I just saved you a considerable amount of prowling, why don't you take a seat? We need to talk."

"I'm sorry. You must have me confused with someone else."

"Do I? That's strange. I thought you were Morris Sankey. The Morris Sankey who murdered his mother by literally scaring her to death and has been living off her life insurance proceeds ever since. The same Morris Sankey who's roamed the eastern seaboard for the better part of a decade, raping and terrorizing women with his unique gifts and sodomizing their dead bodies. Loitering around the town for weeks afterward to revel in the misery he's caused, soaking up the local news accounts, sometimes even attending the funeral and wake, pretending to be a friend of the deceased. Changing up his MO each time just enough to keep the FBI from getting called in."

The peaceful morning ambiance suddenly seemed less so. The chorus of songbirds, the whine and hum of cars, the scrape of the wind, all were screams and screeches now that echoed inside the walls of his head, taking on the rhythm of his pulse. He felt himself trying to pull out of his body, shrug it off like a piece of clothing and have it fall away as he floated into the sky.

This was it. She was a cop. Had to be. But how? He'd always believed he'd been immunized against getting caught. Protected. Even so, he'd never gotten cocky, been persistently careful, never testing his luck, never leaving anything to chance. At least, he thought that was the case. He bit down on his tongue, held it between his teeth. Clamped down hard, feeling the pain. Tasting the blood. Every beat of his heart felt like an icy squeeze, surges of adrenaline spurring it to anxious gallop.

So they were on to him, apparently had been for some time. Tracing his movements, anticipating his next stop. They had to know everything about him. Idiot! Always the same orange coat, same orange hat. What was he thinking?

The pain from his tongue was drawing him back into himself. There was no time for self recriminations. Not now. He felt a tug and his eyes fell to the leash. The dog was pulling on it, circling and whining.

He could strangle her. Yes. Quickly, right here. Use the leash as a garrote. Or just crush her neck with his Hand, since there was no reason to be discreet. Do it and get the hell out of town. Yes, he could do that. *Shit, no.* What kind of plan was that? There had to be other cops watching. *Had* to be. But if there were, where were they? Why weren't they moving in on him? Was she wearing a wire?

"Will you relax, for goodness' sake?" The woman's lips stretched into a crimson slit. Her voice contained a hint of a chuckle, as if at her own joke. One she knew would bring a good laugh later when retold. "Sit down. Just pretend you're planning to rape and kill me, if it makes it easier for you."

Morris stared down at her blankly. Exhausted from panic, and lacking a more attractive alternative, he circled the bench warily and sat.

"You know, you don't have to keep it hidden away like that. Not around me. What you have is a rare gift. A mark of distinction. Must have been hard growing up, though, huh? The other kids either ridiculing you or keeping their distance. Teenage years spent watching others have fun, while girls treated you like a disease. The stuff of urban legends. Quite a word, isn't it? *Deformed.*"

Morris said nothing. He pressed the Hand deeper into the pocket of his jacket.

"But enough pleasantries. You're a hard man to track down, did you know that? Of course you did. That was a silly question."

"Who are you?"

"My name is Katrina. Or Ashley. Or Melissa. What you call me doesn't really matter, but if it helps you can think of me as Deborah. What does matter is, I found you. And now . . . now we can get down to the business of helping you realize your full potential. Your true calling."

"You don't sound like a cop."

"I can't tell you how relieved I am to hear that. Now, if you'll just assure me I don't smell like one, either, you'll have made my day."

Morris stared at her, saying nothing

"I'm not a cop. Have you ever seen a cop that looked like me?" She swept her hand down the length of her body. "Like *this*? I mean, come on."

"What do you want?"

The woman perched an elbow along the top of the backrest. Morris had the momentary impression of an angler setting a hook.

"I told you. To help you realize your potential."

"I don't understand anything you're saying."

"You, Morris. I'm talking about you. You and your one, all-consuming talent. A talent for torture and murder. For inflicting pain. For destroying lives without remorse."

He started to toss out a denial but held it in check. There was something about the woman's manner, the way she spoke with such familiarity. And the way those sunglasses reflected his faces; twin images of himself staring back, like a snapshot of the way she saw him. The way he saw himself. There was a heaviness in the air, a gravity to the moment. This was too much. He needed to stand up and walk away. But then what?

"Would you like to see him?" she asked. "See what he looks like?"

"See what who looks like?"

"Don't pretend you don't know what I'm talking about."

He watched the frozen image of himself stare back in stereo. He wasn't certain how to respond. He really hadn't known what she was talking about, until that last comment.

"That knowledge you've always had, that you were different. And I don't mean just physically. That the world was designed by and for other people, people you understood only the way a human might understand creatures he observed in the wild, or in a zoo."

The trill of a siren grew loud, then just as quickly began to recede. The woman paused briefly to let the noise pass.

"Well, you are different, Morris. You're literally one in a million. A hundred million, actually."

"Different how?"

"You were born without a soul. And that allowed you to bring a little bit of Hell with you into this world."

A long silence between them. Then Morris said, "And how do you know this?"

"You might say it takes one to know one."

"You're saying you don't have a soul?"

"We'll get into that later. For now, I just want you to know that you're here for a purpose, Morris. I can show you that purpose."

"What's in it for you?"

"Maybe I just want to do a good deed, help my fellow man."

"Bull crap. Everyone does what they do for themselves. They just want everyone to think they're doing it for others."

"What a refreshingly candid display of your sociopathy! I regard this as a breakthrough in our relationship. What's in it for me is irrelevant. You wouldn't understand if I told you. What matters is what's in it for you."

Another siren warbled, rising in pitch as it approached, descending as it passed into the distance.

"You never answered my question. Do you want to see him?"

Morris blinked. He started to respond, then stopped, not knowing what to say. The woman seemed to accept that as a yes. She reached into a purse and retrieved a small round piece of glass that at first he took to be a monocle. She held it out to him and realized it was reflective. A mirror set in a bronze frame. Some lettering was inscribed on the back, too small and faint for him to read. But he could make out a symbol etched in the center. It looked like a bird with scorpion's tail.

"Hold it facing this way." She pulled her thumb over her shoulder at an angle as she looked in the opposite direction. "Shut your right eye and look into it."

The object felt heavy in his hand, almost alien in its unexpected heft. He hesitated, then did as she'd instructed. Right eye closed, left hand holding out the mirror. Nothing.

"Adjust the angle left and right until you get it."

He tilted the mirror one way, watched it pan across some trees, a swing set, a water fountain. He was starting to tip it back when he felt himself jump back in his seat, his body reacting almost before the image registered.

"And there he is," the woman said.

Morris stared at the glass, fixated. Realizing it was a reflection, he glanced over his shoulder, then at the mirror, tossing his head back and forth several times before fixing on the image again. He wasn't certain whether he was frightened or elated. Or if this was even real. Maybe he was laying on a hospital gurney, his mind awash in a trauma-induced chemical soup. Maybe the bus had gone off a cliff.

"Here's what's in it for you," she continued. "A chance to be the scion of a new royal line, to take your rightful place as a crown prince in a new order. And all the perks that go along with it. Sex, for example, with women as sinfully hot as me—well, close, anyway—if you want it. I'm throwing that out there, even though I have a hunch you'll pass, because you won't be able to butcher any of us. But there will be plenty of other violence expected of you. And mayhem. Lots of mayhem, with you at the center of it."

Morris set down the mirror and turned to let his eyes roam the area. He could see the trees, the swing set, the water fountain. Nothing else.

The woman was talking again, but Morris wasn't listening. Then something she said got his attention. He looked over to her and asked her to say it again.

"I said, if that's not enough, I should probably point out that you're a wanted man. Those sirens you've been hearing? They're for you. Your DNA has been matched with specimens found at two separate scenes. Seems someone mailed a swab of your saliva to the detective in charge of your last homicide. It came with a note explaining who it belonged to. An anonymous phone call a little while ago tipped off the same detective that you just arrived into this town. By bus. They must have just got word here. I imagine the police switchboards were lighting up."

"You're saying if I don't do what you want, you'll turn me in, is that it?"

"No, Mr. Sankey. That was just a stick meant to dangle a carrot off of. You can run off and be a fugitive if you want. But what I'm offering is to get the police off your back. Permanently. To let you shape the world that is to be, a world suited for someone like you. Aren't you the least bit intrigued about fulfilling your destiny?"

Morris looked down at the mirror. "What do I have to do, exactly?"

"First, you have to put your particular talents to work in sending a certain troublemaker to Hell. You're uniquely qualified for the job."

A moment later she added, "You, and your guardian demon over there."

CHAPTER 5

HATCHER SWUNG A LEG OVER THE CONCRETE BENCH AND
reached over the concrete table. Vivian slid her cell phone out of
the way to make room for the pair of coffee cups. The phone
was in a small leather case with a wrist loop. Hatcher hadn't had
a phone in a while. He could think of lots of reasons they came
in handy, but the reality was they seemed to bring him nothing
but trouble.

A voice inside his head chided him that the same could be
said of women. Especially considering the bombshell this one
had just dropped.

"So, Bartlett kidnapped my nephew."

He paused, letting his own words sink in. The notion sounded
more believable the way he'd put it, minus the sugarcoating.
Vivian lowered her head. Even trying to soft sell it, she seemed
more disturbed by the thought than he was. And she was right to
be. By any objective measure it was beyond the pale. Susan
Warren had been a few months pregnant with his brother Garrett's child last he'd seen her. That would make it still a baby.
Bartlett wasn't messing around.

Hatcher said, "And that's intended to ensure my cooperation,
I suppose. Did it ever occur to them that kidnapping is a federal
offense?"

"I didn't use the word, Jake. 'Kidnapping' makes it seem
like he's the bad guy and you can just call the police. I don't
think it's that simple."

She gazed up at him with glassy eyes, the sea breeze wrapping strands of hair across her face that she repeatedly had to
hook with a finger and slide back over her ear. Except for the
serious cast to her lips, she had the soft, sultry look of a woman
who'd just had sex. She'd protested that they needed to talk first,

that she had things she needed to tell him, urgent things, important things, but the taste of her, the scent of her, the feel of her when she'd kissed him had been too much, and he'd practically ripped her panties off. Hatcher could still smell her on him, smell the fleshy, earthy scent on his lips from when he'd gone down on her. He knew that was probably just his imagination, but it didn't make it any less real. Sort of like the way knowing some things weren't imaginary didn't make them seem any more real.

"But you also know that's exactly what it is," he said, lowering himself onto the cold rough slab.

"Well, of course I know it's not good. I'm afraid for the boy, for his safety. And I didn't even find out about it until a few days ago, until Edgar more or less confirmed it. But I don't think William will harm him. Not unless he believes he has no choice."

"People only convince themselves they have no choice when they know the one they're about to make is wrong."

Hatcher's cup made a grainy, scraping sound as he slid it closer. He picked it up and absently swiped his hand across the surface of the concrete. A gust of wind pelted his eyes with a few invisible bits of sand, forcing him to turn away and blink.

The first streaks of daylight crawled overhead from the east. The morning air flowing in from the Pacific was cold enough to bite. Cyclists and joggers were starting to appear on the Strand fifty yards away. A guy in gray sweats was stretching his back. Hatcher wasn't sure which beach this was. They'd walked a long way before they found a place open for business.

He wiped the back of his hand across his face and lifted the coffee to his lips. The steamy heat felt good on his face but made him think twice. Better to let things cool down before you commit. Always good advice. Almost always.

He started to say something, then stopped when he saw the way Vivian was looking at him.

"What?"

"Nothing."

He set the coffee down. "Tell me."

"It's just . . ." She smiled with her eyes even as her lips formed a tight little frown. Hatcher thought he caught her chin quivering. "Your eyes were watering."

"It was just sand."

"It looked like you were crying. I've never seen you cry. I don't think I could have even pictured it till now. Couldn't have imagined how it would look."

"But I wasn't."

"I know. That's not the point."

Taking a sip of his coffee, Hatcher checked his response. The hot liquid burned his tongue and stung a spot on the roof of his mouth. Damn it—he knew he should have waited. He hated that feeling.

"You're angry. I know. You want to go and hurt someone."

Hatcher grunted. It didn't take a genius to figure out she would much rather be talking about *them*, about the future of their relationship, about the months apart and the feelings they shared and the violent and tender sex they just had in that motel room. But this wasn't the time for that. Of course, it hadn't exactly been the time for sex, either. Priorities and emotions don't always play nicely.

"You make it sound like I'm prone to random acts of violence."

"Okay, you want to go hurt William."

"Wanting to hurt someone and hurting them aren't the same thing."

"Maybe for most people. Please, Jake. Don't. Don't respond that way. It won't help. He may be going about this wrong, but I'm worried the threat is real."

The sky was brightening by the moment. Hatcher scanned the distance for anything suspicious. The morning denizens seemed split between those on two wheels and those on two running shoes, both tending to be dressed in a uniquely California look of sweatshirts, running shorts, and knit beanies. The only one who drew Hatcher's attention was the guy in the gray sweats stretching about a hundred yards away. Seemed to be doing an awful lot of it and very slowly, the way someone trying to look like he was doing something would when all he was really doing was hoping he wouldn't stick out.

"Explain it to me again," Hatcher said.

"What part?"

"The whole thing. Start with why you think I can do anything about this."

"Because you've dealt with the Carnates before. And

because, like I told you back at the motel, William is convinced the Hellion is your brother Garrett."

"Okay, stop right there. You're acting like they formed a fan club or something. The Carnates used me. I was a pawn to them, and I'm sure they hate me for spoiling their big event. If anything, I'm the last person anyone would want as a point man if they're involved. And that stuff about Garrett, I don't know what to make of that. I never even met him. Not when he was alive, anyway."

"Jake, you don't understand. Nobody else—at least, nobody I know of—has the kind of experience with the Carnates that you do. Hardly anyone knows a thing about them. William and his men seem to know only what I could tell them, which wasn't much. Before that, they had only heard the most vague of rumors, combined with what William knew. I just don't think they know what they're up against."

"And yet he thinks the Carnates will want to stop this Hellway from opening," Hatcher said, stating it as a question without asking one. "That they'll want to help me stop Garrett—who's now a Hellion, whatever that means—from causing a demonic jail break."

Vivian gave a tilt to her head and hitched a shoulder. She broke eye contact and stared at the cup of coffee in front of her, thinking.

"That's what he told me, yes."

The tension coming off her was palpable. This was more awkward then he'd anticipated. It was clear she had things she wanted to say, but couldn't. It was just as well. She'd left to go back to New York months ago to wrap up some matters with her former order and tend to some personal issues, but Hatcher knew there'd been more to it. Much more. And now they were picking up right where they'd left off, baggage and all. The big question loomed, hovering like a swollen storm cloud. If she came right out and asked him, something he doubted she would do, he wouldn't know what to say. He didn't think he'd ever loved anyone. Not his parents, not any girlfriends. Some fond feelings, maybe some fantasies, but that was about it.

But Vivian was definitely in love with him.

She'd come across the country for him, to thank him, she

said, to pour her soul out to him about what happened in the way all those letters she wrote couldn't.

The letters. Hers were the only ones he'd opened. He still wasn't sure why. Not Amy's, not his mother's, not those from some lawyer or the one from the *New York Times*. But hers, he did. Perhaps out of simple curiosity.

And after he wrote back, they kept coming. Not e-mails, a privilege he refused. Not phone calls. Letters. He never thought of himself as the letter-writing kind of guy. But he kept responding.

She wrote of her faith and her doubts, of her gratitude and her fears. She urged him over and over to not give up hope, to not believe his soul was lost.

He didn't have the heart to tell her whatever happened to his soul happened long before he touched the demon-prince known as Belial.

His last letter to her was supposed to be a farewell and a thank-you. But then she showed up in Phoenix, found him bouncing at a bar, not too different from the one he bounced at now. She said she wanted to talk, to actually say the words, face-to-face. And he listened, listened to her explain the fear she'd experienced, the transformation she'd undergone, how her faith evolved from one indulged by dedication to her Order to one demanding a personal quest for answers, answers well beyond the scope of any convent. Within a couple of days she was touching his hand often, caressing his face, and she confessed she had strong feelings for him, feelings she wanted to explore. He'd resisted at first, but she'd dismissed his concerns about her emotional state, insisted she wasn't confused. Told him she felt a connection.

So he let himself become involved, and the inevitable question presented itself, the one about whether he felt the same thing for her. He didn't know the answer. It felt good to be with her, to be in the moment when they made love. But he couldn't tell her what she wanted to hear, because he wasn't sure. He didn't even understand why someone like her would want to love him. He certainly didn't love himself.

When she told him the desert wasn't for her, and that she'd always wanted to live in Los Angeles, he said okay and packed up the few belongings he had. A couple of months later she left, told him there were things she needed to take care of back in New York, and he couldn't help but think it was because he wouldn't say the words.

As if picking up on his thoughts, Vivian smiled in the sad, sober way only a woman can. She reached across the table and patted his hand, taking a sip of her coffee. Hatcher let his gaze drift over her shoulder to the guy in the sweats again. Still stretching, but a second after Hatcher looked his way he bent down and picked up a basketball. Started dribbling toward the cement courts separated from the Strand by chain links.

"What are you looking at?" Vivian asked. Hatcher appreciated that she didn't turn to look herself.

"Not sure."

"If you think you see one of William's men, you're probably right. They're keeping an eye on me. For my own protection."

"Uh-huh."

"Honestly, Jake, I'd be surprised if some of his men *weren't* nearby. He thinks I might be in danger. He doesn't leave much to chance."

Danger. Hatcher pondered how many times in his career a man like Bartlett would have used the pretext of danger to justify his actions, to manipulate others, sometimes entire populations, to fall in line. Times when the biggest danger to those he was "protecting" was actually Bartlett himself. For years he had been a high-ranking commander of a world power engaged in global conflicts. That was the nature of the beast.

"How does he even know anything about this? About the Carnates, what happened in New York . . . about any of this?"

She sucked in a terse breath, released it audibly. As if she'd been dreading this part. "Through glossolalia."

Hatcher stared at her. "Are you actually going to make me ask?"

"He said a message was sent to him in church. His church. Assembly of God. It's not uncommon for members to spontaneously start speaking in tongues during services."

"Now that's just fucking great."

"Jake, please."

Hatcher took another sip of his coffee. "Sorry."

"He said one day a woman stood up, and he suddenly understood what she was saying. Same with the next one, and the next. One by one, people in the congregation would stand up, two or three during a sermon. Other members would offer an interpretation, but he realized they were all wrong. He could understand everything they said, clear as if they were speaking English. But he didn't dare say anything."

"And why is that?"

"Because the message instructed him not to."

"And from the mouths of random babblers came orders to kidnap Garrett's son? To stop him from opening some door to Hell?"

"Like I told you, William seems to think of it as protective custody. That's the term I heard. I would be willing to bet anything he *believes* that's what it is." Vivian paused. "How about the boy's mother? Have you heard from her, Jake? Do you know how to reach her?"

"No. I haven't spoken to her since before you and I even met." He took a long gulp of coffee, draining the cup before crushing it in his fist. He tossed it at a nearby trash receptacle. It fell short and bounced off the wire mesh.

"I take it *she's* not in 'protective custody,'" he said, lowering his tone at the sound of his own sarcasm. "Maybe they just considered her collateral damage. Have they mentioned her?"

Vivian stared at her hands. "I don't know where she is. Or if anything's happened to her."

"But they nominated you to explain it all."

"No. That was my idea. I was scared how you'd react. I wanted to tell you myself." She raised her eyes to meet his again. "And it was an excuse to be alone with you."

Hatcher shifted focus to the guy in sweats. He was still shooting baskets. He supposed Vivian was right, that having someone nearby wasn't unexpected, wasn't even that big a deal. But that didn't mean he had to like it. He kept the guy in the corner of his eye.

"Do they know about us?" He remembered the way Mr. E had made that comment about having a hand in her divorce. The words certainly reeked of innuendo, but there was also an ambiguousness to them that smacked of fishing.

The question seemed to surprise her. She took a few seconds to mull it over, then shook her head.

"I don't think so. No, I would say definitely not. William

sought me out based on the message. He didn't seem to know anything else."

Hatcher dropped his chin and gave his head a different sort of shake, weary and exaggerated. "The 'message.' The one in tongues."

"Yes. After what we've been through, Jake, all the things that we've witnessed, I don't think you should be so dismissive. He knew about what happened. Knew where to find me."

"All right, so why you? Assuming the glossy-lollypalooza stuff—"

"Glossolalia."

"—assuming it's all true, what do you have to do with this?"

"I don't know. Neither does he. Not that he'll admit. According to him, the message said I was in danger and that he needed to find me."

"Did it also tell him to sic Sherman the Tank on me?"

"No. I'm so sorry for that, Jake. He didn't want to get you involved. The message told him to organize a team and not tell anyone about its purpose. But I knew I had to get you involved, knew it because of your nephew, and because you're the only one I trust to deal with these kinds of things. I had to convince him you were the key. I told him that's why the message told him to find me, because I knew how to find you. He didn't want to do it."

"Why not?"

"From what I could tell, he had you checked out. Maybe even knew something about you before. He kept saying you were a loose cannon. That you wouldn't be willing to take orders. I didn't know anything about the plan to have Sherman confront you, not until it was about to happen. I don't know where they got the idea."

The sun was over the horizon now, creating an explosion of golden colors. Southern California was the only place Hatcher had ever been where the air was cool and the sun was warm virtually every day, the only place where you could wear a bathing suit or a leather jacket and be equally comfortable. There were a lot of things people could bitch about when it came to SoCal, from the politics to the traffic to the obsession with appearances, but the weather wasn't one of them.

"And you really want me to do this?"

"No, Jake. I don't. Not even a little. But I know you have to. I know it in my heart. I'd do anything to believe you could walk away and that everything would turn out all right. I've prayed about it more than you would even believe. This is the only way. It's all part of God's plan."

Those lines had been rehearsed, that much was clear. Hatcher pictured her practicing in front of the mirror. She probably had for days. And right now, she was wondering how she did. Searching his eyes for a sign. Rather than look away, he let his gaze fold into hers. The blue was so pure, so uncommon, they looked artificial. Like some visual prosthetic fashioned out of cubic zirconium. She didn't have a movie star's face or a porn star's body or even the kind of gorgeous hair that gets a woman noticed. But those eyes were otherwordly, he had to admit.

"What makes you so sure?" he asked.

"I just know it. You're one of God's warriors, Jake."

"Please, Viv. In case you weren't listening when all that crap was going down, I'm going to Hell. According to Valentine and those gals in Satan's Harem everyone suddenly wants me to start making nice with, there's nothing anyone can do to change that. So if He really wants me to be in His army, I'd say He needs to work up a better benefit package."

"Please don't talk that way. You can't believe there's no hope . . . you just can't."

"To be honest, I don't know what to believe, but let's be logical here. In for a penny, in for a pound. Cherry-picking what you want to believe out of it is a form of denial."

"I don't understand how you can be so . . . calm about it all. Don't you understand what it means? To be damned? To spend eternity, all of forever, stretching out to infinity, in never-ending torment?"

"No, I hadn't really thought about it. But thanks for reminding me."

"You don't know how much it hurts to hear you joke like that."

"I don't know what you want me to say."

Her gaze sank into her cup, like she was trying to read something at the bottom. "Does it scare you?"

"Vivian, honestly, I try keep it out of my mind."

"Maybe they were just trying to get in your head. Sap your will, crush your psyche. Maybe it was a cruel lie, and that's all."

"Valentine sure seemed to believe it. Besides, whether any of it's true or not, I don't think God needs someone like me to be His special agent. There are plenty of people out there with military backgrounds who are in church every Sunday, guys who would literally kill for such an assignment. Sucking up to command has always worked in the past, so I don't see why it shouldn't now."

"But don't you see? The fact you fought for what was right, fought to prevent that evil man from fulfilling his plan, even though you didn't necessarily believe you were saving your own soul, that's what makes you such a warrior for Him. He knows your heart, Jake. He knows the kind of person you are, that you don't act out of an expectation of being rewarded in the afterlife. You're better than that. Better than most of those people who sit in pews out of self-interest."

His neck popped as he twisted it. The motion was uncomfortable, sent a twinge radiating into his back. He was sore, and the soreness was just beginning.

"Even if all that's true, what do you expect me to do?"

"I expect you to do what God put you here to do. To follow your conscience. To use your God-given abilities to help people. Your nephew's life is at stake, whether because of William and his men or whoever he thinks he needs to protect him from. But if William is right—and I think he is, Jake, at least partly—this may be much, much bigger than that."

Hatcher said nothing. His gaze drifted over the concrete surface of the table. It ended up resting on the cell phone.

"Vivian, I wouldn't know how to find the Carnates if I wanted to. They're not exactly in the phone book."

"You found them before. You're good at that kind of thing."

"I literally wouldn't even know where to begin."

"Why do you keep looking at my cell phone?"

It took a second for the question to register. It was true, he had been staring at her cell phone. He wasn't sure why. He raised his head but found himself looking past Vivian again. The guy in the sweats shooting hoops. Something had caught his eye, maybe a few times now, but he wasn't sure what.

"Jake?"

Just as he started to pull his gaze back to her, he saw it once more. A glint. He watched for it this time. The guy put up a shot, trotted over it recover it, then turned to dribble away. There it was again. A tiny flash of sunlight. Reflecting off his ear.

He looked down at the cell a final time. He gestured with his chin toward it, lowered his voice when he spoke. "Did they happen to give you that, by any chance?"

Vivian started to speak, then stopped. "Why?"

He picked up the phone, slid it out of its leather jacket. "You said you were pretty certain they didn't know about us?"

"No," she said. "I mean, yes. I don't think so."

The phone was new. He ran his finger over the top, pressed a button to wake up the screen. He groped around the menu until he found the call log. Last call listed was from a private number. The entry indicated it ended less than a minute earlier.

Hatcher's head snapped up. A basketball rolled slowly across the cement court until it gently bumped against the chain-link fence. The guy in the sweats was gone.

"If they didn't before, they sure do now."

Hatcher stood, scanning the distance. Joggers, cyclists, a few skateboarders. No guy in gray sweats.

He glanced down at the display again. The call that just ended had lasted for over forty minutes. The prior three calls were from the same number. Given the time intervals, it seemed Bartlett had the decency not to let anyone listen, including himself, while Hatcher and Vivian had been taking the edge off their pent-up libidos.

"I don't understand," Vivian said. "You think the phone has a . . . what, a bug? That they bugged it?"

"Didn't need to. All they had to do was program it to be on silent mode and to automatically answer. It basically turned itself on whenever they called it."

"Why would they do that?"

"Because it's just like you said. People like Bartlett don't like leaving things to chance. He wasn't about to take anything on faith. They would want to know if I was in, was *really* in. Or if I was intending to head over their way and start popping caps. They'd want to know if you and I were planning something. If you had found out where they were holding my nephew. They want to know everything. Bartlett understands better than most—information is power."

Hatcher kept studying the Strand as he spoke, watching for some sign of the man. "I'll bet that guy is still close."

"Jake."

Hatcher moved out from behind the table. "Probably just around that corner. If I—"

"Jake."

"Relax, Viv. I just need to get some more infor—"

"Jake." Hatcher felt Vivian's grip on his arm. "Remember how you said you wouldn't know where to begin?"

She raised a hand and pointed into the distance. "I don't think that's going to be a problem."

She looked past him, moving her eyes from his in the direction of her finger, peering out over the Pacific at the brilliant morning sky. Hatcher turned to look over his shoulder.

A small plane was flying above the water, maybe a thousand feet in the air. A banner trailed behind it, carrying a message:

J.H. LET'S TALK. LOOK UP YOUR FAVE ESCORTS AND GIVE A CALL.

Hatcher watched the words fly by to the south until the angle became too acute and they started to shrink in the distance. Assuming he'd read it correctly, he realized he'd been wrong about one thing.

Damned if they weren't in the phone book, after all.

CHAPTER 6

HATCHER COASTED TO A STOP IN FRONT OF THE SMALL HOUSE
and shifted the car into park. After staring at the porch for a few
moments, he double-checked the number. This was it, all right.
Not exactly what he expected. But when the Carnates were involved, he couldn't think of much that was.

The address was in south L.A., what used to be called south
central, not far from Florence and Normandie. He didn't know
southern Cal that well yet, but even the Jihadis he'd mixed it up
with in Afghanistan probably could have popped off about this
zip code's rep. It was known for having a lot of gangs, a lot of
crack, and a lot of crime. Cheap liquor stores and colorful graf-
fiti. Race riots and drive-bys.

But what Hatcher saw when he looked around was a neighborhood of modest tract homes, mostly Spanish-styled stucco, a
smattering of squat, hardy palm trees lining the street in front of
them. The landscaping was spotty, the majority of lawns a
patchwork of browns and greens and footworn dirt. The assortment of purple and red and yellow paint jobs were probably a
bit loud, too, and the cars parked along the curbs tended to be
either really flashy or really beat up; but notwithstanding a few
of the houses he'd passed with plywood over the windows,
sporting spray-painted initials and monikers, the area didn't
strike him as a ghetto. People owned most of these lots, lived in
these homes. They cared for them and cared about them. People
like that had something to lose, and people with something to
lose usually left everyone else alone.

He reminded himself that unlike them, he didn't really have
anything to lose. It wasn't even his car.

The sidewalks were mostly empty and there was very little
traffic. Except for an elderly black man a few houses down

watering a sprawl of chrysanthemums, nobody seemed to notice Hatcher as he walked up to the house and rang the doorbell.

It was one of the nicer homes, and actually had a fairly uniform lawn. The walls were a powder-puff blue and the wooden porch was painted a gunmetal shade of gray to match the roof tiles. A good half-minute had passed before a black kid glaring out from beneath a do-rag answered. Short, maybe five foot two, but thickly muscled, wearing a tight shirt with long sleeves that was ribbed like thermal underwear. He stood behind a dense screen door with a *fuck-do-you-want?* sneer on his face.

"I'm Hatcher."

The sneer flexed. "Yeah? So?"

"I called. Was given this address."

"Zat a fact? By who?"

It was a good question, one Hatcher wished he could answer. The Carnates hadn't exactly had a Yellow Pages ad, but he'd been able to find one entry for PI Escort Services on a web page dedicated to adult entertainment in the L.A. area. *PI.* That was how these half-human, half-demon women had referred to Pleasure Incarnate back in Manhattan, back when they were leading Hatcher around by the nose and setting him up for Valentine's big finale. Unlike the other posts he'd seen, it didn't promise GFE or PSE or erotic massages. It simply read, *We're No Angels.*

"By the person I spoke to," Hatcher said.

"The person you's spoke to. Know what I think? I think you just another white boy come down to our hood looking to score some rock. Prob'ly knocking on random doors, thinking there's got to be some brother on this street dealing, right?"

Hatcher tried to get a read on the guy, figure out if the vibe he was giving off was for real, but the screen was too dark. The one thing he was relatively certain of was that do-rag wasn't in the business of offering anything like a Girlfriend Experience or a Porn Star Experience. Then again, sometimes it was hard to tell.

"Guess I have the wrong place."

"Damn right you do, racist motherfucker."

Hatcher smiled faintly and turned to leave. He'd only taken three steps when he heard the rack of a charging handle, freezing him in mid-stride.

The voice from the doorway said, "Know what this is, bitch?"

Careful not to move his head, Hatcher swept his eyes from one side to the other, scanning the street. His field of vision was relatively unimpeded, but it didn't offer much consolation. The guy who'd been watering his flowers wasn't there anymore. Nobody else seemed to be around, either. Everything was quiet.

A bird chirped.

"You hear me, punk-ass white boy?"

"It's an Ingram MAC-10. I'm guessing a nine-by-nineteen Luger, because a sawed-off runt like you couldn't handle the kick of a forty-five."

"Aww, idn't that just the cutest. Whiteboy's got a mouth on him."

Hatcher heard a jumble of footsteps, then the squeal of the screen door swinging open, people piling into the yard. He could make out at least three more weapons being cocked. He was pretty sure they were all pistols. At least four guys, at least four firearms. Not great odds.

He was thinking about those odds, and the odds of going to a wrong address where the person who answers the door just happens to brandish an automatic weapon and just happens to have several armed friends with him, when one of them said, "Taze his ghost ass," and he felt a twin set of stings in his back at almost the exact moment his entire body began to vibrate like a funny bone and he dropped face-first onto the concrete walk.

THEY LATCHED HIS WRISTS WITH A NYLON ZIP TIE, PUT A SACK over his head, and threw him in the backseat. He was pretty sure it was Vivian's rental, since it smelled the same and they'd made a point of ripping the keys out of his pockets while he was on the ground. The barbs in his back didn't seem to be going anywhere so he angled his torso, letting his arm and shoulder take the weight against the stiff upholstery. He had half a mind to pipe up and tell them keeping the Taser engaged was a waste. If the drive was going to be any sort of distance the only thing he was interested in was getting some sleep.

But he knew that wasn't going to happen.

Two guys sat in back with him, one on each side. The one to

his right shoved his head down, the one on his left nudged him with something Hatcher realized was the Taser. A reminder it was still hooked to his back, he supposed. He could hear a guy bounce into the front passenger seat, felt the car rock and heard the driver's side front door shut. No one said anything as the car started up and pulled away.

They were good, Hatcher noted. All that jawing at the door aside, these guys were disciplined. Didn't risk a physical altercation, didn't discharge any firearms to draw attention, wasted no time in taking him out with an electronic control device. Quick, clean, quiet, effective. Even now they weren't giving anything up. A few snickers, an occasional whisper. Some likely fun at his expense with a gesture here and there. But they were maintaining an impressive degree of operational security. Hatcher had encountered more than a few military units that could learn a thing or two from their example.

The car drove backstreets at first, judging by the lack of noise and the sense he had they were barely reaching a top speed of thirty. They stopped for a moment and Hatcher realized they were at an intersection. Seconds later his weight pulled as they accelerated into a turn and he could tell they were on a main thoroughfare. Sounds of traffic. Lots of starting and stopping. They spent about fifteen minutes that way before he felt the car pick up speed and merge onto a freeway.

They arrived more than a half hour later. How much more, he wasn't quite sure. All Hatcher could surmise was that wherever they were, it wasn't too far from the highway. The driver pulled to an abrupt stop. The car bounced as the person behind the wheel slammed the transmission into park. Doors opened all around him.

The ground was flat, hard. A path of some kind, strewn with stones and pebbles. Definitely an upward slope to it. His only source of direction was the shoves he received to keep moving. After a while the ground began to feel more like hard-packed dirt. The feel of the sun on his arms was intermittent, and each gust of breeze rustled like a maraca. He could hear tweets and chirps.

They walked for a quarter mile or so, maybe longer. The sun on his arms disappeared, as did the glow of light through the cloth, and he sensed a sudden shift in the surrounding acoustics. They had entered an enclosure of some kind. A kick to the back of his leg and a hard press on his shoulder forced him to his knees. He clenched his jaw as they ripped the twin probes out by the wiring. Once the burning subsided, he could feel the blood seeping into his shirt and running down his back.

The crunch of footfalls echoed tightly around him. Receding sounds, pulling away until they were gone. A hollow silence settled in.

One minute stretched into two, then three.

He reached up with his bound hands and ripped the sack off. There was a sudden brightness immediately in front of him, a concentration of light, maybe more than one, surrounded by darkness. His eyes took a second to adjust. As they did, he saw he was in a cave.

"I was wondering how long you were going to sit there like that."

A woman's voice. The source of it took its time emerging into focus, blink by blink. Platinum blonde. She had buttery skin just this side of pale, swaths of it generously visible with the exception of a few small areas covered by a white, shimmering dress that hung in folds like a satin toga. A brilliant aura of sunlight framed her figure, radiating from the largest of three cave openings maybe ten yards behind her. Every detail of her seemed constructed for stimulating the libido, from her hair to her teeth to the sheen of her toenails peeking out from a back-strapped pair of high heels.

She shifted her weight from one foot to the other, her hips trading angles back and forth. It was almost painful to watch.

He'd forgotten just how beautiful Carnates were in person. But with that memory came the reminder that perhaps *in person* wasn't quite the way to put it. They were, after all, the hybrid spawn of demons. If he were to believe what they'd told him.

She lifted a cigarette to her lips, lighted it with a silver Zippo. The flame threw its glow onto her face, igniting her eyes like a pair of candles. This wasn't the first time they'd met. He searched his memory, came up with a name.

"Hello, Soliya."

"Hello, Hatcher."

"I hope you didn't come all the way out here just because of me. I told you I'd only end up breaking your heart."

She tilted her head and let out a column of smoke. "Always have something funny to say, don't you, Hatcher?"

No, he thought. Not always. "We could have just met over coffee. This really wasn't necessary. "

The woman smiled. "So you say."

She took a step toward him and blew a stream of smoke that drifted over his head. As she did, two forms moved from her sides in opposite directions. With the lighting what it was, they had been mere shapes prior to that, hunched low, obscured by shadow. They lunged toward the cavern walls, then bounded up the rock, taking positions on outcroppings to each side of her, several feet above her head. They let out a series of screeches and hisses in his direction.

"Your pet sitter cancel at the last minute?" he asked.

"You expect me to come alone? A girl can't be too careful."

Hatcher remembered the creatures from the tunnels beneath Manhattan. *Sedim*, the Carnates had called them. Some kind of demon spawn, hybrids, like their Carnate cousins, only without any of the sex appeal. He could still feel the rip of their claws in his back, the stab of their teeth on his shoulder. But these two seemed a little different. They were bigger. Their teeth were definitely larger, the lower ones protruding well beyond their lips, and they had a pair of thick intertwined horns looping down over the backs of their skulls and bending sharply forward. Their eyes seemed blank, like empty sockets stuffed with polished glass, and each of their faces was dominated by a single large nose leaf that groped the air, constantly twitching.

"Okay," Hatcher said, trying to ignore them. "What now?"

"That is the question, isn't it?"

She stepped forward, placed a finger on his head as she circled him. He raised his hands, which were still secured at the wrist and feeling cold and swollen. The things on the walls let out a warning hiss. Deep, piercing. And effective. He remembered his encounter with the creatures in the tunnels beneath Manhattan, made a mental note to avoid sudden movements.

"Am I going to get a little help with these?" he asked, his hands suspended in the air.

"We'll see."

He put out one of his feet, slid himself into a sitting position, careful to keep his motions deliberate and calm. A slight improvement in comfort, but not much. "So, what do you want, exactly?"

"You were the one who placed the call."

"You were the ones who flew a banner telling me to."

A sly grin tugged at her cheeks. "Are you going to pretend you weren't planning on finding us?"

"Now, where would you get information like that?"

Soliya took a long drag on her cigarette, exhaled a plume of smoke out the side of her mouth, then cut a question mark in it with her finger that, in Hatcher's estimation, held its shape for just a second longer than it should have.

"Wouldn't you like to know."

Well, yes, he thought, he really would. But now wasn't the time to ask. Almost as much information could be conveyed with a question as with an answer, and he was already staring down the barrel of a huge disadvantage.

"If you knew I needed to find you, I'm going to guess you also know why."

She looked down at her cigarette like she was measuring it for length. "That would be a fair assumption."

"Then maybe you can fill me in, and we'll both know."

"I take that to mean you cannot fathom a reason we would be willing to help you."

He was inclined to tell her that was a pretty damn accurate interpretation but instead said nothing.

"Your problem, Hatcher, is that you don't understand the nature of the world you live in."

"Tell me about it," he said. "Our foreign policy. The war on drugs. Don't even get me started on health-care reform."

She leveled her eyes at him, eyes that somehow seemed to flash, even in the low light. "Cracking wise won't change things. Nothing is quite what it seems."

Big surprise, he thought. And this coming from someone who tricked him into almost fulfilling a prophecy that would have sent every soul in existence to Hell.

"How about you clear things up a bit."

"I think I'd prefer you stay in the dark a bit longer."

Hatcher tried to figure out what was going on behind those eyes, get a handle on the workings of her mind. Realized it was a futile exercise.

"Then why am I here?" he said.

Eyes trained on his, Soliya walked over to the scalloped wall of the cave, lifted her cigarette and blew on the tip. Then she opened her fingers and let it drop. A small flame erupted where it landed, illuminating a compact heap of pitchwood near her feet. The fire quickly grew, engulfing the wood, shooting flames up along the wall with a loud crackle. The smoke carried a pungent odor.

She slinked toward him, smiling, all curvy sex on two creamy legs, and leaned in close. He reminded himself how the Carnates operated, how they traded on a unique combination of physical beauty and powerful pheromones to manipulate others, told himself to keep in mind it was an unnatural allure that they possessed. That knowledge didn't stop his blood from flooding to his loins, her warmth from causing his skin to flush, her scent from setting his nerve endings on fire. She stroked his face with tender fingers and then cupped his jaw and guided his head to face the opposite cavern wall. The fire emblazoned it with an orange cast, projecting their shimmering shadows onto the surface.

"You think what you perceive is reality, Hatcher . . ."

Her voice was a whisper. Breathy, sensual. It puffed into his ears like the seal on a sacred promise.

"But it's not . . ."

He felt her move behind him, watched her figure on the wall in front of him rise slowly, one hand swirling tightly above her, the other cradling his jaw, keeping his face in place, ensuring he watched.

"You see what you're conditioned to see . . ."

Her shadow swayed with an erotic pulse as she straightened her legs, her hand gradually leaving his face to join the other in the air, the black silhouettes of her arms weaving like courting snakes on the bumpy expanse of rock.

"Understand only what you've been trained to understand . . ."

The play of her arms and body on the wall had him transfixed. The undulation of her torso, the swimming motion of her hands, the roll and tuck of her ass all gripped his gaze like visual hooks set deep into his eyes.

"But how do you know what is real . . . ?"

It struck him that the sights riveting him, even the form of his own shadow, were incredibly crisp in their relief, not vague shapes of darkness but precisely outlined figures. Like entities in their own right, creations existing independently of those who cast them.

"And how . . . do you know . . . what isn't?"

The dark shape of his head began to rise, his shadow body rising with it. The form was so clear, so tangible, he had to lower his eyes, just for a moment. Check himself to make sure he was still sitting. When he looked up again his shadow was standing, an inkblot rendering, moving on its own, hyper-accurate in every detail. Except for the fact he hadn't budged from the cavern floor.

"And what if everything you assumed to be true wasn't?"

Soliya's dark figure slid around his on the wall, bending in a rhythm that seemed to produce its own music. Hatcher watched as she turned his shadow to face hers, and placed her ghostly arms over the form of his shoulders, hips swinging to and fro, knees bending slightly, slithering her body lower.

What looked like the shape of a dagger appeared in one of her hands, but before he could even react he saw her image cut the zip tie from his wrists. His shadow wrists.

He watched his arms spread apart on the rough, makeshift screen, saw her darkened form merge into his. He could almost taste the kisses, the slippery tanginess of her tongue, almost feel her body sliding against him. He watched his jeans get shoved down, the folds of her dress being pulled up. Felt it in his loins as his shadow plunged into her, the warm, gliding slickness of her, her arms gripping his back, her leg wrapping around his.

Then a finger caressed his cheek and the image was gone. The shadows in front of him shuddered with the flames, vague shapes, still recognizable but only just. A man seated, a woman leaning over his shoulder. Practically amorphous, if you didn't know what you were looking at.

She pressed her lips against his ear, almost kissing it. *"People perceive what they want to perceive."*

With a pat on the shoulder, she stood, backing away.

"They have my nephew," he said.

"Do they?"

"Yes. I think you know what I'm talking about."

"Maybe yes, maybe no," she said. She'd resumed her original position, facing him, backlit by the largest of the three cave mouths behind her. From somewhere in the folds of her dress, she produced another cigarette, raised it to her mouth. Lit it with what looked like the same Zippo lighter she'd tossed into the woodpile some moments earlier. As she did, the fire she'd started near the wall died, its orange glow disappearing. His head snapped to look. Nothing. Not even a smoldering trace of ember in the darkness, even though he knew the darker it was, the easier it should have been to see such a thing.

"The question is," she continued, "do you?"

"Look, I'm sure messing with my mind is great fun. But I'd appreciate it if you dropped the whole Sphinx routine for one damn second. They may hurt him. I'm not even sure what I'm supposed to do."

"Is that what they told you? They'd hurt the child if you didn't succeed?"

"No. But I doubt it's the easiest thing to work into a conversation."

"And these people, the ones you say have your nephew, they want you to stop the portal from opening."

"That's what they said."

She stepped back to a point where the cavern divided and leaned against the craggy curve of stone. She tipped her head back, sucked a breath through her cigarette, and blew smoke rings into the invading light.

"Tell me, why does it matter to you?"

"Why does what matter?"

"What happens to your nephew."

He watched the profile of her face as she drew more smoke, then sent it steaming into a cloud overhead. For a second, it seemed like the cloud formed a face looking down at her, moving in for a kiss. But then it disappeared and he wasn't certain it had ever been there to begin with.

"What kind of a question is that?" he asked.

She pulled away from the wall and took a few steps toward him.

"What's his name?"

"Excuse me?"

"The boy. What's his name."

Hatcher didn't respond. There was nothing for him to say, since he didn't know.

"You never even bothered to find out. So, I'll ask you once more. Why does it matter?"

"He's just a child. An *infant.*"

The creatures on the walls let out a pair of hisses. Hatcher took a breath. They didn't seem to like him raising his voice.

"We all were, at one point," she said.

Hatcher pressed his teeth into his lip, stopped himself from saying what he was about to, that he had a hard time ever imagining someone like her as a child, except maybe one that seduced her teachers with dirty pictures and set the house on fire while her parents were asleep. Maybe one who'd convinced her kindergarten playmates to snort a little meth before stabbing the babysitter.

"He's innocent," he said instead.

Soliya dropped the cigarette and pressed on it with the sole of her shoe. Hatcher forced himself to look away from her legs. He kept picturing himself doing the things he saw his shadow doing, reliving it as if it had actually happened. It was all he could do to maintain focus. She even managed to make the twisting of her foot back and forth seem like something out of a porn film.

"That's a temporary condition," she said. "Everyone loses it eventually. And I do mean *everyone.* Wouldn't you say that makes it meaningless? I would."

"What do you want to hear? That it's because I feel guilty? That he's my brother's child, so I feel a sense of obligation? It's a baby we're talking about, for Christ's sake."

"Yes, a baby. What if I were to tell you that the blood of that baby is the only thing that might avert what is coming? That a hellish fate awaits many other *innocents,* many other children, if his blood is not spilled? What would you say then?"

Hatcher started to consider the implications of what she'd said, then stopped himself.

"I don't know. All I do know is, I'm expected to stop someone, someone who may be my dead brother, from opening some sort of a portal to Hell, or else the child might be in danger. And that I was told you might be willing to help me."

"Ah, but you see, what if the child is the only way to prevent it? I'm not saying he is, I'm just asking the question. A truly good man is willing to sacrifice, Hatcher. Not just himself, but the ones he loves. That is the hardest sacrifice of all. To give the life of a loved one, to know they've been deprived of all they have, all they will ever experience, and to have to live with the knowledge it was by your doing."

"I never claimed I was a good man."

"No, I suppose you didn't."

"Are you going to help me?"

She peered down at him with an inscrutable expression. Maybe somewhat amused, maybe somewhat annoyed. Maybe something else altogether that was impossible to pin down. He couldn't tell if she was smirking out of a sense of fondness, or grimacing out of a sense of impatience. Carnates were so damned hard to read.

"Don't underestimate the power of a name, Hatcher. It's more than just some identifying piece of information. It's the essence of a being, carried in a word. Without a name, you can wield no power. Without knowledge of your name, no power can be wielded over you."

"You're saying I should find out my nephew's name?"

"I'm saying his name is Isaac."

She dropped into a crouch, curling her finger under his chin, propping his face with her knuckle.

"And if you knew your Bible stories, you'd know that was the name of Abraham's son. The one he laid across an altar, knife in hand, to sacrifice to God."

"Did my brother really escape from Hell? Some kind of Hellion?"

"Whether he escaped from Hell or merely managed to avoid it, the one you're looking for is definitely your brother."

Hatcher lowered his eyes and stared at the cave floor. Then he raised them again.

"Are you going to help me?"

The Carnate stood and let out a sigh. "If you wish to understand your nephew's fate, there's a woman you need to find."

"Who?"

"Are you asking me for a name?" Her lips peeled back into an impish grin, her perfect teeth glistening.

"Touché."

"She calls herself Nora. Nora Henruss."

He searched his memory, came up with nothing. "How do I find her?"

"That, my dear Jacob, is up to you."

She walked past him, her scent overcoming his nostrils and coursing through his system, the scent of Amazon warriors in heat, dropping behind his lines of defense, riding a battle wave of air. He started to look over his shoulder, twisting his body, only to be stopped by an almost deafening shriek of hisses.

"You'll find your car at the end of the trail," she said. "You live in a world of illusions, Hatcher." Her voice grew fainter in the distance, even as she continued to raise it. "Most are easy to spot. It's identifying the truth that's the challenge, because a man who rejects the truth deceives himself."

He heard what sounded like a car door shutting, then the hum of an engine, the crunching of rock beneath tires. The engine noise faded away as the much closer hissing grew louder.

Louder, then louder still. A harsh growl, like something between a cougar and a bobcat. Hatcher scanned the shadows along the wall, could make out the shifting of dark shapes within. Predatory movements. Muscles coiled, readying themselves. Then the hisses vaulted in pitch and one of the creatures leaped out, followed by the other.

A surge of adrenaline accelerated his heart. The one from the right landed in front of him bursting into the light, front paws padding first, rear paws following and springing past him to his left. The other shot from the left in almost identical fashion. They almost touched as they crossed.

Cats. Run-of-the-mill, garden-variety cats. Tabbies. Maybe a tad on the large side, but no bigger than plenty of others he'd seen.

He peered up into the recesses along the walls. Nothing. There was just enough diffuse light for him to trace the contours of shadow. The only thing hiding there was rock.

He stood and turned to look back where Soliya had left. It was the same direction from which he'd entered. There was a single large opening at that end, more like the mouth of a tunnel than a cave. He walked toward it, exited out into the light. A rocky, sandy path the width of a road curved out and down, descending through hill country. Gnarly shrubs and clumps of tall grass staked claims between boulders of varying sizes.

Above the mouth of the cave, patches of dead brush dotted the craggy hill face. Hatcher studied it for several seconds, then checked the surrounding area again. The location looked vaguely familiar.

Using his teeth, he ripped through the plastic ratchet case of the zip tie and freed his hands. He glanced once more at the opening, then walked through it again, heading toward the largest of the three openings at the other end. He ran a hand against a wall as he moved. It really was more of a tunnel than a cave, he realized, barely fifteen or twenty yards deep. Man-made, blasted out of the rock. He kept walking. It emptied on the other end into a quarrylike area between hills that resembled a canyon. Hardy greenery and burned-out sagebrush competed with chunks of fallen rock for space.

He stepped out into the expanse of dry hardpan and took in the view. *I'll be damned,* he thought, shaking his head.

His mind wrestled with a number of things as he inspected himself. His jeans were incorrectly buttoned, as if carelessly refastened. There was a lingering taste of something like tobacco mixed with a honey sweetness in his mouth. He could smell the gamey remnants of sex wafting off him as he fixed his pants.

He stared down at the pool of his shadow around his feet, thinking. Then he took one more look at the view, running a hand over his hair. A chuckle started to surface, but died somewhere in his throat.

In the distance between two of the slopes was another hillside. From just below its peak a word blared out at him in blocks of enormous white letters:

HOLLYWOOD

CHAPTER 7

❖

HATCHER WAS TEMPTED TO STRETCH OUT IN THE CAVE FOR A much-needed nap but drove back to Venice Beach instead. He stopped off at a Target on the way, bought a couple of prepaid disposable cell phones using his debit card, and headed to his apartment. He dropped into bed as soon as he got there and managed to get three hours' worth of sleep before a knock woke him.

The room was bathed in angled sunlight, forcing him to squint. He heard another knock. The tiny alarm clock on his nightstand told him it was late in the afternoon. His head and body ached when he stood. Stretching, he staggered on stiff legs toward the door.

His landlord was standing on the porch landing. Guy named Ling. Short, Asian, mid-sixties. A bad comb-over and liver spots on his cheeks and brow. No surprise it was Ling, because no one else ever came to his door. Practically no one knew where he lived.

Ling looked up as Hatcher leaned a forearm against the jamb.

"You look awful," he said. "Did I wake you up?"

"Don't worry about it. I'd still look awful hours from now."

The man didn't smile. Never changed expressions, as far as Hatcher could tell. He had affable eyes, but that was about it. It was like talking to a friendly robot. A friendly Chinese robot with a bit of a lisp.

"That your car in the back? Thought it must be yours."

"Do you want me to move it?"

"No. I just wanted to tell you, someone came by looking for you. A man. Cop maybe. He was wearing a sport coat and tie. Shoes needed a shine."

"When?"

"Earlier. Before lunch. Thought you should know."

"Did he say what he wanted?"

"No."

Hatcher dragged a hand down his face. "What did you tell him?"

"I pretended I didn't understand a word he was saying, told him 'no speak ing-rish.' He left."

"Thanks, Ling."

"You in trouble?"

"Not the way you're thinking. It's complicated. I appreciate you keeping quiet about me."

"You kidding? You pay your rent on the first of the month, in cash. No worries about a check bouncing that way. You never make a sound that I can hear, and you somehow manage to use less electricity than when the place was vacant. Last tenant I had, place smelled like pot all the time. Always had music shaking my windows in the middle of the night. Always had a sob story about why the rent was late. If someone's looking for you, they're not going to get any help from old Ling."

Even though Hatcher always assumed Ling was his last name, he had no idea whether it actually was or not. He had never had a long enough conversation with him to find out. Part of him felt bad about that, but part of him also figured Ling was better off that way.

"If he comes back, let me know."

Ling waved in agreement, headed down the wrought-iron staircase.

Hatcher shut the door, listened to the receding steps. So, he thought, somebody, maybe a cop, is looking for me. Bartlett? No. He obviously knew how to find him. Had to be someone else. He had no idea what that meant, but doubted it could be anything good.

He made his way to his kitchen space and mixed a protein shake, chased down three Advil with it. He would have loved to have gone back to sleep, but he knew if he crawled back onto the bed, he would just lay there with his eyes open. The restlessness that had given way to exhaustion earlier was back in full force. He finished the drink, rinsed out the glass. With the tap running, he peered down into the sink. Watched the water circle the drain, thinking.

The studio apartment he rented sat over his landlord's garage. After Vivian had left, it was just what he needed. Modestly furnished, utilities included. Saw an ad in a local sheet, put up two months' rent as deposit. It was small but more than adequate. Private, functional. And after months of confinement and a dozen years of army life, the place seemed practically palatial. There was a small flat-screen TV on a stand and a combination radio/CD player on a bookshelf. A laptop computer sat by itself on a small desk in the corner. Cable and internet were part of the deal, though he rarely used either.

The laptop was almost forced on him by Denny. It was a few years old with a full few years' worth of use but worked fine. He'd given it to Hatcher instead of cash for helping him clean out a storage unit. It'd only taken a couple of hours, so Hatcher didn't object, even though he saw no need to own a PC. Denny had disagreed, and seemed to take his lack of a computer personally. Hatcher had figured he could use one at the library if he had to and didn't have the slightest interest in idling away time surfing news sites or chatting with strangers.

But here it was and he was glad to have it. He fired it up, waited for it to boot, then jumped on the internet. A Google search for "Nora Henruss," found nothing. Couldn't find anyone with the name "Henruss" at all. He tried "Isaac Warren," and had the opposite problem.

He'd finished Googling local pizza deliveries to his zip code before he finally admitted he was procrastinating. He fetched one of the new TracFones from next to the bed and cut open the packaging with a pair of scissors. He followed the instructions to activate it, then fished a business card out of his wallet.

He lowered himself into one of the chairs of his dinette set. He tapped the edge of the card several times against the tabletop with the other, staring at it. The laptop made a noise in the background as it slipped into hibernation mode, nudging him back into himself. His eyes jumped to the phone and he thumbed the number into the keypad. He hesitated for several seconds before pressing send.

Three rings. Four.

"Hello?"

Hatcher took in a breath and held it, steeling himself. "Amy."

"Yes?"

"It's Jake."

The line went quiet, time dripping from one moment into the next. He listened to the digital hum coming over the connection and waited.

"Jake . . . Hatcher?" she finally said. It wasn't so much a question as it was questioning.

"Yes."

"Wow. Didn't expect this one."

"How've you been?"

"Good. I'm good. I didn't think I'd ever hear from you again. Considering you never called. Or returned any of my letters. Or even made the slightest effort to get in touch with me."

"I know. I'm sorry."

He could hear street noises in the background, the bleating of horns, the din of voices. Sounds of the city. For several seconds, that was all he heard.

"I don't suppose you called just to apologize."

"No. I didn't. But that doesn't mean it's not real."

"Right. So, why are you calling?"

"I need a favor."

She seemed to digest that for a few moments before responding. Something about the pause told him if it wasn't the worst thing to say, it was probably pretty close.

"Where are you?"

"Venice Beach. California."

"Was that the farthest place you could find?"

Actually, he thought, yes. That was always the reason he figured Vivian had suggested it. But he doubted that would go over well. "The weather's nice."

"I'm sure it is."

"I know this is awkward. I need some help, Amy."

"Are you in jail?"

"No, nothing like that. I need you to help me find someone. You're pretty much the only one I can think of who can do that kind of thing."

"You mean, like, a driver's license search? NCIC?"

"Something like that."

The silence that followed was deep enough he could almost hear her thoughts echoing across the airwaves, thoughts about the nerve he must have, calling to ask such a thing, what a callous schmuck he was, how only someone with an incredible ego and no regard for the feelings of others could be expected to act this way.

Then he heard her exhale into the phone as if she'd been holding her breath.

"I don't know, Jake. It's not like on television. They've cracked down on that kind of thing. You have to log in, have a case number. They don't like us fishing and won't tolerate us using police resources to help private investigations."

"I wouldn't ask if it wasn't important."

"Is this connected to . . . what happened? The stuff with Valentine?"

"Sort of. Maybe. I don't really know. It's similar. I just need to find this person, and I'll be out of your hair."

"Don't put it that way."

"I'm just saying I won't ask for anything else."

"What's the name?"

"Nora Henruss." He spelled it for her.

"Anything I should know about her?"

"Remember Susan Warren? She had a son. There might be some connection."

"Okay. I'll see what I can find."

"Thank you, Amy. I mean it."

"So," she said, her tone softening. "How are you, Jake? Are you okay?"

"Not ready to throw in the towel just yet."

"Jake . . . I have to know. Was it something I did?"

"No."

Neither of them spoke for a moment.

"I'll see if I can find something. Can I reach you at this number?"

"Probably, but I'll call you back in a day or two."

"That your way of saying, 'don't call me, I'll call you'?"

He pinched the bridge of his nose, suddenly wishing the call could be different, that he could be different. "I'm sorry. I didn't mean it that way. I'll explain some other time. Call me if you find something."

"Sure."

"Thank you, Amy."

"One more thing, Hatcher."

He listened, waiting for her to finish the thought.

"I never believed Dan committed suicide," she said. "Not for a second."

Hatcher struggled for a response until he realized the phone had gone dead in his hand.

PERRY CHECKED HIS WATCH AS HE EXITED THE FREEWAY onto San Rafael and turned right on Colorado. Knowing he was on schedule seemed important. He just wasn't sure what the schedule was for.

All he knew was he wanted to step back into his old life, immediately. Go back to being who he was, what he was. Forget as much of the past night's events as he could. Go back to the Game.

He turned onto Melrose, and almost as soon as it merged into Sixty-fourth Avenue he saw the church on the left.

There was a lot across from the building that was almost empty. He pulled into it and parked. The car whined as its systems shut down and was still whining when he picked up one of the envelopes from the seat next to him. He counted the wad of bills inside, ticking through them with his thumb. Then he did the same to the cash in the other envelope. It was a lot of money, but a fraction of what he was willing to pay to be free of this.

He read the note one more time before stuffing it into one of his pockets along with the envelopes and getting out of the car. The early evening air was cool, but heat rose from the asphalt beneath his feet as he retrieved the long duffel bag from the back of his car. He stood there looking down at it, feeling its uneven weight, simultaneously thinking about and trying not to think about its contents for several moments. Then he shut the trunk and crossed the street.

Perry had always considered places of worship to be a joke, but even he had to admit the Victorian architecture of this one was impressive. Nestled among trees on a lush residential hillside, the building appeared to be an example of nineteenth-century Gothic revival with hints of Spanish and other influences, sporting rugged, dark sandstone, Tudor-style timbering and a five-story clock tower as its centerpiece. Arched windows and a steep roof completed an Old World look.

A sign identified it as the Church of the Ascension. A white shield with a red cross and blue design in the upper left quadrant. It looked familiar to Perry, but he wasn't sure of its meaning.

He followed a circular drive and ascended through stone archways onto a large porch. The main entrance seemed to be to an oversized set of double doors to his right. He wasn't certain whether to knock. He tested the thumb latch, found it wasn't locked. That seemed to answer the question. He tugged the door open and entered.

The interior was dark after the brightness of the late sun. A feeling of foreboding settled over him. He had never gone to church, not once in his life. He'd always assumed it to be nothing more than a way for the masses to fill worthless time, part of the ritual habit of sheep. He was forced to concede that the events of the prior evening might require him to rethink many things, but he didn't intend for that to be one of them.

Even so, the hard, sterile stillness of these surroundings was discomfiting. Wooden parquet floor, walls of pressed dark brick, arched redwood ceiling; it all seemed so . . . alien. Like a museum exhibit showcasing life on another planet.

His instructions were to take a seat in the nave near the altar. He wasn't certain what a nave was, but as he wandered further into the building, he assumed it was the main area with all the wooden benches. On the way to the aisle he passed an ornate fountain with a white marble statue, a long-haired child with wings. The child was kneeling, holding a cross. He could feel its eyes on his back as he made his way toward the altar.

There is no God, he reminded himself. Whatever the explanation for what happened last night, it wasn't that. He muscled his thoughts along, moving them past the subject, telling himself he'd have plenty of time to figure all that out. Right now, he just needed to get this over with.

He took a seat in the second row of pews, setting the duffel bag down in the aisle. A large stained-glass window dominated the area beyond the altar. It was almost impossible to take his eyes off it. The liquid colors seemed to blaze like neon. He wasn't certain what the scene depicted, but the most prominent image had large bat wings. He supposed it was an angel. But it reminded him of what he'd experienced, so despite the attention it demanded he forced himself to lower his head and stare at the floor.

The day had been the most harrowing he could ever remember. He woke that morning on the sofa in his bedroom coated in blood, his mind still reeling from the prior night. Darin's dismembered body was in his bed, wrapped in cellophane. The kid's arm, the tattooed one, had been cut off, bundled in towels, and placed in a duffel bag. The note on the coffee table left explicit instructions on how to dispose of the rest of the body. Instructions for that, and for what to do next. Instructions for his entire day. Instructions he didn't dare ignore. The final task was to show up here and wait. With the cash. And with the arm.

That arm sent feelings through him he could only shake off with a shudder. It wasn't the thought of a severed limb that bothered him. He'd cut off many in his life, some from living subjects who screamed and pleaded as volcanoes of blood erupted from their wounds, but just thinking about this one induced something akin to a panic attack. At times when he'd looked at it, it seemed . . . different. There was something wholly unnatural about it, not just its appearance, but its texture, its musculature, its very presence. Other times, it just looked like an arm.

But he couldn't think about it without being reminded of that terrifying figure that came through the mirror, stretching out over him. It was an image that kept rushing into his head faster than he could bail thoughts of it out. He didn't want to think about that thing, or what it meant; not at all, not ever. That wasn't part of the Game, that wasn't part of anything he accepted. There was no Hell in his reality. And he'd always known, *always* known, that his awareness was supreme, absolute, defining. God Delusions were for those pieces of meat who existed to populate his world, whose purpose was to provide him meaning, to serve as his entertainment.

Unless . . .

Stop thinking about it! It wasn't Satan! There is no devil! There is no God! There's only the Game! Stop, stop, stop!

He clenched his eyelids shut like teeth and tapped his forehead against his knuckles. Faces of all the young men he'd murdered were popping into his thoughts like raindrops on a window. Memories once so elusive, so fragile, that he would prompt himself with photos and objects to help him retain them, now were coming unbidden, vivid like never before. Visions of hellfire and damnation took shape alongside them, endless parades of unspeakable horrors, of indescribable tortures presided over by the demonic figure from his mirror. He began to rock back and forth, trying to clear everything away.

There is no God, there is no God, there is no God, there is no God—

His head snapped up. A middle-aged man with dark hair, salting at the temples, was in the aisle looking down at him. Colorful robe, gold trim. A cross hung down the front of his garments on a large chain.

"I'm sorry," the man said. "I didn't want to interrupt you."

Perry rubbed his eyes, glanced around the church. He swallowed.

"Interrupt me?"

"Your prayer. It seemed so intense. I'm Father Medina. The rector."

Perry nodded. He scrambled to reorient himself, to remember his instructions. "I'm, uh, from the Foundation," he said, following the directions contained in the note.

The priest nodded. He had dark eyes, darker than his hair, and a round face with broad cheekbones. The man's expression remained pleasant, but even in Perry's distracted state he thought he detected something beneath it. Something like distaste.

"I assume you have a donation."

Perry removed one of the envelopes from his pocket and handed it to the man. He could hear the intake of breath, prelude to a sigh, and watched as the priest peeked inside before letting his hand fall to his side, gripping the envelope tightly.

"The church greatly appreciates the Foundation's generosity. Please remember to check the door."

Perry stared up at the man, unblinking, but said nothing.

"When you depart, that is. After I close. I assume you want time to reflect in solitude. I normally leave about fifteen minutes from now."

Perry recalled his instructions. The note said to wait in the nave until after sunset, which was almost an hour away. It hadn't mentioned anything else.

"Yes," he said, because it seemed like the thing to say.

The priest tensed his lips into a grim smile, gave a single nod, and began to cross in front of the altar. "Exit through the tower entry here. It will let you out if you press on the bar. The door will lock behind you. Please make sure it's completely shut."

"Okay," Perry said. He watched the priest start to leave again, then blurted out, "How did you know?"

Father Medina paused under an archway and looked back, his brow folding into a quizzical expression. Perry immediately regretted asking, an accidental spillover of all the paranoia and involuntary curiosity bubbling inside him.

"Know?"

"That I would want . . . time alone. To reflect."

"Because," the priest said, pushing open a large door, sounding both puzzled and wearied by the question. "That's what all the others have wanted."

CHAPTER 8

"OH, FUCK, MAN," DENNY SAID. "YOU CAN'T DO THIS TO ME."

Hatcher frowned. "Wish it didn't have to be this way. Don't really have a choice."

"How long did you say?"

Denny was leaning over the bar, pretending to wipe it with a small towel. He liked to play bartender sometimes, and this was one of them. But Hatcher knew he never actually tended customers, even when the place was busy and shorthanded. Especially when the place was busy and shorthanded.

"I don't know. A week or two. Maybe less. Maybe more."

Hatcher had driven down to the Liar's Den just before seven to tell Denny he was going to be taking some time off. He figured he owed him that much. He told Vivian to meet him there on the hour, but it was a couple minutes after now.

Denny leaned an elbow on the bar, surveying the few patrons seated at tables.

"I knew something was up when you disappeared last night. You're the only fucking guy I can count on, you know that? The only guy, and now you're just walking on me. Leaving me in the lurch."

That was a hard one to refute. Mostly because it was true. At least technically. He was the only guy Denny could count on, because none of the waitresses were guys. One other bouncer was always late, another was brand-new, and the only male bartenders were part time.

"If I can come back sooner, I will. We'll watch one of those Mark Specter DVDs you're always wanting to show me."

"Yeah, sure." He flashed a sullen look, then seemed to perk up. "You really gonna come back? You bugged out on me last night."

"I know. I'm sorry. Something unexpected came up."

Denny snapped his fingers, then stood up and reached into his pocket.

"You want to see it now?"

"I don't really have time to watch a DVD, Denny. Not now."

"No, not that. The gun."

Hatcher had to think a moment about that. "You mean that little toy thing? Looked like a monopoly piece?"

A grin stretched across Denny's jowly face and he withdrew his hand from his pocket, pulling out a key chain. It was connected to a miniature holster that looked like brown leather. He flicked open the strap with his thumb, unsnapping it, and removed a miniature firearm. It was the kind of thing Hatcher imagined you'd find in an expensive hobby shop, a place that specialized in tiny replicas. A classic-looking revolver, like a stainless-steel Smith & Wesson with a wooden grip. Denny stuck out his hand, displaying it in his palm.

"What d'ya think?" he said, beaming. "It's real."

Hatcher studied the tiny metal object. "What do you mean by 'real'?"

"It's a Swiss mini-gun." Denny leaned over the bar and lowered his voice. "They're illegal here," he said, popping his eyebrows as if he'd been waiting to say those words all day.

"Looks like you took it off an NRA Barbie."

"Ha! This ain't a toy!"

"Wait a sec . . ." Hatcher raised his eyes to look at the man. "You're saying this is a functional firearm?"

Denny nodded. "I looked it up on the web, thinking it was a joke. But it's not. It fires a 2.34-caliber bullet. It came with a dozen of them."

Hatcher wasn't inclined to believe it, but the more he looked at it, the more details he noticed. Like moving parts. And a serial number. Hatcher couldn't imagine who would buy such a thing. You'd need a perfect shot from rather close range, and even that was unlikely to do much damage. It would be like firing a pellet gun. Only less accurate.

"I'd be careful trying to fire that thing."

Denny shrugged. "My brother got a bunch of stuff from a guy who owed him. I was thinking maybe I could use it for self-defense."

Right, Hatcher thought. He wanted to tell him that at least it was small enough that it wouldn't hurt when someone shoved it up his ass, but he managed to stop himself.

"I'm guessing these are intended more as conversation pieces. Guns are only good for two things, deterring people or disabling them. That's unlikely to do either. And didn't you say something about them being illegal?"

"Yeah—hey!" Denny said, snapping his fingers again. "That reminds me. Someone came by here earlier, looking for you."

Hatcher didn't like the sound of that. "Who?"

"Some guy."

"Cop?"

Denny scratched his beard, eyes reading the air above him. "Cop-ish. But he didn't flash a badge or nothing. Just asked if you worked here."

"What did you tell him?"

"I told him you come in sometimes, but you weren't a regular employee. Guess I was being more honest than I realized, huh?"

Hatcher said nothing. His phone vibrated in his pocket. He pulled it out, saw he had a text.

Running late. Want to meet here?
I'll be in the lobby in 30.
xxoo

"Hey," Denny said. "Is this guy looking for you the reason you can't be around to work?"

"Honestly, I don't know who that is. And frankly, I can't deal with whatever he wants right now."

The folds beneath Denny's chin jiggled as he shook his jowly head. "I'll just pretend you're going on vacation for a week. After that, well, obviously I'm going to need to hire someone else to man the door."

The words came out like someone auditioning for the part of "Boss." Hatcher felt for the guy. It was never pleasant to see someone letting themselves get walked all over, even if you were the one doing the walking.

"You do what you have to. No hard feelings."

Denny pointed the tiny gun at him. "Don't forget," he said, grinning. "I'm the one with the gun!"

Hatcher gave him a friendly nod and left. He crossed the street, headed up an inclined drive toward Viv's rental. There were several cars on the street. Hers was an inconspicuous shade of silver but, being a PT Cruiser, easy to spot.

He was within a few feet of it, thumbing the key fob, when a man called to him from across the street.

"Mr. Hatcher?"

Great. The man jogged toward him. Hatcher didn't break stride. He reached the car and opened the door with a few yards still separating them.

"Are you Jake Hatcher?"

It was tempting to ignore him. Simply start the car and drive away. Tempting, but not necessarily prudent. Hatcher stood in the wedge of the door with one foot on the running board. He hadn't made eye contact yet, so it wasn't too late to keep pretending. He gave serious consideration one more time to getting in and shutting the door, but instead he lifted his gaze as the man reached the curb in front of him, watched him curve around the car toward him.

The first thing Hatcher noticed was that the guy certainly didn't look like a cop. He was a bit thin, a bit soft, and dressed in a ridiculous bright orange jacket. A bright orange jacket with an even brighter orange hat, like something you'd see on a commercial fisherman who was color-blind. The man slowed down as he approached and audibly tried to catch his breath. Hatcher took him to be in his late twenties or so, on the tall side, and somehow managed to have a skinny body and a fleshy face. He stood there with his hands in his pockets, panting. Not in the best of shape.

Hidden hands were not a good thing. He studied the pockets for signs of a hard edge pressing the fabric. Couldn't find one. But the right-hand pocket was definitely stuffed with something, even if he was pretty sure it wasn't a gun.

Of course, he'd just learned that guns could be pretty damn small.

"Are you Jake Hatcher?"

Hatcher stared at him for several beats. His best guess was process server. That would explain the bulging pocket. Sort of. But he had no idea why anyone would want to serve him with anything.

"If I say no, will you leave me alone?"

The man gaped slightly, crinkled his eyes. He sucked in a few more breaths with the same look on his face. Hatcher knew that hesitant look, that hazy way the eyes get. Mr. Orange was trying to figure out what to say.

No, he realized. Not what to say. Rather, what not to say.

"What do you want?" Hatcher asked.

"I just need to talk to you for a few minutes, that's all."

"About what?"

Several beats passed in silence.

"Can we go somewhere? Maybe sit down?"

Hatcher gave the man a hard stare. Wasn't going to happen. Even if he had a few minutes to spare, which he didn't, the guy was plain creepy. His mouth was shaped in a plastic smile and his demeanor was jittery, eyes staring one moment, darting the next. Like something was distracting him.

"I really don't have time," Hatcher said.

"Are you in a hurry?"

"I'm going to ask you again. Just who the hell are you?"

The man shrugged. "Someone who's interested in getting to know you."

"You're starting to annoy me. That's not a good idea at the moment."

The plastic smile stretched wider. "Should I come back when it is a good idea?"

Hatcher clenched his jaw and resisted the urge to put the jackass in his place. He slid into the driver's seat and started to shut the door. He had no idea who this guy was, and at the moment he didn't have it in him to care.

"Deborah told me to say hello."

The name made him stop. It was obvious he'd dropped that for a reason, and it worked. Orange-guy had his full attention.

Hatcher pushed the door back open and got out. Orange backed away as Hatcher closed in. Movement in the right pocket of the man's jacket caught his eye.

A piece of Hatcher's brain registered a threat and he lunged forward, clamping down on the man's arm with one hand and spinning him around. He knifed the back of his other hand under the man's chin and drew his head back. Almost instantly, all resistance ceased.

"Who are you?" Hatcher said, yanking the man tight against him, spreading his thumb wide, the triangle of his wrist pressed against the man's throat. "I won't ask again."

"M-Morris," he said.

"And what do you want, Morris?"

"Just . . . just to talk. That's all I'm here for. Just to talk to you."

From somewhere in the fold of the jacket, Hatcher heard a faint scraping, could feel movement in the muscles and tendons of his forearm. He squeezed his fingers into the man's arm, forcing a gasp.

Before he could ask what the man had in his pocket, a clipped siren blasted a descending note from the street, loud and close.

Hatcher looked over his shoulder to see a black-and-white Crown Vic pulled up near Vivian's rental at an angle. A voice blared out through a PA system.

"Sir, take your hands off his person and place them on your head. Then lower yourself to your knees. You in the orange coat, back away and do the same."

Hatcher complied, letting go. But he did it with enough of a tug on the arm and bump with his chest to send the man stumbling a few steps.

The cop got out of the patrol car and stepped forward, one hand resting on the handle of his holstered pistol, the other draped over a tonfa-style baton hanging through a loop in his belt.

"It's okay, officer," Morris said, waving a hand like he was cleaning a window. "It was just a misunderstanding."

"Is that so?"

The cop turned his attention to Hatcher, who placed his palms on his head and lowered himself to his knees, one at a time. The last thing Hatcher wanted was trouble with the law, especially with everything else he had to worry about. The patrolman was reasonably stout. Short dark hair, black Ray-Bans. Bland facial features, chiseled lines worn into his expression by frowns and sneers. Average height with a cop's somewhat bloated upper body. Hatcher had seen that build often. Swollen arms and chest and shoulders. Lots of time at the gym, but not the greatest diet. Very little lung work.

"Face the other way."

Hatcher turned a few degrees, sliding his knees, waited to be patted down. He wondered if the cop was keeping the creep in view. Wondered if he had enough situational awareness to be paying attention to the other guy at all. But the vibe he was getting told him to keep his mouth shut.

The cop said, "You military?"

"Former," Hatcher said.

"I'm going to need to see some ID."

Hatcher brought a hand down to remove his wallet and felt his right shoulder ignite and collapse under the pain. A second later, his upper body jerked and fell forward, the harsh chop of a blunt object slamming into the space between his neck and shoulder.

"Did I tell you to move?"

The side of Hatcher's head pressed into the sidewalk. His right trapezius muscle was in serious agony, stinging jolts of fire shooting up his neck and into his head. Using that arm anytime soon was going to be difficult. He lay there wincing, the ridge of his orbital socket grinding the flesh around it against the rough cement surface.

"Get up. And from now on, you only move when I tell you to, got it?"

Hatcher pushed himself off the pavement. Slowly. The smell and taste of cement lingered. A tendril of bloody saliva stretched from his lip. Second time in the same day he'd been dropped face-first.

"I see rejects like you all the time, losers who think they're shit-hot badasses, jacking up guys smaller than them. That how you get your kicks? That make you feel like a big man?"

The problem with fighting cops, Hatcher knew, was that you couldn't win in the end. The worse you beat them, the more they would send after you. Lot of wannabe tough guys were attracted to the badge, and that was why—to be able to act tough without necessarily being tough. He remembered some of the kids from high school who wanted to join the force, had seen the same kind in the MPs. Lot of low achievers with high opinions of themselves. Not all cops were like that, but enough to constitute a trend as far as he was concerned. They were a lot like some of the guys he'd met in prison. Mirror images, in many ways.

Of course, tossing them off a tall building wasn't advisable, either. And he'd gotten away with doing just that to one of them. So far.

Back on his knees, Hatcher put his left hand to the top of his head. His right hung limp, slightly crooked at the elbow, pressed across his abdomen. He couldn't get it to cooperate yet.

"Yeah," the cop continued. "Seen plenty like you. What were you? A ranger or something? That supposed to impress people?"

Hatcher said nothing. He felt the end of a tonfa-style baton poke him in the kidney for emphasis. Hard.

"Well, you're not *shit* here, in my town. Just a bad seed, no better than any of those saggin' punks toting a gat around, demanding respect. The biker detail books troublemakers like you every day. White guys with nothing but contempt for everyone else. Think going to war means you've done all you ever have to, that no one else can ever tell you what to do. No respect for authority. No respect for the badge. Got cop killer written all over you."

You don't know the half of it, Hatcher thought. Anger was welling up inside him. He could feel it in his face, the hot swell of it in his cheeks, felt the pressure mounting in his head. He knew he had to keep it in check.

"Only matter of time with your type," the cop said. "Only a matter of time."

A pain in his rib forced him to suck a sudden breath. The shock of it knocked him back to the cement. He pressed a hand to the point of impact. Pictured the end of the baton, punched into him, a lot of leverage behind it.

"You are one lucky lowlife, you know that? Assault of a pedestrian, felony menacing, disturbing the peace—all witnessed by a peace officer, no less. Dead to rights. But wouldn't you know it, seems the vic got scared. Fled before I could ascertain his identity. Can't be wasting the taxpayers' money. No vic, no stick."

Hatcher's scalp scraped the sidewalk as he shifted onto his side. His back was arched, the bony curve of his wrist pressed against his rib near the spine. He opened his eyes, could see the span of pavement down to where it ended at the street. Morris was gone.

The officer dropped his baton into the loop on his belt. "I'm going to let you off with a warning. Don't let me catch you up to no good again."

He opened the door to his cruiser and flashed a row of teeth. "Otherwise, enjoy your stay in the City of the Angels."

MORRIS DUCKED INTO A YOGA STUDIO THREE BLOCKS FROM where he'd just left Hatcher and the cop. The vestibule was small. Bamboo flooring, wicker furniture. Water trickled audibly down a section of rock from the ceiling to the floor. Piped music competed with the babbling water, instrumental, new age stuff. A harp being strummed and plucked.

No one was at the reception counter. He tried to remember specifics about what he was told. She'd said yoga, but he wondered if he might have the wrong place. This was California, after all. There might be another right next door.

But he couldn't imagine not being warned about that.

He waited until he didn't feel like waiting anymore, then circled behind the counter, passed through an access to an inner corridor that led to an open room. It had mirrored walls and a smooth wooden floor littered with mats. She was in the middle of the room, kneeling over a dark container, peering down. The container was shaped like a cauldron.

"I did it," he said.

The woman didn't move. The harp music kept playing. The water kept trickling.

He started to speak again, but she flung up a hand, showing her palm. She held it that way for almost a full minute before lifting her gaze and directing it toward him.

"You were saying?"

"I did as you asked. You didn't tell me he'd be so quick to get violent. What was I supposed to do? You said you didn't want anyone to see my hand."

She ran her eyes down to his shoes, then back again. "You don't look beat up to me."

"A cop showed up. He started questioning him. I got out of there." Morris thought for a moment. "Was that something you arranged?"

She stood, ignoring the question. "What did you find out?"

"What you wanted me to. It worked."

"Are you sure?"

Morris nodded. "I heard it, plain as day. Like a loud whisper in my ears. I'd never heard that before. The whispering."

"But you did. You just didn't realize you were hearing it. Like the subliminal messages department stores send out, telling you not to shoplift."

He wondered what subliminal messages he was hearing now through that piped music. Not ones telling him not to shoplift, he was pretty sure of that.

The harp finished its melody, started a different one. *Shoplifting.* The word reminded him. He removed his right hand from his pocket, wresting it through the tight opening, and held it out. At the end of his wrist, two impossibly long, unnaturally thick fingers unfolded, resembling a pair of arachnoid limbs.

The Hand.

Ectrodactyly, the doctors had called it. Lobster Claw Syndrome was the term most people used, though he'd always thought that was a stupid name since his looked more like a sloth's claws than a lobster's. Morris's was a severe case, manifested in a unilateral malformation of the right hand. His mother had tried to persuade him to have it altered surgically after finally locating a specialist willing to try, practically begged him from the time he was a small boy. He had steadfastly refused, telling her that was the way God had made him, and that no one should interfere with His will. But that was merely talk meant to shut her up. He'd never believed in God, not that he could remember.

And besides, he'd hated his mother. The way he saw it, she was the one who did it to him. If she hadn't been such a whore, he wouldn't have been born this way. He wouldn't have been born at all.

"What the hell is this thing you gave me, anyway?" he asked. Something that looked like an ancient marble, rough and petrified, sat in the narrow depression that was his right palm.

The woman produced a small leather pouch from a pocket hidden in the folds of her skirt and took the object from him. She cinched the pouch closed with it inside. "You don't need to know."

He didn't like that answer. "It looks sort of like an eyeball."

"Does it, now?" She crossed the room and set the pouch in a small wooden box. "Okay. Tell me."

Morris slid his hand back into his pocket and told her. She listened.

"How very, very interesting," she said, after a long pensive pause.

"Really? I was thinking you might be disappointed."

"Why would you think that?"

"Because that's a strange thing to have as your innermost fear."

The woman smiled. "Not when you're convinced you're going to Hell, it's not."

Morris thought about that, decided he didn't care. He had a more pressing matter on his mind.

"I'm overdue," he said, feeling the itch in his Hand. "You promised."

"You're going to need to control yourself. Just a little while longer. Maybe if things go well tonight, we can arrange something."

"What's happening tonight?"

"There's something I need you to do for me. Something I believe you'll find quite interesting."

"And what would that be?"

"Very simple," she said. "I want you to go to church."

CHAPTER 9

HATCHER FLINCHED. VIVIAN PRESSED THE COTTON BALL TO his forehead, unperturbed.

"*Ouch*. You know, that really hurts. I'm not kidding."

Vivian dropped the cotton onto a washcloth, picked up a bottle of isopropyl alcohol. She reached for another ball, held it against the opening, and gave the bottle a quick tip.

"Hush," she said. "You always hurt the one you love."

Hatcher wasn't certain how to respond to that, whether it was intended to get a laugh or start a discussion, so he said nothing. He was leaning sideways across the bed, propped up on an elbow. It was a nice room, with clean sheets and upscale décor. Lots of polished marble and deeply colored woods and shiny smudge-free surfaces. A balcony that overlooked the ocean. The Santa Monica pier was maybe a two-minute walk. Given the price of dirt in that area, he guessed one night in that room was as much as he paid for rent in a month. Maybe more.

The general was taking good care of her. Expensive care. That was troubling.

"I don't like seeing you like this," she said.

Shrugging, Hatcher said, "Is this where I say something like, you should see the other guy?"

"Didn't you say he was a cop? If he's as bad off as that monster Sherman, I'm sure he's in the hospital."

Hatcher started to respond, then stopped. It occurred to him just how conflicted Vivian must have been. Sherman was the one who'd abducted her for his boss, Valentine. She was the pure heart to be raped and dismembered by a creature of Valentine's own creation, an animal designed to be possessed by a demon. During that fight on the roof, she must have been hoping Bartlett's guy would take the shot. Even though that wasn't her nature.

"What?"

"Nothing. You're sure Bartlett's not in this hotel?"

She placed a hand on his face, pulled her finger and thumb apart to spread the skin around his eye flat.

"Positive. Close your eye."

He held up a palm and waved her off. "Let me do it."

"You wouldn't be able to see what you're doing. You have to clean these scrapes. They're filthy. Are you sure you won't let me take you to a doctor?"

"You stood next to me while I washed my face," he said. "How filthy can they be?"

She inspected his eye without looking into it. "Very. I can see dirt in the cuts. Little specks of grime and rock and God knows what."

"Hydrogen peroxide would be better."

"I don't have any hydrogen peroxide. I have alcohol. Now close your eye."

Hatcher bit down on the inside of his mouth and closed his eye. He flinched again when she wiped the ball across his skin. It stung, kept stinging after she was finished. She blew on it, gently. The stinging disappeared.

Her breath was moist and sweet and cool. Her skin felt warm next to him and soothingly smooth where it touched him. It was an unusual feeling, having her fuss over him. A sort of pleasant discomfort. He wasn't sure which dominated, the pleasure or the discomfort. He'd had medics stitch him up, doctors look him over, nurses relieve his pain. But he couldn't remember anyone taking care of him like this. Tend to his needs out of affection. It occurred to him Amy probably would have. Then he killed her lieutenant, and any chance they had to be together splattered on the sidewalk with him. He'd decided it would have been too much of a risk to see her again. Not for him, but for her.

He tried not to think about that.

"There," Vivian said. "At least I don't have to worry about you getting an infection."

Hatcher opened his eye, blinked it a few times. "You do realize 'no pain, no gain' only applies to weightlifting."

"Tell me what happened, again."

"I got rousted by a cop."

"But why?"

"I'm not sure. He saw an altercation between me and another guy. But I don't think that was it."

"What kind of an altercation?"

"Somebody's been asking around, looking for me. He caught up to me as I was heading to the car. I didn't like his attitude."

"What did he want?"

"I don't know. The cop stepped in before I could find out."

"Maybe you should file a complaint. With the police department. Police officers shouldn't be going around beating people up."

"I don't think you get how these things work. Besides, I don't even know his name. I'm not sure he was even wearing his nameplate. This was a setup. It has something to do with the Carnates. That much I know."

Vivian said nothing. A shadow seemed to sweep across her face, like a cloud passing overhead. She dropped her eyes.

"Relax. We knew they'd play games. I just have to figure out what their angle is."

She replaced the cap on the bottle of alcohol and pushed herself off the bed. She brushed her dress off, then carried the bag of cotton balls and the bottle into the bathroom.

"I don't like you getting hurt," she said, her voice carrying from around the corner.

"I made contact, by the way," he said, thinking there was no way he was going to get into that story any deeper than he had to. "With the Carnates. Earlier. Before this happened."

A pause. The sounds of movement from around the corner stopped. "And?"

"Does the name Nora Henruss mean anything to you?"

"No." She stepped out, leaning past the wall to look at him. "Why?"

"She has something to do with my nephew. That's all I know."

Vivian said nothing. She withdrew back into the bathroom, shut the door. A trail of light spilled across the carpet from the clearance below it.

"What do they want from you?" she asked. Her voice was muffled coming through the door.

Hatcher got up and walked over to the door. "The Carnates?

It's hard to say. The one I talked to today had been in New York. They're up to something. One thing is for sure, they can't be trusted."

Seconds passed before she responded. She cracked the door a bit, just enough to peek through. "What do you mean?"

"I mean, the way you know they're lying is that their lips are moving."

"But what if you were giving them something they wanted? Wouldn't they honor a deal?"

"You never can be sure *what* they want. I mean, what they *really* want. I learned that the hard way. And I wouldn't trust them to honor anything. Ever."

She blinked. The point of her chin twitched. "Even if they were your only hope?"

"Why are you asking this?"

"Because I'm worried about you getting hurt. What do you *think* they really want?"

"I don't know, but they seemed to know an awful lot about my nephew. I need to speak with Bartlett."

"Maybe this wasn't such a good idea, Jake."

"Maybe what wasn't such a good idea?"

"Any of this. Let's just go. Leave. Go somewhere far away. Miami maybe. Or Maine. Or one of those islands in the Caribbean. Just you and me."

"What's gotten into you? This morning you were giving me a John Wayne speech, telling me to cowboy up."

"This is starting to scare me, Jake. I'm getting a bad feeling."

"I've just got to find my nephew, make sure he's safe. Then we can talk about our next move."

She paused, letting the door bleed open a little wider.

"But maybe we should just leave this to William and his men. They can protect him."

"You were the one telling me he was in danger."

"Yes, I know, but now I'm not so sure. I just . . . I mean, really, there's no reason to believe William would hurt the boy."

"Did Bartlett threaten you?"

"No. I just . . ."

"Look, Vivian—I've had a hell of a day. Just tell me what's going on."

She peered intently through the divide, her focus shifting from his left eye to his right and back again. He realized she'd been holding her breath when he heard a lengthy sigh escape and she lowered her gaze.

"Nothing," she said. "I'm just worried about you."

"Speaking of Bartlett, if you want to get this over with, maybe we should quit tiptoeing around. Tell him I want to meet again."

"He won't agree to it."

"Why not?"

She backed away from the door, out of view. "Because he thinks you'll start trouble. Maybe kill someone."

"You could say you need to see him. I could just show up. Take it from there"

"He's too cautious for that to work. I don't even know where he is. We just talk by phone, until he wants to meet. Besides, he would have his men there. Someone would get hurt. You're hurt enough as it is."

"I need to have a talk with him."

"He won't do it, Jake. I doubt he'd even meet with me now under any circumstances."

"Then why is he paying for your room?"

No response. Hatcher retreated to the bed, sat at the foot of it, resting his face in his hands. A few moments later, she emerged wearing a matching set of lingerie. Slinky, with frilly trim. The kind modeled in catalogs by airbrushed sexpots with angel wings and a halo. Demi bra, thong panties. All white.

"This is unexpected," he said, standing up.

"I thought maybe you'd like it."

"You thought right."

"How are you feeling?" she asked.

"Suddenly invigorated."

"Be honest."

"Tired," he said. He rotated his shoulder. "Sore. And generally miserable. But I'll manage."

She crawled onto the mattress with a feline motion, padding on hands and knees.

"I want to make you feel better," she said, looking back at him over her shoulder. "If you're up for it."

He moved to the bed, climbed on one knee at a time. She

rolled onto her back and he leaned over her, felt her ankles creep over his hips, slide down his legs.

"You nuns," he said, staring down into her eyes, "have the funniest way of putting things."

HATCHER SLEPT FOR AN HOUR AND A HALF, THEN SHOWERED and left Vivian in her room. She protested meekly, half asleep, but let her head settle back down into the pillow with a dreamy hint of a smile on her face as he gave her a kiss. He was fidgety, juiced with the knowledge things needed to be done and that lying in a hotel room wasn't getting him closer to doing them. The compulsion to move around made it difficult to think.

He didn't know what to make of Vivian's sudden change of heart. She was holding back a lot of things, that much was obvious. But it was hard to get a good read on her because she was clearly in love with him. Love had no respect for rules. Made people do strange things, act in strange ways.

Like throw a cop off a roof.

He pushed the thought out of his mind, looked down at the keys in his hand. He didn't have time to think about any of those things. There were too many more pressing questions that needed immediate answers.

It occurred to him that there was one place he might find some, so he got in Vivian's car and drove. As he pulled out onto the street, he realized he'd been heading to the parking garage before he'd even thought about where he was going.

The Pacific peeked out from between hotels, an expanse of darkness to the west, a hint of a glow from where it swallowed the sun. Its waves crested white in the distance, a nonstop churning. Just as restless as he was.

Nora Henruss. Nothing more than a cipher to him, but one somehow connected to his nephew. But what kind of a connection was it? Did Bartlett know about her? And why would Bartlett kidnap the boy, and possibly his mother, in the first place and still let himself be talked into letting Hatcher get involved. It didn't make sense. Someone was playing him, no doubt about it. Nothing new there.

The question was, why? Even if he could stop this Highway to Hell from opening, assuming there even was such a thing, how was he supposed to find it? And who was that skinny prick who approached him earlier? What was his game? And was that thing with the cop something arranged? Or had someone dialed 911 right before he made contact, told them an assault was in progress? What the hell was that all about?

His head started to hurt, a sign he needed to stop beating it against a wall of thoughts. The way to overcome your limitations, he knew, was to recognize them. He wasn't an investigator, didn't know the first thing about analyzing forensics or piecing together clues. He had limited access to law enforcement data through Amy, but who knew how much and for how long, and even that required more to go on than he had. What he needed was more information. He found the thought semi-comforting. When it came to obtaining information, he wasn't without skills.

Vivian didn't want him to confront Bartlett. Obvious, that. The more he thought about it, the more he couldn't blame her. She was right. It would probably not be pleasant. It was just as well, because before he did anything like that, he wanted to have a better handle on things. If he was going to make the follow-up worth the hassle, he needed to figure out how much there was he didn't know.

And there was only one source of information for that he could think of.

He headed over to Venice, parked on a side street off Pacific, one of those ubiquitous alley drives between the backs of homes and duplexes. Tiny parking alcoves and garage doors lining a narrow lane. More than a driveway, less than a street. Good place to tuck a rental for a little while.

Three blocks south sat what looked like a former drugstore, made over into a clinic. The marquee-like sign over the entrance read MEDI-GREEN, with the words WALK-IN CLINIC in smaller letters beneath.

The number of medical marijuana dispensaries in the region had exploded a few years earlier, taking advantage of a permitting loophole, only to be shut down when local lawmakers realized how many had popped up. But there were still plenty around, and it was only natural that a pay-as-you-go, no-hassle medical clinic here and there would figure out they could pad their revenue by providing easy prescriptions, and a few did.

These were places used to dealing with people who didn't feel comfortable with a lot of questions. People who liked to pay in cash. People who needed a doctor, and wanted something nearby, convenient, quick.

People like Sherman.

Even for a relatively short fall like the one he took, Sherman would have needed medical attention. The math wasn't that hard, especially since Hatcher had been forced to memorize it. Basic rappelling, instructors drilling into your head the physical dangers of not controlling your descent. A one-story fall was assumed to be twelve feet, producing a velocity of about twenty-eight feet per second. Two stories was shorthanded as twenty-four feet, velocity around thirty-nine feet per second. He guessed the effective distance of Sherman's fall was about fifteen to twenty feet. A one-story building, but some extra distance due to the parapet and the fact it was from a roof, not a window. That put the height somewhere in between. A one-story fall created an impact of around forty-eight g's; a two-story fall, around ninety-five g's. So Sherman had probably sustained a sixty to eighty g crash. Headfirst, solid concrete landing. Probably twisted in flight, so his back absorbed some of the blow, avoiding a melon splatter of brains. But even so, instant deceleration. Nothing hits quite as hard as the ground.

And that meant serious pain when he finally regained consciousness, possibly severe injuries, even for a freak like Sherman. He'd need treatment, drugs at a minimum, probably stitches for his scalp in addition to a number of them for the rip up his arm. But he'd want to avoid a hospital. Too tied in to the bureaucracy. Too cozy with law enforcement. Too reliant on things that require ID. Too likely to result in outstanding warrants popping up on some screen when they processed his paperwork.

He'd want a clinic like this. No frills, just a doc earning a buck. Four blocks from the scene. Open until two a.m. The only place like it nearby. Denny mentioned it often. Claimed four doctors owned both it and the medical pot dispensary across the street. According to him, they were the ones who paid for the banner ad along the side wall outside the Liar's Den.

The doors opened pneumatically with just a nudge, and a blast of air-conditioning hit him. The reception area was a

collection of cold, smooth surfaces designed to look antiseptic
but, under the harshness of the fluorescence and the absence of
natural light, seemed naked instead, as if the illumination was
part of a video-taped crime-scene display, intended to expose
the subtle trails of grime and smeared handprints. Layers that
had been cleaned and repeated in ritual perpetuity but never
quite erased.

A black guy with long dreads and a tight beard stood in the
corner. He was a good two-eighty with an aggressive stare,
dressed in gray cotton pants and a blue long-sleeved shirt. Dark
sunglasses curving around his eyeband. Hired muscle written
all over him.

A young woman in a white coat sat behind a counter. She
looked up with a perfunctory smile through the open square of
a partition window.

"Yes?"

"My cousin was in here last night. Early this morning, actually. I'm sure you'd remember him. Big guy, huge. Bald.
Squeaky voice."

"Oh," she said. "Him."

Bingo.

"Yeah, him. Did he give you a hard time?"

She arched an eyebrow and mashed her lips together,
shrugged as her gaze drifted down.

Hatcher constructed a mental image of Sherman, pictured the
condition he would have been in. Concussion, possible skull frac-
ture. Severe laceration along his forearm, not to mention contusions and possibly a broken collarbone or dislocated shoulder. At
least a cracked rib or two. Angry, impatient, unable to think
straight. Having to sit still, head pounding, while some doctor,
most likely Indian or Chinese with a pronounced accent, stitched
him up out of a sense of professional obligation, being told over
and over again that he needed to go to a hospital and be admitted.
Getting more pissed off by the minute as the ibuprofen or acet-
aminophen they'd given him started to dull the ache in his skull
just enough for him to think, listening to rote explanations of why
he couldn't be prescribed anything stronger without a more complete examination and medical history. Telling him they could
give him a scrip for marijuana if were able to relate some chronic
pain symptoms or other qualifying condition, but that he wasn't

going to get any opiates, because they couldn't be seen as catering to drug seekers. Then being handed a bill.

"Knowing him, I'm thinking he stiffed you."

The woman sucked in a terse breath. "I really can't say anything. The police called and told us not to talk about it."

Police, Hatcher thought.

"Did he get rough?" Hatcher glanced over at the ebony Sphinx in the corner who was eyeballing him. "Maybe hospitalize your other security guy?"

"I'm sorry, I can't say anything. You can come back tomorrow when the manager is here."

"How much does he owe?"

"I'm not allowed to discuss patient information."

"That's a shame, since I'm just trying to make sure you get paid. He's got problems. Cleaning up after him is sort of a habit. How is it going to look if it comes out someone tried to pay his bill and was refused?"

The woman pursed her lips tightly. She tapped a few things on her keyboard, scrolled her eyes up and down her screen. "He doesn't owe anything."

Hatcher took a moment to think that through. Sherman caused trouble but didn't owe anything.

"I just hope you understand, he's a troubled person. If you help me find him, it might stop him from killing himself."

"He doesn't owe any money, and I can't give you any information. To you or any of his other friends."

Hatcher nodded, took a breath. It was a good idea on paper, but good ideas were like battle plans. Few survived contact with the enemy.

He turned to leave, then stopped. "What friends?"

"Excuse me?"

"You said, 'or any of his other friends.' What friends?"

"Please, just leave. Talking about patients could get me fired."

"I'm just trying to understand. Did another person come in asking about him?"

"Go."

Hatcher felt Mr. Dreadlocks stir from his perch.

"I need to know who it was, so I can . . . coordinate with them. They may not realize I'm looking for him, too."

"It was just some guy, okay? He didn't give his name. Just paid the bill. I checked to make sure there was a zero balance."

"What did he look like?"

She tilted her head and made a gesture directed past him. Hatcher felt a hand tap his shoulder.

A baritone voice said, "You need to leave."

Hatcher threw up his hands, patted the air in surrender.

"Last question, I promise. I just want to know what the guy looked like."

"Why don't you just take a picture . . ." She glanced over his shoulder, gave a thrust of her chin toward the entryway. "Or ask him yourself."

Hatcher turned, looked through the glass. Saw him standing at the curb, leaning back against his motorcycle. A winning smile on his face, not a hair out of place.

Mr. E raised a hand, gave a little wave.

The pneumatic door hissing closed behind him, Hatcher stepped out into the night air, leaving Dreadlocks staring at the back of his head and making a comment about not showing his face again. Mr. E's smile contracted into a smirk as Hatcher got close. Cocky pose, Hatcher noted. One heel on the sidewalk, the other wedged against the side of the bike beneath his rear.

"I thought California had helmet laws."

The man kept his gaze fixed on Hatcher for a moment, then reached down, pulled up the flap on a saddlebag. He scooped out a small black curve of fiberglass that glinted in the light from the clinic.

"Take it. I've got another. Then hop on and we'll go to your car. You can follow me."

"I'll walk, thanks. Not that there's anything wrong with that."

The man dipped his head, nodded with a hint of a laugh. Hatcher tried to remember what Bartlett had called him. Edgar, maybe. Yeah, that was it. Not very mysterious. He could think of better names for him. But those wouldn't be kind.

"Well, that's too bad," Edgar said, some contempt showing in his eyes. "I was really hoping to tell all the guys about you riding bitch."

"What do you want?"

"Right now, I just want you to get your car and follow me. There's something I need you to see."

"Why should I trust you?"

"I don't care whether you trust me or not. As long as you follow me."

Hatcher took a step forward, sliding to within an arm's length. "How about instead you explain to me why I shouldn't cause you an unbearable amount of pain until you tell me where my nephew is."

"For one, because you know I'd probably kill you."

Those last words hung out there for a moment, like a mist of breath on a cold night. Hatcher's eyes floated down to the curb, lingered over Edgar's boot. Edgar started to say something else, but before he could, Hatcher was on him. All one fluid motion, just the way his mental cues told him to do it. Lunge, grab, twist. His right foot shifting across as he spun his body. Simple physics. The tight arc of his torso around the axis of his spine leveraged his power, the large muscles of his chest, back, and abdomen doing all the work. He triggered himself to point his right shoulder to the ground, swim his right arm past it, feeling the smaller man rise, the fistfuls of shirt he had yanking the body in it forward, felt the man's weight lift, then tip over his hips. Edgar's breath escaped in an audible grunt as he landed on the sidewalk.

Hatcher lifted Edgar's torso off the ground by a clutch of cloth and buttons. "I hope for your sake explanation two is better."

Edgar gasped, coughed as he tried to speak. Said something Hatcher couldn't make out.

"What?"

"I said . . ." The man raised his eyes, peered straight into Hatcher's. "I don't know where your nephew is."

Although he was well schooled in the art, determining whether a person was lying was not easy. Under certain conditions, it could be almost impossible. Hatcher trusted his ability to read verbal and nonverbal tells, but the practice of discerning lies from truth was far from foolproof. Stress, emotional connections, the subject's own belief in the righteousness of his cause, all those and a thousand other factors could have an effect.

The eyes staring up at him were unwavering. He knew that contrary to popular belief, a practiced liar was more likely to look the other person in the eye when telling a lie. He also knew that in a high-stress situation like a street fight, those nonverbal cues were all but worthless. He was going to have to go with his gut. His gut told him to believe it.

"Besides," Edgar said, regaining his voice. "I wasn't kidding."

It took Hatcher a second to feel it. He lowered his head, saw the blade resting sidelong against his shirt, kissing his abdomen. The edge so sharp it had sliced a clean slit in the fabric.

The security guard was standing at the door, staring through black lenses. The gal from the counter was on the phone behind the security glass, out of her seat and looking alarmed. She was holding the handset with two hands and her lips were moving rapidly.

Hatcher unclenched his fists, the cloth of Mr. E's shirt slipping free as the smaller man stood. Edgar tucked the blade into a pocket, smoothed out the clumps of linen with his free hand, seemed to frown at the bunching and wrinkles left behind.

"So," Edgar said a moment later, flicking a hand in the direction of the clinic. "Are we going to wait for the police? Or can we go now?"

CHAPTER 10

❖

THEY DROVE FOR MORE THAN TWO HOURS, EDGAR ON HIS
Harley, Hatcher following. Hatcher knew they were heading
east, but had no idea where. The area was remote, all rolling
prairie and farmland. He weighed competing ideas on how to
proceed, such as simply veering off to the shoulder and taking a
wide arc to turn around and head back without giving any signal, or creeping up to the rear of Edgar's bike, flooring the accelerator, then leaving whatever twisted mangle was left of the
snot and his motorcycle in the road and heading back. Before he
could come up with any more options, Edgar pulled into a gas
station and coasted to a stop. It was the only business Hatcher
had seen in miles. He watched Edgar park the bike near the tiny
clerk's booth, exchange some words with the guy behind the
glass, then walk over and sit himself in the passenger seat of
Vivian's rental.

"What the hell are you trying to pull?" Hatcher said. "The
middle of nowhere isn't what I agreed to."

"Keep on going the same direction. It's not far now."

Hatcher pulled back onto the long stretch of highway, toward
the ghostly silhouettes of mountains, just dark shapes beneath
an only slightly lighter sky.

At least he didn't say "trust me."

A few minutes later, Edgar stiffened a bit in the seat, leaned
forward.

"There," he said, pointing through the windshield at a spot
ahead. "Turn left right there."

The turn was a swath of unpaved road, cutting through the
rolling, prairielike terrain. The road took them into the foot-
hills, terminating at some sort of small utility station, maybe
twenty-five-feet square. Pebbles jangled off the undercarriage

and the tires crunched as Hatcher pulled the car to a stop. A white metal sign with red letters on a chain-link perimeter fence surrounding the structure warned of no parking and no trespassing.

"This is just where we ditch the car. We're walking from here."

Hatcher shut off the ignition and got out. Circled the car and waited for E to lead.

"You're a clever guy," Edgar said. "I'll give you that."

Hatcher said nothing.

"You started that fight at the clinic just to cause a scene, didn't you?"

"Why do you say that?"

"Because it's true. You wanted witnesses, a police complaint called in. People who saw you and me in an altercation. You wanted to see where I wanted to take you, but wanted a little insurance that I wasn't just luring you out for a kill."

"Is this where you show me how smart you are by telling me what I overlooked?"

"Not at all. But I am curious. Do you really think a description by a couple of people who don't know me would be enough? What if you just disappeared?"

"Your motorcycle."

Edgar cocked his head a bit. He smiled in the way of someone who wasn't quite sure what he was smiling at.

"You've got a Harley that looks maybe a year old," Hatcher continued. "Pretty distinctive color scheme on it. Not to mention a personalized license plate. The security guard was holding his cell phone. You couldn't be sure he didn't snap a picture with it. Someone would eventually connect us."

"Like I said, smart guy."

Hatcher hitched a shoulder. It sent a pain down his arm that made him wince. He wished he'd gone into the gas station and bought some Advil.

Edgar said, "Okay, so maybe there are a couple of things you overlooked."

"Such as?"

"For one, that bike's not registered. I mean, it is, but the records aren't in the system. One of the bennies of having a former general as your boss. Know the right people, they can fix things with the state. At least they can in this state, where government officials are used to doling out special privileges."

Hatcher said nothing.

"And for another, how do you know that security guard's not one of ours?"

Hatcher stopped walking. Edgar's words swirled in his head. At first blush it seemed far-fetched to the point of paranoid fantasy, but then he realized the only reason that was so was because he assumed they couldn't possibly know he'd be going there. Yet obviously, they did know, otherwise Edgar wouldn't have shown up.

Edgar looked back at Hatcher after a few more steps and waited. His eyes caught just enough moonlight to glisten wanly. His face was barely visible, and stayed that way for several seconds, until the whites of his teeth flashed.

"I'm just fucking with you. I never saw the guy before." He turned and resumed his pace. "C'mon. Not much farther."

Watching Edgar pull ahead, Hatcher realized he could get back to the car and take off, leave the man out there with a long walk back to his bike. But he could have done something like that a number of times, could have run Edgar over on his bike, or at least knocked him off and left him stranded. Then, as now, it wouldn't have accomplished anything, so he decided to keep following. As much as he hated to admit it, Edgar had piqued his curiosity. The little shit.

The trail inclined, ascending into the hills. They walked for over a mile, closer to two, before Hatcher saw Edgar climb up toward a ridge and crouch just below the ridgeline.

He urged Hatcher to join him, whispering forcefully and waving him closer.

After a moment's deliberation, Hatcher climbed the slope, set himself down on his elbows a couple of feet away, and peered over the edge of a berm.

Edgar pulled out something that looked like a cigarette case. When he slid a lever along the side, the top and bottom expanded to reveal a pop-up set of binoculars. He handed them to Hatcher.

"Take a gander," he said, his voice low but audible.

Though they looked like a child's toy, the heft indicated he was holding expensive equipment. Hatcher gave them a once-over, then raised the upper half of his head over the edge of earth. There was activity about half a click away. He put the lenses to his eyes.

Serious optics, that much was obvious. Strong magnification. Image stabilization. Good brightness. The features combined to provide a crisp visual, allowed him to see clearly in the low light.

But he was having trouble figuring out exactly what he was looking at.

There were men. At least a half dozen of them, though it was hard to tell exactly how many, because they kept moving in and out of view from behind utility trucks with trailers. Athletic, well-proportioned group. They were carrying things, boxes and crates. Setting them down one at a time near a large opening in the ground at the base of a hill.

"Okay, I give up," Hatcher said.

"What do you see?" Edgar asked.

"I see a bunch of guys unloading a couple of moving vans."

"What else?"

"A cave, or cavern, or something." ˙

"What else?"

Hatcher looked over at Edgar, feeling the side of his face contort in disdain, then raised the binoculars again. Everything looked the same.

Before he could speak someone emerged from the opening, head bobbing up into view. Somebody not too tall but solid, an authoritative bearing to him. Gray hair a shade that seemed to adore the moonlight. The man kept glancing at something in his hand, checking it every few seconds.

"It looks like Bartlett," Hatcher said.

"That's because it is."

"What's he up to?"

Edgar ignored the question. "What else do you see?"

"Will you just tell me what the hell I'm *supposed* to see?"

"Let me ask this another way, what don't you see?"

Wagging his head, Hatcher peered through the lenses again. Same image. Guys in T-shirts, walking between trucks and hole, moving through the horizontal spray of brightness from the headlights of the trucks, Bartlett watching over them.

What don't I see? I don't see much. I can barely see—

Then it clicked. Snapped into place like a molded part.

"I don't see their legs. I mean, I do, but not very well."

"Imagine that."

"I don't see them," he continued. "Because they're camouflaged."

"And?"

"They're camouflaged because they're all wearing battle dress trousers."

"Ya think?"

"Recent stuff, too. It's dark, but I can see a bit when they cross through the headlights. I'm going to guess MultiCam."

"And who wears MultiCam?"

Hatcher turned and slid down below the ridge. "Special Operations. Stateside, at least."

"And why would guys like that be out here with a retired general?"

"Because," Hatcher said, piecing it together as he spoke, "he's not really retired. He's gone black. And SOCOM unit COs would be among the handful of people he could call to borrow some muscle, because they're one of the few who know units like his exist."

Edgar held out his hand for the binoculars, grinning. "Very good. I might even have to give you extra credit."

"There could be other explanations," Hatcher said.

"Like?"

"Anybody can order them. Or he could have swiped them from a supply depot."

"Do you believe that?"

Hatcher didn't answer. If those trousers each guy wore were full waterproof MultiCams, he guessed they'd cost almost a hundred bucks a pair. The MultiCam boots they were wearing, probably another hundred at least. That's not including tops, jackets, and headgear. Outfitting even a few guys with that would cost thousands. And stealing them sounded a lot easier than it actually was. And why the expensive stuff? Simpler camouflage made of good material can be found for a lot less money.

"Mind telling me why you're showing me this?"

"Maybe you're not the only one he's tricked. Maybe he recruited guys like me without telling us the whole story. Maybe—"

"Maybe you can cut the crap."

"I have my reasons. I just thought you should know."

"What about Isaac?"

A few beats of silence, then Edgar crinkled his eyes. "Who?"

"My nephew."

"I don't know where he is. That's the truth."

Hatcher dragged a palm down his face. "So, what now?"

"Now, you know."

"What did he tell you you were signing up for?"

Edgar twisted away, raised his head above the ridge and put the binoculars to his eyes. "I think we've had enough revelations for one night."

"Listen, I'm getting sick of—"

"Ah, perfect." Edgar passed the binoculars back to Hatcher. "Take a look at the mouth of the cave."

Hatcher peered through the lenses. Two men set down some boxes, then stepped out of view. The cave entrance was just a black hole. Wisps of dirt and dust and debris, illuminated by the car beams, danced in the space in front it.

"I don't see anything."

Adjusting the focus, Hatcher panned left, then right.

"What am I looking for?" he asked.

The silence seemed to echo, broken only by the faint scraping of wind. Hatcher snapped his head around, shot glances in every direction, almost immediately he realized his mistake, knew there was no point.

Edgar was gone.

But he couldn't have gone far. Several thoughts flashed. The car, the head start, the motorcycle. Hatcher patted his jeans. Keys were in his pocket. Would he try to hot-wire it? He couldn't have more than a thirty-second lead, and without the car, how would he make it back to his Harley?

Unless someone was waiting back where they parked, ready to pick him up.

Hatcher burst into a sprint, negotiated the path in the low light. He crested a hill in time to see vehicle lights in the distance. He picked up his pace for a few seconds, then slowed to a walk and caught his breath. There was no chance. Running was a waste of time.

When he reached the car, he saw he'd been right. A flashlight was on the ground, bulb burning bright, pointed at the rear passenger tire. A knife handle protruded from the sidewall.

The flashlight came in handy as he changed the tire. More than a half hour had passed by the time he got to the convenience store. He pulled along the side of the building, drove by where Edgar had parked the Harley. The headlights illuminated a white rectangle on the ground.

Hatcher got out of the car and picked it up.

The note inside read, *Maybe next time.*

THE INSIDE OF THE CHURCH WAS QUIET ENOUGH THAT EACH footstep seemed a cavernous, amplified clomp, jarring enough to make Morris wonder how resounding a scream might be in such a place, feeding his imagination with fantasies of terrified shrieks bouncing off all the hard wood and marble. It was such a solitary place, dark and still. He paid special attention to whether he could hear any other footfalls, ones more subtle than his own, uncertain if his guardian demon, as Deborah had called it, was able to enter such a place.

But, why wouldn't it be? The place was nothing but a building. Just because demons may actually exist, it didn't mean there had to be a God.

He walked the aisle, scanned the rows of pews. He stopped a few feet from the altar, stared up at the stained glass beyond it, the colors softly glowing with moonlight. Twenty-four women, and not once over the years did he ever think of killing any of them in a church. That was something he was going to have to add to the list. Maybe even before he was done with this venture.

Treated like a god, she'd said. *That hand is godlike, and so shall be the bearer of it.*

It was his destiny, according to Deborah.

She had promised him it wouldn't be much longer. He looked down at the bulge in his jacket, thinking, *it had better not be.* It had been a couple of months, and now he was long overdue. Three months, that was the max it could wait. He pulled his Hand from his jacket pocket and scratched the back of it. The skin covering it was tough and smooth, never quite dry, but often peeling. And when he went a while without indulging it, it started to itch. Like it was now.

Oh, but how just plain fucking *beautiful* it was. Holding it up to silhouette it against the stained glass, he flexed and scissored the twin appendages that were his fingers, a pair of enormous, curving digits that extended outward in a crustacean motion. The fused bones of those digits made the skeletal structure incredibly dense, and the confused biology had resulted in abnormal growth. The length from the bend of his wrist to the outermost tip at the longest point was a hair over fifteen inches. No thumb, no fingerprints, just two massive, prehensile phalanges connected to a padded section of bone that was harder than rock. Long, and strong.

He'd lived with it all his life, but he still couldn't get over how much he loved it. It never let him down.

And there was nothing like the sensation of running it down a woman's body. *Nothing*. It was as if the senses of touch and smell and taste combined to form some inexplicable sensitivity, one that filled him with awareness and feeling and excitement, every moment of contact mainlining a powerful drug directly to his brain. The silky warmth of their flesh, the salt of their sweat, even their fragrant aromas were more than just felt, they were absorbed by each and every touch, flooding his consciousness until his mind was awash in them, with that added bonus of pure delight sizzling through his nerve endings, the experience that made it all so irresistible—the tactile taste of fear.

How indescribably delicious it was, how literally mouthwatering. His marvelous extremity—an extremity in every sense of the word—sliding over their beautiful bodies, the sight and feel of it creating waves of terror that his own, special flesh could actually ingest, a taste it chemically identified like a tongue slathering over something oh-so-sweet, oh-so-sour, a tanginess that reached up and tingled through his taste buds even as it bathed some magical part of his brain. It was the very best part of him, and always had been. By the time he was four, maybe even younger, it was something he knew made him unique, something he couldn't imagine being without.

But he also knew that while his limb was a many-splendored thing, it was thrust upon him against his will, and he was not surrounded by those who appreciated such exceptionalism. By kindergarten, it was obvious he was never going to be accepted as normal, and yet his mother kept talking about surgery? To remove the only thing he cared about? What should have been a gift was treated like a curse. His mother had made him this way, and he was still a boy of fifteen or so when he decided she would have to pay. His Hand was a thing of wonder, but everything bad he suffered, the taunting, the names, the constant stares, the looks of such utter disgust from girls, those were all her fault. She had not equipped him for childhood, had set him up to be tormented. The Hand made him special, but she had made him different. Yes, she would have to pay.

And pay she did.

Morris was thinking about that, remembering the rush of touching her with It, the sexual thrill that coursed through him as he held the knife to her throat, the surprise of finding It running over her breasts, almost with a mind of Its own, the dizzying cocktail of sensations, culminating in the satisfying crunch as he tightened those tentacle-like digits around her throat, recalling all the vivid snapshots of memory, reliving each moment, especially that one—that special, all-important one—when he realized he could use the hand on other women, women like those he had spent all those hours sitting and watching at the mall, dreaming of those legs, of It running up the silky interior of their thighs, burrowing into that special opening . . . no, not just women, mothers . . . *that* was the epiphany. Young mothers, young mothers with young children, children who would grow up suffering, damaged, always and forever tortured inside. Always different. It all became clear to him, not so much knowledge but understanding, not so much a thought but a feeling, an orgasmic convergence, where he saw the color of ecstasy, saw it, felt it, comprehended it. It was the red of his mother's blood, and the yellow of a school bus filled with children, children staring hopelessly, robbed of their childhoods like he had been, a color emerging from this epiphany, swirling inside him, painting itself over his brain as It indulged in a feast of sensations from his mother's body, his mind drowning in it, it and all it stood for, that brilliant, rapturous shade of orange . . .

He stiffened. Someone was there, next to him. The presence abruptly registered, jolting him out of his reverie.

"How long have you been here?" the man asked.

Morris whipped his Hand down and back into his jacket, blading his body to block the view as best he could until It was concealed. This had to be the guy, the one he was supposed to meet. He didn't have a description, didn't even know his name. But who else could it be? Before he could say anything, the man started to walk away.

"Follow me," the man said, tossing his arm ahead of him, gesturing forward.

Yes, Morris thought, had to be the guy. He looked like some businessman, all gussied up in a suit and tie, black trench coat hanging open. Not what he expected, but what, exactly, did he expect? Horns and a goatee?

"Where are we going?" Morris said.

The man stopped at a large wooden door, opened it with a tug and a long pull.

"Downstairs."

As soon as the man finished saying the word he was through the door, descending into a dark stairwell toward a faint spill of light. Morris watched him, watched the top of his head bob downward, swallowed by the shadows in long, slow gulps. Then he followed.

Seconds later, Morris stepped into an impressive basement, spacious and finished with an institutional look: functional floor tiling, a corporate shade of eggshell wall paint, fluorescent lighting. A hallway stretched back beneath the church. He could make out a doorway to what looked like a classroom.

A few steps ahead of him, his guide headed to another door in the opposite direction, this one leading to an unfinished storage area, rough concrete flooring cluttered over with many years' cumulation of junk. A yellow bulb cast an uneven light from the ceiling, leaving most of the perimeter in a dusky mélange of indistinct shapes. The man picked up a flashlight from the top of a nearby box, Morris realizing a beat later he must have left it there himself to retrieve. He flashed it toward the far wall. The beam shone down a narrow space that cut between crates and boxes and stacks of chairs that had been pushed aside. The makeshift path led to another door, an old, imposing piece of antiquity, solid planks of arched wood that looked like railroad ties, secured to each other with wrought-iron bands bolted through. The man headed straight for it, then gave it a solid tug. It swung slowly.

The air was thick as they descended, like the darkness had

substance to it. The faint light cast down from the open door pulled away, growing smaller with each downward step. The man pointed the flashlight ahead into the pool of inky blackness, illuminating their path. Morris noticed a few empty metal torch mounts tracking the stairs along the right side, but there was little else to see.

The beam glanced across walls of stone to each side that curved in front of them, but those soon gave way to rough swaths of vertical earth. The air grew more damp and cooled steadily as they progressed.

"Where are you taking me?"

"By the time I explained it, we'd be there."

They continued down the stairs for another minute or so, until the last step deposited them onto a rocky landing, a chamber carved out of the substrate.

The man crossed the area to a door that was a bit smaller than but just as imposing as the last one. It was coated with dirt, its features obscured except where some recent hands had been at work. He strained it open, leaning back with his body to keep it moving. The hinges groaned as it drew, an almost nautical sound, deep and scraping. The void behind it came into view like a puddle of crude, thick and opaquely black.

"What's down there?" Morris asked.

"The future," the man said. "To end all futures."

CHAPTER 11

❖

HATCHER HEADED BACK TOWARD L.A., UNCERTAIN WHETHER to go to Vivian or just head back to his place. He still needed to think, but he wasn't sure all the thinking in the world would do him any good without some answers. What he'd learned tonight only raised more questions.

Given his lack of understanding, he'd considered driving back and crashing the general's party, just to force the issue. But that was a nonstarter. He was unarmed, one man, against a squad. That kind of math never resulted in anything good. Besides, his only advantage now was that he knew something the general didn't know he knew.

But what exactly it was he knew, he couldn't say.

None of it made any sense. What did Bartlett want from him? To find out about this Hell Gate from the Carnates? And then what? Pass the intel along? Act on it and stop whatever it was from happening?

And what was the deal with Edgar? The guy struck Hatcher as a sublimated psychopath, and Hatcher was inclined to think he was more the latter than the former. He'd seen his share of them in combat, guys who enjoyed it, who lived for the kill, jumped at any excuse. Doing the right thing was not high on their agenda. So why was he helping him? And was "helping" even the right word? There had to be a hidden motive of some sort. Maybe some vendetta against Bartlett. Maybe something impossible to even guess.

A bunch of men moving things from trucks to a cave in the hills of nowheresville. Bartlett supervising them. General Bartlett, maybe not retired. The more he chewed on it, the more he could feel another headache circling his brain, looking for a place to burrow in.

He decided to let Vivian sleep and go straight to his place.

He was a few minutes away when he checked his cell phone. Amy had called. Shit.

It was unforgivably late, or unforgivably early, depending how you looked at it. He thumbed the button to dial her anyway. She answered on the fourth ring.

"Do you have any idea what time it is?"

"Yes."

"Why doesn't that surprise me?"

"I figured you wouldn't have called unless you had something."

"What I have is a big fat nothing. But I thought that was unusual enough to be something."

"Nothing?"

"As far as I can tell, your Nora Henruss doesn't exist. No social, no driver's license. Nothing."

"That's strange."

"Yes. Needless to say, I couldn't find any connection to Susan Warren."

"What about the baby?"

"Checked that, too. Found the birth information. Isaac Garrett Rohner, born January twelfth."

"Rohner?"

"Her maiden name. She changed it to Jordan when she moved to New York, then took the name of Warren when she married. It was on the birth certificate, née Rohner."

Hatcher thought about that, wondered if he'd heard that name before. Decided he hadn't.

"Anything else?"

"No."

"Thanks for doing this, Amy."

"You're welcome." She paused. "Hatcher . . ."

He waited for her to finish.

"You should have told me."

This was the subject he was dreading. Playing dumb wasn't even an option. He kept his mouth shut and said nothing.

Amy said, "You should have trusted me."

"I did trust you, Amy. I still do."

"I know why you did it. Or at least I think I do. But you didn't have to. If you would have told me, we could have figured something out."

Hatcher didn't respond. The road seemed to ramble in front of him, like a carpet rapidly unrolling, keeping one step ahead of his beams.

"I know you don't believe me, but it's true."

"Thanks again for checking, Amy."

"You're welcome. Again. Can I ask you a question?"

"Maybe."

"That baby . . ."

"It's not mine, if that's what you're asking."

"I know. I was going to ask if you'd seen him yet. Your nephew."

"No."

"Oh. Sorry. Well, maybe you can soon."

"Why do you say that?"

"Because he was born in Orange County. That's right by where you are, right?"

"Born here, huh?"

"Yes. You didn't know that?"

"No, I didn't."

"Sorry I couldn't be more help."

"Don't be. You were."

He dropped the phone on the seat next to him. *Isaac Garrett Rohner.*

The name bothered him. He wasn't sure why. It tumbled over and over in his mind as he drove, like the contents of a dryer.

Isaac Garrett Rohner.

He picked up the phone, pulled up the call log, hit send. Amy answered.

"That didn't take long."

"How did you know he was my nephew?"

"Because of what the birth certificate said."

"What did it say?"

"That the father was Garrett Nolan. Your brother."

Hatcher thanked her again and she grumbled a good-bye. A few minutes later he was turning onto the alley lane behind his place. He parked tight against the wall of a garage and put the car into park.

Rohner.

Why was that name bugging him? He pulled the envelope

Edgar had left for him from his pocket, checked the glove compartment for a pen. Nothing. Just a brochure and a folded rental contract. He checked the seats, then the middle console, flipped down the visors, finally found one beneath the driver's seat.

The tiny light above the rear view mirror focused a yellow glow toward his lap. The envelope was folded into a stiff and bulky rectangle. He scratched a few test lines on it to make sure the ink flowed, then wrote the name.

Isaac Garrett Rohner.

He stared at his own writing for almost a minute, then below it, he wrote:

Rohner.

A few moments later, he wrote:

Susan Rohner.

He flipped the envelope over and wrote it again.

Susan Rohner.

His hand moving almost automatically, he wrote another name a few inches lower.

Nora Henruss

Hatcher picked up his phone, redialed.

"First I couldn't get you to call, now I can't get rid of you."

"One more thing," he said. "I just need one more thing."

He told her what he wanted to know, then stared down at the envelope, studying the names.

Jesus, he thought. *I really am stupid.*

MORRIS FOLLOWED THE MAN THROUGH A LIGHTLESS TUNNEL deep beneath the church, holding on to his coat. He'd never been anywhere so swollen with darkness, where the tarry mass of shadows enveloped him like a liquid, a tangible substance soaking every crevice, a presence he could feel as he swam through it, filling his lungs with each breath. Darker than sleep. Almost as dark as his thoughts were when he was able to relax and allow them to roam free. Almost.

"Why did you turn it off?" he said. He'd whispered the words, but they took on an artificial volume in the confines of the tunnel, magnified by the surrounding walls.

"The light bothers them."

Morris didn't know what he meant by *them*, but decided there was no point in asking. He would find out eventually.

Less than a minute later Morris felt a change. The lightless air seemed to expand around him, a sensation of space, coupled with a shift in ambient sounds, a stretching of echoes. He felt the man ahead of him—Perry, he'd told Morris to call him, but he didn't say it like it was his real name—straighten up.

"Wait here," Perry said, placing a hand on Morris's arm. Morris let go of Perry's coat.

Morris realized his own Hand was tingling. Blood pulsed through it, forcing him to flex his digits. Something was exciting it.

Several yards away, a flash of light ignited, the sizzle raking through the silence. For a moment, Perry's front half was aglow, illuminated by the tiny flame of a match, which he lifted to the end of a torch. The torch lit with a whump, tossing shadows across every surface, where they shuddered in spasms.

They were in a chamber. Morris didn't know much about architecture or history, but it looked ancient to his eyes. Ancient and enormous. The size of an arena. A wide circle of polished stone, with arched passageways at regular intervals and a vaulted dome ceiling. There were images on the ceiling that were hard to make out.

In the center of the chamber stood a round platform of rock, carved from the substrate of the floor, a chair of solid stone perched on top of it.

Perry set the torch in a wall mount and moved to another. The area brightened with another whump.

The images above gained detail. Morris stared at them, trying to discern the particulars. Another whump, and they came into full view.

Devils, frolicking in a sea of fire, their faces barely containing their glee. Eyes more intense than the fire licking their hooves. The heads and arms of people were reaching from the flames, and Morris understood it was on them the devils were prancing, hopping from one to the other, smashing them down to drown in the blaze, to drown and burn forever. Demonic creatures lined the perimeter of the scene like gargoyles, batlike faces staring down, drawn in such detail they looked three-dimensional.

Morris felt a powerful twinge in his Hand. Then he saw something that caused him to rub his eyes with his other hand, and look again. He could have sworn one of those gargoyles had blinked.

And just like that, they leaped. All of them, at least twelve, hurling themselves from twenty feet, plummeting down toward him. A shower of creatures dropping like paratroopers. The shock knocked him off his feet. He lay there on his side, instinctively closing up into a defensive curl, knees pulled in, arm raised to protect his face.

The things landed around him with a feline grace, leg muscles bulging with coiled power, absorbing the impact.

Thunk! Thunk! Thunk thunk thunk!

Dozens of eyes gleamed in the torchlight, regarding him with something more intense than curiosity. Slowly, the things began to close ranks.

He snapped his head in the direction of Perry, found him looking on dispassionately. An ambiguous smile played across the man's lips.

The things closed in. What began in Morris's throat as a plea came out a mere groan. Taloned hands gripped his arms, yanked him to his feet. Within a few seconds, his scream died out, the force behind it dissipating. They weren't ripping at him or biting him or slashing his throat. Now that he was on his feet, they were gently stroking him.

No, he realized. Not him. His arm.

"Go ahead," Perry said. "Show it to them."

Morris swallowed. His Hand was throbbing insanely. The sensation had been overshadowed a moment earlier, drowned out by his survival instincts. Now it was impossible to ignore.

He took a hold of his jacket with his other hand and tugged

the clawlike appendage from his pocket. The creatures made a strange noise as he unfurled its prongs, tiny grunts erupting like exclamation points as he flexed it open and shut. Sounds of reverence.

The Hand was practically humming now, purring with a satisfaction beyond anything he'd ever felt. Whereas killing and maiming sent thrilling sensations through his nerves, this seemed to supercharge him with a feeling of well-being, of purpose. Of belonging. His entire body was like a tuning fork in reverse, absorbing the intoxicating series of vibrations that emanated from it.

Low on their haunches, the creatures seemed transfixed.

"If you're through being admired," Perry said, pulling a cover of dark cloth off a large section of wall. It was smooth and black and polished to a sheen so slick it was practically mirrored. "I'm going to need a small amount of blood."

"Blood? You mean, mine? Why?"

"It's complicated. Blood is like a scent marker. And a lubricant. Relax, I only need enough to mark this once. Then you'll be recognized."

Perry smiled, showing a row of perfect white teeth. "Just think of it as lending me a hand."

CHAPTER 12

❖

HATCHER SAT IN A BOOTH NEAR THE BACK OF THE DINER AND waited. He'd told her to be there at noon. It was now quarter past.

A small pocket of gas gurgled across his stomach. The burger hadn't tasted bad, and he'd really needed something, but now it was feeling a bit dense in his belly.

The few remaining fries on his plate didn't look like they would last much longer no matter how slowly he tried to eat them, so he ordered a cup of java. Lots of cream, lots of sugar. The waitress pointed to a small silver pitcher and a container stuffed with packets of sweeteners. She was smiling, but she clearly wanted the table. The lunch crowd was heavy.

His appointment showed up before his coffee, a green sun dress clinging to her curves beneath long, straight hair so black now it shimmered blue, like raven feathers in a summer Kansas field. He saw her cross in front of the windows before walking through the doors. It only took her a moment to spot him.

The waitress escorted her to the booth. Jake stood and gave her a hug. She declined a menu and asked for an iced tea as she slid onto the banquette.

"Jake Hatcher," she said, shaking her head. Her smile seemed genuine.

"Hello, Susan. Looks like you're holding up well."

"I wasn't sure I'd ever see you again."

Hatcher shrugged, offered a what-can-I-say frown as he tilted his head. Back in New York, he'd told her he would call when the coast was clear, leave her a message how to reach him, but he never did. He told himself it was the right thing to do, that it was a way to keep things from getting weird, and her from getting hurt. But he knew those were rationalizations. Following up wasn't his strong point, and he would readily admit putting it that way was being generous.

"I hope your sister isn't too pissed."

"She'll get over it. Judging by what she wrote, she was mostly scared."

Hatcher nodded. "Sorry. I didn't want her to know more than she needed to."

"How did you find her?"

"I had Amy—Detective Wright—check on your family. As a favor. You remember her, from New York. I figured you would let someone know how to get in touch with you. It seemed like a sister would be the most likely."

"Detective Wright?" Susan arched an eyebrow. "She doing favors for you now?"

"It was the first I'd spoken to her since that whole . . . thing up there."

"Yeah, I followed what I could in the news." Her gaze dropped to the table. He could tell by her tone that she'd pieced together some of what happened after she'd left. If he had to lay money, he'd bet it all that she figured out what he'd done to that cop. Not the details, maybe, but the gist of it. After all, she knew exactly what Maloney had done to Frederick. Had seen his throat-slashed body, soaking in a pool of blood.

"I wasn't sure if it was safe," she added. "I've been very careful. I pay everything in cash. Use ATMs, and never the same one twice. Fortunately, I've got a lot of money in the account, so I haven't had to work. I even sublet an apartment, so it's not in my name. Nothing is."

"I understand. And your sister didn't admit a thing. Insisted she hadn't heard from you, had no idea where you were or how to get in touch with you. I just told her my name and where I wanted you to meet me."

"She has a private e-mail address I use. Untraceable, I think."

The waitress returned with his coffee and her iced tea. Hatcher poured some cream from a miniature pitcher, then tore open a few sugar packets and watched the granules disappear into the cloudy surface.

She was putting on a good front, he told himself. Maybe

she'd been warned not to say anything. Or maybe she believed what Vivian had suggested, that the boy was being protected. That it was for his own good. It was hard to tell.

"How are you holding up, Susan?" he asked. "Or is it Nora now?"

"Nora? How did you find out about that?"

"I was told I should look for Nora Henruss. It took me a while, but eventually it hit me. Same number of letters as Susan Rohner. And when I saw it wasn't just the same number, but the same letters arranged differently, that sealed it. It was you I was looking for."

"I used one of those internet anagram makers . . ." Susan furrowed her brow, her lips bulging a bit as she mulled what he said. "Why were you looking for Nora? I haven't used that name in months."

"Because of Isaac."

"Isaac? What about him?" She paused, eyes almost bulging. "Is he in danger?"

"That's what I'm trying to figure out. I need you to tell me what you know about who has him, where he may be."

"I . . . don't understand."

"The people who took him, the ones holding him. Bartlett and his gang. I need you to tell me everything you know about them."

She stared blankly, her eyes searching his face. "Who?"

Hatcher shifted in his seat, pushed his coffee out of the way. "Susan, maybe you should start by just telling me what happened."

"Jake, you're not making any sense. What happened to who? Isaac? Why do you think something's happened to Isaac?"

"Hasn't he been, you know, taken?"

"Taken? You mean, like, kidnapped?" She glanced around after the word came out, ducking her head.

"Well, yeah."

"Why would you think a thing like that?"

"Wait a second . . . When was the last time you saw him?"

Susan blinked, lifting her palms from the table and letting them drop as she spoke. "When I left him asleep in his little port-a-crib, with my neighbor. About a half hour ago."

*   *   *

AFTER PARTING WITH SUSAN, HATCHER HEADED BACK TO FIND
Vivian. He had to find out more from her about Bartlett, press
her for details, dig for things she may not have even realized
were important.

Or did he?

This wasn't his fight anymore. Without Isaac, Bartlett had no
leverage. Maybe it had been a bluff, a way of pressuring him to
do what Bartlett wanted. He used Vivian to convey the info so
he could have deniability. Vivian, who said she'd only found out
days ago, but was vague on the specifics. Maybe that was the
case because there were no specifics, just information carefully
fed to her by Bartlett.

Crude and at best only semi-effective. Hatcher expected
more from a man of his background and reputation. Did the
man really think he wouldn't try to find the boy?

Susan had been upset, and Hatcher felt bad about that. She
was paranoid enough as it was. But a call to her neighbor's cell
confirmed Isaac was okay, still sleeping. She gave Hatcher her
address and a number before hugging him. She said to call
soon, because she'd probably be moving now and switching
phones.

The Carnates were obviously playing games again, but when
did that become a surprise? It's not like he made himself hard to
screw with. He didn't even know as much about his own nephew
as they did.

That thought seemed to create an echo, not wanting to go
away. Didn't even know as much as they did.

Didn't. Know. As much.

Hatcher stomped on the brake pedal, the car slamming to a
stop. A horn blared behind him, but he ignored it.

No.

He yanked the steering wheel and hit the gas, U-turning
abruptly into a stream of swerving traffic.

No, no, no.

He punched the address into the car's navigation system. It
calculated the route, estimated his time of arrival to be in
twenty-two minutes. He wrestled his cell phone out of his
pocket and dialed the number. No answer.

The closer he got, the less he observed traffic laws, driving like he was racing every car ahead of him. He'd been speeding the whole way, but now he was running red lights with only the briefest of pauses, screeching through turns, weaving through traffic.

It took him seventeen minutes to get there. He sprinted to the front door and pounded on it.

He heard Susan's voice, asking who was there.

"It's me, Hatcher. You need to get out of there. Now."

He heard a deadbolt being disengaged, a latch being turned. Susan yanked open the door, eyes round.

"What is it? What's wrong?"

"We need to go. And by that I mean *you* need to go."

"Why?"

Before he could respond, a car skidded along the curb in front of the town house. Two men in matching tracksuits leaped out of it, drawing weapons, their faces covered. Another car pulled to a stop a few lengths behind it. Hatcher bulled his way into the apartment, knocking Susan back, and slammed the door. He bolted it shut behind him.

"Back door?"

Susan blinked, standing still for a moment, before shaking her body and hands as if trying to free herself from a thought. Then she nodded and pointed to the rear of the town house.

"Grab Isaac and lock yourself in the bathroom. And call nine-one-one."

"But—"

"Just do it!"

Hatcher sprinted through the living room toward the back. Susan protested, but he wasn't listening, his mind focused on sealing off all points of access. A few steps, and he was passing through a kitchen that opened to a dining area. The wall of the dining area opposite the kitchen was mostly a sliding glass door, hidden behind a row of parallel blinds. Hatcher saw the latch, exposed in a sliver of space between the last blind and the wall edge. He lunged for it.

The door slid open before he reached it. The barrel of a large-bore semiautomatic pistol appeared. Thin stock. The recognition was instant. Colt 1911. Forty-five caliber. Distinct, unmistakable.

The guy wielding it pushed through the louvers. He was wearing a black ski mask above a gray tracksuit.

"Don't move," he said. His voice was low, loud, and harsh, the words forming a command. "Heroes die."

Hatcher didn't move.

But in his mind, he was urging the gunman to. Just about a foot closer.

The man stayed put, his intense gaze tracking Hatcher from one hand up to his eyes down to the other hand and back. He stayed that way for about a minute, following the same visual pattern the whole time, as if he'd been counting down the seconds, then slowly retreated. The blinds swung in his wake, knocking together.

It was nice to have the gun out of his face, but something told Hatcher right off this couldn't mean anything good. He barely had time to lower his arms before he heard a scream from the front. He ran back to the living room. The door was wide open. He barreled up to it, slapping his palm against the jamb to keep from careering off the front stoop, pausing to take in the scene. Susan was waving her arms hysterically in the yard as the cars sped away, engines snarling. Both cars swung left at the end of the block and disappeared before he could even reach her.

The screams had deteriorated into moans and yells by the time Hatcher grabbed her by the arms.

"Isaac?" he said.

She pointed in the direction the vehicles had fled, sobbing.

Hatcher stared down the road. The cars were already long out of view. He glanced over to the PT Cruiser. They hadn't even bothered to disable it. There was no way he could catch them and they knew it.

As if to acknowledge the point, the squeal of tires taking another sharp corner sounded in the distance. The fading distance.

"How'd they get in?"

She fought to stop crying. It took her several attempts before she finally managed to say, *"They didn't."*

Another round of sobs began, only to be choked off in her throat as she looked past him.

"Oh my God," she said. "Patti . . ."

He turned to follow her gaze and saw the door to the town

house two units down was open. Hatcher hesitated briefly before sprinting to it. He paused at the threshold, glanced at the
living room, then headed up the stairs, taking them two at a
time.

The first room was empty. A woman in jeans and a sweat-
shirt lay on the floor in the second one, unconscious. Her pale
blonde hair was lumped in blood. Hatcher knelt next to her,
checked her wrist for a pulse.

He looked up to see Susan in the doorway, a hand to her
mouth.

"Is she . . . ?"

"She's got a pulse. It's steady, but we need to get her an
ambulance."

"I tried to tell you, she was watching him for me. I called her
on the way, and she said he was still sleeping, told me to get
some rest. She said she enjoyed having him around."

Hatcher nodded.

"Will they hurt him?" she said, wiping away tears, her body
convulsing in sobs.

"I don't think so," Hatcher said. It felt like a lie. Truth was,
he had no idea what Bartlett was capable of.

"What do they want him for? He's just a baby." Her eyes
squeezed shut, forcing long streams to roll off her lashes. "Just
a sweet little baby . . ."

"I don't know, exactly. But I'll get him back."

"Promise me you will, Jake. Please promise me you won't
let them do anything to my baby."

Hatcher slumped down onto the floor. "I promise," he said,
having no idea how he would, wondering if that word even
meant anything coming from him.

CHAPTER 13

VIVIAN SAT ON THE EDGE OF THE BED IN HER HOTEL ROOM, kneading the flesh of her palm and chewing on her bottom lip while she listened to Hatcher's rendition of the day's events.

"I left her with the police," he said. He'd related most of what happened, keeping it simple, finishing with the police arriving and being led to Susan's neighbor.

"Do they think you had something to do with it?" Vivian asked, swallowing.

Hatcher shrugged. He rubbed his clenched eyelids with his thumb and forefinger and leaned back in his chair. The police had grilled him for over an hour before letting him go. They knew something didn't jibe, that was for sure. Lying to them had been Susan's idea.

"We didn't tell them about the boy."

Vivian didn't react. Or, at least, didn't react more. She continued to rub her palm and dig her teeth into her lip.

Susan's logic was simple. If Hatcher told the police everything, they would consider him a huge liability and someone who needed to be kept under a watchful eye, and that meant they'd do their best to keep Hatcher from interfering with their investigation. She didn't want that to happen, because he was the only one she trusted to get her son back.

Hatcher didn't argue the issue. Truth was, telling the police was a bad idea for more reasons than that. Reporting that her son had been kidnapped meant the FBI would be called in. Bartlett was likely to have serious pull with the federal government, friends in high places who had friends in higher places. Somebody from the DoD, like an Undersecretary of Defense, calling someone at Justice, like a deputy director of the Bureau.

And given what he'd gleaned about Bartlett, there was always the possibility this was somehow part of a government op. Not likely, perhaps, but not something he could rule out.

Either way, Bartlett would be insulated. Maybe become the subject of an investigation, maybe not. Maybe forced to change his plans because of police attention, maybe not. But the bottom line was, Susan was right. Regardless of whether it affected Bartlett, Hatcher's ability to do anything would be extremely limited if the police were involved, especially if they started to take an interest in him.

He also couldn't help but wonder if that's what Bartlett had been counting on in his planning, to operate behind the cover of an investigation, to keep Hatcher away, buy him all the time he needed. He'd gone to elaborate lengths to find the boy; he could have easily factored that kind of response in.

"If they figure it out," Vivian said, staring at her lap, one hand still wringing the other. "They'll try to blame it on you, won't they?"

Hatcher swallowed a glass of tap water. "Maybe," he said.

"This woman," she said. "The neighbor . . . was she hurt? Is she going to be okay?"

They'd kept the story simple. Susan and Hatcher told them he had stopped by to visit, Susan called her neighbor to say they were coming over to get the baby, and found the neighbor unconscious on the floor. Some kind of robbery.

The baby, she claimed, was sleeping in his room at Susan's place, just as fine as could be. The risk was that at least one cop would want to see the child, have it examined by a doctor or at least take a look at it to see if there was anything relevant to document. But no one did. They bought the robbery story.

Patti, the neighbor, had briefly regained consciousness, but just barely, and wasn't in any condition to talk. She voiced a groggy concern about the baby, and Susan told her everything was fine. EMTs took her in an ambulance. Hatcher's presence seemed to bug the cops more than the woman's injuries, so they spent most of their time questioning him, which more or less confirmed that Susan's instincts about not mentioning the kidnapping were on target. No, he didn't see anything except a car speeding away. Yes, it was quite a coincidence this happened right after he arrived. No, he didn't hit the woman or know the person who did. They checked his cell phone, took his ID like it was a credit card they were revoking, and ran his name through a database. If they realized he was an ex-con recently released from an Army Regional Confinement Facility having served a two-year felony sentence, they didn't show it. They were just as hostile before they ran the check.

"I think so," Hatcher said. "An ambulance took her."

"You don't know if she's okay?"

"Viv, there's nothing I can do for her. From what I could tell, she should recover. In the meantime, I need to find Isaac. And that—"

"But what about when she is able to talk to the police? Won't she tell them she had . . . tell them what really happened?"

Hatcher rolled his head back until he was staring at the ceiling, then closed his eyes. "Maybe. But that shouldn't matter if I find Isaac." He leveled his gaze at her. "That means I need to get to Bartlett. Now."

"Bartlett? Why?"

"Do I really have to spell it out? He used me, used me to track down Isaac. That means he used you, too."

"Jake, please. You're going to get yourself killed. Or hurt. Can't you just . . ."

Hatcher tossed his hands into the air. "What? Let it go? Jesus, Vivian, what's gotten into you?"

"I . . ." She lowered her gaze to his shoes. "Nothing. This is spinning out of control, that's all."

"I don't understand. Yesterday, when you thought he had Isaac, you were all for me 'doing what I do.' Now we know he does, and you're all timid about it."

"How do you know?" she asked, deep furrows creasing her brow. "You said they had masks."

Hatcher lowered his head, swinging his jaw slowly from one side to the other several times. God, women could be stubborn.

"And yesterday," she continued, "I was telling you to do what Bartlett wanted, not to go against him."

"Look, Viv, you need to be honest with me—did he threaten you?"

She shut her eyes, let out a weary sigh. "No."

"Well, he's done something. You can spin it all you want, but he's gotten in your head somehow."

The words seemed to frustrate her. She reached forward,

placed her fingertips on his knee. "Jake, don't. You can't be sure it was him."

"You know something? You're right. I can't. Not until I confront him. So, I need you to tell me how to find him."

"I told you before," she said, withdrawing her hand. "I don't know."

"Vivian."

"Please, Jake."

He rocked forward out of the chair. He took hold of her upper arms and lifted her. Not much, but enough she wasn't quite sitting anymore. "Tell me."

"Jake . . ."

"Tell me."

She turned her head and shut her eyes, a pained expression tightening her face. She seemed to think long and hard before answering.

"He's rented a house. I heard a couple of his men talk about it. They said it's a big one, a corner lot. On Mulholland Drive."

THE PLACE WAS LESS A HOUSE THAN A COMPOUND. FULL PErimeter wall, iron gate complete with guardhouse. The guardhouse looked empty, but there was a CCTV camera pointed at the drive.

Through the twisted curves of the gate, Hatcher could see a bald guy in camouflage pants and a dark shirt walking a circuit. He had an earpiece over one ear with a flex mike curving down to the side of his mouth. One hand rested along the top of an M4, with the other loosely wrapped around the grip, trigger finger resting on the guard, strap pulled taut over his shoulder, holding it across his body in a ready position.

Sometimes, Hatcher figured, the direct approach is best.

He parked Vivian's rental along the street and walked toward the gate. It had enough play for him to move it open and walk through. He walked straight toward the sentry with the M4.

The guard eased the muzzle of the rifle in Hatcher's direction. Not quite at him, but close enough to make the point.

"That's far enough," the man said.

Hatcher took two more steps, stopped about ten feet away. "I'm here to see Bartlett."

"Get down on your knees, hands clasped behind your head." The guard raised a hand to his earpiece, was about to speak into the mike.

Rolling his eyes and his head in an exaggerated gesture, Hatcher frowned and moved a few steps closer. "Look, my name's—"

The man snapped the weapon up, staring through the sights. "I know who you are. And I gave you an order. On the ground."

"If I can just—"

Hatcher slapped a hand to his neck. He pulled it away and looked at his palm, then held it out to show the guard. Blood, and a metal dart. Then he collapsed.

The guard covered him with his rifle, approaching cautiously. He looked down at the dart, warily glanced to each side. He nudged Hatcher's body with his foot, then gave it a prodding kick. Nothing. He swept the perimeter with a quick rotation of his head before taking a knee and reaching for the dart next to Hatcher's palm. He raised his other hand to his earpiece, started to speak.

He never got the chance. Hatcher launched his legs over the man's head, scissoring his neck. He grabbed the rifle stock in the same motion, pointing the muzzle away from his body, and gave a violent twist of his hips. Both of them came crashing to the concrete, Hatcher's lower body slapping flat, the guard slamming down onto his back. Air blasted from the guard's lungs with a loud grunt. Hatcher released his grip, spun himself around, and flipped on top of the man, punching him once, twice, three times, each blow causing the back of the man's skull to bounce off the concrete.

The guard's eyes rolled back. Hatcher ripped off the headset, unfastened the rifle sling, and took the M4. He shot looks front and back, side to side, checking for movement. Nothing.

His best assessment was there was really no chance that they didn't know he was there, though he figured there were still two ways to play it. But it didn't matter, because anger was making the choice for him. He grabbed the man by the back of his collar and yanked him to his feet.

A body, especially one of a grown man, is heavier than most people realize. The key to forcing someone's body to do what you wanted was getting them to assist you with their own movement. That meant a state of dazed consciousness worked best, the kind where the person would try to stand, use some of their own balance and leg strength to achieve the goal. Though he was a little too wobbly to walk smoothly, the man offered just enough of an effort at keeping his feet for Hatcher to push him toward the house, rifle in his back. The man staggered forward, his head bent into his hand.

The front door to the house was constructed of ornate panels of etched glass set in a cherrywood frame. Hatcher dug his hand deeper into the man's shirt, bunching more cloth into his fist and clenching as tightly as he could. He pulled back slightly, then thrust forward, running the stumbling man into a near sprint, propelling over two low steps, across the porch, and smashing him headfirst through the designer glass.

Two of the glass panels shattered in a burst of shards. Hatcher jumped through the opening and shouldered the rifle. The guard lay on the floor of the foyer, having cleared the door. A spill of blood leaked over the sand-colored tile beneath him.

The foyer was massive. A wide wooden staircase the color of tea wound around a baby grand piano and fanned onto an open stretch of second-story hall. There was an overlook, fenced by a decorative railing that matched the banister.

To the left was a study, or perhaps a library. To the right, a spacious dining room, elegantly furnished with service for ten or twelve. Beyond the staircase, the area opened into a room so bright it almost hurt his eyes to look at. Hatcher could see the backs of a sofa and chair, white and puffy. A huge window took up most of the far wall. Beyond it, the glistening water of a pool reflected the azure California sky.

What Hatcher couldn't see, or hear, was any sign of people. No footfalls, no shuffling, no bumps or knocks or sounds of hushed voices. Only the light whistle of a breeze through the smashed glass door behind him.

One step, then another, swinging the rifle along points in a pattern to cover every angle. He continued creeping forward, passing the piano, dropping down one step, then another, into a living room.

The furniture was so white it seemed to require a power source. Accent tables of chrome and glass added to the brightness. White marble statues and colorful pieces of artwork, little more than random brushstrokes on canvas to Hatcher's eye, rounded out the decor. Beyond the room to the right, an expanse of kitchen stretched out behind a half wall, spilling into a breakfast nook. To his immediate left stood a fireplace. A flat-screen television, large and conspicuously black, hung on the wall above it. The screen was blank, but with a subtle glow to it, like someone had left it on.

Hatcher moved through a doorway to a bedroom. Fourposter bed, neatly made. A spacious bathroom with dark tiling. All empty.

He passed back through the living room and into the foyer, looking up the stairs. He doubted anyone was up there, but he knew assumptions like that got people killed. He was going to have to check.

Or maybe not.

The guard was still on the floor. He was pushing his chest up, trying to raise his head off the tiles and having a tough time of it. Blood was dripping off his scalp and puddling along the grout.

Hatcher gave him a firm kick to the ribs.

"Where is he?"

The man fell off his hands and onto his side, coughing.

"I asked you a question."

Another cough, then a low groan. *"I don't know . . ."*

Hatcher put a heel on his shoulder and shoved him into his back. "Don't make me get creative."

"I don't know . . . go back and ask him . . ."

And just how am I supposed to do that? Hatcher started to say, but his head snapped up before he could.

Either his ears were playing tricks on him or he'd heard a voice. Someone speaking. There was an artificial aspect to it, like a recording, or a phone call. He waited, listening.

There it was again. This time, there was no mistaking it. Faint, but distinct. Someone calling his name.

He hurried back to the living room, M4 up and ready. Nothing.

"Hatcher."

Hatcher spun, muzzle up and aiming. General Bartlett was there, wearing a gabardine suit coat and a turtleneck, staring down from the television screen.

The general frowned. "I have to assume that's Engel's weapon. I hope you didn't kill him."

"He'll live."

"Given the look on your face, I suppose I should be grateful. You should know he was instructed to alert me regarding your presence, then escort you into the house. There was no need for violence."

"In that case, why have an armed guard at all? And why aren't you here?"

"Because you, Chief Warrant Officer Second Class Hatcher, are prone to breaking bones first and asking questions later. I can see I underestimated your proclivity for recklessness."

"That's sort of funny, coming from a lying sack of shit like you."

Bartlett bristled at the words, shifting his body and cocking his jaw to one side. "I like to think of myself as a patient man, Hatcher. But you're testing me."

Hatcher ran his eyes around the edges of the monitor. The camera had to be embedded. "What have you done with the boy?"

"Nothing, Hatcher. That's what I'm trying to tell you."

"Where is he?"

"I have no idea," the general said, shaking his head slightly.

"Suppose I dragged your man Engels in here and started planting rounds in his body until I started feeling better about your answers."

Bartlett stared down from the screen as if he were on the other side, looking directly through it. "Are you saying you'd just kill a man rather than believe me?"

"Not right away."

"No," he said, shaking his head again. "I don't think you would. Engels doesn't know anything, and you're smart enough to know that. That's precisely why I brought him in. Besides, you *Kittens* pride yourselves on your ability to sniff out deception. You can see it in my face. Hear it in my voice. I'm not lying."

Hatcher knew it shouldn't bother him to hear Bartlett refer to him as a Kitten—Coercive Interrogation Tactician—but it did. Few people were supposed to even know such a program existed, and while a general like Bartlett would be one of them, the fact he knew Hatcher had been one meant he'd dug way deeper than a personnel record.

"Well, you sure as hell aren't being candid. How's that?"

"Candid? Please. Candor would mean putting all my cards on the table, and you of all people understand that is not a luxury I can afford. I'm not going to let you know where I am, so you can cause more trouble and get someone killed. And I'm not going to jeopardize an operation by letting you know too much. But a lack of candor doesn't mean I'm lying when I tell you I have no idea where the boy is."

"And I'm supposed to believe you didn't take him?"

"Yes, because it's true. I didn't take him, and I didn't authorize anyone to."

"Then why did you lead me to believe you already had him?"

Bartlett stiffened in his seat. "When did I do any such thing?"

Hatcher watched the screen, studied the man's expression, took a measure of his body language and demeanor. He didn't like what he saw, because there was nothing there to indicate his indignance was feigned. Had Edgar played him?

"I think I see what's going on here," Bartlett said. "*She* told you that, didn't she?"

Hatcher said nothing.

"I think you've been misled, son."

No, he told himself. No way. Vivian? But even to his own mind, it was a weak protest.

"Why would she do something like that?"

Bartlett remained silent, he looked on pensively, as if it were a rhetorical question. It wasn't.

"What do you want with me, General?"

"I didn't take your nephew, Hatcher. I'll let you draw your own conclusions about who put it in your mind that I did. Let me leave you with this—there's a reason I didn't invite you to join my team. You're too much of a wild card. I can't have some cowboy with oppositional defiance disorder disrupting things, substituting his own judgment for mine. This situation is a perfect example of your lack of discipline. Try not to make any more rookie mistakes. Next time, you might get yourself killed. Good luck, soldier. Godspeed."

The general leaned forward, looking down toward some point beyond the bottom of the screen. Hatcher raised a hand, lunged toward the image.

"Wait!"

Too late. The screen flickered once, then went dark.

Goddamnit. Hatcher rolled his head back and stared at the ceiling, gritting his teeth. What did Bartlett mean by that last crack about rookie mistakes? What had he missed?

Shit.

He sprinted toward the foyer, letting his momentum die as he got there. A small pool of blood on the floor, with some smears and streaks near it. But no Ellis. He walked past the blood, looked through the door.

Out on the drive, the headset was gone, too.

He hadn't secured his prisoner. Hadn't secured him or killed him. Bartlett wasn't just talking. Under different circumstances, such an oversight could have gotten him very dead.

The general was right, but he was also hiding things, things more relevant than what he would have Hatcher believe. Selective honesty couldn't be trusted. Unfortunately, there was one thing Bartlett alluded to that he couldn't dismiss.

He wiped down the M4 with his shirt and left it in the foyer, then hurried to the Cruiser. It took him almost forty-five minutes to reach the hotel. He banged on the door, phoned the room from his cell, and with a small bribe and some begging, finally persuaded a housekeeper to open the door for him.

The housekeeper screamed before he was even across the threshold.

A body lay on the bed, naked save for the rolled silk red panty around one ankle. The smooth white skin of her legs was marred by red streaks along the inner thighs. Thick strings of damp blond hair obscured her face, allowing just a glimpse of eyes that beamed a vacant, milky stare from her skull. It sat atop a crimson pillow almost a foot away. Perched in a splash of blood, balanced upright on its stump. One bloody arm lay along the edge of the mattress.

That was all there was. Her entire torso, along with her right arm, were nowhere to be seen.

Hatcher fell back against the wall as the frantic housekeeper pushed past him, still screaming wildly. He squeezed his eyes shut and lowered his head against the heel of his palm.

Oh, God . . . Vivian . . . what have you done?

CHAPTER 14

HATCHER GOT TO THE CAVE JUST BEFORE SUNSET. HE PARKED
in the same place from the night before, pulled the flashlight out
from beneath the seat, and walked to the same spot Edgar had
led him. He followed the same path. Climbed the berm and
crossed the rocky flat. There were no vehicles he could see. No
one was around.

He stood at the mouth and peered inside. There was something inviting about an opening in the ground like that. It made
you want to go inside, even if it might be dangerous. Maybe
because it might be.

Two days had passed since he'd found her body. This was the
first time he'd emerged from his apartment. Other than eating
and sleeping, both of which he'd engaged in minimally, he divided his time between staring at the window thinking of Vivian
and staring at the ceiling plotting his next move.

It would have been easy to wallow, to swim in an emotional
cocktail of guilt and loss, and he was tempted to do just that.
While he wasn't normally the type to allow his feelings to run
wild, hating—fearing, even—the lack of control that implied,
he couldn't pretend what happened hadn't produced a painful
mix of anxiety and grief, topped off by fury and hate. It was a
potent blend that churned uncomfortably through his chest,
worming its way to his core.

But by the end of the first day, anger and determination were
the last men standing. What had started as a sense of urgency
grew into something he found himself needing to keep in check.
Whatever course of action he was going to take, he accepted
that it would have to be thought through first.

The police might be looking for him. Not just a man described by the housekeeper, but him specifically. He couldn't

rule it out, and couldn't waste the countless hours it might take for them to finally realize he didn't kill her, if they ever realized it. But even if they weren't looking for him yet, they were probably looking for her rental car. He was trying to figure out what to do with it, his gaze was fixed blindly on the ceiling as he pondered whether to use the car for a while and try to keep a low profile, leave it somewhere with the keys in it, or park it at the rental agency, when something clicked.

Barely thirty seconds later he was rummaging through the car's interior, first the glove box, then the center console. He found it in the console, neatly folded into three sections. The rental agreement. She hadn't rented the car. Bartlett had. Using the Mulholland Drive address.

It didn't give him the info he'd hoped for—a fresh address to check out—but it did convince him the car was probably safe to drive. Maybe.

He started to get out of the car, return to his room to do more thinking, but stopped. He reached over to the glove box again and dropped it open. There were only two items inside. One was a map from the rental car company. It was the other that had drawn him back.

A brochure. Glossy, tourist type, like the ones near motel check-in counters. Only this one happened to be for the Los Angeles Natural History Museum, advertising a touring exhibit that ended over a month earlier, the next stop being San Francisco. The name of the exhibit was a single word, presented in large red letters across the front fold, stylized to look both ancient and ominous.

Apocalypse.

Below the word was some sort of painting, a depiction of Christ with people ascending toward clouds and others held back. Near the bottom center was a dark opening in the ground.

So he drove back to the cave and now found himself standing at the mouth, staring.

There were footprints all over. Boot over boot over boot, a fresh trail worn into the ground. Hatcher turned on the flashlight, raised the beam along the trail into the blackness. He paused for a few seconds, then followed it inside.

The entry was a steep incline that leveled out after a few feet. He saw them right away, the conical stretch of light bouncing

over one, illuminating several others. Crates. Stacks of them.
He swept the beam into the distance and back. Two rows, each
taller than he was. Each two crates wide.

The light flashed off a metal cabinet in the distance, throwing its shadow on a wall of rock behind it. There didn't seem to
be any descending tunnel. The cave simply stopped about
twenty yards in.

The crates were nailed shut. Reaching up to the closest stack,
Hatcher tried to move one from the top. It was heavy. He put the
flashlight down and managed to slide it over the edge of the one
beneath it, then tipped it until it fell. The casing splintered on
impact.

Hatcher removed the broken pieces of wood, yanked a few
more planks off. Inside were boxes of ammunition. Nine milli-
meter. Plain brown cardboard, simple descriptive print. Government issue.

He moved down the row to where the crates were slightly
larger. The next one didn't break, but he managed to kick the lid
with his heel hard enough to open it on the fourth shot. U.S.
Army–issue MREs. Meals ready to eat.

At the rear, eight metal containers were wedged between the
last set of crates and the back wall of the cave, four on each side.
About six feet tall, maybe three feet wide. Each had a combination dial and a large wheel latch. Solid steel walls and doors.
Gun safes. A ninth one, slightly larger than the others, stood in
the middle of the aisle, backed up against the cave wall.

Running the flashlight along the rows, he did some quick
math. Hundreds of thousands of rounds of ammunition, at least.
Probably a hundred thousand MREs. Maybe more. Dozens of
weapons in each safe.

What the hell was Bartlett up to?

He walked the aisle between the stacks, probing them with
his flashlight. There only seemed to be the two types of crates.
The rows terminated at the end of the cave.

His foot caught on something as he started walking back. He
shone the light where he'd stepped, crouched down to take a
closer look.

A piece of metal, protruding slightly. He flashed the light
along the cave floor, toward the mouth, saw the slope, and that's
when the realization hit him. The interior didn't just level out. It

had been leveled. The floor of the cave was flat. He aimed the flashlight at the metal, rubbed his thumb along it. Rebar.

Cement. Relatively fresh.

He stood, walked back toward the opening, sweeping the light over the crates. Something flashed between two of them. He backed up, pointed the light into the space. It looked like a piece of glass. He bent down and reached as far as he could, grazing it a few times with his fingertips before he was able to scoot it close enough to pick up. A shard of broken mirror. About six inches long and a few inches across at the widest.

Hatcher swept the area one final time, the light moving unevenly across the crates.

If nothing else, Hatcher told himself, at least he'd come back and torch this place.

AFTER THE CAVE, HATCHER DROVE TO SAN FRANCISCO. HE LO-cated the museum easily enough, but it was three o'clock in the morning when he got there. He found a parking space, reclined the seat as far as it would go, and tried to sleep.

Sleep didn't come easy, but he managed a little over an hour's worth. The sun woke him, and his first thought was San Francisco was damn cold. The museum didn't open until ten, so he walked to a nearby breakfast place, steeling himself against the chill, and forced down some eggs and toast and a generous amount of coffee.

When ten o'clock arrived, he was the first one to buy a ticket. The only one, as far as he could tell. A young Asian gal sold it to him, smiling broadly, as if she were almost embarrassed for him. He didn't smile back.

He followed some velvet cordons to the entry under a large sign for the exhibit. It fed him into a corridor that took a sharp left after a few yards. The first display was at the corner, a glass case containing several tall tablets. The tablets were arranged like pages, with lines and columns, each filled with small symbols that Hatcher took to be glyphs and colored etchings of masked individuals in ornate feathering and primitive attire, all rubbery limbs and monstrous faces. There was a quality to the drawings, a cluttered arrangement of asymmetrical shapes that looked familiar in an abstract, academic sort of way. Like stuff he'd seen pictures of in textbooks. The information plate below identified the tablets as replicas of a Mayan codex.

Above the display, a flat monitor ran a video. Images of ancient texts and artwork cascaded through the screen, each one zoomed in upon slowly before dissolving to make way for the next. A sonorous narrator provided a voice-over:

> *Throughout history, humankind has tried to imagine its ultimate fate, with many devoting a lifetime's worth of mind and spirit to the task of interpreting a divine plan from the evidence available, often making great sacrifices for the gift of revelation, the power of prophecy. The word "Apocalypse" is commonly used to describe scenarios causing or envisioning an end to the world as we know it, or, at least, an end to humanity's sovereign rule over the planet. Deriving from the Greek term for "revelation," most of us now associate the word with the biblical prophecies attributed to John the Apostle, whose visions have provided centuries' worth of fodder for historians and theologians and authors regarding their meaning. The turn of the millennium saw increased attention focused on the year 2012, a time some believe to have been forecast by the Maya of Central America as the End of Days under the Mesoamerican Long Count Calendar.*
>
> *Join us now on a journey through belief and legend as we examine the historical record for predictions of what is to come, visions of what the Christian West thinks of as Armageddon, forecasts as varied as a war between Heaven and Hell where mankind stands in judgment, and a war between nuclear powers ending in annihilation, a journey from mythology and religion and the wrath of gods, to science and technology and the wrath of nature. Come explore the persistent anticipation of the Apocalypse . . .*

Hatcher left the entry display and entered the exhibit hall. He forced himself not to think about Valentine and the freak creation he called the Get of Damnation, or the psycho's ramblings about prophecies and Hell. He had to keep himself focused on the task at hand.

Bartlett had mentioned this exhibit during their first meeting, when he was explaining about the Hell Gate. If there were answers here, clues as to why Bartlett would want his nephew, he was determined to know what they were. Even if Bartlett was telling the truth, the more he knew, the more he might be able to figure out how to track down who did take the boy. And doing that would likely lead him to whomever was responsible for Vivian's death.

And then there was really going to be hell to pay.

He entered a wide room with black walls, a black ceiling, and black carpeting. Dim red lights guttered in the corners to create an ominous mood. There were pictures on the walls, with information plaques beneath or next to them, illuminated by LED spotlights. Tiny rows of bulbs along the ground marked a path around glass display cases in the center of the room, each in its own cone of light from lamps suspended overhead.

The paintings were of gods and devils, weighted heavily toward the non-Christian religions in what was obviously a conscious effort at inclusiveness. The cases housed various artifacts. A small sculpted fetish from the Middle East, a wood carving from the Middle Ages, a scroll of parchment. Several displayed books; small, dark tomes dating back centuries. Hatcher glanced over all the items but began to feel impatient. He realized this was going to take much longer than he'd anticipated. The fact he really had no idea what he was looking for didn't help.

He exited the first room and found himself in a much more open, brighter area. The displays here were larger, grouped together in segments along the wall or in stand-alone cases. He passed sections labeled Greece and Rome, Native America, Egypt, Persia, Islam. The area curved around a display on Millennialism, veered into another area with a large sign that read REVELATION. Hatcher walked past it and leaned through a passageway toward the next area. He could see a plaque that read DOOMSDAY CULTS and another that referenced Beliefs in the New Age. What looked like a mock nuclear test bunker was set up in a far corner. An entire half of the room seem dedicated to Global Warming and Climate Change. Even people who didn't have religion had a religion.

Hatcher stepped back toward the Revelation section. The painting from the brochure was there, as were various other artifacts and drawings and scrolls. He scanned them all, then leaned against a wall. Frustration was starting to well up inside him. This had been a long shot and was now starting to seem ill conceived. He couldn't tell what, if any of it, was relevant. Maybe if he could just remember more of what Bartlett had said. He lowered his head and rubbed his eyes. There had to be something that made the man mention this place, some detail.

He looked up as a museum attendant, a young black woman in a uniform blazer and white shirt, approached. She showed a row of imposing white teeth. Her smile was friendly but practiced.

"Can I help you?"

He doubted it. "I'm doing some research. For a blog. I'm just having a little trouble finding what I was looking for."

"What is it you're researching?"

Good question. He inhaled sharply, pulling himself away from the wall. "A particular prophecy, one found engraved in a tablet."

"Oh, well, did you look through the Revelation display?"

"I'm still going through it."

"Okay. If you can't find what you're looking for, maybe you can talk to Dr. Pitsch."

"Dr. Pitsch?"

"The exhibit coordinator."

"Is he around?"

"She. I don't know. She's in the hall a lot, checking on things."

"What do I need to do to talk to her?"

The young woman pulled a small walkie-talkie from her belt. It squawked as she thumbed the push-to-talk button. She raised the transceiver to her face, turned away as she mumbled a few words in shorthand. Another squawk, and a voice came back with a response Hatcher couldn't understand.

"You're in luck," she said. "My supe says Dr. Pitsch is on her way down."

He spent the next few minutes staring at the painting from the pamphlet, now before him on the wall. It showed a complex, sprawling scene, depictions of a hovering Christ surrounded by saints, with numerous souls climbing and riding clouds around them, ascending, others left behind in anguish and torment. But Hatcher's attention was quickly drawn to the lower center, the part that caught his eye in the brochure. An opening in the ground at the end of a snaking tube of raised earth, like a gopher trail. The entrance to a cave. A pair of eyes no larger than dots of light peered out of the darkness, set in a cadaverous head. Suggestions of other bodies, tumbling into oblivion, haunted the shadows. It was the reason he'd come.

"The damned, swallowed by the mouth of Hell."

Hatcher snapped a look toward the voice. A woman stood a few feet away, a pleasant expression on her face that didn't quite amount to a smile. No need to practice one, he guessed. She was tall, sporting a pair of large round glasses, maybe a few pounds overweight. But not unattractive. What she lacked in beauty and figure she made up for in attitude, which beamed off of her like a heat signature. He could tell this was a smart woman who knew just how smart she was.

"You're the man who needs help with his research."

"Good guess."

"Well, you are the only person here."

Hatcher glanced around. "I suppose I am."

"It's early, on a weekday," she said, hitching her shoulder. She held out a hand. "I'm Gladys Pitsch. So, how can I help you? Do you have questions about *The Last Judgment*?"

"The last judgment?"

"The piece you were just viewing. It's by Michelangelo. This, of course, is merely a print. The original is on the wall of the Sistine Chapel."

"What was it you said about the mouth of Hell?"

She gestured toward the painting with her chin. "The opening in the ground there. It's called a Hell's Mouth. I noticed you were staring at it."

"You could say it looks familiar."

"Depictions of a Hell's Mouth were very common in these types of paintings. They're called Dooms. The walls of almost every church had them, prior to the Reformation. Is this what you want to ask me about? Natalie said you couldn't find what you were looking for."

"I'm trying to find what I can about a tablet, something that talks about opening a gateway to Hell. I was told you have a display here that would shed some light on it"

Her eyes dimmed slightly and her mouth hardened. She stared at him and blinked. "What kind of tablet?"

"I don't know much, except that it was engraved in some weird language spoken by Solomon. And found somewhere in the Middle East. Jerusalem, maybe."

The woman seemed to take a few moments studying Hatcher's face, sizing him up.

"Did I say something wrong?"

"No." She took in a breath and her demeanor appeared to relax. "A gate to Hell, you say."

"Yes. One that would allow demons to pass through. Set them free on the earth. Ring a bell?"

Without responding, she pivoted and started walking back the way Hatcher had come. Hatcher followed.

She led him back to the open exhibit area and zipped around a tall glass enclosure surrounding some sort of primitive stone carving.

"Here we are."

A large poster of a sketch adorned the wall, the view of it blocked from his prior vantage point by a vertical plenum. It was an image Hatcher was already acquainted with, the depiction of a winged creature with a goat's head and a human body. The same picture Bartlett had showed him in the motel room. The poster towered over several smaller plaques surrounding it. Next to it, a column of words running down the wall asked

Hell

on

Earth?

"This is probably what you're looking for."

"I've seen this before," Hatcher said.

"That's not surprising. This is a very popular occult symbol, one that is often used to represent evil or demons, or even Satan. We sort of hid it back here, since it has a tendency to upset children. And some adults. It's called the Baphomet."

"So I've heard. What the hell's a 'Baphomet'?"

"It depends on whom you ask. No one is quite sure where the term comes from. Some say it's a corruption of the name Mohammed, others have proposed various Latin or Arabic roots. One scholar theorized it comes from the Greek word *Sophia*, meaning 'wisdom.' It's been around for centuries as a pagan conceit, though this particular likeness was the creation of a nineteenth-century French occultist named Eliphas Levi. It is said the Templars worshiped an image much like this, that being what led to their persecution."

"The Templars? Weren't they knights? Crusaders?"

"Yes, but much more. A number of people believe they discovered the secret of King Solomon's power, which is why they were so wealthy. And so feared by the ruling class."

"And these people, they think this Baphomet thing was the source of that power?"

"No, just a symbol of it."

She took a step to the side and gestured toward a compact glass cube on a pedestal. Inside the casing, a small item, green and corroded, sat on a black velvet lining. It took Hatcher a second to realize it was a ring.

A poster above the display read THE LEGEND OF THE RING OF AANDALEEB.

"Ancient lore tells of how Solomon was given a ring containing a mystical seal."

"This ring?"

"Good heavens, no. This is merely a representational artifact. It was unearthed in a dig near Jerusalem and dates back roughly to the time of Solomon. So there's a good chance his ring would have looked something like it."

"And what does that have to do with goat head over here?"

"If you were to believe the legends, the ring gave Solomon the ability to control demons."

"Control them?"

"Yes. Summon them, and command them to do his bidding. All their dark magic and knowledge were at his disposal. It was the source of his power and wisdom."

"And the Baphomet?"

"Some say the seal on the ring was a pentagram containing the name of God." She gestured toward the forehead of the creature in the image. "Just like that one, there."

"I don't understand. If Solomon controlled these demons, are you saying the Templars found his ring?"

"These are just stories, Mr. Hatcher. And completely separate ones, at that. They overlap mostly because of the speculation of conspiracy theorists. But to answer your question, no, the Templars wouldn't have needed the same ring. They would have needed to discover the seal."

Hatcher glanced at the shape on the Baphomet's forehead. "That thing? It doesn't look too complicated."

"Neither are passwords or combinations, if you know them. And it's only because of some evidence from the trials of the Templars and pictures like this that didn't even exist at the time that it seems so simple."

Parts of what she said raised even more questions and didn't make much sense to him. But Hatcher got the impression her patience was already starting to fray.

"If they could control demons, why would they worship one?"

The woman shrugged. "That was what they were accused of, but it doesn't mean the accusations were true. Maybe they came to associate the image with the source of their vast wealth and decided to adorn items with it. Maybe they saw demons as a fountain of forbidden knowledge and decided this 'Sophia' was a fitting symbol for their new wisdom . . ."

Hatcher perked up at the sound of her words trailing off.

"What were you going to say?"

"Nothing."

"You wanted to say something else."

"Really, it's nothing."

"Come on, now." He forced a smile, willed himself to have it reach his eyes, even though he was in no smiling mood. "Don't make me turn this into an interrogation. I didn't bring my thumbscrews."

She grinned and looked away. "Apparently, there's a legend about Solomon. How he began to regret his dealings with demons, gave up his ring toward the end of his life. He'd decided any interaction with such creatures corrupted the soul."

"Okay."

"According to this story, Solomon decided no one should have the kind of power he'd wielded. So he fashioned a spell and used the magic he had learned to trap the most powerful demon and all his minions."

"The most powerful? As in, Satan?"

"Satan was forbidden from walking the Earth. This demon

was more akin to his first in command. His name was Asmodeus."

"Let me guess. This spell was inscribed on a tablet."

"According to what I was told, I think so. Yes."

"So, if you didn't have this tablet, you couldn't summon the demon?"

"I suppose. That's why they would fashion an image of it. Try to communicate, bring it close, even if they couldn't raise it. Reportedly, Asmodeus is extremely vain and demands proof of your worship for him in the form of a sacrifice and a graven image of itself. Look, this is more like a rumor. I only heard this story recently. From a museum visitor, no less."

It took a second for the words to reach the right spot of his brain. "Visitor? Who? Was it a woman, by any chance?"

"No. A young man. He was quite interested in these objects. Very knowledgeable."

"Short guy? Hair teased up like some salon model?"

"Not too short, no. Almost as tall as you. I didn't notice anything about his hair. Why are you asking about him? Do you think it's someone you know?"

Hatcher dipped his head ambiguously and waved the question off. He took a closer look at the drawing. Atop the head a torch burned between its two horns. One arm was pointed up, the other down. Each forearm had writing on it.

"What are these words?"

"*Solve* and *Coagula*."

"Is that Latin?"

She nodded. "*Solve* means to dissolve. *Coagula* means to congeal. It's from an expression used by alchemists, referring to the idea of breaking something down into its base elements, then reconstituting it in a purer form. Here it probably refers to purification through knowledge."

"Knowledge of what?"

The woman shrugged. "Your guess is as good as mine."

Something she had mentioned earlier was scratching at his brain. *Sophia.* His eyes abruptly fixed on the thing's bare torso. He leaned in closer. "Are those . . . breasts?"

"Yes."

"This Baphomet is a woman?"

"Not exactly. More like an androgynous entity. A hermaph-rodite. Really, it has no sex, no gender. It's not human."

Hatcher's eyes took in every detail of the sketch, moving from top to bottom and back up. "How would someone go about stopping it?"

"Excuse me?"

"This Baphomet. How would you kill it?"

"Mr. Hatcher, this is a just a drawing. There is no such crea-ture. It was only intended as a symbol."

"A symbol for what?"

Her eyes seemed to swoon at the question. "Forbidden knowledge, the expansion of the mind. Defiance of orthodoxy. Moral liberation. Take your pick."

"So you're saying it's not an actual demon."

"Some would say yes, but I would tend to think not. More like, the ideal demon."

"And what about the ring? What happened to the real one?"

"No one knows. No one knows if there even was a real one. These are just legends, Mr. Hatcher. They're not even what one could call biblical."

Hatcher stared at the depiction of the demon. The intense gaze of the goat's head, eyes that were human, but not exclu-sively so, came close to giving him the creeps. There was some-thing authentic about its features. Too authentic. Drawings of the Devil that he could recall tended to look like cartoons. Not this one.

"Did that guy tell you anything else about this?"

"Nothing I care to repeat."

"I'd really appreciate it."

She made a face. "It's . . . gross."

"I can handle it."

The woman sighed, and Hatcher could tell whatever remained of her willingness to indulge him left her with the breath. "He said the Templars never found the tablet but were successful in communing with Asmodeus because of their show of respect."

"Respect."

"Yes. He claimed the image they worshiped wasn't merely an image at all, but an actual figure. An exact replica. One con-structed of human and animal body parts. Specifically, the left arm of a male murderer, the genitalia of a rapist, and the female

body and right arm of a whore. He said the replica was this being depicted in the drawing."

Hatcher said nothing. The brochure wasn't a coincidence,
that much he knew. Someone was trying to tell him something.
Images of Vivian's remains slammed into his thoughts, darkening them.

The woman glanced down at her watch. "I hope you found
this helpful. If you don't have any more questions, I—"

"Just one."

The woman looked on as Hatcher moved closer to the picture. The eyes of the Baphomet peered down at him. He gritted
his teeth.

"Would this thing live in a cave?"

DURING THE DRIVE BACK TO L.A., HATCHER TRIED TO SIFT
through what he knew. It didn't take long, because he didn't
know much.

Bartlett had used him to find the boy. The man could deny it
all he wanted, but Hatcher was sure of it. Almost sure.

But why? What was the boy to him? How much of that story
he'd told when they'd met was real? And what was Vivian's in-
volvement? Since they already had the boy, why kill her? Were
they using her body to create some sick Franken-statue? Why
her? And what did Bartlett mean when he intimated there were
things she wasn't telling him?

He thought about his meeting with Soliya. How did she
know so much about what was going on? How did the Carnates
know where and when to fly a banner?

Figuring out what he wanted to know was easy. Finding answers was proving decidedly more difficult. So was determining
where to go next. He tried dialing the number from the ad the
Carnates had placed. No answer. Not even a voice mail. HUMINT
required sources, and he had none. He was going to have to find
someone in the know and extract whatever information they had.

That meant starting somewhere. He could think of only one
place.

It was early afternoon when he arrived in South Central. He
parked in front of the house, walked straight to the front door.
He didn't see any advantage in not being direct.

He knocked and waited. Nothing. He knocked again.

"Ain't no one home."

Hatcher glanced in the direction of the voice. It was an older black man, with powdery white hair. He recognized the man as the neighbor who'd been watering his lawn the last time he'd been there. He was standing at the edge of his lawn one property over, wearing a wifebeater tank top and blue pants.

"Any idea when they'll be back."

"If you's looking for who I think you is, no time soon."

Hatcher said nothing.

"Woman name of Georgia owns that house. She works all day, takes an extra shift early evening. She ain't the one you want."

Hatcher stepped off the porch. "Who is the one I want?"

"Her kid brother. Name's Floyd. Goes by T-Bone."

"He live here?"

"No. She kicked him out long time back. Doesn't stop him from using the place when she's not around, though. That boy some bad news."

"Do you know where I can find him?"

The man scratched his head, then ran a long middle finger down the side of his nose, thinking. "You know, I called the police"—he said the word with the accent on the *po*—"the other day. Told them I saw a white man being assaulted."

"Thanks."

"You don't need to be thanking. I'm just telling you. No one showed. Didn't send no car, didn't send nothing. Then a couple days later, badge comes by and wants to know what I saw. One cop, by himself. White as you. Asking me what I saw. I told him I didn't see nothing, just heard a commotion."

"I won't let him know you told me anything, if that's what you're saying."

The man shook his head and looked at the ground, a rueful smile creasing his cheeks. "That ain't what I'm sayin'. But you's white, so you don't get it."

"You know where I can find Floyd?"

"Try Chesterfield Square Park. Boys call 'mselves the Chesterfield CPs."

"Thanks."

"Man's gotta be crazy, going down there. Certain kinda crazy."

"I'll watch my step."

"No, you won't. I can see it on you. Coming here, walking up to the door like that. Revenge crazy, that's what you are. Them's the craziest."

Hatcher said nothing.

"Just remember what I said. Po-lice didn't show. Think about it."

"Yeah, well, I was thinking I'd just as soon leave them out of it, anyway," Hatcher said.

The man walked back toward the front of his house. He picked up a hose with a spray nozzle, bent over to turn on the spigot, shaking his head.

Hatcher was rounding the car when he thought he heard the man say to himself, "Crazy people don't ever listen."

HATCHER SAT IN THE PARK FOR MORE THAN AN HOUR, WATCH-ing from the car, before he spotted the one the neighbor said called himself T-Bone. Recognized him by his do-rag. That, and the fact he was a good six inches shorter than everyone else. He was rolling through with a crew, sauntering down the sidewalk, strutting and laughing. Four of them, plus him. Yellow Lakers jersey with the number 8, baggy jeans that sagged way below a pair of purple boxers.

They headed into the park, draped themselves over a pair of benches.

They were probably armed, so Hatcher waited. His opening came about fifteen minutes later. A car pulled up along the curb and stopped. One of the crew flipped open a phone, started talking. T-Bone started walking toward the car just as a little kid about seven years old got out from the rear passenger side. He passed T-Bone without looking at him and headed toward the bench. The rest of T-Bone's crew moved away in a gaggle, making a show of joking around. The kid bent down next to the bench and retrieved a lunch pail from beneath it.

The car pulled away just as T-Bone drew close. T-Bone knelt down and tied his shoe at the curb, then casually reached over and picked up an envelope as he stood. He crossed the street and kept walking.

He glanced in the envelope as he walked, then scratched the back of his head with a pronounced motion. The rest of the crew moved off the path and the little kid resumed walking. The car pulled up to the curb on the opposite side of the park just a few seconds before the kid got there. The boy hopped inside and the car sped off.

This was as good a time as any. Hatcher started the car and headed to where T-Bone had crossed, turned down the street. The area was the product of unplanned growth probably half a century ago, maybe more. It was mostly residential, small weather-worn cottages with graying paint and sagging wood. A small apartment building mixed in on one side along with a pair of plain commercial structures so fortified it was hard to tell what they were used for. A few people were sitting on porches in front of a few houses, a handful more were in a gaggle near the next corner. Hatcher spotted T-Bone immediately. He was the only one who looked like he had somewhere to go.

There were two options. He could pull past, turn at the next street. He guessed T-Bone was making a circuit, heading back to the park, or near it, to hook up with his crew again. But pulling past him risked being noticed, since T-Bone already knew the car.

So that left the other option. Hatcher parked along the side of the road next to a no-parking sign. T-Bone was about thirty yards ahead, talking on a cell. Hatcher got out and popped the hatch. He lifted the floorboard and pulled out the tire iron. Then he headed up the street behind T-Bone at twice the kid's pace.

When he got within a few feet, he lowered his shoulder and closed the gap in a sprint, slamming into the boy. T-Bone's phone rattled and cracked against the sidewalk and he went stumbling forward. Hatcher took a fistful of jersey and jerked him onto his toes before shoving him into an alley drive behind the apartment building, getting him off the main road. Away from porch-bound spectators and passing cars.

T-Bone regained his balance and tried to yank himself away, stretching his shirt. He clenched his fists and batted at Hatcher's arm, bouncing on the balls of his feet like an amateur pug.

"What the fuck?"

Hatcher let go of the jersey and with a tight, quick swing smashed the curved end of the tire iron into T-Bone's cheekbone. The boy dropped to the ground on his side, holding his face. He let out a loud, angry-sounding groan.

Another groan, and he tipped farther over. Then he spun back, yanking a pistol from the sags of his jeans. Hatcher was ready for it. He brought the tire iron down hard on the back of the kid's wrist, latched his other hand onto the barrel of the pistol. One firm twist, and it tore loose.

A Glock 17. While T-Bone babied his wrist, howling, Hatcher tucked the tire iron under his arm, dropped the magazine from the gun and ejected the chamber round. The cartridge plinked off the asphalt and rolled in a semicircle until it bumped against the kid's foot. Grabbing the pistol from the back, Hatcher gave it a tight squeeze and pressed the take-down lever above the trigger. He pulled off the slide and tossed it onto the roof of the apartment building. He dropped the remaining half of the pistol onto T-Bone's lap.

"I need to find the women who hired you," Hatcher said.

No response, barely a sneer. Hatcher rapped him on the cheek with the back of his knuckles, same spot the first blow from the tire iron had caught.

T-Bone barked, dropped even lower to the ground. He rocked, trembling in pain, his hand covering up everything just below his eye. "Crakka, you fucking crazy! Ain't no damn women hired me. Goddamn! Fuck you do to my face, motherfucker?"

"Tell me where to find them."

"You hard a' hearing, Jack? I said I don't know."

A kick to the ribs, once, twice, then Hatcher snagged the boy's wrist. The tender one. The kid winced and tried to jerk away. Hatcher lowered himself to one knee and leaned his weight into it, stretching the arm out against the ground, until the hand was extended. Then he hammered it twice with the tire iron. Bones shattered each time with the crack of a subdued gunshot.

The sound T-Bone let out was halfway between a scream and a snarl. "Shit, nigga! What the fuck! You broke my fuckin' hand!"

"You could say I'm not in the mood for bullshit. Next wrong

answer, I break your other one and you can jack off against plaster for the next couple of months. If you still haven't sung me the right tune, I start using the sharp end of this to remove your eyes. Leave me pissed off at that point, I'll finish by making you useless to a woman. Which, now that I think about it, wouldn't be much of a change."

"I told you! Ain't no bitches hired me!"

"Then who told you to grab me and take me to that cave?"

A long pause, panting. "Fernandez."

"Who the hell is Fernandez?"

"A fucking cop, that's who."

"A cop hired you? Why?"

He rolled his eyes up at Hatcher, sneering. "Fuck should I know?"

"You better start telling me what you *do* know. This is heavy, and I'm feeling the urge to swing it again."

"'Dez just said he had a job for us. Wanted us to be at my sister's place, jack up some dude be coming there. Said take him to Bronson Caves, drop his car there. That's all the shit I know."

"Did he tell you why?"

"No."

Hatcher slid the tire iron higher in his hand, cocked it back.

"Whoa, damn! Hold it! He said there'd be a woman there, to leave her alone. Said if we even looked at her, he'd dump us in La Brea."

"Why you? You owe him?"

"We do shit for him. Run shit."

"Run shit? Like drugs?"

"No, Gomer. Like Amway. Course like drugs. He gets two bits off the top."

"Two bits?"

"What are you, ignorant? A quarter." T-Bone cupped his jaw, worked it side to side. "Shit, man, it hurts to even move my mouth. I think you broke my fucking cheek, too."

"This guy Fernandez, what does he look like?"

"Fuckin gray boy, man. 'Bout as Mexican as Ward Cleaver. Shit, you all look alike to me."

Hatcher held out the tire iron for T-Bone to see, rotated it as if there were writing on it he wanted him to read, then cracked it off his forehead with a flick of his wrist.

"God*damn*, man! Knock that shit off!"

"I'm not in the mood for banter. What does he look like?"

"Short hair, like a marine or somethin.' Big ol' arms and chest. He looks like a big dick, which he is."

"Where do I find him?"

Grimacing, T-Bone pushed himself into a sitting position. He touched the side of his face gingerly. "It's Thursday. Tuesday 'n' Thursday afternoons he teaches some karate bullshit or something. Told us not to bother him when he's there. Or else."

"Where."

"Shit if I know. Go hassle some slant 'n' ax them."

Hatcher grabbed him by the head, pointed the wedge end of the tire iron toward his eye.

"Fuck, man! Some joint over on Santa Monica Boulevard! Aint got no fuckin' address! Never even seen the shit!"

Hatcher stood. "If you're lying, I won't leave you breathing next time."

"I ain't lying." The kid touched his face again and winced. "Go, see for y'self, sadistic motherfucker. You two deserve each other."

Hatcher turned to leave, took several steps, then walked back as if remembering something. He kicked T-Bone hard across the face, knocking him off his ass onto his back, causing his skull to bounce off the concrete.

"That's for using the N-word, you little shit."

CHAPTER 15

❖

THERE WERE AT LEAST SIX MARTIAL ARTS SCHOOLS ON SANTA
Monica. Two were Brazilian jiujitsu, one was Kempo, one was
kung fu, and two had generic signs that said KARATE.

But only one had a patrol car in front of it. Three patrol cars,
in fact.

The place with the cruisers out front was a low-slung stand-
alone with a single row of parking The front was mostly window, broad sections of it painted over with the yin-yang symbol
and the Korean flag. But there was enough clear glass to see
inside from certain angles, and from what Hatcher could tell,
there were three guys in there. Three guys, three squad cars.
That meant three cops.

Hatcher checked the time on his cell phone. Just after four.
Three cop cars, no one else. Odds were Fernandez either ran the
place or taught classes. Probably showed up for a workout with
some buddies before the first evening session. That would start
at five or five thirty, at the earliest. Just enough time.

Traffic was a bit heavy, but it only took him five minutes to
double back to an electronics store he had passed. Ten minutes
to buy a mini-DV camera. He found one on sale for a little over
sixty bucks. Pink, on closeout, about the size of an iPod. Half
the time was spent making sure it had the features he needed,
the other half hoping he had enough money in his account for
his debit card not to get rejected, since he'd been using it lately
without keeping track. He took another five minutes to stop at a
convenience store on the way back and pick up a large pack of
Big League Chew, scooping a bunch into his mouth that made
his cheek bulge.

Then he parked on the far end of the parking lot away from

the cruisers and out of easy sight, powered up the camera and checked the battery, and walked into the dojo.

The three guys were to the left, in a large workout space, separated from the no-frills reception area by a low wooden divider. Looked like two of them were doing some light sparring, practicing kicks and blocks. The other one was doing forms a safe distance away, kicking and punching in a prearranged series of moves. Each was wearing a white *gi* held closed by a black belt. Fernandez's *gi* top was so wide open he was practically bare-chested, something Hatcher didn't think was by accident since his pecs were shaved smoother than a lingerie model's ass. The other two were a bit taller than Fernandez, but neither looked nearly as built. The one sparring with him was lean and angular. The one doing kata was thick and a bit puffy, carrying a gut that looked like he'd swallowed a medicine ball.

Hatcher blew a bubble, let it pop loudly.

Fernandez looked over. He gave him the just-a-minute gesture with his index finger as if Hatcher were a prospective student, not recognizing him. It wasn't mutual. Hatcher had already expected as much based on T-Bone's description, and now he had confirmation. This was the same cop from the other day, the one who had knocked him around for no apparent reason.

But now it was obvious there had been a reason.

Fernandez said something to his sparring partner, a bit of instruction, pointing to his leg and pantomiming a block, then gave the man a pat on his shoulder and headed Hatcher's way. He slowed down after a few steps, finally realizing who it was.

"You," he said.

"Me," Hatcher said. He spit the wad of gum into his hand and smacked it down on the wooden railing. Then he took out the mini-camcorder, started it recording, and wedged it standing up into the sticky mound.

Hatcher made eye contact with Fernandez, then let his gaze drift around the practice area. Two duffel bags were stashed against the wall on the far side, near the corner. As far from the entrance as possible, but not out of sight. He programmed the location into his mental hard drive. His first rule of engagement: keep the party from drifting in that direction.

There were plenty of reasons he was reluctant to confront Fernandez at a martial arts studio. He knew there would likely be other people around, people probably inclined to fight, people like cops, and even if there were no cops or anyone else anxious to get involved, witnesses wouldn't make the going any easier. The larger the number of people, the harder it was to control the situation.

But on the drive over, he warmed up to the idea. There were some definite advantages. The most significant one being, this would be one of the few places a cop wouldn't be armed.

The guns, however, wouldn't be kept far away, or out of sight. Hence the duffels.

There were other cops, as it turned out, but three unarmed cops instead of one armed one was a trade he was happy to make.

He passed through an opening in the divider and walked out onto the practice floor.

"Forgive me if I don't take off my shoes." Hatcher raised his arms and turned full circle, showing his waist band. "No gun, no knife."

Fernandez shot a furtive glance over his shoulder at the others, then pointed a finger. "You better just turn around and get the fuck out of here."

The guy who'd been Fernandez's sparring partner moved closer. "There a problem, Joey?"

Fernandez took in a breath, then smirked. Couldn't sell it, though. Too much tension behind the lips.

"Looks like we have ourselves an unhappy citizen," he said. "I witnessed him assaulting a pedestrian a couple days ago. Vic fled, so I let him off with a warning. You'd think he'd be grateful."

The third guy stopped his kata, walked over slowly.

Normally, three on one presented bad odds no matter how skilled you were. Real fights weren't choreographed sequences like those in movies or TV shows. People wanting to pummel you didn't politely wait their turn to attack. When there were three, usually the first one engaged for only a few seconds before the other two dove in. All it took was someone to grab the legs or waist from behind and drag you to the ground. And cops in particular were trained in how to subdue people once they got them to the ground. Normally, that wouldn't make for good odds.

But three was practically a magic number today. Three was just enough numerical superiority that none of them would feel compelled to make a dash for his weapon, just enough to make them feel comfortable moving in the opposite direction from the duffels. But not enough to make the disparity overwhelming.

As long as he cut the total to two before they could take advantage of their number, that was.

The kata guy to the rear bothered him. Not because he looked particularly formidable but because he was hanging back. Closer to the duffel bags. Not much, but enough.

Hatcher pointed a finger at him. "Hey."

The cop's eyes narrowed as he shifted his weight.

"You look like you'd have a coronary if you so much as listened to someone talk about a fight." Hatcher jerked a thumb over his shoulder. "Just waddle your fat ass out of here."

The man stomped forward several steps, only to bump up against Fernandez's outstretched arm.

"You're here to fight?" Fernandez said. "Is that what you're saying?"

"Call it a challenge. This is a dojo. I'm saying you're a punk." Hatcher spread his hands vaguely, then dropped them. "So, what now?"

Fernandez said nothing. Hatcher looked to the sparring partner. The skinny one. He was the closest.

"I have to assume you're all as crooked as your buddy, so I'm guessing you'd prefer not to have me showing the video I have of him taking his money from the Chesterfield CPs." Hatcher's eyes shot back to Fernandez. "What are they moving for you? Rock? Meth? Smack?"

Fernandez started to say something, then glanced over at the camera. It sat erect on the wooden rail, protruding from a wad of pink.

Hatcher said, "Here's how it is. You win, you get to keep the video, destroy or erase it or whatever, throw me in county lockup if you want. Inflict as much damage to me as it takes to get you off, brag to all your precinct buddies. I win, you tell me what I want to know. And I keep the video as insurance."

The sparring partner shot an exasperated look at Fernandez. "Why are you taking this shit off him? Let's just run him in. You asked him to leave, and he refused. We got trespassing, disorderly conduct, felony menacing."

Hatcher looked at the man, thinking, *well, that's a shame.* That was the reaction of an honest cop. Or not a crooked one, at least. Maybe even the two of them, him and bowling-ball gut, were straight. Didn't matter, though. They could be saints with badges and it wouldn't make a difference. He needed Fernandez to talk.

He felt a twinge of anticipatory guilt, a sense that maybe he should've given this more thought. But then he thought of Vivian, and everything soft inside him hardened.

Extracting what he wanted to know meant getting Fernandez under control, and that meant incapacitating all three of them. The first step toward that end was leveling the odds. There was only one way to do that.

Though the average person tended not to realize it, a fight against multiple opponents was actually several individual fights happening simultaneously. The key to prevailing was to remember you weren't in one fight against three guys; you were in three fights and against three separate guys that just happened to be occurring at the same time. Prevailing in two out of three of them wasn't good enough. The only realistic way to manage the street math was to reduce the number of fights by winning them as quickly as possible.

Hatcher raised his fists, squared his body to the sparring partner. He made sure to raise his elbows high, exposing his midsection. He locked onto the man's eyes and, with an exaggerated motion, lunged forward.

Most fights were effectively over within thirty seconds, and often the outcome depended on who had more information about the other person or who made the right guess. Boxers could be expected to fight in a certain way, requiring a different strategy than what might work against a grappler. Knowing what to expect from an opponent was a tremendous advantage. If your information was accurate.

The Korean flag on the window meant the art practiced there was Tae Kwon Do, not actual karate. Tae Kwon Do people liked to kick above the waist. During the little bit of sparring Hatcher had seen, this guy seemed no exception.

The man cross-stepped toward Hatcher, blading his body,

and loaded a side kick. Hatcher cut on a diagonal the moment the guy committed, swung his rearmost arm under the extended leg as it fired past him, and grabbed the collar of the man's *gi*. Using the momentum of the kick, he swung his arm up and launched the man off the ground. The man's leg acted like a lever and Hatcher held him aloft, turned him over, and slammed his upper body face-first against the wooden floor. The sound of breaking teeth cracked the air like a whip. Hatcher sprang up and stomped his heel against the back of the man's head, once, twice, before immediately circling toward the middle of the dojo, his back to the front window. Facing the other two.

The cop he left behind sprawled on the floor didn't move.

One down.

Surprise had clearly been in his favor, but that was gone now. The guy with the large girth stared at his fallen brother officer for a moment, then struck a stance, one foot forward, fists up. He glanced uncertainly over to Fernandez, looking for direction. He was unlikely to find any. Fernandez's face was flush with rage, but his eyes moved erratically. Hatcher took note. The man was already thinking about the cover-up, putting together some plausible scenario to pitch. Good.

Two fights on his hands now, and his job was to reduce it to one. Hatcher circled farther to his left, placing belly cop in between himself and Fernandez. The movement created a small window of opportunity, a brief moment where the angle would place them in a line and block Fernandez off. But it was only a moment. Hatcher couldn't afford to keep circling. Giving one of them a quicker route to the duffel bags could ensure things would end badly.

Belly cop turned in place, keeping a squared-off stance. This time, Hatcher kept his hands a bit lower, palms out, and bounced on his feet. He made a sudden feint forward, and the guy bit. He charged Hatcher, barking a *kiai* shout, and threw a straight punch. Not a bad punch, all things considered, but exactly the move Hatcher had expected. Hatcher dropped low, letting the man's fist pop into vacant air just above his head. Pivoting on the way down, he thrust his forward leg out, smashing the hard edge of his shoe against the man's shin, just below the knee. The guy's leg buckled and he took a wobbly step back. Hatcher launched himself forward and up, rotating at the hip, drilling an uppercut against the man's chin. The blow snapped the cop's head back and sent him sprawling into Fernandez, who caught him under the arms.

Hatcher followed the man's fall, moving forward with it, and planted a hard pendulum kick right between the man's legs before Fernandez was able untangle himself.

Fernandez let go. The man curled into a lump, his face contorted, holding his crotch. Blood ran out of his mouth onto the floor, connected to his lips by strings of saliva.

Two down.

Fernandez barely gave the guy a glance. He was breathing in angry pants, lips pulled back, baring clenched teeth.

"You're never gonna be heard from again. You hear me?" he said. "When I'm done with you, you'll be disappeared. Vanished. Poof."

"When you're done with me? We haven't even had dinner and a movie yet."

"Fucking idiot. You should have just left it alone. But no. Had to be a hero. Well, you're not shit. And you're about to become less than shit."

Something dawned on Hatcher at the words, something that hadn't clicked until that point. But before he could let the thought play out, Fernandez made his move.

A straight, plain bull rush. Nothing fancy, and not exactly Tae Kwon Do. But that didn't make it any less effective. Hatcher knew he should have been ready for it, should have realized the anger would have made the guy abandon disciplined kicking and punching, but knowing what he should have done didn't change anything. Fernandez moved fast for a beefy guy, quicker than Hatcher expected. All that muscle translated into velocity, momentum.

Enough velocity that Hatcher was caught flat-footed when the muscular cop lowered his shoulder and exploded into his midsection. Fernandez wrapped his arms around Hatcher's upper legs and lifted his feet off the floor, drove him down, and landed on top of him.

In the real world, almost all fights end up on the ground. End up there, and end there. Quick knockouts were the only real exception. If a fight lasted more than five seconds, it was going horizontal nine times out of ten. At some point, one guy will take the other down, whether by tackling or dragging or throwing him, and that's where it will finish. The guy on top usually wins.

Unless the guy on the bottom knows what he's doing.

The impact was jarring, but Hatcher had exhaled hard on the way down. One of the quickest ways to lose a fight, and maybe your life in the process, was to get the wind knocked out of you. If your lungs are out of sync with your diaphragm, you can't fill them with air, and if you can't fill them with air, you can't get oxygen to your muscles. No oxygen, and your body shuts down, leaving you at the mercy of your opponent. But you can't get the wind knocked out of you if you don't have any in you.

Hatcher's first move after hitting the floor was to wrap Fernandez up. He clamped his legs around the guy's waist, threw his arms around his neck, and squeezed. A fighter on top could rain blows down with weight and force, battering your skull against the ground, if he wasn't tied up in a clench. The key was to keep it tight but not expend much energy. And to breathe. Always breathe.

Fernandez pulled and clawed for a few seconds, then started going to the body, a volley of hooks to the rib cage. They didn't tickle, but without him being able to put his body into them, they were just arm punches. Hatcher could take them. For a while.

In a sign of frustration, Fernandez went wild, launched a rapid-fire barrage of shots to his kidneys. Hatcher winced and sucked in some sharp breaths, but knew he needed it to happen. The man was shooting his wad, making an amateur mistake. No doubt holding his breath, running on adrenaline. It would only be seconds before the adrenaline wore off and the guy bonked.

Only Fernandez didn't bonk. He kept punching, alternating between unleashing a torrent of blows, resting the arm for a few seconds, then following up with another flurry of strikes that penetrated Hatcher's oblique abs, battering his floating rib. It occurred to Hatcher the guy wasn't holding his breath after all. He was just breathing softly. Calmly. Apparently the cop's cardiovascular system was in a lot better condition than Hatcher had presumed.

The rib shots were taking their toll. Hatcher was forced to tense his body rigid, use his musculature to fend them off. But ab muscles were poor shields. The design of the human body delegated that responsibility to the arms. Problem was, Hatcher's arms were busy holding on, preventing an even worse beating to his face. One thing was certain, something was going to have to give. Not only were his sides starting to ache, but each thump was a knife to the kidney. His guts were starting to churn to where he could feel them in his throat. Another minute or so, his muscles would begin to slacken from the exertion. Nausea would probably set in. Fernandez would be able to wrest free from Hatcher's arms and start to land strikes to his head, maybe slip past his guard and into a mount, where he could pound Hatcher's skull into the floor.

Since he knew he couldn't let that happen, Hatcher decided he would have to get mean.

He tightened up as another five slugs banged off his ribs, then he mustered his reserves and groped a hand along Fernandez's scalp, sliding it across the sweaty buzz of the cop's flat top, until his fingers brushed against the man's ear cartilage.

The ear was slick. Hatcher dropped his hand onto Fernandez's shoulder, wiped it against the cloth of the man's *gi*. The *gi* was damp, having absorbed a good deal of sweat, so he quickly dragged his fingers around until he found a spot that seemed relatively dry. It would have to do. Before Fernandez could load up for another round of hammering, Hatcher pinched the leafy part of the man's ear between his thumb and the knuckle of his index finger as tightly as he could, and gave it a hard, quick yank. A very hard yank.

The exact amount of force necessary varied from one person to another, but it normally took around ten to fifteen pounds of force to rip off a human ear. That took more strength than it sounded like, akin to picking up a dumbbell by a shoelace held between fingertips, but it was definitely an amount that could be generated by a grown man's arm and two fingers. And a lot less force than Hatcher used.

The ear separated from Fernandez's skull with an audible rip.

Fernandez jerked his head in the opposite direction, started to punch again, then stopped.

"What the fuck?"

Hatcher could feel the blood running down onto his own

body, wetting his shirt. He held on, keeping the man close, waiting for the eruption.

Fernandez screamed. Half pain, half anger. He raised a hand to the side of his head, felt around, screamed again.

His ear was hanging by a flap of skin near the lobe.

"Jesus Christ! What the fuck did you do to me?"

A wave of bucking and struggling, flailing punches and attempts to claw at Hatcher's face. Hatcher felt him try to bite, locked the side of the man's head tightly against his chest.

Fernandez was gunning it on a pure rush of adrenaline now, wasting precious energy. And, more important, he wasn't focusing on the ribs anymore. His punches were wild, half of them bouncing off Hatcher's shoulder. All Hatcher had to do was hang on until the surge wore off. Problem was, he was about out of gas himself. The body shots had bled the energy out of him.

Just as his arms started trembling from the strain, he felt Fernandez's body sag. His fists continued to knock into Hatcher, some even catching the ribs, but now they were coming without any snap. Hatcher relaxed a bit, let his muscles rest. As soon as he felt his arms and shoulders had recovered enough, he slipped one arm across the front of Fernandez's throat and took a hold of his *gi* collar, keeping the other arm behind the the back of the man's head. Fernandez raised his face, looked Hatcher in the eyes as he tried to hook his hands over Hatcher's arm and push it away. Hatcher levered his wrist, twisting the curve of it into the man's neck, pressing his forearms together against the cop's throat with every bit of strength he could muster.

Fernandez started flailing again. A last-ditch effort. He scraped at Hatcher's hand, grabbed at his hair, even made a desperate play for his eyes, but couldn't apply enough energy to do any harm. The whole time, the curve of Hatcher's fist pressed into his artery, shutting it down. Less than thirty seconds later, the man was out.

Hatcher rolled Fernandez onto his back and lay there, eyes shut, trying to catch his breath. After a few seconds, he sensed movement nearby, glanced over to see cop number two, the one with the gut, manage to get on one leg and start hobbling toward the duffel bag. Hatcher popped to his feet and broke into a sprint. He slammed into the guy the instant before he reached the bag, knocked him against the wall just past it. The man bounced off and crumbled to the floor, grimacing and holding the shin Hatcher had caught with a kick earlier.

Hatcher put his foot on the leg, eliciting a howl, and picked up the bag.

The duffel contained two pistols, a couple of clips, two badge holders, a set of cuffs, and a Taser. Hatcher eyed the Taser, glanced over toward Fernandez, then scooped out the cuffs and pocketed them. Each badge case case had a picture ID. One was for Joseph Fernandez, the other for Lou Humphrey. He glanced down at the face moaning with each breath on the floor a few feet away. Definitely Humphrey.

Fernandez and the other cop were out cold. Hatcher turned Humphrey onto his stomach and cuffed him.

"Sorry, pal."

It took Humphrey several seconds to respond.

"Not as sorry as you're going to be, asshole." He paused, eyes, nose, and mouth wrinkling in pain. "You fucked with the wrong guys."

"Great line. I'd love to sit here and let you bask in the glow of it, but I'm afraid I have less time than I do questions."

"Questions? Are you out of your mind? Do you realize how long you're going to go away for? We're cops!"

"*Dirty* cops. At least one of you." Hatcher glanced over his shoulder in the direction of the other two. "Tell me what you know about your buddy Fernandez."

"I ain't telling you shit."

"Wow. Never heard that one before." Hatcher put a hand on Humphrey's shoulder to hold him still and lowered himself onto the man's back in a sitting position.

Humphrey grunted. He squirmed and kicked and bucked, but couldn't get Hatcher off him. When he spoke, it was in clipped pants. *"What the fuck are you doing?"*

"I thought cops were supposed to be trained observers. What does it feel like I'm doing? I'm sitting on you."

More grunts. "Wh-why?"

"Because, a couple of hundred pounds bearing down on you, pressing your sternum against the hard surface of this floor, is making it impossible for you to breathe. For the moment, you can force air into your lungs using a combination of the muscles in your chest and abdomen. But the space available for that air is compressed, and it's already putting a strain on your diaphragm. In about fifteen seconds, your ability to support my weight will start to shift from your muscles to your bones. The bones of your chest cavity, your rib cage, they're flexible. They'll start to sag. Each breath is taking in less air than the one before it. Feel it? You're suffocating. And the pace is speeding up."

"You're out . . . of your fucking—*huff*—mind. You can't . . . kill . . . a cop."

If you only knew how wrong you were. "You're wasting the little air you have left. Why did Fernandez have a bunch of bangers abduct me?"

Humphrey strained to get out the words. "What the hell . . . no idea . . . what . . . talking about."

"You know, I'm willing to bet I can stay like this longer than you can."

Hatcher felt the man take in a long, strained breath, then immediately let it out in a frantic blurt. "I don't know what the hell you're talking about!"

"All right then, give me something on him."

"Huh?"

"Fernandez. Give me something. Something I can use. Dirt."

"I'm not going to—"

"Fine. Little tip—in a minute or so, if you don't see halos and harps and clouds, you went to the other place."

"Ungh! Fuck! Okay! Gimme some air!"

Hatcher shifted some of his weight to his feet and arm, heard Humphrey suck in a couple of breaths. He sat back down before the man could get a third.

"Talk."

"I know he has those spooks doing stuff for him," Humphrey said, forcing out the words. "But Norwood and me don't have anything to do with that. Some guys supplement." *Huff, huff.* "Others look the other way."

"Noble. But tell me something I don't know. Something he'd never think I could know. Preferably something he doesn't know you know."

"What? How am I—"

Hatcher lifted his feet, pressed every ounce of weight he could down.

"Okay! Okay! But I . . . can't . . . breathe!"

"You're going to have to earn your next shot of air."

"Can't."

Rolling his eyes, Hatcher slid off Humphrey's back and bar-reled him onto his side. He clamped a hand on the man's throat and gave it a gentle squeeze.

"Now you can breathe."

Humphrey's face was a shade of crimson. He coughed trying to suck in air.

Hatcher tightened his grip for a moment, then let go. Humphrey coughed some more. He shook his head when Hatcher made like he was about to grab his throat again.

"I busted a tranny a couple of years ago. Solicitation, lewd and lascivious. Looked like a gal, but I realized it was a guy when I saw his DL. Offered me a blow job to let him off. I laughed, asked him what he took me for. He told me another cop had let him go a few weeks earlier for one."

"Fernandez."

Humphrey's nodded.

"Confirmation?"

"It was him. I brought it up to him, told him I'd arrested a whore who turned out to be a dude and gave him the location. Showed him a phone pic. Wanted to see his reaction. He turned whiter than a sheet. Didn't say a word."

Hatcher chewed on the info for a moment. "Thanks. Now, tell me where there's a closet."

"Why?"

"Because you're not going to want to watch what happens next."

THERE WASN'T A CLOSET, BUT THERE WAS A BATHROOM AND A dressing room in the back of the dojo. Hatcher dumped Humphrey into the bathroom on the floor and closed the door, then found another pair of cuffs in a jacket in the dressing room. The jacket had the name NORWOOD stitched on the front left. He put those cuffs on the unconscious guy and dragged him back to the dressing room.

A schedule was tacked on the wall near the front of the dojo. According to the block for Thursday, the first class started at six fifteen. Hatcher figured some early bird or assistant instructor would probably be showing up by five thirty. Maybe earlier. That meant he had twenty to thirty minutes, barring some random walk-in or unscheduled activity. He needed to make the most of them.

Fernandez looked pretty bad. He lay on his back, motionless. His left ear dangled next to his head, just over a spill of blood.

Restraining him posed a momentary challenge. Hatcher was short a pair of cuffs and didn't have any zip ties or cord. After thinking about it for a few seconds, he removed Fernandez's rank belt. The floppy *gi* would only get in the way, so he took that off him, too. The white of it was splattered with bright blood.

The choke Hatcher had used was actually a strangulation, since it didn't cut off his airway but instead compressed the carotid artery. Shutting off the blood flow to the brain deprived it of oxygen, causing him to pass out. Even though the brain was getting sufficient oxygen now, that kind of choke induced a state of unconsciousness that tended to last. Hatcher was going to have to revive him.

Hatcher tied the belt around one wrist, then raised Fernandez to a sitting position. Kneeling behind him, he lifted the man's other arm over his lolling head, laid the forearm across his crown. He slipped his arms in a hug around the man's torso, hands meeting right beneath the breast bone. He straightened his back and he lifted and squeezed, lifted and squeezed, lifted and squeezed. He counted to ten, then repeated. After the second time around, Fernandez's hand started to twitch, then his head began to move. Hatcher could hear the rough gasp of a waking breath.

Fernandez groaned, made a noise like he was trying to say something. Hatcher shoved him forward onto his stomach and yanked his arm down and behind him. He wrapped it snug against the other arm with the belt, wrists crossed. Tied it off with a tight square knot. A bit bulky, but it would have to do.

There was a bottled water fountain near the changing room. Hatcher walked over to it, filled a paper cup from a dispenser. He started to return to Fernandez, stopped. He glanced over to the exercise area, then to Fernandez, who was stirring slightly but clearly not ready to move on his own. Hatcher placed the cup down and went into the changing room. Norwood was still out. Hatcher untied his rank belt and pulled it from around the man's body, flopping it over his shoulder. Looking around, he grabbed two others, one brown, one green, from wall hooks before returning to Fernandez with the water.

He took one of the belts and knotted the end around Fernandez's ankles. Then he pulled Fernandez up into a sitting position and put the cup to his lips.

"Drink it," he said.

Fernandez took one sip, followed with a larger one. He blinked his eyes, choking on some of the water. A few more sips and the cup was empty. Hatcher crumbled it and tossed across the room in the general direction of a wastebasket.

"Your ear is detached. A hospital can reattach it and you'll barely show a scar, other than one no one will see unless you show it to them. But you've only got about a half hour before the tissue will be too far gone. So you'd better talk."

The man blinked again. His eyes were straining sideways, trying to see the side of his head. His ear hung there, swinging slightly with every movement. Hatcher was sure Fernandez could feel it brushing against the side of his jaw and neck.

"It's still there," Hatcher said. "For now."

"You're fucking crazy!" Fernandez took a few more breaths, his eyes clearing. "Attacking three cops? You'll do twenty years. You hear me? Your life is over. *Over.*"

"I don't think so, but right now let's talk about you. Why did you come after me the other day?"

"I don't have to answer shit."

Hatcher said nothing. He locked his gaze on Fernandez's eyes, raised a hand slowly toward the dangling ear.

"You were assaulting someone," Fernandez said, jerking his head away. "I thought I'd teach you a lesson. Now let me go, before you're looking at twenty-five to life."

Hatcher frowned, wagged his chin in a slow pantomime of disappointment. "Even if I wasn't able to tell you were lying from giveaways like the movement of your eyelids right before you spoke, or the way you swallowed midway through, or the tension in your vocal cords, I would still know. Because you've got to be the lamest-ass liar ever."

"Says you." Fernandez swallowed to clear his throat. "That's what happened."

Hatcher stood and stepped behind Fernandez, leaning down to grab the man's bound wrists. He clamped down on the knotted clump of belt and dragged Fernandez toward the exercise area.

"*Sunuva . . . !* Jesus! That hurts!"

"Okay, let me explain how this works," Hatcher said. He stopped just beneath the pull-up bar, dumped Fernandez on his stomach. "What you're about to experience is called *strappado.*"

"What? Hey! What the *fuck!*"

"Strappado. Should I spell it?"

Hatcher removed a forty-five-pound plate from a weight rack and balanced it on its edge near Fernandez's feet. The cop tried to roll onto his buttocks, but Hatcher shoved him back onto his chest. He took the loose end of the cloth belt he'd tied around the man's ankles and threaded it through the center hole of the weight. There wasn't much slack left after he finished tying it off, with the plate almost touching Fernandez's feet, but after he saw how it looked he decided that was probably ideal.

"This was very popular during the Inquisition," he continued. "It was one of the few ways to break a body, but still leave the person alive to confess. And it was simple."

"What the . . . ?" Fernandez twisted to look back over his shoulder. "What the hell are you doing?"

Hatcher knelt next to Fernandez and slid the remaining belts off his shoulder. He secured the end of one to the end of the other with a sheet-bend knot. It was clunky to use a nautical knot with thick cloth, but he knew it would do the job. When he was done, he fed one end of the double length belt between the man's forearms.

"At the moment, I'm tying this belt around the one holding your wrists. Then, I'm gonna toss it over this bar here and lift you by your arms, still reversed and tied behind you, just as they are now."

"What? You can't—"

"Eh, no need to worry. Other than twist your joints and pop your arms out of their sockets, stretch your tendons and ligaments beyond tolerances, and probably cause significant, irreversible nerve damage, it probably won't do anything except cause more pain than you've ever experienced in your life. Oh, and there is a real chance some of that damage will be to the brachial plexus nerve cluster, which would likely result in permanent paralysis. But other than that, you should be fine."

"You can't fucking do this!"

Hatcher shrugged. "Call a cop."

With the belt secure, Hatcher stood and fed the other end over the bar. He pulled down on it with all his weight, checking the hold. Fernandez's body pulled up, hips rising and legs sliding across the floor. The bar looked like it could handle the weight with no problem.

The knot connecting the belts seemed solid, too. Hatcher paused, leaning his weight against the rope but not pulling. Anticipation was crucial. The mind was the ultimate instrument of torture. Bodies could only be broken. Minds could be manipulated in a thousand different ways.

"I mean it! You better fucking stop!"

Hatcher yanked again on the belt, one hand climbing over the other, pulling down using his weight. Fernandez's arms extended and his body pitched forward. He rolled to his knees to keep from being lifted, then hopped to his bound feet, standing as quickly and as tall as he could, supporting his weight with his legs as long as possible.

"Generally speaking, there are two types of torture. The first type is to inflict pain. It's punitive. The goal of that torture is to simply heap as much suffering on the individual as possible."

"Ahhh! Christ! My shoulders! That hurts!"

"No kidding. That's sort of what people in my line of work call 'the point.'"

The heavy plate anchored Fernandez's legs, keeping him from flipping forward. That forced his reversed arms to lift his entire body weight from behind his back, pulling them in ways they weren't meant to rotate. Something popped audibly in one of Fernandez's shoulders and he screamed.

"The other type of torture is designed to break the individual's resistance. This is the type that requires an understanding of the human psyche. Ya see, it's not pain that causes someone's will, their spirit, to break. It's fear. Pain can be endured. But it's the fear that there will never be anything else that really gets them. That this will become a permanent condition, one that can only worsen. Repeated over and over and over forever. It's the anticipation of that, of the repetition, of the worsening, of the permanence—that's what causes people to crack. Funny thing is, that happens even though they know it can't go on much longer."

Hatcher lowered him back to the floor. Fernandez slumped onto his side, clenching his teeth.

"Almost forgot," Hatcher said.

He walked over to the reception area, rummaged through a small wooden desk in the corner. He returned a moment later with a letter opener.

Crouching next to Fernandez's head, he said, "Couldn't find scissors, so this will have to do."

The cop tried to pull away, but Hatcher yanked him back. "What the fuck?"

"Your ear. Since you don't seem interested in saving it, I figured I'd just remove it and flush it down the john. Permanent disfigurement is a good way to make sure you don't harbor any illusions about how far I'm willing to take this. Don't worry, once I flush it, I'll hoist you back up."

Hatcher reached down and picked up the loose flap of ear. It was connected by little more than the earlobe, looking rubbery and fake and every bit as detached as it was. He moved the letter opener toward it.

"No! Okay! I'll tell you!"

"Tell me what? That you were doing your duty as a public servant, protecting a pedestrian?"

Fernandez huffed several times. His jaw was bulging, the muscles of it visibly working beneath the surface.

"Speaking of permanence," Hatcher said. He shot a glance over to the camcorder. "This is being recorded. If you don't want to answer these questions, soon as I'm done introducing your ear to the L.A. sewer system we could talk about the hummer you got from a dude in drag."

"What the fuck are you talking about?"

"Oh, yeah, I know all about that. *All* about it. And by the time we're through here, I'll know a lot more."

"You're crazy. I didn't get a hummer from no fucking guy."

"Fitting double negative. Save your denials. Bottom line is, I can make you talk. Question is, do you want to talk about things like why you had a bunch of bangers kidnap me and why you beat a rendition of 'Wipe Out' on me with your tonfa the other day, or should we explore how you let some swingin' dick-wearing lipstick blow you in your squad car. Either way, the camera's running. And my patience is, too. Out."

Fernandez sucked in a hard breath, whiffling it through his teeth. "I did it for some gal, okay? Happy?"

"Afraid you're gonna have to be more specific. Let's start with the gal. Who is she?"

"Some chick. Met her a couple of months ago. We've been going out."

"What does she look like?"

"Brunette. Smokin' hot."

"Name?"

"Deborah."

Second time he'd heard her name, Hatcher thought. Had to be the same one. Her and Soliya, both in L.A. Him in L.A. Not a coincidence, that was for sure.

"How hot?"

"Eat-a-bucket-of-shit-just-to-sniff-her-asshole hot."

Hatcher let the information sink in. That sounded like her, all right.

"What did she tell you?"

"First time, said she needed someone picked up. That he wouldn't go peacefully. Needed to be done clean and controlled. Told me to have it ready to go, then called with the when and where. Bronson Caves."

"Why?"

Fernandez rolled his head, grimacing. "You did something to my shoulder, you asshole. It hurts like hell."

"Given where you're headed, my advice would be to get used to it. Now, I asked you a question. Why?"

"She didn't say," Fernandez said, sneering. "And I didn't fucking ask."

"And that shit with me on the sidewalk?"

Blinking at the ceiling, Fernandez huffed out some halting breaths. Talking was clearly a chore. The pain and overall dis-comfort were causing his respiration to be labored.

"She wanted me to roust you. Said a guy was going to be

with you. She told me to make sure he could walk away, not get roughed up or followed."

"Who is he?"

"No idea." Fernandez glared up at Hatcher, his chest heaving. "What about my ear? I need a doctor!"

"What's she got on you?"

"Got on me? I don't know what you mean. Look, if you don't call me an fucking amb—"

"Yes, you do. You know exactly what I mean. Those kinds of favors don't just get asked out of the blue."

Fernandez said nothing, just kept huffing. He stared at the floor, crunching his eyes in pain every few seconds.

"Okay. If this dislocates your other shoulder, just scream the way you did before. I won't let you down, but it'll make me feel good."

"Hey!"

Hatcher grabbed the end of the belt that tied off Fernandez's wrists. "Hope the skin and muscle on that one are strong. There are stories about arms ripping off."

"No! Wait! Jesus! She's got a bunch of girls who hire out as escorts, all right? Top dollar. I provide security."

Hatcher let the belt slacken. "For a percentage."

Fernandez glanced over at the camera, then looked away. He shrugged and dipped his head in a way Hatcher took as a nod.

"What do you know about William Bartlett?"

"Who?"

"Two-star general, retired. Gray hair. Looks like a politician."

"Never heard of him."

Voice was steady. No obvious signs of evasion in the eyes, no unnatural facial expressions. If anything, he looked relieved at being able to answer honestly.

"What about my nephew?"

Fernandez raised his head, one cheek tensing up toward his eye like he couldn't understand the question.

"Baby boy named Isaac? Ring a bell?"

"I didn't know he was your nephew."

"What did they say about him?"

"Only to make sure he didn't get hurt."

"Say again?"

"They told me to make sure he didn't get hurt. And not to hurt you, either."

Showing surprise at an answer during an interrogation, unless you were feigning it, was usually a tactical blunder. But Hatcher couldn't help himself. "What? When?"

"What do you mean, when? When I was heading out with the group."

"The group."

"To get the boy." A look of dismay, mixed with incredulity, washed over Fernandez's face. "You gotta be kidding me. You didn't know?"

Hatcher ignored the question. "Why did they want him?"

"Couldn't tell you. Guy said to make sure no one got careless. Kid wasn't to get hurt."

"But you have no idea why you were taking him?"

"They told me they had to protect him. That he was in danger. That's all."

"Protect him from what?"

"They didn't say. I'm telling you the truth."

"Where did you take him?"

"Handed him off to some gal. Blonde. She got in the back of a car and took off."

Soliya, Hatcher thought. Maybe.

"Who was driving?"

"Didn't see. Didn't care."

Hatcher stared at the floor for several seconds, then looked over to a clock on the wall. Someone would be coming soon. He sensed he'd used up all the time he had.

Standing, he glanced over at the phone. He was about to say something, then stopped. He squatted again.

"You said, 'guy.'"

"Huh?"

"Guy. You said, 'Guy said to make sure no one got careless.'"

"Yeah?"

"Guy, as in male."

Fernandez winced, squirming in place. "So?"

"Who?"

"I don't know his name," he said, letting out a breath.

"What did he look like?"

"Short. Spent a lot of time on his hair."

Hatcher stared down at the man for a long moment, thinking. "What kind of ride?"

"A Harley."

"Why were you taking orders from him?"

"What do you mean? Because she told me to."

"Deborah told you to?"

"Who else."

"How do you get in touch with her?"

"E-mail. Sometimes by text. She told me not to call anymore. Said it wasn't safe. She changes phones like every day."

"Where do you meet?"

"Different places. Never the same place twice. Hotels, mostly."

Hatcher said nothing for several seconds. Then he stabbed a finger toward Fernandez's face. "You're holding out on me."

"No! It's true! She always picks different places!"

"But you're holding out. You're a cop. You wouldn't be screwing some gal and committing felonies for her without knowing something more, something you were confident she didn't know you knew. You'd have checked her out, ran a plate, traced a number. Something."

Fernandez stared up at Hatcher, then his eyes wandered like he was thinking and he shook his head slowly.

Hatcher reached for the belt, started to stand.

The man stiffened, spoke quickly. "Wait! I tried to check her out. All the stuff came back phony. Name, everything."

The last word hung out there, an expectancy to it. Like it wasn't the end of the thought.

"But?"

Fernandez took in a deep breath and let it out in a sigh. "But I slipped a GPS pusher into her car, tracked where she lived. Or at least where she would go after she left me."

"And where was that?"

"Some mini-manch. Up on Mulholland Drive."

CHAPTER 16

HATCHER LEFT THE DOJO AND HEADED BACK TO HIS PLACE.
His side hurt and he needed sleep. He didn't feel any closer to
the answers he needed, but there was no shortage of new
questions.

He was reasonably confident Fernandez would keep quiet
and stay out of his way. More confident about the quiet part. The
video was his insurance, and he made it clear what would happen if he was arrested or if he met some untimely demise. He
guessed the man was more concerned about word of the blow
job making the rounds than he was about having confessed to
serious corruption.

Of course, there were two other cops to worry about. But
they wouldn't be sure who Hatcher was, wouldn't have a name,
and he figured Fernandez would persuade them to let him handle it on the QT. At least, he hoped that's how it would play out.

But Hatcher's biggest concern was figuring out what to do
next. If Fernandez was telling the truth, and Hatcher had to as-
sume he was, the Carnates were actually behind the kidnapping.
But if that were the case, how did Edgar fit in? And why was
Deborah going to Bartlett's place? Bartlett and the Carnates?
That didn't make sense. The Carnates seemed to have their own
reasons for wanting to end the world, one way or another, but
Bartlett? And what had that stuff with Edgar been all about?
Was he playing him? For what?

He needed some rest. A few hours, at least. Time to recover,
think things out. There had to be another person to hit up, someone who could point him in the right direction. He just had to
put his mind to it.

Fernandez's cell phone sat on the passenger seat. Hatcher
had scanned the phone's contents briefly, looking through the

contacts and saved texts. The man had been careful, which meant whatever might be helpful would be hard to find. After he got back to his apartment, he'd go through it carefully, scrutinize every name and number. At the very least, he figured being able to see the incoming calls might be useful, as would the ability to make calls from it. He doubted Fernandez would have the time to cancel his service for hours, if not days. Not while he was racing to have his ear reattached.

But he resigned himself to getting some sleep first. He was having trouble focusing. The mind was a stubborn thing. He knew he needed to let it wander through some REM or it would refuse to cooperate.

Good habits can allow you to avoid bad situations. Hatcher was thinking of a number of things when he arrived at his place, but his autopilot mode had him drive past the alley-drive to get a look down the narrow lane before turning into it. It usually took an extra minute, having to cruise a block past after taking a peek, turn around, and then double back and pull into the drive. It was a minute usually wasted. But today it paid off.

He only caught a glimpse, but that was enough to register. Nondescript silver gray sedan. Single occupant, seated in the driver's seat. Visible for maybe two seconds as Hatcher rolled by, but he looked to be male, largish head, short hair. Probably middle-aged. Probably a cop. Probably there to talk to him about Vivian. Or maybe it was the same guy who'd been asking around about him.

If there was one thing Hatcher did not have time—or energy—for, it was more cops.

He kept driving, taking the first turn he could, making his way to the highway. He checked his rearview several times. Nothing.

So, his place was hot. The bar was an option, but not a good one. He needed a place to think, to stretch out and crash. Denny might let him use his place, but dealing with Denny in this situation might be more trouble than it was worth. Man would ask too many questions, and either bug the heck out of him to work tonight or treat it like a slumber party. He could go to a motel, but they would require a swipe of his debit card and that would, potentially, at least, send a beacon out to anyone looking for him. Resting in the car wouldn't let him work the kinks out of his aching muscles and would almost guarantee a stiffer neck than he already had. There was only one place he could think to go.

It took almost forty minutes to get there. Susan answered on the second knock. She was holding a tissue. Her nose was red and her eyes were puffy. She wore a pale blue housedress with sandals and looked like a woman who hadn't slept in days. Which, he was sure, she hadn't.

"Oh, Jake," she said, dread coloring her voice. "I've been so worried. Do you have news? Have you found him?"

"Not exactly. Can I come in?"

Susan worked her brow, frowning and nodding at the same time. "Of course. Please. You'll have to excuse my manners."

The town house was dark and cool. Hatcher stepped past the foot of the stairwell and into the living room. Susan shut the door and moved by him to the middle of the room. She stood there for a few seconds, facing the opposition direction, before saying anything.

"Just come out with it . . . do you have something bad to tell me?"

"No. I think he's still alive, if that's what you mean."

The sound of her letting out a breath was audible, and Hatcher could see her body sag in relief. She lowered her head and dabbed the napkin to her eyes. Her body shuddered slightly in a sob.

Hatcher said nothing.

As if sensing the silence start to accumulate, she straightened her back and turned to him.

"I'm sorry," she said.

"Don't be. You have every right to be upset. Actually, you seem to be holding up well. I'm the one who should apologize. It was my fault. I led them to you."

Susan nodded in a way that indicated she wanted to believe him but didn't.

"Do you think you'll find him?"

"I know more about who was involved. I have to figure out where they're keeping him. I'm doing all I can. I promise you."

"I believe you. How about you? Are you okay? I see marks on your face. You look like you've been fighting."

"I just need a place to rest for a while."

Another nod, this one more ambiguous. "Why don't you go lay down? Can I get you something? Would you like something to drink?"

"Maybe some water."

She disappeared and returned a minute later with a glass of ice and a cold plastic bottle of Dasani. The glass had a lemon slice wedged over the rim.

"Let me turn down the bed for you," she said. She poured some water into the glass and set the bottle down.

"The couch is fine."

"Don't be silly." She placed a hand on his chest, ran her fingers down his shirt. "You need to get out of those clothes. I'll throw them in the washing machine."

"Susan, you don't have to—"

"No. I want to. You can take a shower if you want."

He didn't want to. But there was no arguing whether he needed to clean up. Just like he didn't really want to sleep, but he knew he couldn't think straight in the condition he was in. He was worn out from the day's events, and his mind as much as his body needed to shut down, recuperate. A warm shower sounded like a good start.

"Okay," he said. He gulped down several swallows of water. "Thank you."

The bedrooms were upstairs. Susan led him to the master bath, waited outside while he stripped down, had him hand her his clothes from behind the bathroom door.

As he leaned over the faucet to the bath, he heard her yell through the door that she was putting his phones and his wallet on the dresser. Phones, plural. He supposed she knew better than to ask.

The hot splash of water on his face and chest felt soothing, the steam soaking into his nostrils even more so. He turned the heat up and let the stream beat against the nape of his neck and upper back, worked his shoulders in circles under it. By the time he toweled off, he was feeling relatively loose, relaxed.

He padded into the bedroom with the towel hooked around his waist and stretched out face-down across the bed.

He heard Susan enter the room again, the light thump of her footfalls, the rustling of clothes. The mattress shook a bit, springs creaking. He felt her nestle against him, smooth, soft skin. The unmistakable, doughy press of breasts against his back. There was no doubt she was naked.

"Susan—"

"Shhhh. I just want you to hold me. Nothing else. Really. I just want to be held."

Hatcher said nothing. He felt the side of her cheek as she laid her head just below the back of his neck.

"I haven't been with a man since Garrett. And I don't even want that. Honest. If you want me to leave, I will."

Her breath was hot and moist on his skin. He thought about Vivian, about how much he missed her. About how he wanted to love her, tried to, even, but couldn't. And about Amy, whom he also had wanted to love, but couldn't—for totally different reasons.

Vivian, who loved him and was dead. Horribly dead. And he knew somehow it was because of him.

Susan was a beautiful woman, mother of his dead brother's child. Vivian's mutilated corpse was still in the morgue. Jesus, what kind of person was he? Anything hinting of sex right now would be disloyal. Despicably so.

A drop of something ran down his back, across his ribs. A tear.

Tell her to go.

"Susan," he said.

He felt another drop on his back as she moved her head, then the press of her lips against his skin.

"So many scars," she said. "So many little scars. I bet you don't even remember where they all came from, do you?"

Hatcher said nothing.

"Just promise me you'll get him back, Jake. Promise me you'll bring my baby back to me."

Another drop hit his back, then another. He rolled over, took a gentle hold of her shoulders. How could he promise something like that? He had no idea where the boy was. He had only the vaguest knowledge of who took him. He wasn't even sure why. He opened his mouth to tell her that he would do everything he could. That he would give it his all. But he couldn't guarantee anything. He just couldn't.

"I promise," he said.

She closed her eyes, squeezing out tears, and let out a sob

that sounded like a cough. "You must think I'm terrible. Throwing myself at you like this. It's not what you think. It's not that I don't know you won't try your hardest."

"I don't think that."

"It's just . . . I'm so lonely, Jake. I've been so alone since your brother. And you're so much like him. So strong. Yet so caring. I trust you. I don't trust anyone. But I trust you. That makes me a horrible person."

Hatcher dipped his face toward her, put the curl of his knuckle under her chin and forced her to look at him. "That's why I think you should go get dressed. I don't want to take advantage of you."

Susan tilted her head, let out a laugh that shook loose another few tears. She wiped them from her eyes with the back of her hand.

"You take advantage of me? I really am a horrible person."

Hatcher smiled and looked down at the mattress. "No. Ridiculous, maybe. For thinking that."

"Thank you. For promising, I mean. I know you can't really . . . it was just nice to hear it. Reassuring."

Leaning forward, she kissed him on his forehead, ran her fingers down the side of his face in a gentle caress. When he looked up, she peered down into his eyes, told him she was sorry, so very sorry, and dropped her mouth onto his. He felt her tongue barge past his lips, tasted her honeylike sweetness.

Within seconds he was inside of her, straining to go deeper, ever deeper, squeezing the curves of her flesh against his, gnawing at the rubbery bump of her nipple, cramming the sprawl of eternity, every bit that would fit, into a series of guilt-ridden instants that made forever seem like no time at all.

He woke a bit disoriented. Susan was curled against him, her head on his chest. She stirred as he raised his head, looking around. The room was dark. He'd heard a noise.

He heard it again. Some kind of digitized voice.

"It's somebody's phone," Susan said, sounding half asleep.

The room was draped in shadow. A few stretches of silvery moonlight rendered swaths of it semi-visible in a lugubrious blue monochrome. Across the room, he could see a blinking red light.

Hatcher slid out from under her, made his way around the

bed. It was Fernandez's cell. He picked it up, pressed a few buttons until the screen lit up. The message that popped up said there was an incoming text.

"Everything okay?"

Hatcher glanced over. Susan was sitting up in bed, her silhouette barely perceptible.

"Yeah."

He thumbed the screen until he found his way to the text.

Where were you?

The caller ID gave a number, not a name. Hatcher thought for a moment, then fumbled his way to a screen keyboard. The typing was slow, but he realized the phone tried to make it easier by finishing words for him.

Had a visit from your friend. Asking questions. Things got ugly. Okay now though.

He pressed Send, then waited. Seconds stretched into a couple of minutes. Nothing.

"Are you sure everything's okay?" Susan asked. "Does it have something to do with Isaac?"

"No. Not directly."

A long pause. Hatcher could feel her eyes reaching through the darkness.

"Are you coming back to bed?"

Her voice sounded a bit shaky. Hatcher realized she must be an emotional wreck. Her infant son was missing. The boy's father was dead, and she'd just slept with his brother. She had no one to lean on. No one else but him. Was that why she'd done it? Did that make him even more of a creep?

"You think what we did was wrong, don't you?"

Hatcher made his way back to the bed, rolled gently onto it.

"I think seeking comfort in a crisis is something people do."

Meaningless, he knew. The type of pablum intended to gloss over an issue. But it was the best he could muster under the circumstances without just plain lying. And he didn't want to do that.

"Is that what that was to you? A form of charity?"

"No," he said, realizing that, at least, was true. "I needed it."

She seemed to consider his words for quite a while. Then reached out to touch him. "You're a good man, Jacob Hatcher."

He rubbed her arm gently, thinking, *I wonder if you'd say that if you knew.*

The phone indicated it was after nine p.m. He glanced at it again as Susan took it from him, then reached across his body and placed it on the nightstand next to him. With a firm hand she pressed him down onto the bed and pulled close, raising his arm over her head to lay her cheek on him and intertwining her fingers through his.

"You're getting closer, aren't you?"

"It's hard to say. Maybe."

"If anyone can find him, you can. You found me, didn't you?"

Hatcher listened to those words repeat themselves in his head. It was true, he did find her. But not without help.

"That name," he said. "Nora Henruss. When did you use it?"

"What do you mean?"

"When I met you at the diner, you said you hadn't used that name in months. When was the last time?"

"I used it to rent an apartment, right before Isaac was born."

"Why did you stop?"

"Because I had to show them ID at the hospital. Give them a Social Security number. And my address."

"You were that paranoid?"

"I was a little paranoid. But I almost stayed put anyway. But then I got a call from my doctor's office. His secretary wanted to know if I'd gotten the flowers from my sister. The florist tried to deliver them to the hospital."

"But she didn't send any flowers."

"No. Fortunately, I never told my sister where I was, other than on the West Coast. And I had given the hospital a phony address. But it spooked me. So I moved. Switched phones. Covered my tracks to be safe. Changed names again. Found this sublet. I pay in cash. Cable and electric included."

Smart gal, Hatcher thought. Good instincts. Too bad he'd been stupid enough to lead them right to her.

But something about that was bothering him, something just out of reach. His thoughts circled it, trying to close in, but before they could pounce into the brush and drag it out, that digital voice droned out the brand of the phone again.

Another text. Hatcher pressed his way through the screen until it popped up.

Sand Dollar Inn. Room 9. One hour.

"You have to go, don't you?"

Hatcher glanced over to Susan. Her body caught the glow from the phone, giving her an artistic, vaguely pornographic look, like a centerfold. He suddenly found himself wishing he didn't have to leave her, wishing he could stay and hold that body, touch it, kiss it. Absorb the warmth of it as he tried to create something meaningful with its occupant.

But he had to find her son, and he didn't know how much time he had left, if any. And what did that say about him? Wanting her like this? What kind of man does that? It didn't matter what he said earlier, sleeping with her had been wrong.

He needed to drop thoughts of sex, purge his mind of what happened, and focus on the boy. Sex was a distraction. It clouded judgment, muddied priorities. Stoked emotions that could be hard to control. A boy's life was at stake, and possibly much more. The last thing he needed to be thinking about was sex.

A moment later, another text came through:

I'll be in bed, waiting for you.

THE SAND DOLLAR INN WAS A FEW BLOCKS FROM THE SANTA Monica Pier. It was an enclosed square of single-story strips, a dozen rooms per building, rimming a motor court. The most prominent feature of the drive-through entry was a large Coke machine.

Hatcher pulled into the parking lot of a fast-food place across the street. He watched the entry for a while, then went inside and ordered a burger and a coffee. He took a seat near the front window.

The burger was a bit soggy. He bolted it, wiped his mouth, then stared through the glass. If she was already there, she would have to leave at some point.

His options were limited. He could go to the room, see what happened. That, he knew would be unwise. His experience with Carnates was that they were ridiculously strong for their size, possessed amazing reflexes, and were all but impossible to in-

jure. They were also almost impossible to resist. Something
about their demon-hybrid physiology, their genetic perfection,
equipped them to give off overpowering pheromones. That,
coupled with their stunning looks, made them especially dangerous. If Deborah or another one of them was in there, in bed,
probably naked, he would have a hard time focusing on the task
at hand. And if he didn't end up having sex with her, she'd probably just kick his ass.

Yes, that option was definitely unwise, but he still had to
fight himself to keep from choosing it.

The other option was to wait her out. Keep a close eye on the
entry to the motor court, watch for any nubile women driving
out, especially crazy hot ones. The problem with that was he
had no idea how long he'd have to sit there. If she really was
waiting in bed, she may just go to sleep. That would mean loitering until morning, without really knowing if she was even in
there.

He was leaning toward a compromise option. Waiting around
for a couple of hours, then, if nothing happened, heading over to
look around. Play it by ear.

Something was telegraphing to him that the situation wasn't
right. He couldn't pin the feeling down, reduce it to a thought,
but it was definitely there. Fernandez must have held back about
planning to meet her later. Was that due to loyalty? Or just
stress? And could he have gotten ahold of someone after Hatcher
left? Told them what happened? Hatcher doubted it. The guy
was too busy getting his ear sewn on. And something told
Hatcher Officer Fernandez wasn't the best team player to begin
with. Maybe the text just meant she'd gone to find him somewhere he normally would be, and couldn't.

But the feeling wouldn't let up as Hatcher peered out the
window, watching the bugs flit around the fluorescent glow of
the light above the reception window across the street, next to
the bright red-and-white vending machine.

"Excuse me, mister."

Hatcher swung his head at the voice. It was an old man,
maybe late seventies, wearing a few too many layers of clothing
under a black wool beanie and carrying a shoulder pack. He was
unshaven, with leathery, sun-worn skin. Dirt lined the creases in
his neck like grout.

The old man hooked a thumb over his shoulder. "Is that your PT Cruiser out there? You left the lights on."

Hatcher looked the man over, waited for some hint of a scam. The hardship story about running out of gas or losing a bus ticket or having a paycheck stolen, followed by the inevitable request for money.

"Just thought you'd like to know," the man said, before shuffling off.

Strange, Hatcher thought. How could he forget to turn the lights off? He started toward the side entrance, then stopped. The derelict-looking old guy was at the counter, ordering something. Hatcher thought for a moment, made a decision. He headed toward the entrance on the opposite side and pushed through it.

The night air was cool. The sound and smell of traffic rose to greet him as he curled around the door and walked toward the back of the parking lot. He circled around the drive-through lane and stepped beyond the reach of the menu lights into the shadows separating the restaurant's parking lot from an adjoining lot to the rear. He slowed down and walked until he found a decent vantage point that would let him see past the edge of the building to where his car was parked. The front of the car was dark. No lights. The homeless guy had lied.

Before he could react, he heard the cock of a weapon behind him. A flash of red caused him to flinch and raise a hand to protect his eyes. He looked down at his chest, saw a single red dot. Front and back. They weren't taking any chances.

"Don't be stupid."

He heard a vehicle pull behind him, throaty engine, the scraping crunch of tires loud as it circled close.

The voice behind him said, "You've got two weapons trained on you."

He knew that voice. He thought back to the first time he'd heard it, at the bar. First inclinations tend to be right, he told himself.

"Why do I picture you counting them on your fingers with your lips mouthing the numbers?" he said.

"Turn around slowly and get in, smart ass."

Hatcher turned. Edgar came to a stop a few feet to his right. A black Hummer idled directly ahead.

The back door of the Hummer opened, and General Bartlett leaned out, beckoning him in with a wave.

"Will you please just get in, before someone spots us?" the general said.

Hatcher scratched his neck, glanced over at Edgar. He was aiming a Beretta nine mil, with laser grips. He dropped his eyes to his shirt, saw the red dot hovering over his sternum. Another dot scribbled below it. A sniper, hidden in the darkness.

"I'm not sure being spotted would be such a bad thing right about now," Hatcher said.

Bartlett dropped his head, let it swing from side to side. "Good Lord, Hatcher. Do you honestly think we want to kill you? We could have put several bullets in you and driven off before you even knew you were dead. So please, just get in the damn car."

Hatcher shot a look at Edgar and stepped forward. "Since you said please."

The inside of the Hummer smelled like cologne. Hatcher slid into the rear passenger seat. Edgar got into the front on the same side. The driver was little more than a kid. Blond, clean cut. Hair cropped tight in a way that screamed military.

The Hummer pulled around the parking lot, heading away from where Hatcher had parked, and left on a different street.

The general gestured toward Hatcher's lap. "Please, buckle your seat belt."

"I'm good."

"I must insist."

Hatcher watched Edgar stare back at him from over the headrest. He knew that Beretta was aimed at him through the seat. The belt was just a way of making sure he couldn't move too quickly.

Fine, Hatcher thought, pulling the belt over his body and latching it. *I can be patient.*

"Where are we going?"

"There's something I want you to see."

They drove in silence for over twenty minutes. Hatcher stopped paying attention to the route after the first few. Fernandez's phone had a GPS map. And since they weren't blindfolding him, he could just remember the street and number later, if necessary.

When they arrived, he decided it wasn't going to be necessary.

The driver pulled into what Hatcher took to be an abandoned warehouse; plain cement construction, industrial windows, a faded sign for a furniture company Hatcher had never heard of. Formerly abandoned, he realized.

Inside, it was bustling.

The interior was an open layout, two stories high. Six more Humvees, reconstructed military surplus from the looks of them, were parked inside being worked on. The far corner was caged off with reinforced wire mesh and a steel-grate door, housing racks of automatic weapons. Crates were stacked high against the walls. At least two dozen men in battle dress trousers and khaki shirts were tending to various tasks, working on creepers beneath the vehicles, cleaning weapons on tables, taking inventory of supplies. Four of them were on a set of mats, practicing hand-to-hand drills and knife work.

Hatcher realized a number of these were probably the same men he'd seen at the cave.

Edgar got out first. He opened the door for Hatcher to do the same. When the general followed, the men all stopped what they were doing and stood at attention.

Bartlett waved a hand in the air, a gesture that looked almost affectionate. "As you were."

Hatcher followed the general to a door on the opposite side of the vehicle. He realized they had parked next to an artificial wall about ten feet high, running the length of the warehouse. Not just a wall, he realized, a large enclosure. As he drew close, he could smell the paint, noticed the surface still had that clean, moist look. The whole thing had probably been constructed within the last few weeks.

On the other side of the door was an office space. PC workstations, printers, a copier. No frills, no personalization. The upper half of the interior wall of the space was partition glass, revealing what lay beyond. No question what it was. He'd seen many in his time.

A war room.

The set up was functional. A large conference table rimmed with laptops dominated the center of the room. Five flat-screen TVs were arrayed across the top of the far wall, each running satellite news feeds from different networks. A pair of lecture hall dry-erase boards were mounted to the wall below them, names and times listed on one side in marker. An enormous map of the continental United States dominated the wall to the right, covered in a clear panels of Plexiglas peppered with hand-drawn arrows and circles and numbers. To the left, blown-up satellite photos of mountain topography hung like posters. Red Xs marked certain locations, with numbers inked next to them that looked like longitude and latitude designations. To the right, a map of L.A., with four Xs. Hatcher could tell one of the Xs was the house on Mulholland. He assumed another was where he was standing. He wasn't sure about the other two.

A tall black man in fatigues was standing in front of one of the posters, holding a digital tablet in his hand and speaking into a headset. His neck was bandaged. Hatcher recognized him as the guy from the motel room, the one he'd given a shot to the throat. He had to think for a moment before he could come up with a name. Calvin, the general had called him. Calvin glanced over and made eye contact when Hatcher entered. Considering the blow to his Adam's apple, Hatcher thought the man didn't look especially upset to see him. But he didn't look thrilled, either.

Hatcher let his gaze drift the room, ran it over the walls as the general strode past him toward the head of the table. He gestured for Hatcher to have a seat.

Looking at the map of the U.S., Hatcher said, "Are you planning a coup?"

Bartlett bristled, then forced the kind of smile a parent might give a petulant child. "This is serious business, son."

"What business are we talking about?"

"That's what we're here to discuss." He waved his hand toward a nearby chair. "Please."

After considering his options, Hatcher pulled out the chair and sat. Edgar took a seat a few chairs away. Calvin remained standing a few feet behind Bartlett, like an adjutant.

"Why don't we start with why Vivian is dead."

Bartlett's eyes jumped to Edgar. Hatcher shifted to face him. Edgar shrugged and shook his head.

"That one has us stumped," Bartlett said. "But the truth is, she had her own agenda."

Hatcher wanted to react with anger, but the general's voice was too sympathetic. He scanned the man's face for signs of deception. There was some guarding, for sure. A definite attempt to control his nonverbals. But Hatcher couldn't say the man was lying. Then again, it was very hard to tell with some people, especially outside of an interrogation.

"What kind of an agenda?"

"None of us is sure, but we believe it had something to do with you. We know she had contacts with the Carnates that she didn't report."

Hatcher said nothing. Could Vivian really have been up to something? Something he knew nothing about? His mind sifted through a sudden flash of recollections. There had been some signs, he had to admit. But it was difficult in the extreme to read someone you were involved with. The emotional nature of conversations tended to mask indicators, and you tended to ignore tells, unconsciously if not consciously, wanting to give the person the benefit of the doubt. Wanting to believe them. Failing to spot things you otherwise would.

"Why don't you just tell me what's going on?"

"What I told you before is mostly true—"

"Mostly."

"Yes. Mostly. What I told you about a portal to Hell being opened, what Vivian told you about your brother likely being involved. But there are things I left out."

"What kind of things?"

Bartlett swiveled his chair slightly, looking to Calvin.

Calvin stepped forward. "The Carnates are the ones trying to open the passage."

"What a shocker. Why didn't you want me to know that?"

"Because Edgar has managed to gain their confidence. They believe he's working with them."

Hatcher looked at Edgar. "Is that so?"

"That's so," Edgar said. "They love me."

"I have no idea what the hell is going on, but you're bat-shit crazy if you believe that."

Edgar started to protest, but Bartlett silenced him with a hand. "Why do you say that?"

"Because I can't see a Carnate trusting anyone. They play-act. They pretend. But they don't trust. And they only love you the way a stripper loves a guy who keeps feeding her C-notes for lap dances and buys her eighty-dollar bottles of white wine and ginger ale."

"I see," Bartlett said, nodding. "Edgar, why don't you explain the situation?"

"They don't trust me in that way. They think they've co-opted me."

"Co-opted you. Let's back up." Hatcher shifted back to face Bartlett. "What do you have going on here?" He waved a hand, indicating the room. "What is all this?"

"This is our operations center"

"For what kind of operation?"

Bartlett leaned back in his chair, pressing his fingertips gently against one another over his lap. He looked to Calvin.

"Our objective is to find the gateway and destroy it."

"How did you even know about it? About the Carnates?"

"Let's just say, I heard a message," Bartlett said. "From above."

Tongues, Hatcher thought. He remembered what Vivian had told him. How he'd heard someone speaking in tongues. The fact it was probably true didn't make it seem any less weird.

And it created questions of its own.

"I have a hard time imagining the government okaying a covert military op to destroy a portal to Hell based upon you telling them God spoke to you."

"The government? Hardly. This operation is privately funded."

"Privately funded? From the looks of it, you've got a small army. Fully outfitted. They have to eat, and I'm sure they're not working for free. That's got to mean millions. A general's pension may be good, but it's not that good."

"Well, it's actually more than just a small army," Bartlett said, a look of something like pride stretching his cheeks. "And you'd be surprised at how many interests out there would invest in something like this. There are still many powerful people of faith in this country. For now."

"What about the boy? You planning to kill him? Murder an infant?"

"Don't be ridiculous. That's something Vivian told you to motivate you to find him."

Hatcher paused. "Where is he?"

"He's safe."

"I want to know where he is."

"The Carnates have him," Edgar said.

"You mean, you had him, and you just gave him to them?"

"Calm down. I had no choice. It was all part of keeping their trust."

"Worth sacrificing a baby, you sick son of a bitch?"

"He's not in any danger," Bartlett said. "Not right now. They need to keep him alive and healthy."

"So they can kill him."

Bartlett tightened his gaze. "We won't let that happen."

"All right," Hatcher said, his eyes bouncing from Bartlett to Edgar, then back again. "I don't get any of this. Why didn't you just tell me what you were up to?"

"Would you have let them take your nephew? Plus, we knew of your . . . relationship with Vivian. We had concerns about her from the beginning."

"You're telling me you think she was working for the Carnates? She was a nun, for Christ's sake."

"I'll thank you to watch your language, soldier. All I can say is something strange was going on. Like I told you, she had her own agenda. Besides, by not telling you, we could allow you to interact with the Carnates without the risk of them figuring out what we were up to. You of all people should understand that."

Hatcher held Bartlett's stare for a few seconds, then looked away in disgust. He understood all too well. The best person to perpetuate a lie was someone who thought he was telling the truth.

"I don't like being used."

Bartlett nodded grimly. "When the stakes are high, we often have to do things we don't like."

"So why do they need him? What are they up to?"

Bartlett tilted his head toward Calvin.

"Experts in the occult believe there are seven points on Earth where the spiritual plane is close enough to the threshold of damnation for a portal to be established. They are known as the Seven Gateways to Hell. No one is precisely sure where they are. Many urban legends claim one for their town, but it seems likely each is located beneath the surface of the Earth."

Hatcher thought about that. "And one of them is here, in L.A."

"Apparently."

"So why haven't they opened it already?"

Bartlett shifted forward in his chair. "It doesn't work that way. The portal can only be opened under certain circumstances, with the proper artifacts in place."

"How does the boy fit in?"

Calvin took a breath, made eye contact with his boss. "We believe that they intend to sacrifice the boy to open the portal."

"Wonderful. You mean they're going to kill him in some ritual? Cut his fucking heart out or something."

"No," Bartlett said. "More like exchange him for someone else. A truly innocent soul offered in trade for a truly diabolical one. We can't be sure, of course. But that's our best guess."

"What the hell are you saying?"

Bartlett said, "That they plan to send your nephew to Hell, so that they can raise the one true unified demon, the god and goddess of damnation."

"The Baphomet," Hatcher said.

"I'm glad to see you were paying attention."

"When is this supposed to happen?"

"Soon."

"Where?"

"We don't know yet," Edgar said. "They haven't confided the location. But we know it has to be underground. Possibly some cave or tunnel."

"So why the Hell are you helping them get so close?"

Bartlett clasped his hands together on the table and frowned at them. "Calvin?"

Calvin straightened his back. "The objective is to identify the target location, ascertain the time when they will all be gathered for the event, secure the location, remove the boy, and destroy the premises."

"Destroy? You mean, like, blow it up?"

"Yes, if possible."

"And what will that accomplish?"

"If all goes according to plan," Bartlett said, "we'll have

buried one of the Seven Gateways to Hell. And, more important, we'll have buried and destroyed almost all of the known artifacts necessary to open it."

"But how do you know they'll tell you when? Or where? How do you know they're not doing it right now?"

Bartlett nodded to Edgar, who leaned forward.

"Because . . . we have one of the artifacts they need. They can't proceed without it."

"So why not just destroy it? Wouldn't that solve the problem?"

"Not necessarily," Bartlett said. "There are likely others out there, somewhere. Edgar's heard them talking about it. Eventually, they'll be found. In archaeological digs, or by some construction crew excavating a foundation. This is our chance to get all the ones they have."

"How do you know they haven't already found one of the others?"

Edgar smiled. "Why do you think they've been willing to let me so close? They need this one, just like they needed your nephew."

"And you delivered him."

"You have to remember, it's all part of the plan. This is why we couldn't tell you."

"You guys are out of your minds. The Carnates aren't stupid. They barely trust each other. They sure as hell aren't going to trust you."

"They have no choice. We have the artifact."

"So why am I here, if you have it all under control?"

Bartlett exchanged glances with Edgar, then Calvin.

"Well?" Hatcher said.

"We were concerned you were going to interfere with the final phases of the operation."

Hatcher's gaze moved from Calvin, to Bartlett, back to Calvin. "Why would you suddenly be concerned about something like that . . . unless . . ."

Bartlett pushed back from the table, as if ready to leave. "I think it would be pointless to debate side issues right now. We have—"

"Unless you were counting on Vivian to rein me in, and when you heard she'd been killed, you realized I was going to come gunning for you. But you had to figure I'd come looking for the boy, anyway. So why . . ."

Hatcher snapped a glance to Edgar, then back to Bartlett.

"You've been tracking me. A GPS. In the car. The car you rented for Vivian."

Bartlett stared at the table, a sober smile shaping one side of his face.

"And when you found out I'd tracked down the cop, you knew I'd find a Carnate next. And you couldn't be sure what would happen then. Whether I might actually find the boy or start piecing things together. Mess everything up."

Edgar shrugged. "Close enough."

"And you," Hatcher said. "You wanted me to think you were turning on Bartlett's program. Why?"

"Just trying to keep tabs on you."

"No. There were other ways to do that. You were worried. When you saw I was heading to the clinic, you realized I was trying to track down Sherman. But you didn't want me chasing that lead, because if I found him, he might tell me something outside the script. Or he might kill me. Either way, you wanted to distract me, get me back to tracking down the boy. So I could lead you to him."

"You're a smart man," Bartlett said. "Smart enough that you should understand we're working for the greater good here."

"I'm going to ask you again," Hatcher said. "Same thing I asked you the first time we met. What do you want from me?"

"I want you to stand down, soldier. Let us take over from here. Just stay out of our way. Don't interfere with the Carnates. When we're ready to enter the final phase, we'll let you know."

"And then what?"

"Then, we finish what we started."

Hatcher frowned. "*We*, huh?"

"Yes. I assume you want your chance to exact revenge against whoever killed Vivian, don't you?"

"I thought you said you had no idea who killed her."

"No, you asked why she was killed. I said that had me stumped. But we do have an idea who."

Hatcher leaned forward in his seat. "Don't play games with me, General."

"Because I understand that you're still quite upset," Bartlett said, his expression stern. "I'm going to overlook the hyper-aggressive hostility you seem intent on displaying."

"Just tell me what you know."

Bartlett turned a palm toward Calvin, who leaned forward over a laptop and tapped a few keys. He stared at the screen, tapped a few more. Then he turned the laptop around and slid it toward Hatcher.

"We think it's this man," he said. "His name is Morris Sankey."

Hatcher looked at the picture on the screen. It was the lanky guy who had approached him on the street, right before Fernandez showed up.

"He's wanted in connection to several murders of young women. While Ms. Fall doesn't exactly fit the profile, the MO is close enough. Mutilation, rape, sodomy. We can surmise what he's done to her body. The work of a sexual psychopath. A serial killer."

Flashes of light gradually blocked out Hatcher's vision as he stared, until he could barely see at all. His mind replaced the image on the screen with ones of Vivian, eyes bulging in terror, trying to scream through a hand covering her mouth, her last moments alive spent being violated, brutalized. Tortured.

"Why," Hatcher said. He had to struggle to get the word out through clenched teeth.

"Like I said, we're not sure. But Edgar was able to confirm Sankey is here, and that the Carnates have been dealing with him."

Hatcher whipped his head around to look at Edgar. "Now is not the time to be holding anything back."

"Honest, Bro," Edgar said, crossing his heart. "They never said anything about killing Vivian."

Eyes were steady but not forced. Facial muscles tensed slightly, but within a normal range for a tense conversation. Body language was quiet. Posture slightly closed, but not beyond what would be expected. Words were clipped a bit, which tended to show frustration with an accusation.

It was an imperfect science, more like an art. But Hatcher had nothing else to rely on. The man was likely hiding something, but Hatcher couldn't say what or why.

"Where do I find him?"

"That's what I've been trying to tell you," Bartlett said. "As best we can tell, he's part of their plans."

Hatcher looked up to find the general peering at him intently.

"Let me put it this way—when you're there to throw him through the gates of Hell, he won't have very far to travel."

Hatcher said nothing. He let his gaze jump from Bartlett to Calvin, float around the table a bit before settling on Bartlett again. He was trying hard to keep from showing any reaction, forcing himself to act normal while he processed the message. Not the one from Bartlett, the one from Edgar.

The one being tapped out on the side of his shoe by Edgar's foot under the table in Morse code, repeated several times over.

He's lying.

CHAPTER 17

✦

THEY DROPPED HATCHER OFF IN THE PARKING LOT NEAR THE rental car. He slid behind the steering wheel, slipped the key in the ignition, and stared through the windshield.

The GPS was beneath the passenger seat, right where they told him it would be. It was a small black device encased in solid plastic, about half the size of a cell phone. Hatcher looked it over a few times, then opened the car door, leaned out, and tossed it behind the front tire.

What now?

Bartlett and company had demanded he stand down, wait for them to contact him. Fat chance. He had let them interpret his silence on the matter however they wanted. But there was no way he was going to sit around and do nothing, waiting for a phone call.

He started the car and backed up, listened for the satisfying crunch of the tracker beneath his tire. He pulled out of the parking lot, merged into traffic, and drove. He thought about calling Susan. He thought about calling Amy. He thought about Vivian. A lot. If only they'd been tracking her, instead of him.

Almost unconsciously, he yanked the steering wheel and screeched into the parking lot of a supermarket. He slammed the Cruiser into park and opened the door. Crouching on the pavement, he felt under the driver's seat, slid it back and put his head as low in the footwell as it would go. Nothing. He climbed in the backseat, pushed his hands beneath the cushions. He groped the interior lining of the roof, checked every compartment. He thought for a moment, then popped the trunk. He lifted the carpet, removed access panels. He knelt down and ran his hands along the rear underside of the bumper. He bent down onto his forearm and scanned the undercarriage.

Nothing, nothing, nothing. He checked the wheel wells, under the hood, in the grill. Still nothing.

He got back in the car, let his eyes scan the interior. Console, light, shifter, radio, nav system, heat and air controls.

His eyes settled on the nav system. Typical rental car bolt-on, mounted to the front console, protruding on an adjustable arm. *Son of a bitch.* Tactical redundancy. Hide two, in different ways. There was a reason things were always found in the last place someone looked; no one keeps looking after they find what they were looking for. No doubt they had switched out nav systems. This one had a transmitting chip in it. Guaranteed. You could buy them online for a few hundred bucks. If someone did an electronic sweep, chances were they wouldn't think twice about detecting something from it. And it was right there. A GPS unit that didn't even pretend to be something else. Hidden in plain sight.

Hatcher yanked the device off its mount and was about to throw it across the parking lot, but stopped. He got out of the car and scanned for nearby vehicles. It was late, and there weren't many. He settled on a small pickup, crossed the lot toward it. A few discreet glances, then he checked the bed. Nothing but a few ratty blankets and a plastic tarp. He was hoping for a cooler or wooden toolbox, but this would do. He stuffed the device into one of the blankets, bunched the cloth up tight against the sidewall and pulled the tarp over it. Then he wedged his fingers into the front pockets of his jeans and walked back to the car, his pace controlled but brisk.

All nav systems, even regular ones, had batteries. Otherwise the device would be useless unless the ignition was engaged, or if the car was dead. The batteries kept themselves charged off the car's electrical system. Ones designed with covert tracking devices that needed to transmit information would have extra need for battery power. This one should have plenty of juice. Hatcher figured it would give him at least an hour before anyone realized it had been removed. Maybe several.

He started the Cruiser and swung the car around, asking himself where he should go now that he knew no one was following. Not the most legitimate question, he realized, since he hadn't known he was being followed before, but an answer popped into his head nonetheless.

Pulling onto the main road, he headed back the way he'd come. He drove until he reached the Sand Dollar Inn.

The motor court had a single lamppost in the rear, throwing off barely enough light to see the cars, let alone door numbers. Hatcher rolled the car around the perimeter of the lot with his foot off the gas, letting the reflected glow of the headlights off the cars illuminate what it could. Room 9 was the fourth to the last room on the immediate right.

A black Audi rested in the space directly in front of the door, looking uncomfortable and out of place. Hatcher parked several doors down, glanced around casually as he got out of the car, and headed over.

The room had one wide window next to the door. A dim light rose from beneath the curtain and around the edges. He stood in front of the peephole and raised a closed hand. Stayed like that for several beats. Then he reached down and gently tried the latch. It moved but didn't engage. He thought for a few more seconds before raising his fist again and giving two short, hard raps with his knuckles.

He waited. The handle made a mechanical sound and the door moved a fraction of an inch. When it didn't open, he pressed his palm against it. There was some pneumatic resistance as it started to swung, requiring him to push harder.

The only light was from a small lamp in the corner. A sheer piece of red cloth was tossed over the shade, throwing a crimson hue over the room, the shadows it cast darkening the walls like bruises. Deborah was on the bed, settling back down, reclining against a cloth-covered headboard.

She raised a cigarette, wedged between the V of two fingers, and lit it. "Hello, Hatcher," she said, flicking the lighter closed and exhaling a stream of smoke toward the ceiling after the words. She hugged herself with one arm beneath her breasts, cupped the elbow of her other as she kept the cigarette near her mouth. "Nice to see you."

Again with the smoking. He supposed being immune to disease ensures you a spot on Big Tobacco's Christmas list. Hatcher dipped his head in a slight nod, but said nothing. He let go of the door, heard it shut behind him. He tried to stop his eyes from gliding down and back, drinking in everything from her hair to her feet, but couldn't.

She was wearing a black silk bra and matching thong. The bra barely covered the bottom half of her breasts, leaving the top half of each nipple exposed. Her thong was hardly wider than the narrow strip of well-manicured hair that terminated just above her groin, and sheer enough to let him count the strands beneath it. She was leaned back, shoulders propped against the pillows, with one leg stretched straight out, toes pointed, the other pulled up, knee cresting toward the ceiling.

"You might as well look," she said, blowing out another cloud of smoke, this time more to the side with a stretch of her lower lip. She removed the arm from across her ribs and held both hands out. Her stomach was lean and firm. "You're a man. I won't think less of you. Besides, it's not like I don't know you want to."

Her skin was alabaster. Smooth, flawless. He felt like a kid with his face stuck against the window of a candy store. He forced himself to lock onto her eyes.

She titled her head, the hint of a smirk playing across her lips, and shrugged. "Suit yourself."

Hatcher watched her for a long moment, saying nothing. She'd obviously been expecting him, which should have surprised him, but didn't.

"Go ahead and ask," she said.

"Did you kill Vivian? Or arrange for that freak I met the other day to do it?"

Her gaze cut through the ribbon of smoke drifting over from her cigarette. Her eyes were the color of an evening rain cloud.

"No," she said.

Completely inscrutable, Hatcher thought. No reaction, no tells, not even an unnatural quieting of the body. The question may as well have been about the weather. Carnates were impossible to read.

"Where's the boy?" he asked.

"He's safe."

"Let him go. It's me you want."

She arched an eyebrow, held it that way as she watched him. "Is it, now?"

"You know it is."

"What makes you so sure?"

"You wouldn't have gone to such lengths to involve me. I don't know what you're up to, but I know that much."

"So, you're offering a trade. Yourself for the boy. How very . . . cinematic."

Hatcher took a step toward the bed. He let his eye travel down her leg, settled on the perfect shape of her foot, on the bloodred toenails. It took some effort to look away.

"If you didn't need me, I can't imagine I'd still be alive."

"What if I said I'd let him go if you came over here and made love to me?" She ran a palm down over her breast, fingers splayed, kept sliding it down her stomach. "Hard, lustful love. Pornographic, desperate love. Tomorrow-doesn't-matter kind of love."

"I'd say you were lying."

The hand changed direction and went back to cupping her elbow. "Why are you here, Hatcher?"

"You know why. For the boy."

Deborah let out a short laugh through her nose. "You can say that all you want, but it won't make it true. Not completely, at least."

"Are you actually saying I don't know why I'm here?"

"I'm saying the real reason is because you're afraid. And I know what scares you."

"You mean, other than you?"

Deborah smiled, pointed a finger with her cigarette hand and poked the air with it. "Always the charmer. Yes, other than me."

"In that case, enlighten me, and we'll both know."

She took another long drag, closed her eyes, and slid down a bit, stretching her arms out to the sides.

"Tell me, when you walked up to this door, were you thinking of the boy? Or of her?"

The question made the skin behind his ears tingle. There was something about the way she said it, some suggestion in her tone, that indicated she was referring to Vivian, to Amy, to Susan, to all of them, and to none of them. The whiff of intimations in the subtext, the casual emphasis on the word "her." Almost like a challenge. Almost like a warning.

"You know, if you were to believe all that nonsense in the Bible, the Devil was an angel once. His most perfect one. The chosen of God. He had everything. Everything but the one thing he truly wanted. So God gave that to him, too."

"And what was that?"

Deborah didn't answer. She snubbed the cigarette out in an ashtray and swung one leg over the other in slow motion, pulling herself into a sitting position on the side of the bed. She stared up at him with that same smile on her lips, sliding one foot at a time into a pair of heels. Then she stood and turned toward the lamp. Her weight shifted from leg to leg as she pulled her dress off the shade, causing the bare curves of her ass to flex.

She pulled the dress over head and wiggled her body until she'd slithered completely into it.

"C'mon," she said, picking up a purse.

"Where are we going?"

She stopped directly in front of him, parts of her grazing him with each breath.

"You can't get the image of her body out of your head," she said, peering up into his eyes. "You want to confront the man who did it, you want to face him, so you can be who you are. So you can indulge your true nature. You want to stare into the abyss."

Her scent sent his head swimming. It was like inhaling a drug. He could feel his heart pounding against his breastbone, felt the erection he already had swell to an impossible bulge.

She pressed up onto her toes and kissed him gently on the lips. He didn't kiss back. But he didn't pull away, either.

"I'm going to give you what you want," she said.

"EXPLAIN TO ME WHY I'M NOT SUPPOSED TO THINK THIS IS A trap, again?"

Deborah gave her eyebrows a pump, cocking her head and dimpling a cheek. She was leaning against the side of her car. A twin turbo. At least, Hatcher assumed it was hers. Carnates had flexible ethics.

He shut the door to the Cruiser, leaned an arm over the roof of it as he studied the building.

"This is a church," he said. "Last time I was in a church with you, I can't exactly say a good time was had by all."

She pushed off the car and rolled her eyes. "You said yourself, Hatcher—if I wanted you dead, you'd be dead. Do you really think you're a hard man to kill? I could have put a bullet in your head back at the motel the moment you stepped into the room.

Even before that, I could have had you fatally wounded while resisting arrest by a man you've become well acquainted with."

Leveling her eyes at him, she added, "I could have even slipped off my underwear, broken down that willpower of yours, and snapped your neck while we made love."

Hatcher said nothing. It was easy to be lulled by their unearthly looks and forget how dangerous Carnates were. He had fought two of them before, armed with extension batons. They were incredibly fast and surprisingly strong and harder to hurt than a rhino. It was a beating he felt for days. And those two had probably taken it easy on him, since the fight had been all part of their charade at the time. They had wanted him alive.

Just like they did now.

The air in the church smelled vaguely of incense and wood polish. Hatcher followed her as she strode the aisle, the dim glow of candles lighting their way. The clack of her heels reverberated off the wood and marble.

She veered left at the altar and headed for a large door.

Hatcher descended the stairs behind her, thinking, *I must be insane.*

"Is this another toga party?"

Deborah didn't respond. The landing captured some light from an adjacent hallway. Deborah didn't pause at the bottom but headed straight for another door, this one to a storage room. Just enough light leaked in for Hatcher to make out supplies and shelving. A few boxes, a pair of mops, and two buckets atop a dusty floor. Deborah moved swiftly past all of it toward another door on the opposite end, this one much more imposing, an ancient looking piece of heavy wood bound by iron bands.

The door moved with a groan as she tugged on it. Hatcher heard the whisper of escaping air, felt a gust of it reach his face, damp and stale. He wasn't sure what he'd had in mind when he'd agreed to go with her, but it wasn't this.

"I think this is where I stop," he said.

"We both know you don't mean that."

Hatcher raised his hands a bit with a shrug. "Contrary to what you may have observed, there are limits to my stupidity."

"What if I told you your nephew was down there?"

"Then I would bet you a large sum of money you're lying and probably die moments later. A theoretically wealthy man."

"Fair enough. You're right, he's not down there. But what if I told you *he* was down there?"

The emphasis on *he* said it all. "Then it would seem rather obvious you're using me, that you want me to do something to him. And if it's something you want, I can't see how it could possibly be in my best interests. Or anyone's best interests, except maybe yours."

"I'll make a deal with you, Hatcher. Follow me, see what I have to show you, and I promise you, then you can leave. All I need is a few minutes."

"Oh, a promise. Well, in that case . . ."

"I'm serious, Hatcher. You'll want to see this. Like I said, if I wanted you dead, you'd already be dead."

Hatcher said nothing. This was crazy. Whatever she was up to, doing what she wanted couldn't be a good idea. But viable alternatives seemed to be in short supply.

Deborah curled her shoulders around and leaned back against the door. "While you're thinking it over, let me ask you something—what do you imagine eternal damnation is like?"

"Toying with me isn't likely to get me down there."

"No, it's a serious question. Do you imagine a lake of fire? Your soul burning ceaselessly? Never feeling anything but the most unimaginable pain and suffering for every moment that will ever be, forever and ever. Long past the point of forgetting you were ever alive?"

"Gee, when you put it that way, you make it sound so unappealing."

"I'm just curious."

"Why? What does it have to do with anything?"

"You'll find out if you follow me down these stairs."

She delivered the words with a complete poker face, eyes capturing the dim light just enough to give him a clear view. There was no outward indication of anything unspoken, but Hatcher knew she didn't complete the thought. There was an implicit follow up, hanging in the air, waiting to be plucked.

Unless, of course, you're scared.

Saying it would have been absurd, like a child's taunt. But not saying it, he had to admit, had the desired effect. It forced him to wonder.

"What about the boy?" he asked.

"We'll talk about that after."

"Is that another promise?"

"If it makes you feel better."

"If you don't keep your word, I am so not going to like you anymore."

A smile as genuine as he figured she was capable of flashed across her face, even reaching her eyes for an instant, only to disappear in such a way it left Hatcher wondering whether the reaction was out of humor or because he'd just agreed to do something incredibly stupid.

Before he could think much about it, she gave the door another hard tug. The crack widened to reveal a guttering glow. Two more tugs and there was enough space for them to pass.

The torchlight was a sudden change from the semidarkness of the storage room, and it took a moment for Hatcher's eyes to adjust. Deborah pulled the torch from an iron wall mount that looked practically medieval and held it in front of her, moving down a set of stone stairs. Hatcher went after her. The way was steep. There was a palpable sensation of descent with each step, a sinking feeling that Hatcher had to force himself to ignore. The walls got rougher, the air grew earthier, and the darkness seemed to push in against the reach of the flame, as if the utter blackness increased in density, compressing the light, shrinking visibility the deeper they journeyed.

The stairs ended in a small chamber. Deborah opened another door, this one much more compact than the first, and led Hatcher through a narrow tunnel. It was several minutes before Hatcher noticed a pinprick of yellow light flickering in the distance.

They emerged into a vast, cavernous space. It reminded Hatcher of a domed stadium, reduced by half, maybe a bit more. Hockey-sized. Torches rimmed the perimeter. Between two of them were a pair of large cages. One held a huge goat, the biggest Hatcher had ever seen. The other, an enormous bird. Some kind of vulture.

A stone chair loomed in the center, elevated on a platform that could have been carved from the rocky substrate when the space was excavated. Not a chair, Hatcher realized. A throne.

A man occupied it. Even before he was close enough to see

his face, Hatcher recognized the ridiculous orange jacket. The absurd orange hat.

Son of a bitch. Hatcher broke into a sprint. He'd more than halved the distance, some fifteen yards or so, when he saw the first Sedim. It dropped almost directly in front of him, forcing him to stumble a few steps, finally planting his feet as he came within inches of it. It peeled back its batlike lips and hissed.

Another dropped immediately behind it, then another. The sound of them hitting the chamber floor took on a percussive rhythm for several seconds. Thump, thump. Thump, thump, thump. Then it abruptly stopped.

Hatcher steadied himself. He eased one foot back, waited, eased another. There were too many of them to count, well over a dozen, at least.

He moved back one more step, only to have a head punch out of nowhere over his shoulder. His body snapped rigid. The growl was like a feline scream, almost deafening so close to his ear. He could smell it's breath. Hot, almost sweet. A hint of something putrid.

He swallowed and tried to remain still. Sedim didn't react well to sudden movements.

The thing hissed again, then slowly drew back. But not very far. He could still feel its low growls, rumbling across his ears.

Morris Sankey stood. He smiled broadly, hands buried in the pockets of his jacket. His lips revealed a mouth of small teeth.

Hatcher cocked his head slightly, spoke back over his shoulder. "I don't suppose you have any treats you could loan me?"

"No," Deborah said. "So I would suggest you don't try any more misguided heroics."

She walked past him, weaving around several Sedim on her way to the platform. When she reached it, she turned on her heel, a model on a runway.

She rolled a palm toward the man standing behind her. "I'll assume no introductions are necessary."

The man hopped down from the platform. The Sedim parted to make way for him. They seemed to drop their heads as he passed, submissive, almost reverent, in the way they held themselves.

Anger began to well up. The man drew close and Hatcher felt himself tense. Talons immediately dug into his arms, locking onto him. One Sedim on each side. The pain brought him up on his toes. They were so goddamn fast, reacted so goddamn quickly.

"Call me Morris," the man said. He withdrew his left hand from his pocket, then used it to pull his jacket while he tugged the other one. After a bit of effort, it slipped free.

Hatcher recoiled at the sight of it. It was huge. Two long appendages, uncurling, flexing, curling again, like some alien ungues. Segmented lengths of lean muscle, covered by a thick, flaky hide.

Morris held it up, tentacling the digits open and shut in front of Hatcher's face.

"I'd offer to shake, but . . ." He let the words trail off, shrugging.

A pause, then he leaned in, whispering. *"Now you get to see how lucky you are."*

Morris backed away, and movement caught Hatcher's eye. Torches, approaching through a tunnel to his left. All carried by women. Beautiful, radiant women.

Some of them looked vaguely familiar. He had no doubt these were the Carnates he'd encountered in New York. Many of them, anyway. Mixed in with others from who knew where. They marched into the chamber in two columns. Some of the faces stood out. One of the redheads he'd seen before, definitely. He could almost remember the name of the black gal, second from the front. She looked over at him as they entered and winked.

The shape of a larger figure among them started to emerge, its details obscured by the raised torches. Hatcher recognized him the moment he came into view. His enormous bulk slouched forward, prodded to move from behind, yanked from in front, wrapped in chains.

Sherman.

The Carnates flared out of their single-file lines, forming a huge circle. One of the Carnates walked Sherman into the center. The end of a thick chain tugged him from the waist and wrists, tensing across to where it coiled and wrapped around the woman's forearm. She twirled her arm free and let the chain drop, leaving him there.

Sherman took a breath. His bald head glistened in the torchlight. Hatcher could see the long row of stitches along his scalp.

His eyes swam in irritable circuits. His mouth was pulled down on one end, sneered a bit on the other. He looked cranky, wary, generally unhappy.

But mostly, Hatcher realized, he looked bored.

"When are you stupid bitches gonna let me out of this shit? I mean, fuckin' A. They're rubbin' me raw."

The big man glanced around, his expression shifting to one of increasing annoyance. He did a double-take when he noticed Hatcher.

"Him?" Sherman said, mouth widening. "That's why you brought me here? Hell, you didn't have to chain me up for that! I'd have begged for the chance!"

Morris bent his head slightly toward Hatcher. "Watch. You should enjoy this."

As if responding to some unspoken command, the Sedim lined up to form a path from Morris to the circle. Morris strode forward, slipping between two Carnates into the makeshift ring. The Sedim holding Hatcher dragged him closer, taking him almost to the edge.

Morris walked up to Sherman and stopped. Hatcher wondered if, were he to have gone without food long enough, Sherman would simply pick the guy up and eat him, the size difference being what it was.

Sherman looked the much slighter man up and down. "Who the fuck are you? Jesus, what the hell is with your hand? Was your mother an ostrich or something?"

Morris said nothing. One of the Carnates approached Sherman and unlocked the padlock securing the chains. The big man shrugged several times, wriggling his arms, before they finally rattled to the floor in a pile.

Deborah leaped onto the platform and walked her high heels to the edge overlooking the circle.

"You know the stakes."

Sherman rolled his eyes. "Yeah, yeah. You told me a bunch of times."

"The loser forfeits his life. And his soul."

"And all I gotta do is take him?" Sherman shook his head, his face barely able to contain his grin. "You gotta be kidding."

"Without your consent, the challenge has no value. Do we have your consent?"

"Anything to get you crazy broads off my back and get the hell outta here."

"Do we have your consent?"

A disturbing sensation crept down the back of Hatcher's scalp, tingled along his neck. He eyed Sherman, his swollen frame, hard mounds of muscle curving between every joint.

Don't do it.

"*Yes,*" Sherman said, snapping the word. In a lower voice, he added, "stupid bitch."

Don't do it, you gigantic idiot.

Deborah tilted her head with a shrug and dipped her chin sharply.

A smug, self-satisfied grin spread itself across Sherman's face. He raised his hands in front of him, palms out, like a wrestler.

"You know," he said. "I should feel bad about this. But there's just something about your face that pisses me off. So I think I'm gonna enjoy it. Can't say you will, though. Freak."

Sherman feinted, throwing his huge bulk forward, then drawing back. Morris flinched, but didn't move.

A hum filled the air, sounds of murmuring. At first Hatcher thought it was the Carnates, whispering among themselves. But they all were still, calmly watching the men in the makeshift ring. He heard a fragment of the sound right next to him, louder than the din, and realized it was the Sedim. They were making a noise in their throats, a harmony of deep, visceral growls, droning in unison as they watched the fight develop. The sound of dogs staring at a door, hearing something on the other side of it no one else could.

Anticipating something about to happen.

Hatcher tried gently to move an arm. The pain was instant. The talons dug in, the squeeze of a vise.

Then, it was over.

Sherman started to circle to his right a bit, then back to his left, then he pounced. He lunged toward the smaller man, ready to throw his enormous arms around him, only to be met in the face with the deformed Hand.

The Hand slapped down in an arc, the flat of it over Sherman's nose. The two long, tubular fingers spread wide, wedging Sherman's head between them, circling the side of Sherman's skull like ram horns, spiraling in a nautilus curl as if they were screwed into the man's ears.

Sherman grabbed at the arm, started to pull it away, only to stop. His body language abruptly changed. His hands drifted off Morris's arm and hovered unsteadily in the air.

A second later, maybe two, Sherman screamed.

It was a piercing, shrill sound. A vocalization of something incomprehensible. Sherman's hands shot to the sides of his head. He was grabbing at the phalanges on each side, trying meekly to tear them off, screaming that disturbing, inhuman scream the whole time.

Then his hands moved down to his throat. No sooner did they get there than his head ripped off his neck, leaving his fingers to claw at the torn flesh and muscle and bone, a fountain of blood pumping out. His heart beat three more times, judging by the number of gushes. Pump, pump, pump. Then Sherman's body collapsed to its knees and slammed forward to the floor.

Morris held the head up high and started to walk forward. He stepped over Sherman's body, the soles of his hiking shoes trampling through the spill of blood, and kept going. The Carnates moved aside, clearing his way. The Sedim's growls were louder now, reaching a crescendo, and they seemed to be following Morris's movements intently. Sherman's head was still wedged between the tentacled curl of his two fingers.

Hatcher suddenly felt himself being dragged again. The grip on each arm set his nerves on fire, forcing him up on his toes and making it impossible to resist.

They moved him in the same direction as Morris, following in his wake. The man stopped in front of a large section of wall. At first it seemed like a darkened tunnel, completely black. But two Carnates stepped up to it, holding out torches, and Hatcher saw the surface was reflective. Some sort of black stone, like onyx, polished completely smooth. So smooth Hatcher could see vivid reflections mirroring back.

Including the reflection of Sherman's head as Morris held it out toward the wall. Morris turned his clawed hand over and unfurled his longer tendril fingers open until Sherman's skull rolled level, pinched between two curled tips of those insectlike digits, facing its own reflection.

Facing its own reflection, and still very much alive.

The eyes were blinking, the mouth was moving. A silent scream, deafening to watch. Blood dripped from the base of Sherman's neck like crimson rain.

Morris stepped closer to the wall. He glanced over his shoulder, gesturing with his free hand, and Hatcher felt the squeeze on his arms again. Hatcher suddenly found himself bouncing on his toes and forced to scramble forward with the Sedim. They planted him next to Morris Sankey, still holding tight. He tested the grip, tried to pull free, but the pain stopped him dead.

Morris looked at Hatcher with a sober face, but his eyes twinkled and his lips couldn't resist a smile.

"I never dreamed it had so much power. That I had so much power. Watch."

Hatcher said nothing. His arms were growing numb, his shoulders searing in pain. Sherman's skull was a few feet away, suspended in midair, clearly visible in the reflection. Working its jaws. Trying to say something. Or maybe just still screaming.

Morris walked forward until Sherman's face was practically touching its reflection. After a brief pause, he took another step, stiffening his arm and pressing Sherman's face against the surface. The wall seemed to ripple, like a vertical plane of liquid. Hatcher noticed Morris's hand change color, turn a strange shade of green, as if it were glowing. Then it pressed into the reflection, taking the head with it.

"Look!"

Even though the wall didn't show any sign of changing, the mirrored surface seemed to have disappeared. Now the section resembled an asymmetrical panel of smoky, charcoal glass. Transparent, though still a bit reflective. Hatcher could see Morris's hand protruding through on the other side. Still glowing. Still holding Sherman's skull.

Hatcher could make out movement along the bottom, bright enough to see by, a luminescence, like water flowing over lights. No, not water. Molten rock. Burning bright and hot.

Something approached. Something on the other side.

A colossus of a figure, probably seven feet tall. It was cloaked in shadow, barely more than a silhouette. Hatcher could make out spired horns protruding from its head, a long face, the reversed legs of an animal.

"It appreciates early delivery," Morris said. "Not having to wait for a man like this to die years from now. He'll be pleased."

The thing strode across the molten floor, coming into view with its last step. Its face was like a hide stretched over a skull, two sunken eye sockets, rimmed in shadow, a pair of teardrop-shaped nasal passages instead of an actual nose, a mouth full of teeth that reminded Hatcher of some sort of deep-sea fish.

It took Sherman's head from Morris's hand, held it to the side, examining it. Hatcher could see Sherman's face. It was still animated, eyes bulging in horror, mouth and jaw flexing and wriggling in an extended scream.

Morris reached his other hand over and placed it behind Hatcher's head, cupping the curve of his skull above his neck. Hatcher squirmed, but the Sedim maintained their painful lock on his arms.

"In just the past few days, I've learned the beautiful, amazing thing about Hell. It's all about customization. That was the word he used, when he explained it to me. Customization."

Hatcher felt Morris start to press his head forward. He held his breath and strained until the burn in his arms was unbearable.

"You know, he told me all about you."

"Who?" Hatcher asked, gasping.

"Your brother. He said you more than most would appreciate its ability to inflict torment like few others could."

Hatcher felt himself being moved toward the wall. He continued to resist as much as he could, but the creatures were too strong, the agonizing pain in his arms too much to bear.

"Everybody's experience is unique. Everybody's eternity is their own. Same place, different worlds."

The wall was just a foot or so away now. The tinted-glass look of the surface became less and less opaque, more and more transparent the closer he got. He could see the thing on the other side with increasing clarity, seemed like he could almost touch it. Or it, him.

It reached out a hand, a large, taloned hand, not unlike the one Morris stuck through the wall. Hatcher thought it was going to reach for him, push through the wall the same way Morris did, only in reverse. Place those claws on his head and drag him through, straight into Hell.

But the hand didn't reach for Hatcher. It took hold of Morris's deformed hand, the claws of both interlocking, and as soon as it did, everything changed.

The world threw itself into sharp relief. The wall obstructed nothing, because there was no wall. There was only Hatcher, Hatcher plunging a knife into the sternum of a sixteen-year-old Taliban fighter on a perimeter watch, Hatcher hooking a car battery and telephone to the genitals of an Iraqi insurgent, Hatcher hammering tacks through the fingernails of a man identified as having been the one in a video of cutting the head off a kidnapped American contractor with a knife. Seamless transitions from one scene to the next, more like a vivid, three-dimensional dream than a movie, realer than real, realer than life, Hatcher both observing and participating, seeing and feeling, over and over, atrocities perpetrated, atrocities forgotten. Atrocities enjoyed.

Then the scenes began to repeat, same setting, same action, same sequence, only the subject of the treatment was different. The boy with the dagger plunged into his heart was now Amy, eyes wide with shock and betrayal; the electrocution was being performed on Susan, who screamed and pleaded for him to stop; the hammering through the fingernails was happening to Vivian, who cried and begged him to just tell her that he loved her, please, just once.

Hatcher doing it all, Hatcher watching it all, Hatcher experiencing it both ways at the same time.

It seemed to last forever, so many scenes of horror, so many third-world hellholes, so many blood-spattered floors, always the same, always different. Always torturing or killing someone. Always being tortured by it.

And yet, he could tell what he was seeing was only a glimpse of this world. His world. For him, of him, by him. A world where every shadow, every crevice, every moment harbored an unbridled nightmare, ready to pounce.

Then it was over. He felt himself snap back, like out of a daydream. He sucked in a breath, staring at his own see-through reflection coming off the shiny blackness of the wall, the burning eyes of a demon looking right back at him from the other side. His body felt drenched in sweat. He realized he was trembling.

Morris was no longer touching the thing, his claw-hand

sticking out there on the other side, empty. The demon drew back and turned, carrying Sherman's head. The head was still trying to scream, its face red and burned and blistering, its eyes scalded but wide and moving. Sherman somehow still quite conscious.

Slowly, Morris withdrew his arm, pulling it back out of the wall. It came out like it was oozing, small rings of disturbance echoing in tremors as it moved, waves radiating across a liquid surface. Finally, his deformed hand came through, and the wall instantly darkened. There was no hole where he'd inserted it, no blemish of any sort to indicate he'd put his arm through it. Just smooth, prehistoric blackness.

The images were scorched into Hatcher's mind. Sensations still pulsing through him, like aftershocks. Time had seemed not so much to stop but to disappear. As if he'd been adrift in an ocean, no sign of land in any direction, no breeze and no current. Surrounded by forever, lost in eternity. Nothing existed but the experiences, observed and performed at the same time, to be repeated over and over and over. No chance of relief. The brink of insanity, always to be chased, never to be crossed.

Morris let go of the back of his head. "How did you like it?"

Hatcher said nothing. He was still shaking. Tried to stop, couldn't.

"That's what you have to look forward to. You know how they explained it to me? It's like you have a lawn that goes on for miles and miles and miles, hundreds of square miles of nothing but green, like an entire continent. And a bird picks up a blade of grass from it and starts to fly around the world. By the time it gets about ten feet, that's your life. The time you're in Hell after that is that bird flying the rest of the way around the world with that blade of grass, then getting another and flying around the world at like fifteen miles an hour, then getting another piece of grass, and another, until it's flown every blade of grass there is, trillions of them. And then the bird just starts over, bringing all the blades back, because Hell for you never ends. Pretty neat, huh?"

Hatcher shut his eyes. He was losing control of his thoughts, his mind running wild. He had to clear it, had to focus on other things, things that would get him through this. There would be plenty of time for Hell later.

The boy. He was there for the boy. He was also there to kill this creepy little abomination, though that was starting to look a lot more difficult than he'd anticipated.

But the experience would not be pushed aside so easily. He could still feel himself there. In the past, but not the past. The future, but not the future. He could sense the flames of damnation, the pits of despair, even as he was immersed in other horrors. Like he was in multiple places at once. Torment in stereo.

Focus on the objective.

God, what a horrible feeling it was. Unbearable agony. Worse than any physical pain. The feeling that this was all he was, all he ever was, all he ever would be. An instrument of suffering. Inflicting it, experiencing it, watching it, projecting it, redirecting it, inflicting it on those close to him. Hating it, cursing it, fearing it. Enjoying it even as it terrified and agonized him and robbed him of all memories of joy. Every moment frozen, swollen with the knowledge that was all there would ever be.

Perpetual torture.

The boy. You're here for the boy.

All of it serving as proof, an unending verdict. His life had been a waste. Damnation wasn't the result of contact with some demon in the flesh. It was what he deserved. No more, no less.

Vivian died because of you. Don't let it happen to the boy. If you can save the boy, it won't be a waste.

He bit down on his tongue, used the pain to scramble his thoughts. He breathed once, twice, then wrapped himself around those thoughts and buried them. Straightening his back, he opened his eyes.

"You promised me you'd let me go," he said over his shoulder, practically yelling.

He heard movement to his rear, strained to see Carnates moving, clearing a pathway. Deborah strolled through them. She placed a hand on Hatcher's head, stroked the sweaty strands of hair to one side.

"And if I don't, does that mean you're not going to like me anymore?"

Hatcher said nothing. His jaw tightened until he felt something pop beneath his ear.

Deborah tipped her head back and let out a laugh. "You are so amusing, you know that?"

She glanced at one of the Sedim holding him, then the other. A look heavy with meaning. Hatcher felt his arms suddenly drop to his sides, a rush of cold through them. Blood began to surge into his hands. The numbness started to give way to pins and needles, then waves of pain. It took him a few tries before he could flex his fingers with any strength.

"I'm keeping my word, Hatcher. Now, before you leave, there's something we should discuss."

Hatcher studied her face, filled with self-loathing over how he couldn't muster the kind of anger toward her that he wanted to. She was simply too attractive, too beautiful. He didn't trust her in the least. But her looks, her scent, her *presence* were so damn disarming his fury just seemed to dissipate. In its place brewed a storm of disgust. With himself.

"Bartlett is not who you think he is," Deborah said.

Hatcher rubbed his arms. "Why doesn't that surprise me."

"Let me guess, he's told you that he wants to stop us from opening The Path."

"You're saying he doesn't?"

"I'm saying that's not the whole truth. He wants to have a say."

"I'm not sure I follow."

"He's been negotiating with us, Hatcher."

"Why?"

"Because like everyone, he has an agenda."

"Why should I believe you?"

"Why would I lie?"

"Because you want the tablet."

"Let me ask you something. What does it matter? What do you care if we open some silly portal to a place you don't believe in?"

Hatcher glanced over at the smooth black wall. "You've got a funny way of making me not believe in something."

"Oh, that. Sure, eternal damnation and all. But do you really believe there's an actual Hell? A place where devils with pitchforks and goatees walk around? I would think a worldly man like you would chalk it up as a creation of the mind."

"I don't know what I believe. I just know I don't believe you."

"Fine. Then what say we just make this a straight business proposition. You deliver the tablet, we won't touch the boy."

"What's the catch?"

"No catch."

"You didn't go through all the trouble of finding him only to hand him over to me."

Deborah hitched a shoulder, tilted her head. "Okay, we'll need a tiny bit of his blood. And his right hand. And an eye."

Hatcher stiffened.

"I'm kidding! You really need to lighten up."

"I'm not exactly feeling jovial."

"I promise you this, Hatcher. Get us that tablet, and the boy will be exactly where he was a few days ago, before you ever found his mother. Nobody will lay a hand on him."

"And in exchange for that, I help you end the world?"

"Don't be so melodramatic. The world won't end. It will just add a few demons to its population. The Path has been opened before. The world survived."

Hatcher let his gaze drift past her. Morris was standing a few feet back, admiring his deformed limb. Scores of beautiful women, insanely attractive women, stood in loose gaggles, occasionally whispering to each other but mostly silent. Watching.

Sedim lurked in the wings, coiled and ready to pounce. Others spidered up the walls, clinging and crawling like bats, peering down with impassive stares.

"Think about this, Hatcher. Every day, people are murdered, raped, brutalized. Wars are constantly being waged. People are blown up in cafes and bombed in their homes. And, as you're well aware, tortured, for reasons big and small. Do you really think a few demons could make things appreciably worse?"

Hatcher's eyes wandered up to the concave dome overhead, stared up at the images in the circular center, a ringed depiction of devils dancing through flames. He thought about Vivian, knowing that he'd failed her. Then he thought about Susan.

He dropped his eyes back to Deborah. "Where does he keep the goddamn thing?"

CHAPTER 18

HATCHER PULLED INTO THE PARKING LOT AND SHUT OFF THE headlights. He reached over to the passenger seat and picked up the piece of paper that had been tucked under one of the windshield wipers, read it one more time.

> *Across the street from the Sand Dollar. Same place we picked you up.*
> *I'll be waiting. Just me.*
>
> *Mr. E*

Same handwriting as the one he got in the bar, right before Sherman almost punched his ticket. Showing up was not the wisest move, he told himself. If this was some sort of trap, he decided he deserved whatever he got. Only an idiot would fall for the same thing twice.

Hatcher glanced around. It was late, and the lot was empty. A few minutes passed, and he started to wonder if maybe it was a little too late, that perhaps Edgar had given up and left. But then a pair of headlights flashed from the lot behind where he was. A car parked in shadows. Whoever was in it had been watching him the whole time.

Nothing else happened, no movement or signals, so Hatcher got out and walked toward it. The passenger door popped open as he drew near.

Edgar was sitting behind the wheel. He offered a grim smile that was more like a frown stretched sideways.

Hatcher got in and shut the door. "How did you know where I was?"

"I know they have things going on at that church."

"More like, under that church."

"Right. Anyway, after I managed to get away from the others I went looking. Your car was right there."

Hatcher nodded. "Mind telling me what the hell that dog-and-pony show with Bartlett was all about?"

"He was lying."

"Yeah, you tapped it out on my foot a dozen times. About what?"

"Pretty much everything. He has his own agenda."

"So I've been told. The question is, what's yours?"

Edgar's mouth collapsed into an ambiguous shape and he turned his head. Hatcher couldn't tell if it was a smirk on his lips. "I have my reasons for doing what I do. Let's just say I don't want him to succeed."

"And the Carnates? Do you want them to succeed?"

Stabbing a finger toward Hatcher, Edgar clucked his tongue and winked. "I want you to succeed."

"Is that right?"

"Yes." The finger he was pointing snapped off his thumb, made a loud pop against his palm. "Hey, before I forget."

Edgar's hand slipped beneath his vest, produced a long, folded knife. "Take this."

"Why?"

"One thing I've learned about the Carnates, they don't like knives."

Hatcher took it, opened the blade. "*Jesus*. How do they feel about swords?"

"Pretty cool, huh?" Edgard said, chuckling. "It's an Espada. Extra large. Seven-and-a-quarter-inch blade."

He had to admit, it was a serious piece of cutlery. Stainless-steel upturned blade that looked sharp enough to split a hair, aluminum frame, and a polished pistol grip handle, with a sub-hilt. Someone could definitely inflict some damage with a knife like this.

The blade glinted. He remembered holding another one, also glinting in the night, right before he used it to kill the boy.

"This is more your thing than mine."

Edgar waved him off. "Don't be stubborn. I've got plenty of blades."

Hatcher held the edge up to getter a better look. It looked sharp as hell. "And you think they're scared of knives?"

"They seem to get nervous whenever they see one," he said, shrugging. "And whenever they get mad at each other, they threaten a stab to the heart."

"Is that so?"

"What, you don't believe me?"

Hatcher unlocked the blade and folded it closed. "Frankly, I don't know who the hell to believe. Bartlett knew you were going to approach me? And didn't mind you painting him as the bad guy?"

"It was the only way I could figure out how to get to you. I didn't have time at the bar, and plus you'd have had no reason to listen to me. So I convinced him to let me try to gain your trust, find out what you were thinking."

"And he went along with that?"

"I was light on the details until after the fact. Better to ask forgiveness than permission. But it worked."

"What's he doing with that cave?"

"Stockpiling."

"I got that much. For what?"

"What do you think?"

"If he's planning on sweating out the end of the world, he'd need a bit more than that."

Edgar raised his head and looked straight at him. "Would he?"

The expression on Edgar's face told Hatcher he was missing something. He let his mind roll, let it tick through files of thoughts.

"The map," he said. "All those locations that were marked. Those are other caves. Other stockpiles."

Edgar leveled a finger. Hatcher was starting to find that annoying.

"Scores of them. Enough to fight a war."

"So, you're working both sides of this. Yet you still expect me to believe you don't have an agenda."

"Believe what you want. Do you want to stop them from opening the Path, or not?"

"What if I told you my only concern was getting Susan back her child?"

"I feel you, man. While we're on the subject, you should know I'm the one who convinced Bartlett we had no choice but to let the Carnates have him."

"Why the hell did you do that?"

"Because otherwise his bargaining position would have been too strong."

Hatcher studied Edgar's face, scanned his eyes. "How many Carnates have you slept with?"

"What?"

"How many? A dozen? Or are you just hooked on one?"

Edgar wrinkled his mouth, dropping his head and shaking it. "You think I've gone native, huh?"

"Yes."

"They have no effect on me."

"Bullshit. Spending time with them is like taking a drug. You'd have to be gay."

Edgar popped an eyebrow, slanted his head with a shrug. That look said it all.

"Oh. I get it. And they're cool with that?"

"Meh. I've played the pussy-whipped weenie. I went through the motions in bed with one of them a bunch of times. It was even sort of enjoyable. I can go both ways, if I absolutely have to. I'm a great actor. And hey, I've got the equipment and they've got the skills. But I'm not vulnerable to their charms. Why do you think Bartlett let me do it?"

Hatcher wondered how that conversation would have gone, whether Bartlett asked or whether Edgar just told.

"So, you think Bartlett can't be trusted, that he wants to open this Path thing himself."

"Yes."

"Okay, you don't want Bartlett to open it. How do you feel about *them* opening it?"

"How do *you* feel about it? I know about the deal they offered."

"And how do you know that?"

"They've mentioned it. They let their guards down sometimes."

Hatcher had a hard time imagining that. Carnates were nothing if not aware. Every word always seemed calculated, and the more you knew about what they were up to, the more calculated in hindsight each word appeared to be. Especially the ones that seemed off the cuff at the time they said them.

"Anyway," Edgar continued. "I just got off the phone with

Deborah. She said they want me to go get the boy. Bring him to them."

"Did they tell you where he is?"

"They didn't have to. I know where he is."

"Well, let's go get him. Put him somewhere safe."

Edgar shook his head. "We have to get that tablet. Destroy it. Without the boy, the Carnates will try to cut a deal with Bartlett, and he'll end up letting them do it."

"You're sure of that."

"Why the hell do you think he's been stocking weapons and supplies? He's planning for the end of the fucking world. He thinks it's his big chance to remake society."

Hatcher pictured Bartlett holing up, fighting in some posta-pocalyptic wasteland. It didn't make sense. The guy may have been whack, but he was a flag-waver. Then again, he could just be nuts.

More important, Hatcher decided he didn't care.

"It's not worth the kid's life."

"I know you think that. But it's not true. Stopping them from opening the Path is what matters."

"I'm not willing to sacrifice him. I won't do it."

"I don't doubt that," Edgar said, twisting in the driver's seat to face Hatcher more squarely. "If we could just figure out where he keeps the tablet, then maybe we could do both."

"You don't know?"

Edgar shook his head. "He's very secretive about it. I'm pretty sure he had it in a safe at the house, on Mulholland. But there's no way he left it there."

"A safe?"

"Yeah. Big one. Cemented into the floor."

A thought tugged Hatcher's attention, forcing him to look away. He chased it down in his mind, like a piece of paper being blown around a parking lot.

Safe. Floor. House. He did the chronology in his head.

"I think I know where he's keeping it."

"You do?"

"Yes."

"Can you get it?"

"Maybe."

"I won't even bother to ask you where, but if you can get a

hold of it, this could work out. There could be a window where, if we time it right, I'll have the boy, you'll have the tablet."

"You sure you can get the boy?"

"Like I said, they trust me."

"Maybe they do, but why should I?"

"You don't want the Carnates to open that thing any more than I do, that's why."

Hatcher peered out the windshield, thinking. Shadows of trees and buildings, bright points of light along the strip beyond. All of it, he knew, would look a lot different in the light of day. Palm trees and sunshine and women in bikini tops and cutoffs, the occasional seagull crying out as it glided high above.

He lost track of how long he sat there, but finally something prompted him to suck in a breath and turn back to face Edgar.

"Tell me how you see this going down," he said.

BY THE TIME HATCHER PARKED NEAR THE UTILITY SHACK, IT was almost dawn. He pulled the bag from the trunk, hefting it over the edge and tugging its thick strap over his shoulder, then he hiked the same trail he had before, crossed the same rocky flat to the cave.

A dim glow brightened the eastern horizon like a watermark, but the sky was still dark and the cave darker still. Hatcher followed the spot of his flashlight into the mouth, flashed it around the contents once inside. Same crates. Same gun cabinets. What he was looking for wouldn't be in any of the ones lined up to each side.

He walked the aisle toward the rear, stopped a few feet from the gun cabinet in the middle of the aisle, against the back wall. It was different than the rest, a bit larger. Facing a different direction. The only container in the space that wasn't stored in a uniform manner.

The bag made a heavy clanking sound as he set it on the floor.

The front of the gun safe had a five-prong wheel handle and a digital keypad. Hatcher gave the handle a try, just to be sure, then knelt down and opened the bag. The drill batteries were heavy.

There was definitely one advantage to living in a place like

L.A. Only a handful of cities would have twenty-four-hour home improvement centers.

He set out the drill and the bits on the concrete floor. The stuff wasn't cheap. Two bright portable lamps. A DeWalt thirty-six-volt hammer drill with two extra heavy-duty lithium ion batteries. Four tungsten-carbide drill bits. Entire pack set him back almost a grand. Or would have, if he didn't use the debit card Edgar gave him. It had a company name on it, Sunrise Security Services. Edgar said it was for expenses. Bartlett kept track—was quite the stickler, according to Edgar—but by the time the transaction showed up in the records, it wouldn't make a difference.

He turned on the lamps and placed them on top of other gun safes nearby, one on each side. They provided more than enough light to work in.

Expensive safes are designed to thwart crackers. They have steel-hard plate between the dial and the lock, and glass re-lockers that kick in if someone tries to penetrate the locking mechanism. But while good gun safes incorporate such devices, most aren't designed to make it impossible for anyone to crack, merely to make it too difficult for a thief to gain entry. Not without taking too much time, or making too much noise.

Hatcher wasn't quite as pressed for time as a burglar would be, and didn't care about the noise.

The drill's cubed batteries were dense and heavy. Hatcher slid one into the bottom of the handle and snapped it into place. He triggered the drill and listened to it whine. He fit one of the bits in and tightened the chuck.

The safe's weakness, if it had one, would be in the bolts. The average heavy-duty gun safe would have an interconnected set of bolts extending out from the door, pressing into sockets along each side, making the door impossible to open. But on most models, the bolts acted as simple rods that kept the door from opening when extended. They were not designed to resist pressure from the edges. And due to the scissor-extension mechanism that connected them to the handle, the retraction of one forced the retraction of all.

Figuring out where the bolts lined up was the hardest part. Without the designs or specs, it was simply a matter of guessing.

It took him almost fifteen minutes to drill the first hole. He used the line of the door as a guide, tried to drill just past the depth of the edge. The object was to insert a metal rod of a smaller diameter in the hole and push the bolt back. The first try seemed to have missed, since no matter how hard he pressed the rod into the hole, nothing moved.

He tried an inch lower, drilling another hole. Still no good, so he dropped another inch. It occurred to him the design might be more sophisticated, that the bolts may be connected by a cam mechanism, rather than a simple scissor pattern, and in that case couldn't be moved from the side. But he kept drilling. Third hole, and something felt different. He inserted the narrow metal rod and pushed. A heavy, sliding clunk sounded from within the door. Hatcher stepped to the front and tugged on the wheel handle. The door pulled open. A small interior ceiling light popped on.

The cabinet was empty.

Hatcher stared at it for a few seconds, his eyes eventually settling on the bottom. The floor of the cabinet was covered with felt. Hatcher crouched down and leaned in, running his hands over the surface, digging his fingers along the sides where the soft felt met the metal walls. He was able to find a spot that wasn't glued and ripped the felt back to reveal the steel cabinet floor.

In the middle was a small handle, set flat in a form-fitted groove. He got a finger under it, lifted it, then pulled up.

The panel was dense. Hatcher had to stand and get himself in a stable position to move it. He set it down on the cement floor behind him and leaned back into the safe to look.

Another empty space. A cut-out box shape formed in the cement beneath the safe. About three-by-three square. Solid-looking as could be. Nothing in it.

The phone in his pocket vibrated. He checked the screen. A text from the number Edgar had given him.

Got him. Let me know what to do. They'll be expecting me in 20 or 30.

Hatcher sat back onto the cement, hooking his arms over his knees and lowering his head. He stayed like that even though it hurt his tailbone, and even though it made his shoulder uncomfortable after holding the drill so long.

Something made him come back here. Something had made him sure.

He replayed the first time in his head. Relived each part, each segment he could recall. Walking up to the mouth, entering, checking the contents of one of the crates, walking the aisle, seeing the gun safes. Noticing one was out of place. Tripping on the bump of rebar.

Noticing the piece of glass.

Hatcher raised his head.

He stared at the gun safe for several beats, letting the thought take root.

Not just a shard of glass. A piece of mirror. Squared at the edge.

He pushed into a crouch and leaned back into the safe, peered down into the hole. An empty square. No question. There was even a convenient light directly above it, so you could see just how empty it was.

So clearly empty, you wouldn't have to actually check.

Hatcher reached his hand into the space. Another hand reached up from an angle to meet it. A perfect mirror image.

Son of a bitch.

The plate of mirror was tilted diagonally across the space, reflecting the other half and for anyone looking down creating the illusion of a complete square. But really, only half the space was visible. The other was just a reflection of it.

Hatcher pressed his fingers against the glass, tapped it, tried to slide it. It wouldn't budge, so he smashed it with one of the drill batteries.

Behind the mirror was a leather pouch. Hatcher reached in and pulled it out. Something solid and flat. He undid the tie on the pouch.

The tablet was dark and smooth. It was the same shape as the one he'd seen in the motel, but the engraving was sharper, more detailed.

Hatcher pulled out his phone. There was one bar of reception. He thumbed through the screens and called the number that had texted him.

"Did you get it?"

"Yes."

"Really?"

"You want me to send you a picture of it?"

"What are you going to do?"

Hatcher looked down at the tablet. "Destroy it?"

"In that case, I guess I'll go see the boy's mother. Don't fuck up, Hatcher."

The line clicked off and the phone went silent. Hatcher examined the tablet again, lifting it closer to his eyes and angling it toward one of the lamps. There were flecks of something embedded in it, possibly some type of metal.

His head snapped up. Something had moved, something near the entrance to the cave. There'd been a sound, like small rocks tumbling.

He put the tablet in the pouch and turned out the lamps. He grabbed the flashlight and the pouch, left everything else. Keeping the flashlight off, he moved toward the dim glow of morning.

The brightening sky was visible even before he reached the mouth. He paused at the incline, listening. Nothing. No more dislodged rocks cascading across anything. No noise at all.

He climbed out and stepped into the light. The brightness made him squint. He thought about walking to his car, then changed his mind. He reached into the pouch and removed the tablet. If he was going to destroy it, there was no sense in waiting. But then he thought of Edgar, how eager he'd sounded. That gave him pause.

"Hold it!"

Hatcher looked over his shoulder. A guy with an M4 was positioned on the rocky slope over the mouth, crouched and aiming. Out of the corner of his eye he caught another off to the side, wedged in a prone position between two boulders.

"Don't fire! Repeat—do not fire!"

Bartlett stepped out from around a curve in the hillside. He was forcing a smile, but his eyes looked nervous. He held his palms out like he was the one with rifles pointed at him.

"Hatcher, nobody needs to get hurt. Just put it down."

Hatcher stared at the man, then glanced down at the tablet.

"What?" he said, hefting it into the air, acting as if he might drop it. "This?"

Bartlett's arms shot out stiff and the whites of his eyes jumped into view.

"Please, you don't understand what you're holding."

"I don't, huh? And why would that be? Maybe because you lied to me about it? About your plans for it?"

"Okay, yes, perhaps I was less than forthcoming."

"Ya think?"

"Just put it down. I'll explain everything."

"I don't think so. I've had more than my share of explanations from you."

"You're upset. I understand. But face facts. You have two weapons trained on you. There's nowhere to go. I promise we'll let you walk off if you just put it down."

Hatcher looked at the tablet again, then hoisted it high above his head. He expected Bartlett to flinch, but instead the man merely pressed his lips tight and shook his head slightly.

"You won't let your men shoot me because I might drop this. I'm thinking that's just one of several reasons I shouldn't put it down."

"Hatcher, that tablet is the key to everything. It's the only bargaining power we have. If you break the seal, it's useless."

"Tell your men to toss their weapons."

"I can't do that, Hatcher."

Hatcher pressed the tablet slightly higher. "Do it, or they won't have a reason not to shoot me anymore."

"If you'd just let me just explain—"

"You can explain after they put the weapons down and march into the cave."

"Then you promise you'll listen?"

"I'll let you talk till you're blue in the face."

Bartlett eyed him for a few seconds, one eyebrow slightly bent. Then he glanced at his men and gave a stern nod. They each placed their rifles on the ground and climbed down to the front of the cave. They paused to give Bartlett another look, then they shuffled inside, stopping a few feet past the entrance.

"Tell them to keep walking until they can't anymore."

Bartlett glanced past Hatcher into the cave. "You heard him. Do it."

Hatcher kept an eye on Bartlett, waiting until he couldn't hear their scraping footsteps as they descended.

"Now," Bartlett said. "Let's talk."

"Sure. But one thing first."

Hatcher gripped the tablet with both hands, raised up on the balls of his feet, and slammed it down against the rocky ground in front of him.

A piece of the tablet broke off, and a crack ripped down its middle.

Bartlett stood, dumbstruck. He gazed mutely at the tablet, blinked as his eyes followed the crack up and down. He swallowed.

"Now, you can talk all you want."

The general said nothing. He licked his lips a few times as he stared. His chest noticeably heaved with each breath.

"It's over, General."

Bartlett's eyes drifted up to meet Hatcher's. There was none of the anger or hatred Hatcher expected. The man's gaze conveyed nothing but what seemed like a deep sense of alarm.

"No."

"Yes."

"No, you don't understand. It isn't over." Bartlett's eyes sunk back to the ground. "It's just beginning."

Hatcher watched the man watch the tablet. The general looked like someone trying to will a dead thing back to life. "What do you mean?"

"Do you have any idea what I went through to find that? That tablet was the only thing stopping them."

"Stopping who? The Carnates?"

Bartlett spoke as if he hadn't heard what Hatcher had asked. "Now they'll be able to open it. God only knows what will be unleashed."

"If you're really so upset about it, why were you negotiating to let them have the tablet?"

"I . . . had a plan."

"What kind of plan."

"It doesn't matter." He mopped a palm down his face. "Nothing matters now."

The man didn't so much sit as he crumpled slowly to the ground. He lowered his head between his knees. Hatcher wondered for a moment if he might be weeping, but then he spoke.

"Go, Hatcher. Just leave. Whatever happens to you now, know it's all your doing."

Hatcher stood there for several breaths, then started in the direction of his car. After a few yards he heard Bartlett say something.

"What was that?" Hatcher asked, turning to face him.

The general kept staring through his legs at the ground. "She warned me. About you. I was foolish not to listen."

"Who? Vivian?"

But Bartlett didn't answer. He just peered down into the earth as if he had X-ray vision, and he couldn't tear his eyes away from all the things going on beneath the surface.

CHAPTER 19

EDGAR WASN'T ANSWERING HIS PHONE.

Hatcher sped back to town, almost running off the road more than once. He must have tried Edgar two dozen times, starting before he even reached the car. He texted him that it was done, pulled over, and texted him again around the halfway point.

Whether or not Bartlett was telling the truth, Hatcher decided he didn't care. As long as the Carnates didn't have the boy, it wasn't his problem. Bartlett struck him as one of those people who convinced himself of things, someone who believed his own bullshit. They were the best liars, because they didn't always realize they were lying.

But without Edgar answering the phone, he couldn't be sure about the boy. That bothered him.

He tried calling Susan. No answer there, either.

The only thing he could think to do was head to where she was.

It was mid-morning when he pulled up to the curb. He didn't see her car anywhere on the street, but it could have been parked in the back. He headed straight for the front door and knocked. No answer.

He tried the knob. Locked.

Standing on the stoop, he considered going around to the rear, trying the patio door. But what was the point? If she were home, she'd answer. Not having any idea of where else to go didn't make her more likely to be there. Still, he was reluctant to just leave.

A car pulled up to the curb behind his and a heavyset woman with red hair got out. She offered a wary smile and headed toward the town house a couple of doors down. The one where Isaac had been snatched.

"Excuse me," Hatcher said, stepping to within earshot as she flipped through a set of keys. He stopped at a safe distance so as not spook her. "Have you seen Susan?"

"Susan?"

Hatcher tugged a thumb over his shoulder. "The woman who lives there."

"No. I mean, not today."

He thanked her and took a step toward the car before turning back.

"I was here the other day when it happened. How's your roommate?"

"I'm sorry?"

"The woman who was injured. Is she okay?"

Her eyes gazed blankly back at him. "I don't understand. Who was injured?"

"Don't you have a roommate? Or maybe a relative staying with you? Someone who was hurt?"

"I live here by myself. The other day, you say? I wasn't even here. I've been out of town."

Hatcher felt something cold settle in his stomach. "Was someone watching your place?"

"I don't really feel comfortable answering these questions. Who are you?"

"My name's Jake. I'm sorry, I'm not trying to scare you. I just need to find the woman who lives there. When I was here the other day, I thought someone was injured in your unit. An ambulance came."

"Couldn't be mine. Nobody's been here."

With a look that indicated she felt vulnerable, she slipped inside and shut the door.

Hatcher stared at his shoes, not liking where his thoughts were going. He got back in the car and drove.

What did Susan say? She had a bag at the train station, ready to go.

Hatcher pulled out his cell phone, tried Edgar again. Nothing. He drove on autopilot, thinking. He thumbed a call to information, managed to find a number for the NYPD. He didn't have her card, and didn't have her number in this phone, so he had to go through several connections.

He almost sagged in relief when she picked up.

"Amy," he said.

"Hatcher? Where the hell have you been? I've been trying to reach you. You never called back."

"I know. I'm sorry."

"I tried to track you down. I called the number you'd used last time over and over."

"I changed phones. Look, Amy. I need you to check something for me. It's about Susan."

"Hatcher, are you even listening? I've been trying to reach you, and frantic probably isn't too strong a word."

"Oh, right. Sorry. What is it?"

"Remember when I said I found your nephew's birth certificate in Susan's file?"

"Yes?"

"That struck me as strange. I mean, why? Why would someone put it there?"

Hatcher said nothing.

"So I checked, and it turns out a copy of it came in the mail, referencing Susan's file. Technically, she's still wanted on a material witness warrant."

"Who sent it?"

"I don't know, but that's not the point."

"Okay."

"That bugged me enough that I dug a little more. I checked with vital records out there, and it—"

"The birth certificate was fake?"

"No, it was real. But here's the thing—it wasn't the only record they had. There was also a death certificate."

"What?"

"A death certificate. Hatcher, Isaac Warren died shortly after he was born."

HATCHER DROVE BACK TO VENICE BEACH. HE PARKED A FEW blocks away and walked to the Liar's Den. He had nowhere else to go.

It was almost noon, so the place was locked. But Denny unlocked it after about five minutes' worth of pounding on the door. He was winded.

"Jesus, man. Some bosses would get pissed."

"I need a favor, Den."

Denny pulled his head back a bit and pinched his lips together. "You coming back to work?"

"Not yet. I just need to use your computer."

"You're killing me, man," Denny said, shaking his head and looking down. For a moment, Hatcher thought he was going to get some excuse about it not being a good time or it not working, but then Denny stepped out of the way and let him in.

Hatcher followed him through the bar toward the back.

"I really wish you could work tonight. I'm shorthanded."

"Sorry, Den. I would if I could."

Denny mumbled something over his shoulder as they entered his office. He pointed toward a monitor and keyboard on a desk.

"That computer I gave you not working?"

Hatcher hesitated as he circled the desk. "I can't go back to my place right now."

"Doesn't your cell phone have internet?"

"No," Hatcher said, realizing he hadn't even considered that. "Not mine."

Denny shrugged. "Who's that guy been looking for you, anyway? He came by again."

"I don't know. I just don't have time to deal with it right now."

The screen lit up when Hatcher touched the mouse. He clicked on the browser icon and waited.

"Well, I really wish you'd come back to work. That other guy quit, bitched about not getting any days off. And Lori bugged out right after you."

Hatcher wished Denny would leave him be, but it was bad enough showing up like this. He didn't need to antagonize the guy. There weren't many other people he could turn to.

He pulled up Google and typed in a search for the Church of the Ascension. Several came up, so he narrowed it to Los Angeles. He found the link, clicked on it.

There it was, the church he'd been taken to. He read through the history. Not much. He did another search, this time adding the words "underground" and "tunnel."

Several conspiracy websites came up. They seemed to all be talking about lizard people and underground cities. One article talked about a vast subterranean tunnel system and said the only known remaining entrance was beneath the church.

"Is this going to take a long time?" Denny asked.

"I'm not sure."

"Hey, when you're done, you want to watch the latest Mark Specter video? I just got it."

"Next time. I promise."

The portly man sighed. He stayed quiet for a while as Hatcher read but eventually asked another question.

Hatcher glanced up from the screen belatedly. "Sorry, what was that?"

"I said, did you know Lori was just going to up and leave?"

"No." Hatcher lowered his eyes again, scrolled down the screen. "Why?"

"Because she stopped showing up right after you checked out on me. Thought maybe you two snuck off together."

It took a few seconds for the words to reach him as he scanned more text about underground Los Angeles.

"Sorry, what did you say?"

"Man, you must really be out of it. I said, she disappeared right after you checked out on me."

Hatcher said nothing. He let his gaze drift off Denny and float out to the middle of the room.

"I always thought you had a thing for her," Denny added. "Caught you checking her out more than once. And I don't think I ever caught you doing that to anyone else."

Lori. Blonde Lori. The one who reminded him so much of Vivian.

"Can't says I blame you, man," Denny continued, "she was hot. A little trashy, but hot. That's what hurts, since she was good for business. You know, one guy told me he could've sworn she used to be a call girl. Some fancy escort service. Thought she'd done some porn, too."

"When did she disappear?"

"I don't know, a day or two after you did. Like I said, I was wondering if there was some connection. You know, maybe you and her . . ."

Hatcher sank back in the chair. Lori missing. Vivian dead.

He forced himself to picture Vivian—what was left of her—on the hotel room bed. Body parts drenched in blood. Severed head propped on a pillow. Blonde hair, stringy with blood, draped over her face.

Lori missing. Vivian dead.

You live in a world of illusions, Hatcher.

Lori missing. Vivian dead. Or . . .

If you'd only open your eyes.

Vivian missing. Lori dead.

The body and right arm of a whore.

"What's wrong with you?" Denny said. "You look like you just saw a ghost or something."

Hatcher pushed himself off the chair and headed out of the office.

"Not yet," he said.

DETECTIVE WRIGHT ANSWERED ON THE THIRD RING.

"Hello, Amy."

"Hatcher. I'm sorry I had to drop such a bomb on you earlier."

Hatcher shut the door to the rental car and slipped the key into the ignition. "Not your fault. But I could use some help."

"What do you need?"

"There was a murder at the Royal Plaza hotel in Santa Monica a few days ago. Mutilation. Very bloody."

"Okay."

"I need to know if they've IDed the victim. I think it may have been a girl named Lori. Worked with me in Venice Beach at a place called the Liar's Den."

Amy told him she'd have to make a few calls and that she'd call him back. Hatcher started the car and drove. He hated using Amy this way. She didn't know about Vivian and would almost certainly recognize the name the moment she heard it. But he didn't want to explain any of that. He was going to have to take his chances.

He was barely a few blocks from where he started when he slammed his hand against the steering wheel and cursed.

He pulled into a lot and shifted the car into park. He laid his head back and closed his eyes.

What did he know? The Carnates were attempting . . . something. To open a portal to Hell? Maybe. That's what Bartlett would say. But could he believe him? Even if he wasn't lying, did he have any clue what he was talking about?

His nephew apparently died shortly after birth. So why send him on a snipe hunt for the boy? And why would Susan lie?

Susan. How the heck did she get involved?

And was Vivian still alive? Why would they want him to think she was dead? Was she a part of it? Did Edgar know?

Edgar, that was one fucker he wanted to have another talk with. What was that lying son of a bitch up to? The questions were causing his head to swim, and not very well, his thoughts sloshing in rough waters.

Frustration started welling up, turning to anger. Most of it was directed at himself. How could he have let so many people deceive him? Reading people was his best skill. Maybe his only skill.

But he knew the answer, and it made his face flush red.

Vivian was his girlfriend, and she was often moody. Couple that with the fact she always accused him of trying to interrogate her, he never really questioned her veracity. Susan . . . that was a tougher one. He trusted her, but the big thing was guilt. He had led them to her, or so he thought. His own shame made him blind to any signs.

Bartlett. He thought hard about Bartlett and realized Bartlett had been careful to let others explain things. Calvin took the lead in the briefing they gave him. Other questions were handled by Edgar. Bartlett was cautious. Calvin probably had no idea what was really going on.

That left Edgar. Hatcher tried to replay some of their conversations, tried to view them through the lens of what he now knew. He pictured him in the car, the last time they'd met.

I'm a great actor.

Hatcher slammed the side of his fist against the dash. A motivated person could beat an interrogation, if they approached it as a role. Remove the anxieties that are coupled with telling lies—the feeling of shame, the worry over getting caught, the guilt over not being honest—and a good actor could easily fool even the most skilled interrogator. As long as he knew his lines.

Another fist against the dashboard. God, he'd been stupid.

Now what? He stared into the center of the steering wheel

for several minutes, then put the car in gear and pulled onto the road. In the direction of the Church of the Ascension.

His phone chimed out just before he got there. The number on the screen was familiar.

"Amy. Tell me you got something."

"Still no ID. I talked to the detective in charge, pretended I was working a missing person's case. She's a Jane Doe. They managed to keep the details out of the papers. It's just showing up as a woman murdered in a hotel room. The hotel certainly doesn't want anyone to know how gruesome it was."

"Do they have any lead on who she was?"

"I don't think so. I probed a bit. They're cross-checking missing persons reports."

Hatcher stirred the information into his thoughts, watched them swirl in his mind's eye.

"Whose name was the room under?"

"That's the interesting thing. There's no record. Somebody on the staff confessed to taking cash to keep it off the system. They treated it under their celebrity protocol, only they never required an actual ID or credit card. It was listed to a Zelda Zonk. The police actually tried to track the name down and couldn't find anyone. Then someone pointed out it was the name Marilyn Monroe used to travel under."

"I guess someone thought that was funny."

"They also mentioned they're looking for you."

"Swell."

"Don't worry, they don't know your name. And it's only for questioning. All they have is a description. Muscular guy with short hair and a frown."

"I'll try to smile."

"Hatcher, I know it's a waste of breath, but don't go off trying to do everything by yourself."

"You think I should head down to the nearest station, tell them everything? If I don't even believe most of it, how could I possibly convince the police?"

She sighed. *"At least be careful then."*

Hatcher told her he would and started to hang up, then thought of something.

"Amy, one more thing. You said Susan had changed her name when she moved to New York."

"*Yes.*"

"Why?" Even as he asked the question, he knew the answer. Dreaded hearing the confirmation.

"*It was a stage name. She was an actress. Broadway. Had a degree in theater. According to some of the statements, she had a promising future, but developed a drug problem.*"

"Stage name," Hatcher said, mumbling the words.

"*Yes, Susan Jordan. Cleaned herself up, never tried again. Became Susan Warren when she got married. Why?*"

"Nothing," he said, thinking, that was one woman who sure as hell got her tuition's worth.

CHAPTER 20

THE LARGE DOUBLE DOORS TO THE CHURCH OF THE ASCEN-
sion were unlocked. Hatcher stepped inside and walked up the
aisle toward the altar. A priest was lighting candles. He turned
at the sound of Hatcher's footsteps.

"May I help you?"

"Just passing through," Hatcher said.

"I'm sorry?"

Hatcher passed by him, his body angled toward the stairwell.
"Heading downstairs, Padre."

The priest stepped back, a hand on the cross hanging from
his neck, over his shirt.

"I'm not going to hurt you. I just need to head down."

"I don't understand. No one's there. Are you—we have very
little of value. Our collections are deposited immediately."

"I'm not here to rob you. I'm here for the tunnel."

The priest rolled his eyes, let out the breath he'd been holding. "There is no tunnel, son. That's just a local legend."

Hatcher pulled open the door to the stairwell. "You don't
mind if I check it out myself, do you, Father?"

The stairway was dark. Hatcher bounded down them two
and three at a time. He heard the priest following, huffing further objections. When he reached the bottom, he immediately
headed for the storage closet. The knob wouldn't turn.

Behind him, the priest came off the last step breathing audibly. "Please, I don't want to have to call the police. You're not
the first person to come here looking for some tunnel. There's
nothing down here."

"Humor me, Father. Would you mind opening this?"

"I must insist you leave."

"I'm not going anywhere. If you don't unlock this, I'll have to kick it in."

"Okay, this is unacceptable. I'm calling them."

"If there's nothing behind this door, why won't you open it?"

"Because you cannot come into a house of God and act this way. Do you think a man of the cloth should just let himself be ordered around by anyone who wanders in off the street?"

"Please, pretty please, with a cherry on top. Just open it. If I'm wrong, I'll go away. Peacefully."

The priest stared at him with shaky eyes, the set of his jaw giving him a look that was half indignant, half frightened. He stayed that way for a few breaths, then his body seemed to loosen, and he lowered his head, giving it a shake.

"I swear," he said, removing a set of keys from his pocket and stepping forward. "I must convince the diocese to sue all those websites. Lizard people, underground societies. People will believe anything."

The door swung out. The priest moved with it.

"There. You see? It's just a storage room."

Hatcher said nothing. He brushed past the priest and headed straight to the back. Some shelving had been moved to block the large back door. Hatcher slid it out of the way.

"Hey! You promised! I'm not kidding! I will call the police!"

"Good," Hatcher said. "Send them down after me."

"You're wasting your time. That door doesn't lead anywhere."

"Is that so?"

Hatcher pressed the thumb latch and tugged. The large door only moved a few inches at a time. He put all his weight into it, finally getting it open.

"I tried to tell you."

On the other side of the door was a wall of rock. Stones, packed tightly, wedged from floor to ceiling. He reached a hand out and touched one, pushed on it, then pulled. It wouldn't budge.

"I'm told it used to lead to a subbasement of some sort. It was filled in long before I got here."

Hatcher pushed and pulled on random stones. None of them moved.

"Now," the priest said, "will you please leave?"

"Just tell me something, Father. Is there another way down there?"

"No. Listen to me—this is all just legend. Stories."

Hatcher let his eyes run over the blockade of stones. The silence yawned. He heard the priest shuffle his feet, sensed him about to say something. Hatcher held up a hand and turned to go.

As he stepped out of the storage room, he turned back. "What legend?"

"Excuse me?"

"You said it was all legend. What legend?"

"The lizard people. Isn't that why you're here?"

"But what, exactly, is that legend?"

"Some old story about how a race of lizard people was found living beneath Los Angeles. Someone had even mapped out an entire underground city. The mayor had gone so far as to hire some 'expert' to dig to find them. This was many decades ago."

"But what does that have to do with this building?"

The priest let out a sigh that sounded like air escaping a tire. "Someone got it in their head that one of the entrances to the tunnels was beneath the church. Don't ask me how."

"That's it?"

"Yes."

"You hesitated there, Padre."

"It's silly."

"I like silly. Same way I like being humored."

"Local residents have told me stories, things they said they heard as kids, about how another type of church was built right below this one. A place where the lizard people would conjure the Devil."

"Was there a point to any of it? In the stories, I mean?"

"One parishioner told me his grandmother used to warn him that the lizard people were controlled by witches, and if he wasn't good, they would sneak into his bedroom at night and carry him down so they could offer him to Satan. Through a doorway to Hell."

"Again, I'm sensing there's something else. Something maybe you left out."

The priest stared at his shoes, gave his head an ironic little shake. "He said something about a sign, that she'd said they were looking for a sign."

"What kind of a sign?"

"If I tell you, will you really leave? No more questions, no more anything?"

Hatcher held up two fingers. "Scout's honor."

"The arrival of a person. Someone he called the Devil's Right-Hand Man."

Hatcher eyed the priest for a few more moments, then gave a curt nod and headed up the stairs, leaving the man with an unamused look on his face. He took the steps two at a time, thinking about the Devil's Right-Hand Man, and how he knew someone who seemed to meet that description perfectly.

SINCE HE HAD NO WAY OF KNOWING WHETHER THE PRIEST called the police, Hatcher wasted no time driving away, vaguely heading back toward Venice.

His head felt like somebody had scrambled his thoughts. Nothing made sense, and trying to get a handle on what was happening was causing his temples to thump.

Had the Carnates really gone through such an elaborate ruse just to get him to break the tablet? Could Bartlett have been right? Did he just let himself play into their hands?

But no. There had to be a more efficient way to get at the tablet than that. Hell, if Edgar was working with them, he could have destroyed it. Or they could have hired someone. It wasn't like he was the only one in the world smart enough to find it. He was missing something. Probably a lot of somethings.

Why did they kill Lori? And where was Vivian? Did they take her? Was she still alive?

He called Amy, but she didn't answer. A few seconds after he left a message, he got a text from her saying she was conducting an interview and would call him later.

His options were limited. He needed to do some research, maybe get on the internet again. He could swing back by the bar, but Denny would probably give him a hard time. At the very least, he'd pressure him into watching another Mark Specter show, like he'd promised. Obviously, he didn't have the time to sit around and watch some guy create a bunch of—

Illusions.

The word seemed to echo in his head, repeating over and over. No, he thought. No, no, no. No way.

He stepped on the gas and sped toward the Liar's Den.

The door wasn't locked. Some guy he didn't recognize was behind the bar. Hatcher ignored him and headed back toward Denny's office.

"Oh, hey," Denny said, looking up from his desk. "Need the computer again?"

"Maybe in a minute. Remember that video you made me wa—that you, uh, showed me a month or so ago?"

"The last Mark Specter one?"

Hatcher nodded. "There was a particular trick he did, something where he pulled a watch from a store window."

"Oh, yeah," Denny said, his eyes brightening. "That one. What about it?"

"Can I see it?"

"You mean now? You wanna watch a Mark Specter DVD?"

"Just that one trick."

Denny's expression sagged a bit, but the idea of watching even a few minutes of a Specter video with someone seemed to counter the disappointment well enough, and he pushed himself out of the chair and poked through a shelf haphazardly cluttered with books and papers and magazines and DVDs. He sorted through a few piles until he settled on one in particular. He held up a case. It had a picture of a shirtless guy with long blond hair wearing an ankle-length black duster over jeans and biker boots, head dipped slightly as he stared at the camera. There was a burst of flame behind him, and the effect was to make it look like he was walking out of it. The word *Specter* was writ large across the top, beneath it were the words *Extreme Magic.*

Denny popped the disc into the drive of his PC. Hatcher circled around the desk and leaned against a filing cabinet, looking over Denny's shoulder.

The disc menu had the show broken down into sections, titles under thumbnail pictures. Denny quickly found the one he was looking for and clicked on it. The drive engaged and whirred and a video image of an urban street at night filled the screen. A bluesy bass rhythm shuffled in the background.

Specter—Hatcher seriously doubted that was his real

name—walked into the frame from behind the camera, wearing the same duster but this time with a white shirt under it and a straw cowboy hat on his head. He kept going a few yards, then looked over his shoulder at the screen and said something about having a little fun.

A pair of young couples, two guys and two gals, came into view heading toward him, talking among themselves and laughing. Specter gave one more glance over his shoulder, winking, and veered into their path.

After asking what time it was and having one of the men glance at his watch, Specter gave a bit of patter about time and space and the mysterious ways matter can behave. He gestured for the people to follow and led them across the sidewalk toward a storefront one building further down the street. The camera caught up and zoomed in on a jewelry store display. Specter had them all gather around the shop window and gave some spiel about glass being liquid and always in motion and how with enough focused energy you can penetrate it. Then he placed his fist against the glass and pressed it through.

There it is, Hatcher thought. *Son of a bitch.*

The sleeve of his duster bunched up as his arm slid out the other side. He pushed as far as he could, to at least halfway up his upper arm, and reached for a watch. The people gasped and made noises. He held the watch in his hand, letting the camera zoom in some more, before pulling his arm out in one swift motion. He knocked on the glass with his fist, showing it to be solid, and invited the others to check it. Then he handed the guy who'd told him what time it was his watch back. The guy looked into the camera, then back at the watch, and absently muttered something that was bleeped out.

"Neat trick, huh?" Denny said.

Hatcher stared at the screen, or more accurately, stared at the window in the video, until the scene ended.

"Play that again."

Denny shrugged, then gave the mouse another click. Hatcher watched the scene unfold, paying particular attention to the glass. It was the same illusion. No doubt. Only the one the Carnates had performed had another twist.

"Tell me something, Denny. Has this guy ever, like, taken off someone's head?"

"Huh?"

"As a trick. Has he ever removed someone's head?"

"Uh, I don't know," Denny said. He drummed his fingers on the desk and turned back to his computer. "Let's find out."

A Google search didn't pull up anything like that with Specter. But it did find an illusion called *decapitation*. It involved a hollow table, guy in a clown suit, and a space for him to lean his head back. The magician would hold up a clown's head for the audience, while the clown's body remained on the table, his real head tucked beneath the surface through an opening. Sometimes, the clown's head would move its mouth or eyes or both. Sometimes it would even speak.

"That's it," Hatcher said. "Or something like it."

"Looks neat. Is this some trick you saw?"

Hatcher scraped his palm down his face. "You could say that. Maybe."

Denny said something about loving to see it himself, but Hatcher ignored him. He leaned in over Denny's shoulder toward the screen, directing the man's attention back to the PC.

"Search for General William Bartlett," he said. Realizing how bossy that sounded, he added, "Please."

"Who's that?" Denny said, typing in the name. He had Hatcher check the spelling and then hit the enter key.

"Somebody I met recently. Maybe."

A list of search results popped onto the screen. "What are you looking for?"

Hatcher glanced at the entries. "A picture."

Denny clicked on "images" and the results list was replaced with rows of thumbnail photographs. Hatcher scanned them. They all looked like the man he'd met.

"That him?"

"I'd say so."

"Hmmm . . ." Denny said.

"What?"

"It's strange."

"What is?"

"If I didn't know better . . ." Denny hit some keys, clicked through a few screens on his mouse. "These all look like the same person."

"Well, isn't it?" Hatcher asked.

"No, I don't mean the same person in the photo, I mean it looks like all these pictures were posted by the same guy."

"I don't understand."

"Look." Hatcher watched as Denny clicked opened a page. "You've got this photo on a foreign policy blog . . ." A few more clicks. "And this photo on a site called Military News and Events." Another series of clicks. "And you've got this site called Pentagon Watch."

"So?"

"Look at the web addresses. They're all using the same platform. In fact—" He clicked a few more photos, opening additional tabs on the screen. "There are only three platforms I can see. For all these pictures."

"What are you saying?"

"I don't know. Just, it's like the same group of people were posting these photos. Look at the dates." Denny clicked through the pages, reading off date-time markers where he could find them. "They're all within a few days of each other. And it looks like they used the same SEO."

"The same what?"

"Search engine optimization. Someone tagged the sites with terms that make sure they pop up first when you do a Google search."

Hatcher let the information flow over his mind, like he was trying to identify the taste of it. "Scroll down that results page, the one with the photos."

Denny dragged the mouse down the scroll bar, causing the page to roll up. After about two screens' worth went by, several photos suddenly looked different. Similar, but different. They were various shots of a gray-haired man, somewhat rugged, but more politician than soldier. Only it was a different one than Hatcher had met.

"Son of a bitch."

"Hey, is that the same guy?" Denny asked.

But Hatcher barely heard him. He stared at the photos until his eyes hurt. Then he looked at the top of the desk, thought of something that might come in handy.

"Denny," he said. "I have a big favor to ask."

CHAPTER 21

✦

HATCHER PULLED UP TO THE WAREHOUSE AND PARKED DI-
rectly in front of the garage entrance. He didn't care who saw
him.

The double-wide garage door was closed. There was a regular entry door next to it, with a small square of security glass
reinforced by wire mesh. The knob wouldn't turn. Hatcher tried
to peer through the glass, but couldn't see anything.

He circled the building, looking for access. The structure had
a row of windows high off the ground, second-story level. Parts
of the wall had spaces where similar windows had been filled in
with brick on the ground level, probably due to vandalism and
street people gaining entry. There was another heavy-duty steel
door on the other side of the building, but it was locked and built
not to budge.

After surveying the perimeter from every angle, Hatcher
went back to the vehicle entrance. The vertical door wasn't
flimsy, but it was somewhat flexible, moving with a tinny sound
when he pressed it. He pushed his weight against it several
times, listening. Then he got in the PT Cruiser, started the engine, and pulled out into the street. With the nose in the opposite
direction, he lined the car up with the garage door, put the car in
reverse, and took his foot off the brake. He let the car roll back
a few feet, felt some mild inertia set in, then jammed his foot on
the accelerator.

The back of the vehicle rammed into the sectioned door,
slamming him against the seat. He put the car into drive, pulled
out a few feet, then shifted into reverse again. The rear of the car
smashed against the door even harder this time. He inched the
car forward and put it in park.

Several panels were dented and buckled. But it was the

edges that mattered. For a door like that to open and close, it had to ride on a track. A door could be made of the hardest substance known to man, but its ability to withstand force couldn't be greater than the track that held it. Or the brackets that held the track. Or the extensions that connected it to the rollers.

Just as he'd hoped, the force had almost snapped the door free from the track at an edge. An extension rod, bent and loose, the roller wheel acting as hook. Hatcher kicked the spot several times, stomping his heel against it, until the remaining connection broke. Because the door was a stacked series of horizontal sections, it was flexible. He bent the bottom two sections back until he managed to squeeze through, sliding along the concrete.

The inside of the warehouse echoed with the hollow quiet of an empty auditorium. Diffuse sunlight beamed in from the high windows, darkened by coatings of greasy dust. He didn't need much light to see the place was deserted. No Humvees, no paramilitary types in fatigues, no tables displaying weapons. No tables at all. Nothing. The sound of Hatcher's hands slapping the cement dust and grime off his jeans bounced off the walls and windows.

Hatcher crossed to the makeshift office he'd been led through during his visit. He opened the door and reached for a light switch. No power. But the spill of light through the doorway was enough to let him see a little. The computers were gone. File cabinets gone. The desk was still there, but it had been cleaned out.

The war room was pitch black. Hatcher stepped a few feet past the entryway and stood there, letting his eyes adjust. The dim light reaching in from the outer office doorway barely dented the mass of shadows, but he could make out the conference table and chairs, smaller tables along the walls. It was hard to tell what, but there was something still on one of the walls. He groped toward it, felt a surface of slick, coated paper. A map.

It tore away from one thumbtack and popped another onto the floor as Hatcher yanked it off the wall. Hatcher held it open, gave it a snap. It made a loud papery sound and collapsed into a few incorrect folds. He carried it out into the main warehouse, where there was more light, and spread it open on the cement floor.

The map of Los Angeles. It had four red Xs. He read the streets. One was the house on Mulholland. One was the warehouse he was in. Another looked like the location of the church. The fourth was at Fifth and Hope, a spot he didn't recognize.

He lowered himself from a crouch into the floor and sat, thinking. He would have to head over there, to Fifth and Hope, and check it out. But the chances of Bartlett actually being there were slim, especially if he left this map behind. What was bugging him even more was the question of why that location seemed familiar.

The thought of heading back to the bar one more time to do a search crossed his mind, but he knew that would not go over too well. He thought about calling Amy again, when he remembered what Denny had asked him about having internet access on his cell phone. His cell phones didn't, since they were inexpensive disposable ones. But the one he took from Fernandez might.

He folded up the map into fourths, crawled back through the bent edge of the garage door, and hurried to the car. Fernandez's cell phone was in the storage compartment between the seats. Hatcher turned it on, waited for the screen to brighten, then searched the icons. He clicked on one that said "browser." The screen flashed a spinning globe, with a download bar. He muddled around until he found a search function, typed in the streets and the city.

It took a few minutes to load, but he was able to scroll through a list of hits. As best he could tell, it was the main branch of the public library.

Hatcher stared into his lap, raking his fingers back over his scalp. Where had he just seen a reference to the library? Thoughts of the church kept blipping. He struggled to make the connection.

Then it hit him. Those conspiracy websites, talking about lizard people and underground tunnels. One in particular maundered about how there was an entrance rumored to be in the church. But the site also mentioned another.

Hatcher started the car and drove, wondering whether people had to pass through a metal detector to access the Los Angeles Public Library.

THE RICHARD RIORDAN CENTRAL LIBRARY LOOKED MORE LIKE a state capitol than a place for people to borrow books. The building was an imposing structure, vaguely Egyptian in its lines, all smooth and sandy-looking concrete and glass, climbing up in vertical blocky layers to a triangular apex with panels of sunburst mosaics, as if a pharaoh had commissioned an Art Deco pyramid. Hatcher passed between a pair of metal gates, beneath an overhead carving of men inscribing books through the ages, and through an ornate set of glass and iron doors.

No metal detectors.

If the exterior was that of an executive or legislative seat, the interior was more like a museum. Hatcher had to admit he was impressed. From the vaulted ceilings with the enormous decorative windows to the hanging displays to the exquisite sculptures, if budget were an indication, the city sure seemed to take reading seriously. Not sure exactly where he was going other than down, he wandered through the main lobby until he found a set of elevators.

The walls of the elevator car were papered with three-by-five Dewey decimal cards, protected by glass panels. His initial thought was that the last time he'd been in a library, that was the only way you could find a book, but then he realized that wasn't true. The last time he'd been in a library was in Manhattan, researching demons. He pushed the lowest button on the panel, marked with a B.

He stepped out into a narrow corridor bathed in fluorescent light. To each side, books stretched out in rows of vintage shelving that looked like it dated back to the twenties or thirties. A young, rather petite woman was pushing a cart of faded, threadbare texts. She looked up from behind circular glasses the size of drink coasters as Hatcher approached, revealing a gap in her teeth.

"Need some help?"

"I just have a question. Is this the lowest floor?"

"Yes, sir," she said. "It sure is."

"Nothing lower?"

"Unless you want the boiler room."

"How would I get there?"

"Sir, I was kidding."

Hatcher said, "I'm not."

The woman's eyes widened and creases appeared above her brow. She broke eye contact and glanced nervously past him.

"I just need to see the lowest floor of the building. I'm not trying to cause any trouble."

"You can't go down there, sir. Nobody goes down there except maintenance."

"Maybe I can talk to one of your maintenance guys."

She lowered the book in her hands back onto the cart. "Why do you want to see the boiler room?"

"I don't. I want to see the lowest floor."

The woman sighed, eyes rolling a bit. "You're not one of those, are you?"

"One of what?"

"Those. You know. One of those guys looking for the lizard people."

"A lot of people come here for that?"

"You wouldn't believe."

"Do they go to the boiler room?"

"No. They go to Jim."

"Who's Jim?"

A voice behind him said, "I am."

Hatcher spun to see a large man standing a few feet away. Corn-fed midwestern type, with thin blondish hair and a patch of scraggly beard on his chin. Late twenties or so. He didn't look like he spent as much time at the gym as he did at the lunch buffet, but he was several inches taller than Hatcher in addition to having a good thirty or forty pounds on him.

"What can I do for you?" he said.

Before Hatcher could open his mouth, the woman said, "He's here for the lizard people."

She said the words "lizard people" slowly, in the manner of someone pointing a finger at their own head and making circles with it.

"Ah!" Jim said, patting Hatcher on the shoulder. "Right this way."

The man started walking. Hatcher looked back at the woman, who popped her eyebrows with an ambiguous grin but said nothing. Not certain what any of it meant, Hatcher followed.

Hatcher rounded a corner to find Jim already leaning on a wide wooden cabinet that came up to his chest. He gave the top of it a double tap with his hand.

"All the information we have on them is on them is right here," he said.

"Like what?"

"Oh, the usual. Newspaper articles, magazine pieces, old maps. And, of course, books about them. Them, or subjects related to them. Everything you ever wanted to know about G. Warren Shufelt, for example."

"Who?"

"The guy who started the whole thing. The one the city granted a contract to dig for tunnels? To find the gold? The one the *L.A. Times* did that piece on back then?"

"Right."

"Well, it's all here."

Hatcher brushed a hand over the top of his head, scratched at his crown. "I was hoping to get a look downstairs, Jim."

Jim smiled. He had a crooked incisor, which made his smile seem like he was showing it for comment.

"Hate to disappoint you, but I can't let you down there. I'll tell you what I tell everyone, there is no 'secret tunnel entrance.' There's nothing down there but steam pipes."

"I'd appreciate it if you just let me take a look."

"Sorry, I tell everyone the same thing. There is no tunnel running under the library."

"Have you been down there?"

The muscles in Jim's face loosened for a moment. "Well, yeah."

"How did you get there?"

"Sorry, friend." The man shook his head. "You can't go down. There are all kinds of insurance and legal issues involved. If it were up to me, shoot—I'd take you myself. But, like I tell everybody, there's no tunnel."

Hatcher peered into the man's face, then dropped his eyes to the cabinet.

"So," Jim said. "Look through all this as long as you want. If you have any questions, just come find me."

He gave the cabinet another double pat and walked past Hatcher, close enough to brush against him.

"Jim," Hatcher said.

The man stopped, turned around. "Yes?"

"One more question." Hatcher took a step toward him, then jammed a forearm against his chest, spinning him to the side and driving him into the nearest wall. "Why are you lying?"

"Let go of me!"

"Answer my question."

The man gulped audibly. "I'm not lying!"

"Oh, yes, you are. Like a rug."

The man opened his mouth as if to yell, but Hatcher clamped a hand on his voice box, biting deep into his throat with his fingers.

"Look, I don't want to hurt you. Really. But I don't have time to dick around, either. You stood there with a plastic smile handing out rehearsed answers, conveniently qualifying them with weasel phrases about 'what you tell everyone is.' You do that because you can rationalize that it's not quite a lie, since you can tell yourself all you're really saying is that's what you tell everyone. It's literally textbook evidence of deception." ·

A gurgling sound escaped the man's throat. He clawed at Hatcher's arms, but it didn't do any good. He was clearly afraid to try anything beyond that.

"Now, I'm going to let go, and you're not going to make any loud noises. What you are going to do is tell me how I get down to the tunnels. Because I know you know."

Hatcher released the man's throat. He sunk forward, coughing and holding the front of his neck. Hatcher gave him a few seconds to catch his breath.

"Okay, *Jim*. The quicker you tell me, the quicker I'll be out of your hair."

"The board," he said, straightening a bit, hands still rubbing his throat, coughing again to clear his windpipe. "They forbid us from talking about it. They wanted to make sure no one tries to go down there, looking. There are steam boilers and electrical boxes and hot pipes. It's dangerous." He coughed again, hacked like something was stuck. "We could get sued."

"Very noble. I'll sign a waiver. Just tell me everything you know."

"There was a fire in '86," he said, his breaths starting to normalize. "Gutted much of the library. It used to be pretty easy before that, from what I was told. Three or four access points in the subbasement. Ladders down to a tunnel system. Dug right through the earth. Some think the original construction crew dug them, for smugglers." Jim squeezed his eyes shut and worked his head back and forth, massaging his neck. "When they renovated, they included some plumbing and heating upgrades, had the contractor wall them over."

"But?"

Jim made a final wet noise, swallowed, and sighed. "But they missed one."

CHAPTER 22

DETECTIVE AMY WRIGHT NOTICED THE FAX COVER SHEET ON the top of the stack as she slid into the chair at her desk. Her landline buzzed the moment she reached across to her inbox.

"This is Sergeant Wright," she said, putting the handset to her ear and plucking the document from the pile. The cover page bore the words *Office of Vital Records* across the top, along with the contact information and the message, *Requested Document Attached*.

She flipped the sheet over its stapled corner to see the copy of the death certificate. Typical government document. Blocks of identifying information: names and dates and places. Signatures and titles. Her eyes roamed the page, skimming the details. She wished the caller, a detective from the Nineteenth, would get to the point and let her hang up. She was much more interested in the document.

There was an attending physician listed, with a name and address. No phone, but that would be easy to find. She wondered if she should call him. Sure, it was almost certainly a waste of time, but 90 percent of everything was a waste of time, and she felt like she had to do something. A witness interview she'd just concluded in a case she was going to pawn off on someone else the first chance she got had taken hours, and she hadn't even had a chance to call Hatcher back, something she wanted to do now but couldn't because of this yo-yo on the phone pestering her about a training seminar.

She hummed short answers, barely listening. Cold air wafted from the open window, cutting through the stifling artificial heat and momentarily capturing her attention. The detective squad for the Twenty-third Precinct was always too hot in the winter and too cold in the summer. People complained routinely, complaints were ignored routinely. She supposed the higher-ups figured that's what windows were for. But open windows meant the sound of traffic, the distant din of construction, the rising and falling of faint sirens. It meant New York was always in the room with you. Even when you wanted to be far away from it.

"Uh-huh," she said, not having any clue what she was agreeing to. She sighed, attention drifting from the death certificate, checking her watch. She wanted to be talking to Hatcher, not this guy.

She started to reposition the fax cover sheet on top and put the document aside, only to stop as her eyes brushed over a signature in one of the blocks far down the page. She stared at the writing and blinked.

"I have to call you back," she said, cutting off her colleague in mid-sentence and hanging up.

She had to be misreading it, she told herself. It was a signature, flowing loops and curls. Seemed legible enough. But no. It couldn't be.

Trying not to take her eyes off the sheet—part of her worried she might not find what she was looking at again if she did—she pulled open a draw and rummaged for a magnifying glass. The lens expanded the handwriting, moving it in and out of focus as she played with the distance. Except for scratches and flecks, the signature looked the same enlarged. The more she read it, the more obvious it seemed.

She grabbed her cell phone and tapped the screen until it started calling Hatcher's number.

C'mon, answer!

Her eyes dove back to the signature, signing on behalf of Eternal Rewards Funeral Home, as funeral director. Not only did it seem as clear as the printed letters around it now, she was starting to wonder how she could have almost missed it.

Answer the phone, goddamnit!

Nothing. She couldn't just sit there three thousand miles away and do nothing. It was an easy decision, really. A no-brainer. Checking her watch again, she grabbed her purse and coat and headed for the door. She'd take care of the arrangements on the phone, in the cab.

The signature was fixed in her mind. The penmanship was

impeccable. There was no mistaking it, no mistaking that name. And no mistaking what it meant.

Vale N. Tine.

THE SUBBASEMENT WAS DARK AND CRAMPED AND FELT LIKE
a sauna.

Hatcher threaded his way through a narrow labyrinth of gray piping, ducking frequently. Within minutes, his shirt was sticking to his back and chest. Beads of sweat rolled down his nose and hung there briefly before dropping.

He followed the directions Jim had given him, hoping, practically praying, that the information was accurate. He wished he could have dragged Jim down there with him, but there was no practical way to do that, and the man would have understandably thought he'd never be coming back up, so he would have had no reason not to put up a huge fight, kicking and screaming. On the other hand, Hatcher realized some bad directions and a call to security could have been a smart move, a way to end up with the police making a quick arrest.

But nobody came and it didn't seem like anyone would, and Hatcher found the spot more easily than he'd expected. One right turn off the main corridor of piping, then a left into a valve recess, right where Jim had said it would be. A large wheel sat flat over a pipe extension in the recess, protruding from the cement floor. Behind the valve was a vented panel, low to the ground. Hatcher could see how the contractors would have missed it. He barely fit between the valve and the wall.

The panel took some prodding, but Hatcher managed to pry it open enough with the rental car key to wedge some fingers behind it. It popped out on the third tug.

And there it was. A tight square space in the wall, with a metal access ladder bolted to the side, descending into a shaft.

Hatcher grabbed the wheel valve and stuck his feet through the opening, moving them until one touched a rung. He dropped a foot to the next rung, then a lower one, and pushed himself through the opening with his arms. Kept pushing and lowering, stepping down. Once he was vertical enough, he reached an arm inside and grabbed the ladder, letting go of the valve.

The shaft descended into blackness darker than sleep. He'd

climbed down around thirty feet when his foot felt nothing but air. The ladder simply stopped. Assuming he must be close to the bottom, he lowered himself a few more rungs with his arms, stretching his foot down and kicking to feel for a landing. Nothing.

He climbed even lower, finally letting himself dangle from the last rung, pointing his toes, hoping to scrape something. Still nothing.

Well, this sucks.

The burning in his arms told him they wouldn't let him hang like that all day. His options were limited. There were really only two. He could climb back up, try to find another access. But Jim had said there was only one left beneath the library, so in practical terms that meant giving up. Or he could simply take it on faith that the bottom wasn't far below, maybe a few feet, maybe mere inches. The problem with that gambit was obvious. If it was more than ten feet or so, he'd almost certainly break a leg or ankle. More than twenty, he'd seriously injure himself and need immediate medical attention. Either way, he wouldn't have any way out. And a drop in the dark of even a few feet was risky. Not knowing when you're going to hit is a surefire way to blow our your knee or your hip. The rest of your body wouldn't enjoy it much, either.

He hung there a few more moments, thinking. He did a mental inventory of his pockets. The right one contained only one thing, but his left one held a small maglite, two replacement batteries, and a set of keys. The knife Edgar had given him was clipped to his jeans, nestled against the small of his back. His cell phone was stuffed in his left rear pocket, wallet in his left. Light first.

He pulled himself up by his arms several rungs until he could hook a leg. He coaxed the small flashlight out of his jeans pocket with one hand, careful not to drop it. The wash of the beam was bright in the enclosed shaft. He held it bulb-end down and craned his neck to look.

There was a bottom, but it was hard to tell how far away it was. More than ten feet, but he wasn't sure how much more.

He tucked the end of the flashlight into his mouth and fished the keys out of his pocket. He held them out and let them go.

One Mississippi.

Before he finished, he heard a clink. He snagged the light from his teeth and pointed it down the shaft. He could make out the glint of metal in the distance.

That made it simple. The distance was about twelve to fifteen feet. Dangle as low as you can get before dropping, that would make it more like five to eight feet. Maybe.

Piece of cake.

Okay, he told himself, this is seriously stupid. There was no guarantee there was any exit down there, no guarantee he'd be dropping into anything other than a pit. There might be no way out, and there was definitely no way back up. There was a good chance that what he was contemplating amounted to suicide.

He stared down for a few more seconds, before he tucked the light away and lowered himself back to the bottom rung. Arms extended, feet swinging gently, he reminded himself once more what a stupid stunt this was. A long moment passed. He took a breath, exhaled half of it, then let go.

The fall lasted longer than he'd expected. When he finally slammed feetfirst into the ground, the force slammed his knees into his chest. One knee skidded up into his chin. He tasted blood on his tongue, could feel a stinging rawness inside his bottom lip.

Hatcher pushed himself up from the earthen floor, dusted off. He pulled out the flashlight and thumbed the button.

The tunnel was between five and six feet high, maybe four feet wide. Hatcher flashed the light down one direction, then the other. Both looked identical.

Think, he told himself. He closed his eyes and pictured the library, the entrance, fixed the direction it faced. He retraced his steps into the building, into the basement, around the corner, following Jim, back to where Jim opened the maintenance stairwell, down the subbasement corridor and around the bend, into the shaft. Compared that to the general location of the church.

Then he started walking.

The low height forced him to hunch over, almost crouch, as he moved. It was hard to gauge distance. Minutes started to pile up. The muscles in his back registered complaining stabs, but he didn't stop to rest. He walked for over an hour before he noticed a light in the distance. He shut off his flashlight and kept moving forward, eventually reaching a hub.

The hub was smaller than the place the Carnates had taken him, but it was definitely man-made. Or made by something. It was an empty, open area, lighted by torches on the walls. And it smelled. A sweet, pungent odor, sharp and persistent, seeped into his nasal passages, refusing to go away. He sensed it had to be whatever the torches were burning. He put the back of his hand to his nose and surveyed the chamber. Three other tunnels fed into it, but only one was in the general direction he was heading. He grabbed one of the torches off the wall. The light from the flame didn't travel as far, but it was brighter and would let him conserve battery power. He peered as far as he could into the tunnel, then entered.

This tunnel was a bit spacier, probably eight feet high and six feet wide, allowing Hatcher to stand as he walked and to hold the torch above eye level. Any hope this segment would be shorter quickly faded. After the first thirty minutes, the torch felt heavy, causing a pain in his shoulder. He switched arms several times, but eventually put the torch down and retrieved the flashlight. He had no idea how long he was going to have to walk, and certainly didn't want his arms to be dead by the time he got there.

Seventy or eighty yards further on, Hatcher realized he was no longer in a tunnel. The blackness surrounded him, an ocean of it, and his flashlight was hitting nothing as he swept it in every direction. Then he saw the man.

He seemed tall, but it was hard to tell, because he was seated behind a small desk, bent slightly over it, marking up some document. He was brightly lit, as if by a spotlight, but there was no apparent source, just an island of illumination. He had pale skin and strawberry blond hair and a roman nose that extended over a pair of puffy red lips. He was wearing a white dinner jacket.

Hatcher stopped. The man continued whatever he was doing at the desk and did not look up. After several moments, he said, "Just because I've got all day, doesn't mean I have all day."

The man's voice was calm, soft, but it had an edge to it.

"Who are you?" Hatcher said.

The man said nothing, engrossed in his activity.

The entire area was like a void. Even the floor seemed to lack any distinct quality, as if were nothing more than the surrounding blackness somehow solidified. Hatcher glanced over his shoulder, tossed looks left and right. It was the same in every direction. Except one thing was suddenly very different. He couldn't have had his eyes off the man for much more than a second, but when he looked back, Dinner Jacket wasn't sitting at the desk anymore, he was in front of it, leaning back. Screwing the lid onto a red fountain pen. He slipped the pen behind his lapel, then withdrew his empty hand. Both hands found his trouser pockets as he leveled his gaze at Hatcher.

"You know who I am," the man said. It was a statement, not a question.

"Don't be so sure."

"Oh, trust me. You do. Which is why you won't. Trust me, that is."

Hatcher realized that two red protuberances curved up from beneath the guy's hairline. Blood red, almost glossy. How could he have not noticed that before?

The man sighed. Then he wasn't there. He was leaning over Hatcher's shoulder. A huge head of green scales, accented by plump cheekbones and a long chin. Eyes like two malevolent jewels beneath twin red horns.

"Does this help?"

Before Hatcher could do more than flinch, the face was gone. The man was back in front of the desk, half-seated against it as if he'd never left. His face was human again.

Hatcher reached for the knife clipped at the small of his back.

"That won't be necessary," the man said, a patient smile stretching his face. "I won't harm you."

"Just who the hell are you?"

"I'm what scares you."

Hatcher blinked. He started to respond, but stopped.

"Come now," the man continued, "deep down, you know what I'm talking about. My name is Raum. I'm your dedicated demon."

"My what?"

"Demon. Your devil. Did you really think Lucifer himself personally dispenses torment to the damned? Please. He's got enough on his plate, running the place."

Hatcher stared at the man, ran his eyes over the horns a few times. "My own devil, huh?"

"Yes."

"But you mean me no harm."

"Of course not. Not now, at least. Why would I? We have all eternity to get acquainted, after all."

"And I'm supposed to believe this?"

"Well, on the one hand, yes," the man said, shrugging. "On the other, it doesn't really matter."

"Let's say I play along for now. If you're a demon, and demons live in Hell, then what are you doing here?"

"My dear fellow, I'm always here." Raum tapped his index finger against his temple. "The Carnates simply saw fit to let you have a glimpse. Just the right mix of herbs and an ancient incantation. I was more than happy to oblige."

"And why would they do that?"

"To fuck with your head. Why else?"

Hatcher lowered his gaze to the knife in his hand. "So, you're not real."

"Oh, I'm very real. You might say I'm as real as it gets. What is reality, after all? Is the color red real? Does it even exist as you know it? What is anything outside of what your brain tells you it is? How do you know someone else sees the same thing you do? If everyone were color blind, would colors still be there?"

Hatcher rubbed his eyes. "I'm hallucinating."

"No. Deluding, perhaps. But not hallucinating."

"This is not real."

"Here we go with the 'real' again. How's this for real." The man tipped forward and lowered his voice to a whisper. "I know everything that terrifies you."

"Is that so?"

"That's so."

"And I'm just supposed to take your word for all this?"

"No," Raum said. "That would require faith. Not something we deal in." The man's lips tensed into a humorless grin. He raised a hand from his pocket, bending his arm at the elbow, and snapped his fingers.

Hatcher tightened up, surprised and disappointed in himself for doing so. But nothing happened.

"Is that all you got?"

The man didn't move. In fact, he didn't even blink. Or twitch. Or breathe. He was completely still. Unnaturally motionless. Like a statue.

Hatcher leaned closer. Something was wrong. He took a step, then another. Not only was the man not moving, Hatcher realized he wasn't even a man anymore. A two-dimensional, life-sized cardboard cut-out stood in his place, a photograph, perfectly duplicating his last pose. Hatcher took a few more steps, reached out and touched the image.

A pair of arms burst through the picture, long and gray, clawed fingers, raking and snatching. Thick hairs protruded from the leathery skin, the hide pulled tight around narrow ropes of corded muscles and knobby bones. The hands cuffed Hatcher's wrists and jerked him forward into the photo. The picture shattered, cardboard exploding into a thousand fragments of glass, and Hatcher found himself tumbling, flailing, falling. He was passing through himself, through his future, through settings and events he could barely conceive. All of it alien, all of it unreal, all of it chillingly familiar.

Faceless creatures fed on human flesh, close enough to touch, yellow eyes and black gaping maws, heads draped in layers of long, stringy hair, teeth like piranha. He knew these things, had seen them before. Seen them, fled them, feared them. In nightmares, as a child. Same for the things that looked like snakes with daggered limbs and human faces, sporting blue skin and cat's eyes, tearing at a carcass, flinging viscera haphazardly over their heads, an orgy of insanity. All of them things his mind had conjured in his youth, what he pictured the first time he'd heard the word "ghoul," his imagination giving form to the kind of thing suited to such a name. Or the product of a movie he could hear playing on the TV while he was huddled in his bed down the hall and his father snored in the recliner, something about a crazy doctor turning people into snakes.

Even now, these scenes seemed to reach an icy hand inside him and squeeze. He tried to tell himself they weren't real, but he knew better. These were more real than anything else he could think of. Solid. Three-dimensional. Alive.

A crazy woman with matted, wild hair squatted over a corpse, stabbing it with a fork over and over, giggling. The sight revived his fears of insanity he had as a kid, sent the same weak-ening tingle through his spine, the same spike in his heart rate. The thought of a person who wasn't really there, whose brain was not quite human, a person who couldn't be reasoned with, whose homicidal mind he couldn't comprehend, still made his skin squirm with unease.

Each world staked its own claim on him, quickly dissolving into the next, lasting just long enough for Hatcher to take in every detail as he passed through, a piece of him knowing he was damned to return.

The victims all seemed to look vaguely the same, but it wasn't until the last scene that Hatcher was able to recognize who it was. A man, arms and legs missing, two stones in place of his eyeballs, with irises and pupils painted on them. He was being raped by troll-like men with jagged buckteeth as they drooled over his writhing body. The man was Hatcher. So, he realized, were the rapists.

Unable to take it, Hatcher shut his eyes, pushing at them with his fingers, trying to squeeze out what he'd seen. The worst part was the feeling that swelled and churned inside him, a feeling so strong it seemed he was immersed in it, a radio signal bombard-ing every corner and cranny, boosted and rebroadcast internally from his crown to his heels. A jittery, helpless feeling, the result of millions of neurons firing and misfiring, bombarding his senses into overload. The entire universe narrowed, compressing into the space around him, existence now defined as the com-plete absence of anything but horror and despair. Pure terror.

When he opened his eyes, Hatcher found himself balled on the ground, apparently in the same place he'd started.

Raum looked down at him from his position leaning against the desk. There was no indication he'd ever left.

"Hope you enjoyed that. I figured I'd skip the maudlin stuff you saw the other day and go for the visceral thrills. That's the beauty of where you're going. You'll never be bored."

Hatcher said nothing. He shut his eyes, tried to catch his breath.

"I'm supposed to tell you to take the ring," Raum said.

"What ring?" Hatcher said.

"They'll offer it to you. Take it. It will make you powerful enough to do almost anything. I'm bound not to lie."

Hatcher held his breath for a moment. "And if I don't?"

The demon shrugged. "That wasn't part of my message."

The shaky feeling in his gut and limbs started to subside. Hatcher shook his head, trying to clear it, rolled to his hands and knees and pushed himself off the ground. He started to speak as he stood, but stopped before any sound came out. Raum was gone. So was the desk, and the black expanse. There was only the tunnel, flickering in the light of the torch that lay near his feet.

CHAPTER 23

HATCHER REACHED THE NEXT HUB IN LITTLE MORE THAN AN hour. He'd left the torch—again—and was following the bouncing sphere of brightness from his flashlight. Firelight glowed in the distance. As he drew closer, he shut off the flashlight and hugged the tunnel wall. He crept forward until he could see what lay beyond.

A woman was standing next to a stone slab, leaning over it and looking down, her back to Hatcher. Platinum blonde, perfect figure. Tight leather outfit. He had to force himself not to look at her ass. And not looking didn't remove the image of it from his head.

Soliya.

Hatcher scanned the area. This hub was similar to the prior one, just a space with more tunnels branching out like spokes. There was no one else there but her.

To keep going in the same direction, he'd have to take the tunnel directly across. On the other side of her. Sneaking to it looked impossible.

Carnates were tough. Hatcher knew that from experience. They were strong and agile and skilled fighters. He'd seen one flip out of an armlock in a way that had to have dislocated her shoulder. She didn't so much as wince.

His hand slid to his jeans, felt the firm outline of the knife clipped to the belt line.

She didn't seem to be paying attention. He could sneak up to her, slow and quiet, stick the long blade deep into her back, straight into her heart. Would that kill her? Edgar had said it would, but he wasn't sure how much of what he'd been told—if any of it—could be believed.

But he tended to think it was true. They were still living creatures with beating hearts. If it had a beating heart, stabbing that heart would kill it.

The question was, could he do that? Kill a woman in cold blood? Even one that wasn't really a woman? Or at best half a woman?

He slipped the knife out from where it was tucked. He opened the blade slowly, let it lock in place with a muted snick.

An image of that Afghani boy flashed through his head.

Stop it.

Just a kid, and he'd covered his mouth, pulled his head back, and cleaved his arteries open. Stabbed the blade into the space behind his clavicle, worked it forward and back to sever the connections to the heart.

Stop, stop, stop. He was an armed sentry fighting for a bunch of murderous fanatics. Would have killed you, killed any American, without blinking.

He hadn't realized just how young he was, or at least hadn't considered it, until he saw the eyes. So wide open, so terrified. Realizing he was dying, but too young to really grasp it. The eyes of a child. A little boy playing terrorist, recruited by diseased minds. Dead in five seconds.

It was a memory Hatcher had assumed he'd locked away, one he'd gotten rid of a long time ago. He'd gone years free of it, not letting anything remind him. Until that glimpse of damnation at the hands of Sankey.

He closed his eyes. *She's not human, damn it.*

He forced himself to think of Vivian, of Lori. Lori, dead and mutilated. Vivian, possibly still alive.

This was no time to lose his nerve, he told himself. Arm around the neck, pulling her up and back, curving her spine, then one, hard upward thrust of the knife, just to the left of her vertebrae, right below the scapula. Not difficult. Just very hard.

The pistol-grip handle snugly wedged in his fist, he stepped from the shadow of the tunnel into the torchlight.

One step, then another, weight on the balls of his feet, legs bent, ready to spring.

Fourteen. The kid couldn't have been fourteen.

Hatcher stopped, squeezed his eyes shut. He had to quit thinking this way.

He had an AK-47 and was on sentry duty, damn it! The

slightest noise, and the rest of them would grab their weapons, start firing. His duty was to his team, not to some Islamofascist punk who'd put a bullet in any infidel he could, or blow up a nursery school, or cut off a civilian's head. It was war.

He took a quiet breath, let it out slowly. Sure, that was war. And war was hell. But what's this? Is it the same thing? What choice was there? They'd killed Lori, taken Vivian. Who knew what they were up to?

He mopped his face, thinking. Maybe he didn't have to kill her. He had a knife, he could put it to her throat. Stab her in the heart only if she resisted. Riskier, yes. But Carnate or not, she was still an unarmed woman. Sort of.

Another breath, then another step. The decision calmed his nerves, let him focus. She was only a few feet away now, completely oblivious. Unmoving.

One more step, and he lunged forward, thrust his left arm across her neck, cupping his hand back to pull her head and expose her jugular, bringing the knife to it, pressing it just hard enough so there would be no mistake—

The body swung woodenly with his movements, rattling. Stiff arms, slightly crooked at the elbow, pointing outward. A solid, fleshless face. Molded composite material under a wig. A mannequin.

What the—?

"I trust you weren't planning on slitting my throat."

Hatcher dropped the mannequin and wheeled around. Soliya was standing against the rocky wall, hands linked casually behind her waist. Her lips were curled at the edges, a bemused twinkle in her eye. Same red leather outfit.

"I mean, really, Hatcher—after all we've been through?"

First the stuff with Raum or whoever he was, now this. Hatcher fixed his eyes on hers, taking whatever measure he could, then slowly let his gaze drift around the chamber. Three torches guttered on the walls. Nothing else but a slab, and a mannequin.

But it wasn't a mannequin a minute ago. That much he was sure of.

"You drugged me."

"Did I?"

Hatcher said nothing. If she did drug him, she would have

had to touch him, inject him. Give him something to drink. Or inhale. In the cave, it would have been easy. The bangers could have done it on the way. But here?

He glanced around the chamber one more time. Nothing but torches.

Torches.

Fire. She'd lit a fire at the cave, and now torches. The drug was in the smoke. Had to be. He'd even smelled it. Made it easy for them.

"Where is she?"

"It just so happens, I'm here to take you to her." She paused, apparently considering her words. "In a manner of speaking."

She pushed away from the wall, smiling as she sashayed past him. Her eyes dropped to the knife in his hand. She arched a brow and winked.

"Don't cut yourself," she said, stepping up to a torch and pulling it off the wall.

She ventured into a tunnel, an orange glow throbbing off the walls in her wake. The chamber dimmed slightly. Hatcher watched her recede into the distance, shadows filling in behind her. Something had to be in those torches, some fume in the smoke. Something he shouldn't be breathing.

"These are just plain old torches," she said, as if hearing his thoughts.

He didn't have much of a choice. He stepped into the tunnel and followed, keeping his distance and forcing shallow breaths.

They walked for what seemed like miles. She occasionally threw a glance back over her shoulder, rolling her eyes, until finally coming to a stop and waiting.

She set the torch into a holder embedded in the wall of the tunnel. "We're almost there. Stop being ridiculous."

Reluctantly, Hatcher closed the distance, still keeping several feet between them.

"There's something you need to know," she said, on the move again.

The light from the flames receded behind them as they ventured forth. The way ahead was pitch black.

"What's that?"

She reached back and held out her hand. "Remember back at Bronson Caves? Our little interlude?"

The hand was barely visible now, the light fading more with each step. She gestured impatiently and he reached forward and took it. The touch of her skin sent a tingle through his body.

"You mean, your little game of mindfuck?"

"Interesting choice of words," she said, dropping her voice to an almost intimate volume. "You betrayed her so easily. It hardly took any seduction at all."

He pushed her hand away, realizing he was in complete darkness now. He swiveled his head to look behind him. No sign of light. Anywhere.

"You're lying," he said.

"Am I?" Her voice was close, but he could no longer see her. She may have been twelve inches away, or twelve feet. "Don't you remember? Your lips and teeth on my skin? Our tongues and limbs intertwined so deliciously? You don't remember sliding deep inside me with such longing, such hunger?"

"No," he said, without any of the conviction he'd tried for.

"Over and over and over, I kept asking you if it felt good, and you kept saying oh, yes, yes, yes."

"It wasn't real."

"And I asked you—asked you as you thrust yourself into me, as your pulse raced in ecstasy . . . do you love her?"

Hatcher put his hand out, swept it from side to side, groping the darkness. Nothing.

Another whisper, loud enough to echo. "You said no, over and over again."

"That's not true."

"Which part? What you said? Or the fact you said it?"

Hatcher patted his pockets, trying to find his flashlight. It was gone. *Son of a bitch.*

He put his arm out again, crept forward.

"Don't worry," she said. "It will be our little secret."

Her voice was so close. He kept moving, waving sightlessly, submerged in inky blackness.

Then light erupted all around him. Torches blooming in every direction, lining a circular chamber. Illuminating a crowd. Hundreds of women. Blondes, brunettes, redheads. Pale, tanned, dark. Stunningly beautiful, provocative women. Some sitting on the floor or casually stretched out, others standing farther back, all of them forming an audience. A large ring of spectators.

An arena.

Hatcher stood just inside the circle, hadn't moved, taking it all in. In the middle of the chamber, the center of the arena, Morris Sankey sat on the throne, looking down from the raised platform. Orange jacket, orange hat. To the left of him stood a man Hatcher hadn't seen before. A bit older, graying. Well dressed in business attire.

To the right was Edgar. Smiling.

Suspended above them was a figure Hatcher had seen before, but only in sketches. The head, horns, and legs of a huge goat, the body of a woman, naked, a sewn-on penis and scrotum hanging limp between the goat legs. The left arm was pointing up. The right arm was male, stitched to the body, pointing downward. Each forearm had a word tattooed on it. As far as he could tell, it was identical to the drawings in every detail. The Baphomet. Not some living creature, at least, he didn't think so, but rather a grotesque collection of Frankenstein parts.

Below it, in front of the throne, a large ring shined on its pedestal, bathed in a cone of bright light.

Why do I think I've seen this act before? Hatcher said to himself.

"So glad to see you again," said the gray-haired man.

Hatcher ignored him. He set his eyes on Edgar.

"You were their prison bitch all along, weren't you? What did they promise you? Supernatural sex?"

"You'll find out soon enough."

"Where is she?"

Edgar pursed his lips, not quite breaking his smile, and let his eyes roll to the side. He hitched his shoulders in a lazy shrug. "Not my department."

The sound of heels grabbed his attention. Deborah crossed toward him, cutting through the circular space. She was wearing a black dress that barely covered anything. Hatcher tightened his grip on the knife.

She clucked her tongue, wagging her chin in disapproval.

"Is violence your answer to everything?"

"No," he said, his back stiffening. "Just to questions I don't like."

"Well, keep it in your pants. Don't you want to hear why you're standing there?"

"I have a feeling you're going to tell me no matter what I say."

Her face tightened into a smirk, and she crinkled her nose. "You are just so adorable. Did you know that?"

"Tell me where she is."

"Silly man. What do you think I'm trying to do?"

Deborah swept an arm, indicating a direction behind him. He turned to see the section of Carnates part, clearing a wide path. The same path as last time, ending at the wall of black polished stone. Soliya stood in front of it. She stepped to the side, gave a Vanna White gesture toward the wall.

It took Hatcher a moment, but then the movement caught his eye. He squinted, leaning forward. Once he could focus past the reflections, it all seemed to burst into view.

Vivian. She was on the other side, being held by things he could only assume were demons, long-fingered creatures with bestial faces and swept-back skulls displaying enormous rows of jagged teeth. They had her tightly by the limbs, some biting at her, some clawing at her. He couldn't hear any of it, but her mouth was set in a scream, her eyes wide. Her expression twisted. She was obviously in severe pain.

She seemed able to see out, able to see him. Screaming for help. Screaming for him to help her.

"Let her go," he said, gritting his teeth so hard he felt one chip.

"Oh, but you see, we don't have her."

Hatcher tightened his fist around the knife handle as hard as his muscles would allow. "I said, let her go. I mean it."

Deborah made a disapproving noise, tilted her head as if in pity. "That's not the way it works. We really don't have her. She's—how can I put this . . . crossed over."

Hatcher's eyes darted back to the wall. The dreamy, liquid image of Vivian was still there, still screaming in silence.

"You're lying."

"Is that so? In that case, prove it."

Deborah walked over to the pedestal. She gestured toward the ring.

"This ring will allow you to pass the barrier. You can go get her. If you dare."

Hatcher stared at Deborah, then back at the ghostly countenance of Vivian. "I don't understand."

"Yes, you do. This is the Ring of Aandaleeb. Let's not pretend you haven't heard of it."

"Oh, I've heard of it. You made sure I did. All that crap about King Solomon and demons. Then the visit from Raum. If there's one thing I've learned, it's that if you want me to believe something, it's not true. You want me to use it, so I think I'll pass."

"Who said I do? I'm offering you a chance to prove it's all fake. I'm actually hoping you don't take me up on it, lest all these carefully laid plans come to naught."

"That's not the way you work. I may not know much, but I know that."

"So you're admitting that maybe it's not fake, that maybe she really is at the banks of Fire Lake, ready to be dragged to its depths."

"Quit the games. What do you want from me?"

"A fair question. I want you to know that you now have a chance to claim the source of more power than anyone has wielded in millennia, power enough to go get your girlfriend and bring her back."

"Let me guess, if I do that, use that ring to cross over, it will open this Path, some gateway to Hell, so all your demon cousins can come strolling out."

"My, aren't we so convinced of our own cleverness."

Hatcher locked eyes with Deborah, then shifted his gaze to the platform. Something wasn't right, and with so many things already wrong, that was saying a lot. That freak Morris Sankey was sitting there like the crowned prince of some role-playing game. The older guy next to him was watching the goings-on intently, trying, it seemed, to appear only casually interested. Edgar was grinning uncontrollably, practically urging Hatcher on with his body language.

"You should know, *she* came to *us*. Oh, yes. It's true. Months ago. A young woman, intensely in love with the man who saved her. A man she couldn't bear to think of as bound to perdition, a man she believed in. A man she'd do anything for."

"You're lying. She wouldn't have the first clue how to find you."

"Oh, we can be found when we want to be. She was proud at first, brave. Trying to appeal to our sense of decency, I suppose. But by the end she was practically begging. She would have done anything to keep you from going to Hell. Anything."

Hatcher said nothing. The muscles in his jaw started to throb. He realized he'd been clenching them so hard they were cramping.

"Don't look at me like that. It's true. We made a deal. If she helped us, we told her we'd do everything in our power to get Hell to relinquish its hold. Problem was, Vivian started getting cold feet. Seeing you nursing contusions and abrasions didn't help. She began to question whether there was more to our plans than we let on. Mostly, though, she started to worry about how you'd react if you found out. She tried to back out, worried we were going to hurt you. Funny part was, we knew she would. Were banking on it, actually. Ironic, isn't it? Here she was trying to save you from Hell, and now she's on the other side of Hell's door, waiting for you to save *her*."

"I'm not buying it."

"Which part?"

"Any of it."

"Are you sure? Perhaps you should act now, while supplies last. This sale won't last forever."

"This isn't about opening up any portal to Hell. That was all a ruse. An illusion."

"Oh, mercy me. Jacob Hatcher has just had an epiphany. I hope we didn't strain ourselves thinking too hard. Who was it who tried to tell you not to believe everything you've been told? You just wouldn't listen."

"Right. Using a fake general and pretending to have my nephew."

"Fake, huh?"

"Yes. I know all about it."

"There was nothing fake about General Bartlett," Deborah said. "And we most certainly did have your nephew. My word, where do you come up with such theories?"

"I don't want to hear it. Whatever it is you're up to, I'm not playing along."

Deborah's eyebrows popped. "Really?"

"Really."

"I'm telling you that you can use this ring to control demons and to rescue this woman. A woman who loves you."

"And I'm telling you I'm not stupid enough to do anything you want me to."

"Why don't you just take it and try?"

"No, thanks."

"Are you saying you refuse to accept the Ring of Aandaleeb? Even though I just explained that you could use it to save this woman?"

"Yes."

"You, Jake Hatcher, destroyed the Tablet of Hadad,"

Hatcher said nothing.

"And now you're rejecting your claim on the ring? Last chance. Just come up here and get it."

"I don't want it."

Deborah's eyes seemed to sparkle in the flickering light and she moved out of the way. The gray-haired man in the suit stepped forward, his mouth tense, as if he could hardly contain his smile. He approached the pedestal and slid his hand into the cone of light. He hesitated slightly, as if half expecting something to bite him. Then he plucked the ring from its perch and held it high, like a trophy.

"Thank you, Jacob. I can always count on you."

The sound of the man's voice sent a sizzle through Hatcher's spine. Something about the tone.

"I must say, you're looking fit."

Hatcher kept his focus firmly on the man's eyes. "Do I know you?"

"I'm hurt. Of course you do. I'm your brother."

"Garrett?" Even as Hatcher said the name, he realized the mistake. He'd never met this man before, but the icy gaze peering down at him was disturbingly familiar. He tried to tell himself it couldn't be, but knew that wasn't true. *I am so stupid* . . .

"Valentine," he said.

The man wrinkled his brow in a look of disapproval. "Last names? After all we've been through together?"

Hatcher said nothing. Valentine held the ring out, romancing it like a gem, twisting it between his thumb and forefinger.

"You have no idea the power you just handed me."

The platform wasn't far. Maybe ten feet away, maybe three,

three and a half feet high. Hatcher's mind automatically started doing the calculations.

"Look, whatever beef you have with me, fine. Just let Vivian go."

"You know, during my travels, long before you killed me, I once got a valuable piece of advice from an Israeli exporter. He had served for a while in the defense ministry, had dealt with more than his share of geopolitical conflict. Over a plate of foie gras, he told me his country had only two rules for dealing with adversaries." Valentine held up a finger. "Only negotiate from a position of strength." He added another finger, making a peace sign. "And if you're in a position of strength," he said, throwing in a shrug. "Why negotiate?"

He pointed the two fingers at Hatcher to mimic a pistol and dropped his thumb in a firing motion. He clucked his tongue and winked as he did it.

Hatcher had no idea what scheme was being put in motion, but he figured he had one shot to keep it from going any further. The knife, still snug in his hand, seemed like his best chance. He took a breath and sprang forward. Two bounding steps and a leap onto the platform. At the first sign of movement, Sedim began to drop from above, plunging like bombs and landing close by, but he'd managed not to telegraph his attack and was a second ahead of them, on the platform now and still moving. Valentine backpedaled a few feet, but Hatcher closed the distance without any wasted motion. He launched himself at the man, cocking his arm and thrusting the blade toward Valentine's chest.

His arm slammed against something, the impact jarring his entire body to a complete stop. No, he realized, not against something, into something. Something tight, constricting. The something had grabbed his arm near the wrist and was holding fast.

The pain was excruciating. His hand seemed about to explode, the build-up of pressure immediately becoming unbearable. His lower forearm was being crushed with machinelike force. The knife slipped from his fingers. His hand swelled, turning a reddish purple. He could feel the two bones of his forearm grind together.

His body buckled from the force on his nerves and he almost

collapsed. It took significant effort to raise his head. Morris
Sankey had a hold of the arm. Or, more accurately, Sankey's
freakish hand was holding him by the arm. A pair of giant leathery crab legs, each almost as thick as Hatcher's wrist, were
roped around it, squeezing.

And then the fear hit.

It washed over his body, flowing from his skull to his feet, a
shower of dread, drenching him, filling him. Anxiety tearing at
his guts, jolts of adrenaline juicing his heart. His mind racing. It
was like being electrocuted by a surge of everything that scared
him, all at once.

"Let him go."

Hatcher caught a vague image of Sankey's face, the man's
expression registering through the haze of panic and fright, eyes
flashing disappointment, mouth set in a frown. Then he felt
himself drop and he was down, his body curling on its side,
cradling his arm. The fear lingered for a moment, a crush of
madness like noise in his head, drowning him, and then it was
gone. Evaporated. Just a dream, obliterated by a sudden
wakening.

Before he could collect his thoughts he realized he was being
picked up, yanked by a pair of Sedim, one latching on to each
arm. His right arm howled in protest. The numbness of his hand
gave way to razor blades, the bones bathed in electric pain as the
Sedim's taloned grip clamped down. They hauled him to his
feet and off the platform.

"Do *not* hurt him."

Hatcher realized it was Valentine speaking, or whoever the
guy was who seemed to think he was Valentine. Hatcher didn't
know what to make of it, what to make of any of it. He was too
tired to be skeptical, his brain too scrambled to dissect so many
pieces of information. For the moment, he would have to accept
things at face value.

Which meant believing the man stepping down off the platform and walking toward him was Demetrius Valentine, somehow back from the dead.

"To think, you passed this up." Valentine held up the ring,
then caught it in his palm. "You have no idea," he said, shaking
his head. "Do you even understand what this can do?"

Hatcher gritted his teeth, his breath catching from the pain in his arm. He pulled against the Sedim, but they tightened their grips. He'd forgotten how insanely strong they were. Immovable when they tensed up, like a pair of six-foot rocks.

"Control demons," he said.

Valentine's face showed a mixture of surprise and disappointment. "That's like saying a nuclear weapon lets you blow something up. True in a sense, but completely lacking any sense of scale. We're talking about much more than controlling a few demons. This allows its bearer to command Asmodeus, the one who controls all others."

Hatcher said nothing. His eyes jumped from Valentine to Sankey, then to Edgar. Edgar grinned back, as if thoroughly enjoying the events unfolding before him. He held up the large knife Hatcher had dropped, the one he'd given him, and slid it into a pocket.

"I doubt you can even grasp what that means. This ring is how Solomon became the wealthiest, most powerful king the world ever knew. And even though they were unable to unlock its true potential, it was how the Templars became the most feared group of their time."

"Congratulations."

"Oh, I owe it all to you. You see, the reason the Templars— and no one else—could actually take advantage of this is because Solomon grew fearful of what would happen after he died. He began to repent for having strayed from God and relinquished his power. But he didn't want anyone else to have it, either."

Valentine held up the ring, a professor using a visual aid.

"So he used his power to fashion a guard. The Tablet of Hadad. A sealed stone engraved with a language known only to demons. A seal that could only be broken by one man. You."

"I don't believe you."

"No? What if I told you the only person who could break the seal was one who had killed a demon, and only the one who broke the seal could claim the ring? Until your unfortunate meddling, do you know how long it had been since anyone had killed a demon? Take a guess."

With slow, deliberate movements, Valentine slipped the ring onto his left ring finger. The torches lining the perimeter of the chamber flared.

"Solomon was quite clever. Without the ring, it was next to impossible to raise a true demon, so how could anyone kill one to claim the ring? Well, by foiling my plans with Belial, you satisfied the requirement. Fortunately, I had a contingency."

Valentine turned and gestured toward the platform. Sankey hopped off and followed him toward the wall. Hatcher craned his neck to look. He could still see the shape of Vivian there, moving beneath the surface.

Another gesture from Valentine, this one simply a glance and nod, and the Sedim began to move. They pulled Hatcher forward, stopping short of Valentine and Sankey, several yards from the wall. Hatcher looked beyond them, fixated on Vivian's blurry image swimming behind the murky black screen of rock. Hatcher wanted to tear his eyes away, but couldn't.

"So, you want to be king of the world? Fine. You have it. Now let her go. Let me go while you're at it, too."

"I'm afraid it's not that simple."

Valentine stepped forward, holding out his hand. The wall began to glow, and the light brought Vivian into sharper relief. Eyes locked in a hopeless look of terror. Feral creatures tearing at her flesh. Hatcher realized her wounds were healing instantly, or at least disappearing. Torn and restored, over and over. She was enduring a mauling that wouldn't stop.

"You see," Valentine continued, "The deal I cut allowed me to jump from body to body, to occupy vessels of the damned. But all of them have been temporary homes, and Asmodeus's powers are limited by his lack of access to this plane. I have to share my host. I get nights."

He turned to face Hatcher, leveling his eyes toward him. "But once he's free, he can claim the soul of the damned on the spot. And you, dear brother, are damned."

"That's what this is about? You went through all this just to send me to Hell early?"

Valentine let out a short laugh through his nose. "My, don't we think highly of ourselves? No, that's just a happy by-product. The moment he claims your soul, I'll be filling the void in your body. I mean, really . . ." He glanced down at himself, sweeping his hand from his chest past his belt. "Why would I choose soft and middle-aged over young and athletic?"

He's insane, Hatcher told himself. Bat-shit crazy. But then

he realized he was thinking of him as Valentine, and if this was Valentine, he was already in someone else's body. So maybe he wasn't the crazy one.

The mauling behind the wall continued. Vivian's screams seemed all the more piercing for not making a sound.

Hatcher struggled to pull free, unable to resist trying, wincing as the claws dug into arms. "Just let her go, then. For Christ's sake, you've got everything you wanted."

The muscles in Valentine's jaw tightened, and the features of his borrowed face grew hard. "I'll never have everything I want. I have to settle for causing pain to the one who made sure of that.

"Besides," he said. His expression relaxed and he broke eye contact. "The deal I made won't allow it. If it were up to me, I would. But I'm afraid she's a prize. He won't give her up."

Hatcher watched as a chunk of flesh was torn from her neck, ripped by jagged teeth.

"You know," Valentine continued, "you really could have saved her. When Deborah offered you the chance, it was real. You had to give up the ring of your own free will for it to work. We couldn't lie, not materially, or your rejection of it wouldn't have sufficed."

"You tricked me."

"No. We told you the truth when it mattered. That was what was required. You refused to believe it. We may have been prevented from deceiving you, there was nothing to stop you from deceiving yourself.

Valentine stepped back, raised a hand toward Sankey. "But even with the ring, none of this would be possible without this man."

Sankey straightened his back. Though his expression didn't change much, his face seemed to light up with pride.

"Our friend here is very special," Valentine said. "He's the only person who can actually pass through to the other side." He clapped Sankey on the shoulder. "He was touched by an angel at conception. A fallen angel."

The other side. Hatcher thought about Sherman, how Sankey had appeared to hand his head through the wall. It hadn't been an illusion. They simply wanted him to think it all was. Lori must have been a spy, someone who fed them the info they needed, told them about Denny and his magic videos. She probably had no idea what they had in store for her. He bit down on his lips, forcing himself not to look at Vivian. They had laid their cards faceup on the table, and still managed a bluff.

God, how could I have been such a moron . . .

"And now," Valentine added. "With his special gift, he's going to complete our deal."

Valentine pointed, then snapped his fingers. Several Sedim scrabbled over to take places in front of Hatcher, forming two rows. A blockade.

"Sorry, can't afford to have you try to mess anything up."

Valentine tugged his suit coat straight, then nodded to Sankey. He stepped close to the wall and held his hand out. The gold of the ring flashed in the torchlight.

Sankey reached his enormous claw out and took Valentine's arm by the wrist. He guided it to the wall, touched it against the surface.

Behind the wall, the demons yanked Vivian aside, gnawing on her face and neck and breasts, slashing her stomach open with their talons. Hatcher shut his eyes and turned his head.

A murmur rose from around him, a hum that sounded almost like a chant. He felt the Sedim holding him tense up. The ones in front of him were facing the wall, watching intently. Anticipating something. Behind the wall, a shape was drawing nearer, coming into view.

He's going to give him the ring, Hatcher realized. That was the deal. Asmodeus gets the ring, Valentine gets Hatcher's body. Asmodeus could then pass through, walk the earth, without being under anyone's control.

The form began to take shape through the blurry pane of rock. A huge head, imposing horns. A beast with a massive chest and animal legs.

Think, damn it. Do something.

The Sedim clamped down even harder on his arm, causing his knees to buckle.

All right, all right, I get it, Hatcher thought, cursing the Sedim in his mind. His legs gave out and he sunk, but the pain of his own weight on his arms forced him to stand back up. Out of frustration, he gave another violent tug with one arm, paid the price for it, but the Sedim holding it didn't budge. They may as well have been trees for all they moved.

Hatcher's head snapped up. *They won't move.*

Two rows of Sedim stood between him and what was going on. Two rows, two Sedim almost directly in front of him. One was a couple of feet away, the other a couple of feet in front of that one. That forward-most one was about only about five feet from Valentine and Sankey.

None of them was paying any attention to Hatcher. Asmodeus clearly had a lot of fans among the Sedim. They were riveted. A rock star was about to enter the building. Hellvis, live on stage.

Hatcher pulled his arms and pushed back with his legs, endured the pain as the grips tightened again.

They won't move.

The shape behind the wall was now in full view. Hatcher's breath caught in his throat. He hadn't looked this close before, hadn't caught the details of it. The thing was huge, practically prehistoric in its proportions. He could see why the Baphomet was its symbol, but now he knew it was a weak facsimile. The goatlike face was vaguely human, but its mouth was too large, its jaw too long, its cheeks too high, its eyes too angled. An impossible number of fierce teeth extended from its mouth.

It stopped to look at Vivian. The things feeding on her immediately pulled off and backed away. She collapsed, but it caught her by the hair as she dropped and raised her back up.

She was healed already, the gashes and rips all closed. The creature ran a finger down her face, almost caressing it, then yanked her head back by her hair and bit out her throat.

Blood gushed out in a plume. The thing thrust its jaw in the air and swallowed, savoring the mouthful.

With a snap of its head, it looked through the wall. Straight at Hatcher. Strings of blood dripped from its lips, its mouth widened into a smile that was almost crocodilian.

Forcing himself to disregard the pain, Hatcher bucked wildly against the Sedim, shaking and yanking. His face darkened, veins and tendons protruding in his neck as he strained. He heard a scream, someone sounding like they were on fire, realized it was him.

"Relax," Valentine said, glancing back. "She can't be killed in there. Beyond that wall, everything is forever."

The thing held her by her hair, her body dangling, throat torn out. She was reaching to touch it, brushing her hands over the wound in a mindless panic. She was unable to breathe, choking on her own blood.

"Stop it, Valentine!" Hatcher said, his body finally letting loose his lungs and sagging. "Bring her out!"

"Out of my hands, I'm afraid." Valentine dipped his head toward the wall. "Talk to *him*."

Hatcher was breathing in huffs now, chest heaving, jaw clenched.

"That's not even Hell you're seeing, by the way," Valentine said. "It's more like damnation's green room. There's probably elevator music playing."

"You can have me, okay? I won't even fight it! Just let her go!"

Valentine peered back through the cordon of Sedim. "Honestly, brother, I can't. She's theirs now. This ring is the only way out, and I've already promised it in exchange for . . . other considerations. If it makes you feel any better, you'll be joining her momentarily."

He turned back and jutted his chin at Sankey. "It's time."

Sankey nodded. He squared himself to the wall and pressed his arm into it, taking Valentine's with it. The arms sank together, submerging into black Jell-O, stopping at the shoulders.

Asmodeus let go of Vivian's hair and took a long, deliberate step toward them. It raised a hand, reaching toward Valentine. Reaching for the ring.

Hatcher clamped his eyes shut. He could only think of one thing to try, had no idea if it would work. Wasn't even sure if he wanted it to.

There were two Sedim between him and them, one directly in front of the other. Hatcher began to pull again, less violently this time, trying not to trigger too much of a reaction. The pain was excruciating, but he only needed them to tense up. To become unmovable.

Beyond the wall, Asmodeus took hold of Valentine's hand with huge fingers like curved daggers, fingers Hatcher realized were similar to Sankey's, only more numerous. The demon slid the ring off of Valentine's finger.

Hatcher filled his lungs with air, held it there. It wasn't much of a plan, but he couldn't think of anything else to do.

I'm so sorry, Vivian.

With an abrupt jerk of his body, he swung his legs up, pulling his knees to his chest, and exploded them out, smashing his heels into the Sedim in front of him.

The Sedim he kicked whipped forward, head snapping back, slamming into the one in front of him. That one stumbled, trying to catch its balance, head and shoulder lowered, plowing ahead. It rammed into Sankey.

Without a sound, Sankey disappeared through the wall. An orange flash merging into the ebony. Hatcher caught a brief glimpse of Asmodeus, hideously intelligent eyes flaming as the demon looked up. The next instant he caught sight of Vivian, just healed again, still in the clutches of dark creatures, a flicker of understanding breaking through the terror on her face.

And then the wall was just a wall. Solid, opaque. Nothing but smooth black rock.

Only this rock had a middle-aged man sticking out of it, his arm buried past the shoulder, part of his face submerged with it. Like someone stuck in solid black ice. He was pushing against the wall with his other hand, letting out a scream more painful than Hatcher could ever recall hearing. And he'd heard plenty.

The Sedim, including the ones gripping Hatcher's arm, seemed stunned. They stared at the spot where Sankey had stood a moment before, looking on in disbelief. Confused. A low groan started to build among them, rising in volume, until they all threw their heads back and howled in unison.

Hatcher felt the grip on his right arm loosen a bit. Just enough for him to yank it free. The pain in both of them made it hard to even move, but he knew he wouldn't have another chance. Summoning all the strength he could, he lifted his foot and gave a violent stomp to the side of that Sedim's leg. As soon as it released him, he swung around with his free arm and smashed the one still holding him in its batlike face. Once, twice, three times in rapid succession.

The blows seemed to daze it, but only just. It maintained its grip, shaking its head and snarling. It reared back with one arm, talons ready to slash. Its eyes grew wide in a show of fury.

Hatcher launched one more strike, a straight right, only this time, he pointed his index and middle finger, pressed together as one and slightly curved for strength, and stabbed them straight into the creature's eye.

They penetrated down to the knuckle and stayed there for a full second before he tugged his hand back. The thing finally let go, both hands shooting to its face.

He spun to defend against the other one, certain even a well-executed heel stomp to the knee like he'd just delivered wouldn't incapacitate one of these things, only to find that it was limping away. Joining the rest of them as they crowded around the wall. Valentine was still screaming, yelling something unintelligible, but the sound was muffled by the press of creatures around him. A demonic mosh pit. Clamoring for their idol.

"They're mourning."

Hatcher spun to his left at the voice. It was Deborah, standing next to him. She looked down at his hand, blood and tissue dripping off his fingers, and wagged her chin.

"You really are a nuisance, you know that?"

He braced himself, but she made no move. Nothing in her demeanor suggested she was planning anything.

He realized the other Carnates were beginning to disperse. They were breaking up into pairs and groups, shrugging and whispering, looking like people who just realized a show had been canceled.

"Vivian," Hatcher said, a demand, not a question.

Deborah rolled her eyes. "Oh, please. Look at that wall! Do you really think anything is getting through there? Any chance you had of getting her back—and I gave you that chance—went away when the Path did."

Hatcher said nothing. His fists clenched and unclenched as he contemplated whether snapping her neck would kill her.

"Don't look at me that way. None of this would have happened if she had just stuck with the deal. But like I told you, she got cold feet and tried to back out."

"As if you would have honored it. Why don't we ask Lori how trustworthy you are?"

"You know very little, Hatcher. She was trying to save your

soul. The bargain was, we'd see what we could do. The person we'd have double-crossed was Valentine, not her. Once Asmodeus got the ring, what that overbearing boor wanted was irrelevant. As for the other woman . . ." She glanced up, eyes toward the profane idol of human and animal parts suspended near the platform. "That was Valentine's thing, not ours. We tried to tell him that part wasn't necessary, not if he opened the Path, but he was such a nervous Nellie. Not wanting to leave anything to chance. The whole scheme was his idea, so we had to do it his way. Mostly."

"You expect me to believe that?"

"Believe what you want. The ring only works with a human. Few other than him would be willing to hand it over to Asmodeus in exchange for your body and Hell on earth. Nobody but Valentine could have engineered a plan that would have worked. He was essential, to a point, but frankly, he's an ass. Bossy and overbearing. We owed him no allegiance."

Hatcher stared at the throng of Sedim. They were silent now, hunched over. Upset.

"Everything you told me really was true, wasn't it? That's how you tricked me. With the truth."

"Yes. For this to work, none of us could actually lie. Not when it counted, anyway. Not about the ring. It was part of Solomon's spell. He was a cunning bastard."

"Bartlett?"

"The real deal. He's probably bunkered down in the mountains by now, armed to the teeth, a small army with him, waiting for Armageddon. He's been planning for years. All it took was a little pharmaceutically enhanced smoke, and he was hearing the word of God."

Hatcher said nothing.

"Oh, and your nephew is safe in his mother's arms, halfway to Montana by now. Just like we promised her he'd be. All she had to do was dig down and play her role. Quite the little method actress. Though I'm going to guess sleeping with you wasn't too much of a stretch. Don't be too hard on her. We promised her your body would still be alive and kicking when it was all over. We didn't say anything about your soul. But I guess that point is moot."

Hatcher let the information leach down through the layers of his mind. They'd tricked him by being honest, knowing he'd assume it was all a lie. How easy it had been. Plant a bunch of pictures of the general on the internet to look like they were hiding the real ones. Plant a fake death certificate. All an illusion. They didn't need to lie. They could bank on him deceiving himself.

"You don't seem all that upset, considering I messed up all your plans."

"Oh, you didn't mess up that much. Sure, it would be nice to raise Asmodeus. But we've released him from the spell, given him the ring. He'll be more than grateful. The person who's upset is Valentine. He was the one who was supposed to get a new life in your body. Of course, he's got more to worry about now, facing eternal torment and all that. And I'm sure Mr. Sankey didn't wake up this morning with a one-way trip to damnation on his mind. But us? Hell's chief executive officer is pleased. And the second stage of the Prefiguration is complete. That's all that matters."

"The what?"

"I'd love to sit and explain, but at the moment, unfortunately, there's another promise we have to keep."

Hatcher looked at her, trying to infer what she meant. Her expression was unreadable.

"She's talking about me," Edgar said.

The large knife in his hand flashed as he spun it once around his palm. It was the same one he'd given Hatcher in the car. He flicked his free wrist, and another blade appeared in it.

Deborah backed away, cocking her head to the side with a shrug and pursing her lips.

"That was the one thing they had to promise me, that if you lived, if anything went wrong, they'd let me kill you myself. So I either got to see you dragged to Hell or got to send you there personally. All I had to do was feed that tyrant Bartlett a bunch of disinformation. And play the role of a lifetime with you."

Edgar swept the blades in a crossing motion over his chest several times, audibly slicing the air, and twirling each over his knuckles with a flourish at the end of each move. Two different knives, vastly different sizes, but he had no problem manipulating them without a hitch.

"This blade, by the way? Fitted with a custom tracker in the handle. Let everyone know exactly when you'd be arriving."

Hatcher didn't respond. He should have realized something was fishy with that knife. But it hardly seemed like the stupidest mistake he'd made, and he figured he didn't have time to beat himself up over it. Not now.

He bent his knees, adopting a defensive posture. He circled away, continuing to face Edgar as the man moved toward him.

"I've been waiting a long time for this," Edgar said.

Hatcher's eyes never left the blades, but his mind tried to follow the words. He wasn't sure what they meant. They didn't make sense.

"Who are you?" he asked.

"I'm exactly who I said I was. Edgar Evans."

The name meant nothing. He searched his recollection but was certain he'd never met the man before a few days ago.

"Maybe you remember a good friend of mine. A really good friend."

Something vague flickered in Hatcher's memory, something about their first meeting.

"His nickname for me was Mr. E."

Davis. The guy who had fucked up Operation Rose Garden. The guy who cost them the mission, whose antics resulted in three civilians dead and two team members in a medevac chopper. Hatcher was the only one who knew Davis had left their flank open and blown their position by sneaking off to take a piss behind a hut. Where he'd also happened to sneak a cigarette.

And where he'd disturbed a family, a family he ended up killing, trying to keep them quiet. First the man, then the wife, then the little boy who'd seen him kill his mother. All with a knife.

Corporal Ronald Davis's story was he'd left his position to investigate something, stumbled across a family the Taliban had killed, encountered enemy fire. It was complete bullshit, and Hatcher knew it.

Why don't you ever talk about women? the guys always asked him. Because I like a little mystery, he'd always say with a secretive smile.

"You want to kill me because your BF was court-martialed?

I thought they let him plead out to three months and a BCD to make it all go away. That's a slap on the wrist."

Edgar narrowed his eyes at Hatcher. He held his gaze that way for several beats.

"He killed himself the first week behind bars," he said.

Hatcher said nothing. He hadn't known. He'd accepted a special duty assignment he'd been offered, one until then he'd been planning to turn down, and left the unit because of that incident. His new job made him the kind of asset no one talked about. Or to. Regular army news didn't even reach him much the first year in the field, let alone gossip.

Then again, even if he had known, he wouldn't have cared. Davis was an arrogant fuckup, a guy who killed a family of unarmed peasants and tried to cover it up.

Of course, that wasn't exactly an argument he could make to the man's revenge-minded lover, even if he were in the mood to defend his actions.

Edgar scraped the edges of the knives against each other, creating a smooth sound of sliding metal. A sharp sound.

"Do you have any idea what it's like to have to hide who you are? Skulk around in the shadows because you're different? Conceal something you want to be proud of? The way everyone else is? Sure, now they say they've repealed that. But do you really think anything has changed?"

"What happened to Davis had nothing to do with that."

"No? Are you going to pretend you didn't know what he was? That you would have acted the same way if he'd been one of the boys? If he hadn't been different?"

There was no way to answer that, so Hatcher didn't. He'd had his suspicions about Davis but hadn't given it much thought. Had those suspicions influenced how he'd treated the man? How he'd judged him? He suddenly had a flash of a different scenario, one where Davis couldn't rely on his teammates, one where he'd been forced to do things alone, one where cigarettes were taken in solitude, because you couldn't trust those around you not to make a big deal of it. He pictured a soldier surprised by an irate Afghani, shouting in the night. A panic response, wife screaming, child wailing. The cover of night being pierced, certain to alert the target. Him making a split-second decision. Maybe doing it to save himself, maybe doing it to save his team-

mates. Was it possible? Hatcher couldn't say. He'd never considered it before. Now didn't seem like the best time to start.

"You John Wayne types," Edgar continued. "So wrapped up
in your own masculinity, wearing it like a costume to hide your
failures, your insecurities . . ." He twirled the blades again in his
hands, spinning them first in his palm, then tumbling them over
his fingers. "You think life is all one big action film, where
you're the hero. You don't care about anything but feeding your
ego. You think you can just save the day, then ride off into the
sunset. Well, you've watched too many movies."

The blades made a whiffling sound as Edgar slashed the air
in front of him, carving a complex, overlapping pattern in rapid
strokes. He started forward, arms still moving like a threshing
machine.

Hatcher stabbed his hand into his pocket, withdrew it in the
same fluid motion.

"And you obviously haven't watched enough," he said,
pointing the mini-gun and pinching the trigger.

The pop sounded like a firecracker. The tiny flash scalded
Hatcher's finger and a whiff of gunpowder braced his nostrils.
Edgar flinched, then stood motionless, hands swooping low and
hanging there, looking confused. After a few seconds, both
knives slipped to the ground and he raised his hands to his
throat. A rope of blood flowed out of the corner of his mouth
and down his chin.

He gurgled once and sank to his knees. Hatcher couldn't tell
if he was trying to cough or vomit, but he was definitely bleed-
ing. A lot. The shot had caught him directly in the mouth.

*I knew the moment I read that note I was going to have to kill
you, you little shit.*

A sharp noise broke Hatcher's focus. Someone clapping. He
swung around to see Soliya, slowly giving him mock applause.

"Always a surprise when a big man packs such a small gun
in his pants."

Hatcher glanced down at the tiny weapon in his palm, then
stuffed it back into his pocket.

"What are we going to do with you?" she said.

"Vivian," he said. "Tell me how to get her back." He took in
a breath, swallowed. "Please."

Soliya frowned, dimpling her cheek. "We really don't know

of any way. You could pick up where Valentine left off." She glanced over to the wall. The Sedim were huddled low, crouched down as if in prayer. Valentine's body hung limp from its shoulder.

"You know," she continued, "spending millions of dollars trying to find a way? Seems like there are better things to do with money. But to each his own."

"I don't have millions of dollars."

Arching an eyebrow, Soliya smiled and hitched a shoulder.

The light from the torches suddenly dimmed. Hatcher glanced around. Only a few of the torches remained lit. He spotted Deborah pulling one down from its holder, snuffing the flame with a metal damper.

Soliya stepped forward and leaned close, hushing her voice like a coconspirator. "By the way, Deborah and I had a bet whether you actually loved her. I won."

A light moved in his periphery, and he swiveled to see Deborah approaching. She was holding something that looked like a severed hand, burning at the fingertips. A candle. She held the hand out in front of her.

"You know how fond I am of you, Hatcher," she said, her lips puckering slightly into a smile that looked almost affectionate. "So, I'll tell you this. Your deepest fear hasn't been exposed yet."

She raised the hand, blocking the view of her face. "Remember, whom gods would destroy, they would first indulge."

Hatcher opened his mouth to speak, but a thought flitted through his mind, distracting him. He chased it, withdrawing into himself, searching all over, combing memories.

Within seconds, he was exhausted. Something wasn't right. He couldn't remember the thought, or why he'd been chasing it. He realized his eyes were closed. That definitely wasn't good. He needed to open them, and quick. His life might depend on it, on raising his lids, on snapping himself awake.

He decided to lie down instead.

EPILOGUE

WHEN HATCHER WOKE, HE WAS SITTING IN VIVIAN'S RENTAL. Shafts of early morning light were beaming in through the windshield. The car was where he'd left it, parked near the library. He checked his pockets. His cell phone was gone. So was the mini-gun.

He drove back to his place. He needed a shower. He wasn't sure how long he'd been out, but he needed more sleep, too.

The lurking car wasn't there when he got back to his place. He'd almost forgotten about it, the conspicuous surveillance of his rented room. The guy going around asking questions, sounding like a cop. But it had flashed to mind just as he pulled onto his street and parked. The guy's car was nowhere to be seen. That was an instant relief.

Stepping up to the landing of his apartment, he noticed an envelope taped to the door. The envelope had a pair of last names connected by an ampersand in a stylized logo atop a New York return address. Stamped below his name were the words *Personal and confidential*. He opened the envelope as soon as he got inside.

The letter asked that he contact the law firm of Jensen and Powers as soon as possible, and provided a name and number. It used the term "urgent" more than once.

He still had an unopened TracFone and unused prepaid card. He initialized the phone and made the call, flopping down on his bed.

The call lasted several minutes. At first he spoke to a paralegal, who transferred him to an attorney. The attorney was frustrating to deal with, but Hatcher could tell he felt the same way. The point of the conversation was finally revealed, and Hatcher wasn't sure how to react. He lay there, staring at the ceiling, long after the other side had hung up.

No fucking way.

Three knocks rapped on his door. His landlord, he presumed. He tried to ignore it, but the person knocked again. He pulled himself off the bed. His arms ached, the deep gouges in them still stinging. The possibility someone might be showing up to cause trouble was annoying, but part of him was hoping that's exactly what it was. Just to get it over with.

He yanked the door open, started to bark, *"What?"* only to cut himself off.

The woman in the doorway sighed, her shoulders sagging as if she'd been holding her breath.

"Thank God! You're okay!"

"Amy . . ." was all he could manage.

Amy Wright rushed forward and threw her arms over his shoulders, stepped up on her toes to press her lips against his. They stood there like that for a long moment, then he put an arm around her waist and picked her up. He took a step back and closed the door.

Their lips separated, and he let her slide back to the floor.

"It's Valentine! And I think Isaac may not be dead!"

"I know. But how did you figure that out?"

She explained to him about the death certificate, the signature. Her frantic attempts to get ahold of him.

"But . . . you're here?" he said. "How? I don't understand—"

"What's to understand? I got on a plane. I couldn't stand worrying about you, about you facing . . . them again. *Him* again. Not alone. There was no one I could call, certainly no law enforcement agency that would be willing to listen. When I couldn't reach you, I couldn't simply stay put, on the other side of the country. I had to do something."

In some ways, what he was hearing was harder to understand than anything that he'd been though. She'd dropped everything, he realized. Just to be there for him. After all those unreturned letters, after the way he'd just called out of the blue and asked her to use her resources at the department.

"How did you know where I live?"

"You told me where you worked. Your boss is a pretty loyal

guy. I finally had to plead with him that I was your friend, trying to help. He really didn't want to give you up."

Hatcher said nothing. Denny was a good guy, and another person he'd treated like crap. He'd have to make it up to him. After explaining how he'd lost the mini-gun.

A long breath puffing his cheeks, he ran a hand through his hair and gestured vaguely toward the interior of the room.

"You're hurt," she said, reaching for his arm and gently touching the wounds.

"I'm fine. Just a little tired."

She gave him a skeptical look, then took a few steps and glanced around the room.

"I know you'll object," she said, turning back to him. "But I want to help. Let me help you. That's why I'm here."

"It's over," he said, shaking his head.

"Over. Are you sure?"

"For now." He rocked his head noncommittally, almost nodding. "Yes."

"Do you want to tell me what happened?"

Hatcher shrugged. "I'm not a hundred percent certain."

"You look like you've been in a war."

"Wouldn't be the first."

"Oh, you poor thing." She placed a hand on his cheek, peered up into his eyes. "Do you need me to get you anything? Do you want me to leave so you can get some sleep?"

He shook his head. "I need to lie down, but I won't be able to sleep for a while."

Amy let her hand drop and stood watching him. She appraised him with eyes that ran from one side of his face to the other and back.

"I'm saying I want you to stay," he said.

That seemed to be what she wanted to hear. She smiled with her cheeks, set her purse on the tiny dining table. "I can't tell you how worried I was. I still am. Are you really sure it's over?"

"Pretty sure."

"Is it something you want to talk about?"

No, he thought. It's not. "I'm not sure where to start."

"Start at the beginning."

He reached for the letter on the bed. "Maybe I can tell you on the plane."

"The plane?"

"I need to go to New York," he said, handing it to her.

"What's this?"

"It's from a law firm in Manhattan. They specialize in probate."

Her brow furrowed, a hint of confusion, a hint of concern. "Somebody died?"

"Sort of. I just got off the phone with them. They were a little tight-lipped, wanting me to fly out there without telling me much. I finally shook it out of them."

Amy held his eyes, waiting for him to finish.

"According to them, they need a blood test. I've been identified as a relative of Valentine. The way his will was set up, if things check out I'm supposed to inherit what's left of his estate. After creditors and taxes, they estimated that one percent or so would come to me."

"One percent?"

"Yes."

"Wait, wasn't he, like, a billionaire?"

Hatcher didn't answer.

"Are you saying—"

"Yes," he said, nodding. "They're telling me I'm about to come into twenty million dollars."

Amy blinked once, her mouth and jaw loosening. Even as she struggled to digest the information, the machinations were easy to make out. Hastily, silently, she was trying to determine how this would affect them, whether this meant they had a shot. Looking at her, he couldn't help wondering the same thing. Vivian had always been a substitute. Now, the real thing, the woman he'd imagined a hundred times showing up at his door, the one he'd kept willing himself not to think about, was right in front of him.

Vivian, in Hell. Amy, right here.

Deborah's last words began to loop in his head.

He sucked in air until his lungs were full and let himself topple onto the bed.

Amy's voice caught in her throat and she had to clear it before she spoke. "That's really what they said? Twenty million dollars?"

Hatcher nodded, staring at the ceiling. "Give or take a million," he said.

ABOUT THE AUTHOR

HANK SCHWAEBLE is a practicing attorney and former Air Force officer and military special agent. A graduate of the University of Florida and Vanderbilt Law School, he lives and works in Houston. His debut novel, *Damnable*, won the Bram Stoker Award for Best First Novel.